CHANGING
WOMAN

Also by Aimée & David Thurlo

Praise for *Changing Woman*

"The authors present a good look at the complexities of the gaming issue while maintaining the character-driven essence of the series. Ella, balanced between mother and daughter, modernist and traditionalist, job and family, remains the captivating focal point of this excellent series."

—*Publishers Weekly*

"The book is packed with action. I liked the careful attention to police procedure and the detailed description that let me 'see' the crisis at the power station. I highly recommend *Changing Woman*."

—*Mystery News*

Praise for *Red Mesa*

"Fans of Tony Hillerman's Jim Leaphorn and Jim Chee, and of Jean Hager's investigator, Molly Bearpaw, should appreciate the way the Thurlos mix Native American lore with modern situations and forensics technique. Even readers unfamiliar with the Native American subgenre will be intrigued by the richly complex Ella and her fight to bring integrity to her work and personal life."

—*Booklist* ★ *(starred review)*

"A great tale. The Thurlos' talent resides in deep and thorough characterizations that lift their Native American police procedurals to a plane shared by the likes of Hillerman."

—*Midwest Book Review*

Praise for *Shooting Chant*

"Enough background is given to know that this is not the first book featuring Ella Clah, but not so much as to make the reader feel as if they've missed too much to make sense of the characters or plot. *Shooting Chant* is well written, descriptive, entertaining. It will provide readers looking for a suspenseful read with a lead character who is intelligent, dedicated, likeable, and quite appealing."

—*Albuquerque Journal*

"If it's just too long between Tony Hillerman novels, the mysteries of Aimée and David Thurlo will help you bridge the canyons. If you prefer your mysteries with a little green chile and New Mexico grit, you'll want to add the Thurlos to your reading list." —*Rocky Mountain News*

CHANGING WOMAN

✖ ✖ ✖ ✖

AIMÉE & DAVID THURLO

A TOM DOHERTY ASSOCIATES BOOK
NEW YORK

To those Navajo Tribal Police officers who put
their lives on the line every day to serve
and protect the Navajo Nation

NOTE: If you purchased this book without a cover you should be aware that
this book is stolen property. It was reported as "unsold and destroyed" to
the publisher, and neither the author nor the publisher has received any pay-
ment for this "stripped book."

This is a work of fiction. All the characters and events portrayed in this
book are either products of the author's imagination or are used fictitiously.

CHANGING WOMAN

Copyright © 2002 by Aimée & David Thurlo

All rights reserved, including the right to reproduce this book, or portions
thereof, in any form.

A Forge Book
Published by Tom Doherty Associates, LLC
175 Fifth Avenue
New York, NY 10010

www.tor.com

Forge® is a registered trademark of Tom Doherty Associates, LLC.

ISBN: 0-812-56870-2
Library of Congress Catalog Number: 2001054772

First edition: March 2002
First mass market edition: April 2003

Printed in the United States of America

0 9 8 7 6 5 4 3 2 1

ACKNOWLEDGMENTS

✖ ✖ ✖

Thanks to Carl and others with knowledge of the Four Corners Power Plant and the San Juan Generating Station for answering our questions and providing us with the information needed to create the fictional facility depicted in our Ella Clah mysteries.

PROLOGUE
✖ ✖ ✖

Special Investigator Ella Clah of the Navajo Tribal Police turned right at the intersection near the center of Shiprock. The reservation town overflowed the San Juan River valley on both sides and spread onto the higher land to the southwest and northwest.

Ahead of Ella's route were a few more businesses, then the narrow, one-way steel-truss 1930s-era bridge that crossed the San Juan River to Shiprock's southwest side. Alongside the classic old structure, just to the south, was a flat eastbound concrete monster.

It was only four-thirty in the afternoon, but the distant sun was already low on the horizon. It was January, when the snow usually kicked in for New Mexico, but although the twenty-eight-degree temperature outside was cooperating, the sky was dry, and so was Mother Earth.

Ella was looking forward to getting home tonight. The same warm, sturdy house her father had built a lifetime ago was one Ella now shared with her two-year-old daughter and her mother. There was a sense of permanence and continuity about living there that made the place all the more dear to her.

Ella glanced around, automatically studying the surrounding area. As she drove by the Totah Café, she noticed a man in white clothing running toward the back of the building, holding a fire extinguisher.

Ready to help, Ella checked for oncoming vehicles, then slowed and swung her police unit, an unmarked blue Jeep, into the restaurant's parking lot. She accelerated slightly until she caught up with Charlie Jim, one of the Totah's cooks.

"Where's the fire, Charlie?" Ella pulled up alongside him and kept pace, noting that he could barely take a breath. The short run was obviously very taxing to Charlie, a thin, unhealthy-looking man in his late fifties who she knew chain-smoked. Charlie was sweating despite the outside temperature.

He slowed down to a fast walk gratefully, realizing who was speaking to him. "I'd just stepped outside for a cigarette when someone in an old tan pickup came by and tossed something that was still smoking into the Dumpster," he said in a wheezy voice. "I ran back inside and grabbed the fire extinguisher. I think it's those vandals again."

She stopped the Jeep and glanced ahead, but couldn't see any smoke coming from the heavy metal Dumpster, which was screened on the café's side by a high wall of painted cinder blocks. As Charlie approached the Dumpster Ella jumped out of her vehicle and followed him.

Her thoughts automatically shifted to the petty vandalism that had been plaguing this part of the Rez the past few months. Last weekend several vehicles at a local church had their tires flattened by the removal of the valve stems while their owners were attending an evening service. A few days later, a plate glass window at a private home had been broken by a thrown brick, and just last night several mailboxes in a housing area east of Shiprock had been knocked off their posts. The incidents had been increasing in number and severity lately, and she hoped setting fires wasn't the latest escalation the frustrated department was facing.

Charlie set the extinguisher down on the asphalt, then before Ella could stop him, threw open the hinged lid, ducking back in case the sudden intake of oxygen resulted in flames.

"I guess the garbage must have already smothered

whatever they threw in." Charlie peered over the edge into the Dumpster, standing on tiptoe as Ella looked around for something to stand on so they could get a better view. "I don't see—" Looking toward the back of the Dumpster, he cursed loudly. "Oh, crap. Run!"

Ella wanted to take a quick look for herself, but Charlie's expression warned her that there was no time to waste.

"What's inside, Charlie?" she yelled, taking off after him.

Abruptly, an enormous blast punched through the air like a clap of thunder. Ella was thrown facedown onto the parking lot, and a large chunk of torn sheet metal bounced across the pavement like a piece of cardboard in the wind, coming to rest against the side of the building with a loud clang.

A wave of heat blew past Ella, and she stayed down a moment longer.

Ella stood up slowly, turning to look at the damage. The Dumpster had split open like a big, rectangular banana, and the cinder blocks in the wall had been scattered like so many children's blocks. Charlie was still hugging the ground, his arms wrapped around his head and neck for protection. The fire extinguisher he'd carried out with him was halfway out to the street, spinning like a top and spewing its white chemical everywhere.

"Charlie!" she yelled. "You okay?"

"I think so. But my arm hurts, and my chest . . . it feels tight."

"Did you get hit by flying debris?" Ella started moving toward her Jeep to call the fire department as well as a rescue unit. Charlie's face was the color of ashes and, remembering her impression that he was stressed out already, it seemed like a wise course of action.

"No, but I'm feeling . . ." He groaned and clutched his chest, then lay back down on the asphalt.

"Charlie?" Ella ran the rest of the way to her Jeep, and grabbed her handheld off the seat. Requesting the

EMTs and fire department, she hurried back to where Charlie was lying.

"Is Charlie going to be okay?" Mary Lou Bitsillie, a waitress and an old friend of Ella's, asked, running up to join her. "He has a bad heart."

Charlie had already lost consciousness. Ella crouched down beside him, and reached for the cook's pulse. His wrist was so thin she could tell immediately that his heart had stopped. She placed her head down on his chest, but couldn't hear any heart sounds.

"I'm going to have to give him CPR, Mary Lou. Can you help me out?" Ella scrambled around, scooting up close so she could bring pressure on his chest directly.

"We've all had the first-aid course. I'll do the breathing part," Mary Lou said with a nod.

Ella leaned over and began the pressure immediately, working with Mary Lou, who gave him mouth-to-mouth in a steady cycle. Someone came up behind them and placed a coat over Charlie, and one over Mary Lou's shoulders. Ella already had a jacket on.

Ella glanced around, hoping to see or hear the emergency units, absently noting a half dozen restaurant employees and patrons standing outside near the side door, watching the column of black smoke and flames rising from the shattered Dumpster. "Come on, Charlie, give us a heartbeat," she whispered.

At that precise moment, she heard the soft click and whir of an automatic camera. Some tourist had just taken her photo. Looking up, she saw that another had a video camera and was alternately filming the burning Dumpster, then their efforts with Charlie like some amateur Hitchcock. The story and photos would be all over the Rez in a matter of hours, and on the ten o'clock news for sure. Anything that made the Rez cops look like they were losing the battle against vandalism always traveled at the speed of light.

Then Charlie coughed, and opened his eyes, and Ella didn't care about the cameras anymore.

ONE
✕ ✕ ✕

Yesterday's "garbage bomb" and Charlie's near-death had made the evening news, even on Albuquerque TV, and more video had aired of the burning Dumpster and shattered cinder-block wall than of Ella's and Mary Lou's success with Charlie. For some reason any event with fire footage usually made the lead story on the TV news. The photo that had run in the newspaper, unfortunately, was one showing her lying flat on her face with the burning trash in the background.

Since the incident, she'd received thanks from Charlie and his family, but she'd also received four calls from the news people about the bomb. It would take a while before things died down.

Now, alone in her bedroom, Ella sat at the small table that held her desktop computer and waited. She'd have to return to the police station soon, but the only way her contact, "Coyote," ever surfaced was through her Internet provider.

The bitterly cold January winds swept down the hillside behind her mother's home, rattling dust and sand against the window. It was said that Wind carried news, but Wind had met its equal in this age of computers.

Coyote's information so far had been as good as gold, though all she really knew about him was that he was probably an undercover cop—federal, most likely. His knowledge of her background in the FBI and his use of certain terms all supported that theory.

Hearing a soft bell tone, she glanced down at the screen and saw the instant message box. Coyote was on line. As she read the message, she reached over and hit the print command. The message would vanish from the screen the second she logged off, and there would be no record of it anywhere. It was now or never.

Ella thought of the many times she'd tried to track down Coyote, despite his warnings not to try. She'd been discreet, but persistent. Yet, despite all the methods available to her, she'd turned up nothing.

"*Shimá*, come eat," Dawn said, using the Navajo word for "mother" her grandmother Rose had taught her. When Ella didn't stand up right away, Dawn crawled up onto Ella's lap.

"Hi, sweetie." Ella brushed a kiss on her daughter's nubby little cheek as she typed a question for Coyote. If the past was any indication, unless she was fast, he'd log off before she even finished the sentence. "Go back to the kitchen and tell your *shimasání*, your grandmother, that I'll be there in one minute." Ella smiled as her daughter scampered off. Rose wouldn't allow Dawn to call her grandma. The Navajo equivalent was all she would accept.

Ella leaned back in her garage sale captain's chair and read Coyote's message again as she waited for his reply. His warnings were always unsettling, and this time was no exception.

The petty crimes all over the Rez are being engineered to make the cops and tribal government look bad. They want politicians voted out and new people brought in who are more in favor of tribal gaming.

Ella stared at the clear-cut message. Coyote's case was more involved than the happenings on the Navajo Nation. He was trying to find evidence against a group of Intertribal Native American activists he claimed were trying to gain control of gambling operations on tribal lands across the nation. Coyote believed the *Dinetah* was their main target now.

But without more evidence she couldn't do a thing. The question she'd typed was the same as always. What proof could he give her so she could act? But he hadn't answered her and, now, he was off-line.

Ella took the printout and placed it in an unlabeled file folder along with the rest. Sensing that someone had come into her room, Ella turned and smiled as she saw her mother standing inside the doorway.

"Since your daughter's father canceled his visit again, I think we should eat now. You'll have to leave for the station before long."

Ella nodded. Rose Destea, her mother, was in her sixties and her once raven hair was now a dozen shades of gray and white. She'd slowed down some in the past few years, but she was still a force to be reckoned with and had a stubborn streak a mile long.

Rose came up behind her and read the message on the computer screen. " 'Coyote,' huh? That's not a Navajo writing you. Must be an Anglo trying to sound like an Indian."

Ella shrugged. "Maybe. I don't really know. But, Mom, this is confidential police business, so you can't tell anyone. Only Big Ed knows about Coyote, and that's because he's my boss and the chief of police."

"I won't say anything, daughter. But I'm still very worried. You could have been killed by that bomb yesterday."

"I know. The police force is doing its best, but the situation is a lot more complicated than it appears at first glance."

"Yes, I know. I read enough of that message to know that there's more to what's happening than has been made public," Rose answered.

"The bottom line is that we really aren't sure what we're dealing with yet."

"Just remember that you have to be more careful these days. You can't afford to take as many chances as you did before. You now have a daughter who needs you."

Ella could hear Dawn playing with Two, the family dog, out in the living room. The pair had become fast friends. "She's changed everything for me, Mom, but I'm still a cop. I have a duty to the tribe. But it's because of her that I wear a vest practically all the time, even in summer when it's sweltering."

"I wish you would find another line of work."

"Mom, we should all be grateful I have a job that's secure. A lot of our people are scrambling for work right now. If I wasn't a cop, I'd probably be out looking frantically for a job off the Rez, hoping to find something that paid me enough to be able to provide for our family."

Rose sat on the edge of the bed, running her weathered hand over the hand-stitched quilt absently. "Times are especially hard for the *Dineh* right now. Last year's dry winter, followed by a late frost and an even drier summer, wiped out a lot of the crops. When the weather does that to us, people and their livestock go hungry. And, now, when money's tightest and the tribe is least able to handle it, we get hit by another bad winter, the coldest we've had in years. Many of our people are having to choose between food and heat."

Silence stretched out, but Ella waited to make sure that her mother had finished speaking before she said anything. Navajos seldom had rapid, overlapping conversations like some other cultures did. Here, it was a sign of poor manners to speak before another was finished, and long, thoughtful pauses were not unusual.

"It's been miserably cold," Ella said at last, "but we still haven't got much snow to show for it except for a little in the mountains. If we don't get some moisture soon, we'll have another dry growing season ahead."

"I have a feeling it's going to go from bad to worse before it's over," Rose said, shaking her head. "Many of the businesses on the *Dinetah*, the tribal land, have already had to close their doors, and more will soon follow. There's not much money for people to buy things these days. Did I tell you that I saw Dezbah Nez the other day? Her son and his family have gone to Phoenix looking for jobs. They heard that some of our people are finding work there in the fast-food places or cleaning offices at night. It's all minimum-wage jobs, but it'll help them stay afloat with everyone working. It's the ones who can't or won't leave the Rez that worry me the most. The only thing that's abundant here now is hunger and cold. The tribal government has to wake up and try to do more to help our people."

"How? There isn't much money in the tribal accounts either. The tribe applied for federal help, but things like that take forever. State and national politicians are slow to get involved since we don't have enough votes to change any election results, or money to support their candidates."

"We have to do *something*. Many of the older ones in the outlying areas won't make it to spring without help. Did you hear that Jim Joe is sick again? Their old wood-stove has got a crack in the firebox, and he couldn't fix it. It can't be welded, either. With the temperature the way it has been . . ." She shook her head again. "And like many traditionalists, he won't go to the hospital, even though he's running a fever. He said that people die there and their *chindi* stay, ready to get anyone who's still alive."

Ella sighed. The fear that the *chindi*, the evil in a man that remained earthbound after death, would contaminate and harm the living kept many of the old ones away from the hospitals. It was a decision that cost lives every year.

"His son should have taken him anyway," Ella said flatly.

"And end up frightening his father to death?" Rose shook her head. "You forget how things are here."

"No, Mom. I didn't forget. I'm *'alní.*" The word meant a person who walked the line between two cultures— a person who was constantly split in half.

"You are what you've chosen to be," Rose said, then stood, smoothing out the quilt. "Come on, daughter. Let's have dinner before you go back to work. I've fixed your favorite, mutton stew and fry bread."

"I thought that was what I smelled coming from the kitchen. Stew will really hit the spot tonight. I need something warm besides coffee inside me before I go out on patrol."

The simple, traditional meal was especially tasty, or Ella was particularly hungry tonight. She really wasn't sure which it was. As Ella hurried through dinner, her mother fed Dawn as she always did on the days Ella had to go back to work.

Ella looked at Dawn and sighed. These days her cute, black-haired daughter with those big, sparkling eyes that could melt butter wore as much food as she actually ate. At the moment, her little hands were submerged in the bowl even as Rose fed her bite-sized pieces of stew.

"Don't play with your food," Ella told Dawn.

Rose glowered at her. She didn't like Ella to correct Dawn while she was eating.

"Mom, she's making a mess," Ella said, answering the unspoken criticism.

"You were worse at her age."

It was her mother's standard answer.

"*Shizhé'é* come?" Dawn looked up, her chin dripping with broth.

"Not today. Your father was busy," Ella said. "But he told me he'd come by as soon as he can."

Rose shot Ella a look that spoke volumes.

Ella shook her head, and glanced away. She didn't want Rose to ever say anything disparaging about Kevin in front of her daughter. Kevin was, after all, Dawn's father.

Ella finished her meal while Dawn chattered away, ignoring the rest of her stew.

"I want to play, *Shimasání*," Dawn said, sliding off

her grandmother's lap and standing impatiently as Rose wiped her face and hands with a napkin.

"Then go. You've eaten enough."

Ella shook her head as Dawn scampered into the living room. "Mom, you really shouldn't excuse her until we're all finished."

"Those *bilagáana* rules will still be around when she's older. Right now with all her energy, she's doing well just to sit and eat as long as she does."

Knowing the futility of an argument, Ella stood, placed her dirty dishes in the sink, then washed and dried her hands. "My daughter's father said he might come by later. If he does, try to be nice to him," she said, avoiding mentioning Kevin by name out of respect for Rose's beliefs. Her mother was a traditionalist who believed names were endowed with power a person could draw upon in times of danger. But using them often weakened that power and depleted their owner. In this house, only the names of their enemies were used freely.

"He won't come. There will just be another excuse. It makes him nervous to be around her, you know. He doesn't understand her when she speaks, and has no idea what to say or do with a child."

"I'm sure he understands her, Mom. She speaks clearly enough," Ella said. "And two languages. What more can you ask of a two-year-old?"

"I think he wants her to discuss law and tribal politics."

Ella laughed. "Mom, you really shouldn't be so hard on him. He *does* try." Ella knew she wasn't going to change her mother's mind about this or anything else, but she had to say something. "Remember not to discuss Coyote or anything else you saw on that computer screen with anyone."

"I *never* discuss your work, daughter. It's about the only thing I can do to protect you these days."

Ella gave her mother a light kiss on the cheek. "I'll see you later, then. Don't bother waiting up for me." She took her pistol and holster from the top shelf in the kitchen and clipped them onto her wide leather belt. After a quick good-bye to her daughter, she put on her heavy jacket and walked out to her vehicle across the hard, frozen ground.

Big Ed Atcitty would be around the station for another hour or so, which was good because she needed to talk to him.

Fifteen minutes later she walked through the side doors of the Shiprock station. Before she'd gotten more than a few feet down the hall, Sergeant Joseph Neskahi stepped out of the squad room and intercepted her.

"The chief wants to see you before you and Justine go out tonight." The young-looking, barrel-chested officer still wore his hair in a buzz cut despite the winter weather.

"Okay, thanks," Ella answered. Neskahi was a fine officer, and they'd worked well together, sometimes in the most dangerous circumstances imaginable.

As she turned the corner and headed down the hall, she spotted Big Ed Atcitty standing in the doorway to his office. "I thought I heard you out here, Shorty." He'd given her the nickname as a joke since Ella was a full head taller than he was. "Come in. We need to talk."

Ella followed her boss into his office, then sat down as he waved in the direction of a chair. If Neskahi was barrel-chested, then Big Ed Atcitty was a redwood stump, impervious to age and impossible to knock over.

Seeing him close the door behind them signaled to Ella that the discussion was going to be more than just a quick briefing on operations.

Big Ed's expression was somber. "I'm very concerned over what happened yesterday with that bomb. That's not just another prank, it represents a real escalation in the vandalism we've been fighting. Just a few seconds one way or the other, and neither you or Charlie would have been around to tell the story. I want you to track down the explosives and nail whoever was behind this.

Taking a baseball bat to a mailbox is one thing, but setting off explosives is a big step up."

Big Ed leaned back in his chair, rocking gently for a moment. "We need to send out a message to the community that we don't take an incident like this lightly. I just wish we had a clue who's behind it, and why. The whole thing is frustrating, trying to watch thousands of square miles with a handful of officers while carrying out our normal patrols and investigations."

"We're in a bind, that's for sure. I'll put the SI team on it," Ella said. "Is there anything else you wanted to talk to me about?"

He exhaled softly, and nodded. "Let me cut to the chase. I've heard that Officer Goodluck is having a problem qualifying with her weapon." He leaned forward, opening a folder on his desk and looking through the papers briefly. "She barely made it, as a matter of fact."

"Chief, those lowlifes cut off half of Justine's trigger finger. Her hand's healed, but she has to find a new grip." Ella paused for a second. "I know my partner, Chief. She just needs a little more time and practice to get it together, but she *will* make it work."

"How is she adjusting overall? Speak frankly, Shorty. I need to know exactly what the situation is with her. Some of the higher-ups are worried she might be a danger to herself and her partner after all she went through."

"That's baloney. I'm her partner most of the time, and *I'm* not worried. Justine is just frustrated that she's having trouble making the kinds of scores she's used to having out on the firing range."

"All right. But keep me posted."

"You've got it." Ella paused, then continued. "I needed to talk to you this morning about something else, Chief."

"Go ahead."

"It's about my contact, Coyote. He's been in touch again," Ella said, and filled in her supervisor on the contents of his latest message.

Big Ed considered what he learned, trying to put everything together in his mind. "From what you've told me before, he's convinced that the attempt to frame you for Justine's apparent death last year was just the first move by this group. But all we really know for sure, based on the vague testimony we had from one of the perps, is that it *was* an organized effort. To extend that conspiracy to gambling requires a lot more corroborating evidence. But the vandalism is having an effect on the people."

Ella nodded. "It's too bad we weren't able to get any more from that bunch. We might know who to talk to about the bomb, the broken windows, and all the rest."

"But we did catch the perps who framed you. If there *are* others, and they are behind this property damage and the rest, we'll find out about them sooner or later. The one thing I do know for certain is that we can't afford to disregard what your contact tells you."

"Chief, do you know something I don't?"

"I've made a few discreet phone calls. There are a few feds I trust and, from the scanty feedback I got, I think your contact is FBI."

"If what he says is true, then this self-styled Indian mafia has picked a ripe target this time. With all the troubles facing the *Dineh* right now, the potential revenue that gaming could pull in appeals to a lot of people."

"It would create a lot of jobs and generate income for the tribe. No argument there."

"But it would also attract some negative influences the tribe doesn't need," Ella answered.

"The tribe will make its own choice," Big Ed said flatly. "That's not up to the department. Our job is to put a stop to all the vandalism, no matter who is behind it, and make sure the decision to approve gaming, or not, is one our people make freely." He paused, and then continued in a heavy tone. "Now tell me, have you made arrangements for extra patrols tonight?"

"Yeah, we'll have more cops out on the streets," she

answered, "but you know how understaffed we are. Any chance the Tribal Council will find some money this spring to hire more officers?"

"Actually, Shorty, I expect our operating budget to be cut even more. No one in the council is really listening to us at the moment. Rather than admit that our department is stretched to the limit, it's easier to just label us incompetent. They don't have to come up with any more resources that way."

"We'll catch the vandals, eventually, Chief. Sooner or later, their luck will run out," Ella said, standing up. "But I've got to tell you, I still have a problem believing that a little action by a few punks is linked to a huge conspiracy."

"Little connections lead to big ones, Shorty. As Navajos, we're taught to believe that everything is interrelated. Just look for the overall pattern until it all makes sense."

Ella left the chief's office feeling uneasy. Like most good cops, she could feel trouble in her gut before it even happened. Right now, instinct and experience warned her that conditions on the Rez were becoming unstable and, unless they were careful, a lot of cops would go down in the crossfire.

TWO

✕ ✕ ✕

Ella continued down the hall to her office and found her young assistant, Justine, waiting. She'd known Justine all her life—they were second cousins—and the changes Ella could see in her face after several years on the force were startling. Justine was relatively young, in her midtwenties, but the eagerness and the optimism of youth had been replaced by the hardness of a seasoned cop.

"I'm ready to go, are you?" Ella said, anxious to get going.

Less than five minutes later, they were on the road in an unmarked sedan.

"You're awfully quiet," Ella said, glancing over at her partner. She'd noted that Justine wore a black wool watch cap over her long jet hair, and, like Ella, was in street clothes. The Special Investigations Unit was not required to wear uniforms.

"I'm just trying to get a handle on things. It's the dead of winter, Ella. In January, what we usually see in the Four Corners are deaths from exposure, and car accidents from the bad roads, not a rash of petty crimes. Around here, people like to stay inside whenever they can and watch TV. This year, with the Rez's economy nothing short of a disaster, people have cut back on everything—including driving. So what's with all the misdemeanors?"

"Maybe it's just street gang activity," Ella suggested. "Face it. Kids get restless when there's nothing to do."

"I agree that fences being knocked down, dents put in cars, and spray-painted graffiti sounds like gangs. But letting the air out of tires during church? And what happened yesterday to you with that Dumpster being split open like a tin can, that's not their MO at all. Think about it. High explosives with a fuse and detonator instead of gunpowder and a pipe bomb? Uh-uh. Stealing that kind of stuff isn't easy, Ella, and it's a federal crime."

"Somebody's relative could work for one of the mines or a construction company. Or, who knows, it may have come from off the reservation. Blalock is working with the ATF now to track down the lot number from the partial wrapping recovered at the scene. And the residue is supposed to be chemically tagged as well, so it should tell us which manufacturing batch it came from."

"Well, all I can say is that we better get some leads soon. This is making us look like idiots, and a lot of us are getting flak from the community, especially in the Shiprock area, where most of it seems concentrated. I was having dinner with Wilson over in Waterflow and you wouldn't believe some of the snide comments people started making about the department once they realized who I was. It was pretty insulting, Ella. And I'm not the only one that's happened to, either. I've heard the grumbles in the bullpen before briefings. I have a feeling some of our cops would resign if unemployment wasn't so high right now on the Rez."

"We're being run ragged because we don't have enough cops on the force. Everyone's dead tired, so naturally morale's going to take a beating. But squelch the defeatist talk when you hear it, will you?"

"Sure thing. But the only way to really stop it is to catch the vandals. Maybe then we can go back to working single shifts."

"I know." Ella watched out the passenger's side window as they moved slowly through the old tribal housing project on the eastern outskirts of Shiprock. Nearly every one of the small frame houses had a vehicle or two parked on the concrete pad beside it or along the street.

The people in this neighborhood, for the most part, worked at one of the coal mines or power plants along the eastern perimeter of the Rez. Their jobs, for now, were safe.

"How are things going for you, cousin? I hear you've been practicing long hours at the firing range."

Justine nodded, her eyes on the road. "It hasn't been easy." She flexed her right hand on the steering wheel. Her index finger was missing the first two joints, and the stub remaining poked out like it had a mind of its own. "I used to enjoy going to the range to practice, Ella. I've always been a marksman and able to give you some serious competition. But lately . . ." She let the sentence hang.

"What's giving you the most trouble when you shoot?"

"Maintaining control. The recoil from the first round screws up my grip and the following shots go wild unless I really clamp down with my left hand, too. But to qualify we have to be able to shoot one-handed," Justine answered. "It's a trick and a half, Ella. I'm using my middle finger for the trigger. All that's left on the grips are my last two fingers and, of course, my thumb, as it wraps around. I've got small hands, so the extra control that my middle finger gave me before really helped stabilize the weapon in rapid fire. If I could use something other than standard ammunition, that might help, but that's not allowed, particularly when qualifying," she said, frustration evident in her tone.

"How about Pachmayr grips made of neoprene—only custom made to fit your 'new' hand?"

"They might help," she said, considering Ella's suggestion. "I'll check around and see who might be able to work with me on that."

"Maybe we can go out to the range together and come up with a design," Ella said.

"I'd appreciate the help. Wilson has been out with me, and I've been practicing a lot. But I've got to tell you that I wouldn't have qualified at all the other day if I'd had to shoot another round. By the end of the session my right hand was really in bad shape. The hammer kept tearing into the web of my hand every time the pistol recoiled."

"And being in pain didn't help your aim, I would imagine. You might want to look for a smaller-frame weapon, even if it costs you in firepower—less rounds per clip."

"Yeah, that's not a bad idea. But, to tell you the truth, I've been thinking that maybe I should take a desk job."

"Why? You'd hate it." Ella looked over at her, surprised.

"Better than not being able to back up my partner when she needs me."

"You'd back me up, no matter what it took. I know you, cousin. In a firefight, you don't even notice little details like pain until it's all over."

Justine smiled. "I appreciate your faith in me, Ella. I mean that. But unless I can solve this problem soon, I'm going to ask to be taken out of the field. Maybe I can just do crime-scene processing and the lab work."

"That's not really what you want. I think you should give yourself time to learn some new tricks."

Justine started to answer when a call came over the radio. Dispatch came through clearly, though that was not always the case when they were in rough country or around some of the big power lines.

"SI Unit One, this is Dispatch. A resident reports a possible ten-thirty-eight on north Riverside. Perps are southbound in an old pickup. No further description of the vehicle is available. Respond Code One."

Ella acknowledged the call, then racked the mike. "Vandalism—still in progress. If we do a Code One, silent approach, we may just strike paydirt. Let's catch these guys."

"I know that neighborhood," Justine said. "Modernists and new traditionalists live there."

With the red light placed on the dash and no sirens, they sped west into Shiprock along Highway 64, then northwest onto the residential area around the old mesa boarding school.

As they approached via a paved street with lampposts at each intersection, Ella switched off the emergency lights and asked Justine to turn off the vehicle lights as well. "Go nice and easy. I want to creep up on these jerks."

They turned down Riverside, heading south, and immediately saw two suspects in an old beat-up truck cruising slowly down the street on the wrong side of the road. The passenger was leaning out the window, tossing bricks into the windshields of parked vehicles.

"Lights on. They're ours," Ella snapped.

The sight of the flashing lights galvanized the pickup driver, and the vehicle skidded around the next corner toward the east and the main highway.

"Stay with them," Ella ordered, calling for backup. "See if you can close in so I can get the plate number."

Justine hit the siren, then the gas pedal, and the souped-up engine responded. But as they pulled up to less than four car lengths behind the perps, it was obvious that the plate had been intentionally splattered with mud, obscuring the three-letter, three-number code. Ella cursed.

"Should I stay in pursuit?" Justine asked as they swerved south onto Highway 666, heading right into the center of town. "It's late and there isn't much traffic, but we're doing sixty and there's a light coming up."

"Stay with them as long as you can do it without endangering any bystanders," Ella said. "Keep them in sight."

Passing the church at the next intersection, the perps ran the red light, nearly T-boning a car. The panicked driver of the small sedan managed to evade the pickup by swerving left, but that put it head-on with Justine's unit and in the wrong lane.

Justine turned the wheel hard to the right, nearly catching the rear end of the sedan, and hit the brakes, coming to a screeching stop fifty yards past the intersection. The sedan spun a full 360 degrees before jumping the median and slamming into a light pole with a crunch.

"It's your call, Ella. Should I continue pursuit or check out the accident?"

Ella could still see the outline of the pickup roaring east out of Shiprock, its lights off now. Anger tore at her, but her duty was clear. "We stay. We have to check out the driver and any passengers. Even if no one's hurt, something like this often brings on a heart attack."

While Justine got on the radio to request the EMTs, Ella ran over to the sedan. The hood was arched slightly and the front bumper had snapped where it struck the metal pole. But the airbag had inflated, protecting the driver, who'd fortunately been wearing her seat belt. A quick check revealed no passengers.

The Navajo woman in her late thirties was wild-eyed as she climbed out of the car, yelling at Ella. Unfortunately, her radio was blasting a popular, fast-moving country song about a cheating husband, and Ella couldn't hear what she was saying over the din. Seeing Ella gesture, the woman reached back into her car and turned off the ignition and, mercifully, the music.

"What are the police thinking, going on a high-speed chase right through the middle of town? You weren't even looking!"

"We *were* looking. You were the one tuned out. You should have pulled over to the right shoulder and stayed out of the intersection when you heard the siren and saw our emergency lights coming down the hill. But you didn't hear us with the music cranked up so loud, right?" Ella shook her head and asked for the woman's driver's license.

The woman, Arlene Natani, handed it to her, somewhat mollified.

"You're lucky to have survived this without anything more than smeared lipstick and a good scare," Ella told her. Unfortunately, the perps were probably halfway to Hogback by now. They'd go to ground on the Rez long before backup could materialize. The PD was stretched too thin these days.

"The EMTs will be here shortly," Justine said, joining them.

"I don't need them. I'm not injured. I'm a nurse and I know what signs to look for. I just want to go home. I've had a long day."

While Justine canceled the EMTs, Ella requested a patrol officer from the station be sent out to complete the accident report. While waiting for him, Ella and Justine began the paperwork, gathering the woman's personal information and getting her statement.

Fifteen more minutes passed before they were finally able to leave the scene. "That fender bender just cost us the first chance we've had so far to arrest these vandals. All we can do now is go back and see if any of the victims saw something we can use."

They returned to the north Riverside neighborhood and found most of the people outside, looking over their damaged cars. Ella and Justine split up, talking to the residents on opposite sides of the street. People's tempers were short and when word got around that the vandals had escaped, their irritation became even more pronounced.

Canvassing the neighborhood became a long and tedious process. Most of the victims had been awakened by the loud thuds of breaking safety glass and had neither heard nor seen anything useful.

After an hour of going in and out of residences or standing outside in the freezing cold, Ella joined her partner. She could barely feel her hands now. They'd gone numb because she'd forgotten her gloves in her Jeep, which was back at the station.

Ella stood beside Justine as she finished questioning

Myrna Manus on the front porch of her home. The clinic director was always in a foul mood but was at her absolute worst tonight. Her BMW had lost its windshield.

"I called right after I heard the first windshield pop. What took you so long? Did you stop for doughnuts along the way?"

"Actually, we were here three minutes after the call, Myrna," Ella said. "We were the closest unit."

"I still remember when we had that break-in at the clinic last year. The bad guys got away then, too, but at least this time you didn't pepper the entire neighborhood with bullets. I suppose we should be grateful for that." Myrna walked out to her car and stared at the mounds of cubed glass on the hood and dash. "Look at what they did! I saved for ten years to get that car. It doesn't even have a license plate yet."

Justine gave Ella a tight-lipped look. "Look, Mrs. Manus, count your blessings. You're insured. Lots of people on the Rez have to get by without that, even when it's breaking the law, because they just don't have the money."

"Yes, but now my rates will go through the roof. If you'd been doing your jobs properly, these criminals would have been in jail before tonight and none of this would have been necessary."

"We all want to put a stop to this crime wave," Justine began.

Ella tuned her out as an uneasy feeling began to creep up her spine. Losing track of what her partner was saying, she looked around carefully, trying to figure out what was wrong, but almost everyone had gone inside now. Yet, she could feel someone watching them. It was that creepy tingling at the back of her neck that made no sense in logical terms but, on a gut level, she knew not to ignore it.

Once Mrs. Manus went back inside her home, Justine looked over at her partner. "What's wrong, Ella? You've got that look on your face."

"What look?" Ella continued to study the area as they crossed the street, heading in the direction of their police unit.

"*The* look. The one that says you know something's up. What's going on?"

"I don't know yet," Ella answered slowly. She felt the badger fetish she wore around her neck growing warm despite the chill. It was probably just her body heat working overtime when her nerves were on edge but, the truth was, that whenever that fetish felt hot, there was danger close by. She reached beneath her jacket, unsnapping the strap that kept her weapon fastened in place. The metal was cold, almost sticking to her fingers, but the familiar touch was somehow reassuring.

"Let's get back to the vehicle as soon as we can. Step up the pace, but don't run," Ella ordered, quietly. "I think we're being watched."

"By whom?" Justine glanced around casually, careful not to tip off their watcher. "I don't see a soul. Everyone's inside now, smart cookies that they are. It's freezing out here."

"Yeah. But he's there. I can feel it." Sometimes the subconscious mind processed information that was minute by regular standards, but as a cop, she'd learned to trust her instincts. Ella's gaze continued to sweep the area.

As they approached the unit, passing under the illumination of a streetlight across the intersection, Ella saw a flash of light, like a small explosion, from the hill farther east. The stop sign, less than three feet in front of them, twitched abruptly.

Ella dove forward, knocking Justine to the grass as the crack of a distant rifle shot reverberated in the air. Justine rolled into the long shadow cast by their police unit while Ella crawled over to the side of the vehicle.

"Stay low. I'm calling it in," Ella said, reaching for the handheld radio clipped to her waist.

THREE
✖ ✖ ✖

Backup is on the way," Ella whispered, looking around the front tire rather than risking a look over the hood. "I saw the muzzle flash way up on the mesa about a quarter of a mile from here. I'm going over there now."

"We don't have night-vision glasses and it's pitch-black outside. And we'll be sitting ducks in the vehicle. Let's just sit tight until we have backup."

"If we do, and the sniper's patient, he'll have a lot more cops in his sights. But you're right about getting in the unit or even staying near it. With the streetlight overhead, we'd be making ourselves great targets. Put some distance between you and the unit, but stay in the shadows and move quickly. I'll go up onto the mesa on foot while you warn the residents to stay away from their windows. You can direct our backup when they get here."

"If you're going up there, I'm sticking with you, Ella. You'll need someone to divide the sniper's attention. I'll advise dispatch where the muzzle flash came from using the radio and, as far as the residents go, I'll warn the ones in the closest house and have them pass the word."

Before Justine could grab her handheld, Ella realized that the lights inside the two closest homes had come on, and people were peering cautiously from the edges of their windows. "There's a sniper! Stay away from the windows and doors and tell your neighbors to do the same!" Ella yelled at the person inside the home behind her. "And turn off your lights."

Immediately the figure watching them disappeared.

The lights in the house were quickly turned off, and others down the street followed suit a short time later.

"Okay. Let's go, and follow an unpredictable course. It'll be harder for him to track two moving targets, especially ones who aren't coming at him in a straight line. Let's just hope he doesn't get lucky," Ella said.

Ella led the way up the wide alley behind the row of houses, running the entire length up the slight incline, zigzagging at random intervals. Justine followed several steps behind, using the same tactics but different moves.

They reached the last of the houses within five minutes, then came upon several stunted trees. Ella kept her eyes peeled on the outline of the mesa above, looking for an easy way up the fifty-foot-high cliff as they got closer. She paused at the foot of a well-traveled trail, probably used by the kids on the way back and forth to school, and took out her handgun.

"Unless he's moved over to the edge of the mesa, he can't see us at the moment, and won't know which way we'll come up," Ella told Justine. "Give me a ten-second head start," Ella added, her breath rushing out in clouds of water vapor now, "and look around before you expose yourself at the top."

Ella was nearly out of breath by the time she approached the top of the mesa and peered over cautiously. A hundred feet ahead she could see a cluster of crosses and low stone markers surrounded by the remnants of a white picket fence. "What the . . ."

"You don't remember the graveyard?" Justine asked in a whisper as she caught up with Ella.

"No. Did you?" Ella whispered back.

"Yeah, I sneaked over on a dare when I was a kid, and I never forgot it. There was a church here once but it burned down and they never rebuilt it. No one comes into this area anymore, except maybe *chindi* and skinwalkers."

"Then why is that housing development so close by?" Ella asked, then shook her head, suddenly understanding. "Never mind. I get it. The residents are mostly modernists and new traditionalists, right? Even if they could see this place clearly in the distance, they probably wouldn't care." Ella paused, her gut coiling into a tight knot. "I'm not thrilled about walking across a graveyard, but if we go around it, it'll take too much time. The muzzle flash I saw came from that little rise over there. We have to cut through."

"Yeah, okay," Justine said.

Ella didn't have to look to know her partner would follow her as she stepped over a section of flattened fence.

"It's not as big as I remember it," Justine said, suppressing a shiver.

"Less than twenty graves, I figure. But be careful where you step, so you won't trip on one of the metal markers and fall on top of one of the graves." Ella looked around cautiously. "The problem is that not all of the graves have permanent markers."

"Great. Just what I needed to hear," Justine replied, stepping around a wreath of all-weather plastic flowers that must have been blown away from a grave.

They made their way across the concrete pad that was once the floor of the church, crouching low. As they left the church ruins and the graveyard behind them, the wind carried the sound of a truck engine starting somewhere down the hill, then a heartbeat later, screeching tires on asphalt at the highway below. The roar of the engine quickly faded away to the north.

"That's probably him," Justine said, slowly standing to full height. "I have a feeling he was watching us all the time from the truck, wondering if we'd cross the graveyard or not."

"Maybe, but he's long gone now. The only chance we had of taking him by surprise was to come up on foot." Ella holstered her weapon, unhooked her radio from her waist, and advised Dispatch.

Once finished, she took out her flashlight and made

her way to the area of high ground that would have made the best vantage point for the sniper. Working methodically, she searched the ground with Justine's help. "Let's see if we can find the spent cartridge or something that will help us track the sniper, the weapon, or both."

After several minutes of fruitless searching, Justine looked up, teeth chattering as the wind whipped against them. "I'll come back tomorrow after daybreak. If there's anything here, I'll find it then."

"There's the Stop and Go further ahead, on the north side of the bluff near the main highway," Ella said, pointing. "You can see the parking lot sign easily from this high spot, and I think the tire marks veer off in that general direction. Once we get back to your unit, we'll go talk to the night manager. Maybe he saw the guy racing by."

By the time they'd walked back down to the neighborhood and had reached Justine's unit, backup was already at work. Most people had stayed inside, not willing to risk having a sniper use them for target practice—all except for Myrna Manus, who was walking toward them now.

Ella heard one of the officers who was searching the intersection for evidence speak to his partner. "I knew she was itching to come out. A woman like that doesn't fear anything. Hell, one look from her, and the bullets would fly into each other."

"I can't believe this! Somebody is taking potshots at us down here and our alleged police force is standing around in the street chatting! What are you people waiting for? Go and arrest whoever's doing this."

"We will as soon as we know who to take into custody," Ella said patiently. She couldn't help but notice that Justine had slipped away and was doing her best to avoid eye contact with her. She was trying hard to appear as busy as possible near the stop sign as she helped the ongoing search for evidence. "Since we were unable to catch the sniper, we'll have to collect what evidence we can find here and up on the hill, and search for clues and a motive."

"Then get busy!"

"As a concerned citizen," Ella added pointedly, "do you happen to have any useful information you can share that will point us in the right direction? I know this is a real reach, but does anyone have a reason to consider you their enemy? Or maybe you know of someone else in the neighborhood who's pissed someone off recently? Do you know anyone who might be inclined to pick up a gun and start shooting at people?"

"From what I heard, the sniper was shooting at *you*, not one of my neighbors. Of course he might have easily hit any one of us. If I had to lay odds, I'd say it was a recent vandalism victim upset because none of you cops are doing your job."

Seeing other people starting to come outside, Ella hardened her expression. "Go back inside, Myrna, and quit distracting us with your unproductive dialogue. Give us a chance to work here."

"That's just it. You're not *doing* anything."

"Are you going home under your own power, or would you prefer that I escort you there myself?"

Myrna's eyes grew wide. "You'll hear about this, Ella. I promise you that," she said and stalked back to her house.

"You'd think the cold weather would freeze that tongue," Sergeant Neskahi said as he walked up to Ella.

"Nothing would freeze that tongue. It's always moving too fast. She's a pain in the—neck."

"Sure that's the place?" he said with a chuckle.

Leaving a team to continue processing the scene, Ella gave Neskahi and another officer instructions to take lanterns and check out the suspected sniper area once more tonight. Once that was covered, Ella joined Justine in her police unit and they drove toward the Stop and Go, about a half mile north of the shooter's position.

"Ernest Ration, the night manager, is no stranger to

violence," Justine said. "If he heard the gunshot he would have recognized it for what it was and grabbed a weapon. He wouldn't stand around wondering what was going on."

"How well do you know him?"

"Not that well, actually. He's never paid much attention to me. He's an ex-Ranger and friend of George, my oldest brother."

"But you would have loved a chance to get to know him better, right?" Ella teased.

"Maybe at one time," she admitted. "But he's dating a tall blonde from Farmington these days. My brother described her as having legs that took a week to get to the ground."

Ella smiled. "I'm getting the picture. What is it with our men and blondes? They see yellow hair and salivate."

"I think it's got something to do with testosterone. Anglo men show a preference for yellow hair too, I'm told. Look what they're missing," she added, making Ella laugh.

As they pulled up to the small convenience store, a stocky, broad-shouldered Navajo man carrying a carbine came out. He held it with both hands, ready to fire from the hip or bring it up to his shoulders. Ella tensed, and reached down to unsnap the strap of her holster.

"Easy. That's Ernest. He won't shoot. I'd bet he was expecting us," Justine said.

Justine stepped out of the car. "Hi, Ernest. Remember me? I'm George's sister—the cop. Would you put the rifle away, please?"

He nodded once, lowered the weapon so he was holding it in one hand down by his side, then gestured for them to come inside the store.

Ella looked him over carefully. He wasn't tense, the way an amped-up shooter often was. He was simply carrying the carbine as casually as a hunter might on the way back to camp. Yet there was something about him that made her uneasy. She didn't refasten the strap of her holster as she left the car and went inside.

"I was wondering if something happened up there," he said. "I heard the shot, definitely from a big, high-velocity weapon. Then I saw a silver pickup come hauling down this side of the mesa cross-country, hit the road burning rubber, and take off toward Cortez."

"Did you notice the make and model?" Ella asked.

"No, but I think it was a big Ford or Chevy. He was hauling ass and, in the dark, there was no way I could get a better look."

"Call the Colorado state police and put an APB on a metallic gray or silver large-frame pickup," Ella told Justine.

"What about a roadblock?" Justine asked.

"I doubt we have an officer between here and the Colorado state line right now. But, in this case, it doesn't make any difference. Face it, the perp could take one of a dozen side roads along the way and we'd just waste manpower running up and down the highway."

As Justine went back to the unit to put in the call, Ella studied Ernest, who was taking off his brown leather jacket now that he was inside again. He still wore the military buzz haircut and had the confidence of a man who didn't have to work up much of a sweat to get troublemakers to back down. "You always keep that carbine handy?"

"Yeah, as a matter of fact, I do. If I hear shooting, I don't wait to see how close it can get before I'm ready to deal with it."

"You might end up walking into a really bad situation someday."

"I was trained to deal with that. The other guy's going to be the one in trouble."

His eyes were focused and direct. He might have been the man who'd fired at her, though it would have been a nearly impossible shot over open sights, especially with a carbine. "Would you mind if I took a look at your weapon?"

He handed it to her.

Ella opened the bolt of the semiauto, sniffed for the scent of burned gunpowder, and found none. There was a round in the chamber so she unloaded the weapon by pushing the round back down into the box magazine with her thumb, then closed the bolt on the empty chamber and snapped the trigger. Then she handed the weapon back to Ernest.

To her, this was a guy hoping to find trouble—a bored serviceman who still hadn't readjusted to civilian life. "If you don't mind my asking, what are you doing clerking at a convenience store?"

"That's where the action is late at night." Ernest smiled and shrugged. "Actually, I'm just making a living while I'm trying to figure out what to do next. I may even join the Tribal PD."

She studied him for a moment before answering. They could use more manpower, but instinct told her he wasn't cut out for the job. "Police work takes a lot more restraint than the kind of missions you had in the armed forces."

"Yeah, I know. That's why I'm still thinking it over."

"Stay out of trouble," Ella said, and headed for the door.

Ella met Justine back at the unit. "Drive back to that stop sign. We need to track down the bullet that was fired at me. By tomorrow, kids will be all over the place and evidence will disappear."

Joining the officers already there, Ella and Justine studied the size of the hole in the metal stop sign. Only a large, powerful weapon would be capable of punching a hole that big.

"What do you think, an elephant gun?" Justine asked.

"Could be, and because of the range, it had to be high velocity as well. Maybe more like a fifty-caliber. It looks like we're dealing with one heck of a marksman, too.

He didn't miss me by much, despite a good cross wind." Ella studied the copper traces around the puncture. "It was a jacketed bullet."

"A few manufacturers make sniper-style weapons of that caliber, but they're big, heavy, and *very* expensive. Around these parts, they're primarily used for long-range competitions. But, even so, they're few and far between," Justine said. "That should help us."

Seeing Officer Tache, Ella joined him. The round-faced crime-scene investigator was taking photographs with a flash. Seeing Ella, he looked up. "I came up with an approximate trajectory by shining a narrow flashlight beam through the hole in the sign from the direction you indicated the shot had come from." He pointed toward three white stakes he'd placed in a line on the big lawn across the street. "It's the best we can do for the moment. But I haven't found the bullet yet. Any suggestions?"

"No. Let's work together walking down the sight line. I don't think it would have ricocheted off the street or sidewalk, judging from the angle."

Justine stayed close to Ella as they worked, trying to watch Ella's back. Justine had been bloodied, but her spirit was strong, and her determination and instincts were still 100 percent cop.

"He's long gone, Justine. You can relax," Ella said quietly.

"We're *assuming* he's long gone. He could come back, or have an accomplice. Obviously, shooting at a cop isn't a problem for him."

They used their flashlights to look for indications along the stunted grass that it had been disturbed or gouged. "Ration seems eager to find trouble," Ella commented. "What's your brother say about him?"

"Not much, but I'd have a hard time believing he was the shooter, if that's what you're thinking. Talking from strictly a cop's point of view, the carbine isn't a sniper's weapon of choice—not for a target at that range."

"He could have switched weapons before we got there

to throw us off. Maybe he's talent someone hired. Some of the gung-ho types harbor the notion of becoming mercenaries."

Justine hesitated. "Taken from that perspective, he could have been the sniper, I suppose. He's got the skill level. He went to one of the turkey shoots last Thanksgiving with one of our patrolmen and won two birds with two shots."

"But you're not convinced?"

"No, not really. From what I know and have heard about him, he's the type who likes having people know all about his accomplishments. My feeling is that becoming a hit man—a job where he couldn't brag about how good he was, or at least get a pat on the shoulder—isn't his style at all."

Ella nodded thoughtfully. That fit her impression of him as well. Cocky and not subtle about it. "Okay. I just wanted to sound you out on that. Let's keep looking."

"Whoever took a shot at us wasn't playing around, Ella. Somebody's gunning for a cop, and a jacketed round like that would pierce our vests."

"I know," she said in a taut voice. "Front and back."

After searching for over an hour with a metal detector, they found nothing except roofing nails, a few coins, some bottle caps, and several of those aluminum lift tabs that would probably be around for the next millennium. Disappointed, but hoping they'd have better luck after sunrise, Ella made arrangements to have a two-man team remain in the area to discourage scavengers until the crime-scene team returned at dawn. The residential street couldn't be completely cordoned off without preventing people from getting out of their homes, so Criminalistics would have to work quickly tomorrow.

Twenty-five minutes later, her hands wrapped around a Styrofoam cup of coffee, Ella sat down at her desk at the station. Justine took the chair across from her.

"I was right beside you when the sniper fired, but you

were his target," Justine said, voicing Ella's thoughts. "The stop sign was on your side."

"Maybe it was a random decision."

"I don't think so. My guess is that somebody with a grudge is gunning for you."

"You could be right. I'll make a list of my known enemies, and we can check on those people first," Ella said.

Justine left Ella, intending to work in her office on the crime-scene report, but returned a few minutes later, paper in hand. "This just came in on the fax. Artie, one of Jeremiah Manyfarms's twin sons, escaped from a federal prison in California."

Ella noted that Justine's hand was shaking as she handed her the bulletin. Artie had been one of the men who'd kidnapped her and cut off her finger in an elaborate plan to frame Ella last year.

"Don't let them get to you, cousin."

"Easier for you to say." Justine's eyes blazed with fire. "That ordeal is over as far as you're concerned, but I'm still paying for what happened."

Ella glanced down at the fax. The twins, twenty years old now, had apparently used the fact that they were identical to confuse the guards. It had taken a fingerprint comparison to confirm which of the two was missing. The escape had gone undetected until a few hours ago and, in that time, Artie would have had plenty of time to fly to New Mexico and take a shot at her.

"I think we just identified our sniper," Justine said, voicing Ella's thoughts.

"We don't know for sure that this was Artie's work," Ella said slowly.

"Sorry, but I don't buy it as an amazing coincidence."

Ella nodded. "It's true that all the Manyfarmses hate my guts. They blame the department, and especially me, for their troubles, especially now since we busted the lot of them and sent them to prison."

"If Artie Manyfarms is our sniper," Justine said, "he's

acting alone now. Jeremiah Manyfarms was placed in a different lockup in the Midwest because the authorities felt he was too dangerous to put into the same prison as his sons. What we're probably seeing is a plan the twins hatched up to exact revenge, as opposed to their father's more sophisticated schemes."

Ella was considering Justine's words when she heard someone knock on her open door.

"Hey, Ella," Dwayne Blalock smiled as he walked into her office carrying a large duffle bag. "Justine," he added, nodding to Ella's assistant.

"It's one in the morning. What brings you here now?" Ella asked with raised eyebrows.

"I just heard about Artie Manyfarms. He's gone fugitive."

"Yeah, we got the fax."

"Let me guess. You didn't find out until *after* the sniper incident?" Blalock asked.

"Yeah."

Dwayne Blalock hadn't changed much physically since Ella had first met him during the investigation of her father's death several years ago. The tall senior FBI agent had grown a little thicker around the middle and his brown hair was now tinged with gray, but otherwise the years had been kind to him. Known as FB-Eyes to the people on the Rez, a nickname he'd earned because one of his eyes was brown and the other blue, he sometimes put in longer hours than Ella did. If he had a personal life, Ella certainly didn't know about it.

"Deputy Marshal Harry Ute is already en route to New Mexico from California. If Artie Manyfarms has returned to the Rez, we'll catch him before long."

The news about Harry's return cheered her up a bit. It would be good to see him again. Lately, her thoughts often turned to her former special investigations team member. There was a new awareness between them these days that was sexy and exciting. She'd hoped for a chance to be around him and see if the spark she'd felt last time was still there.

"Harry will catch up to you sometime tomorrow. And Ella, what have you got by way of a vest?"

"Department issue. You've seen them."

"That's not good enough—not anymore." He unzipped the duffle bag, and brought out a thick, black bullet-resistant vest that looked more like a ski jacket. "I'm going to give you this on loan. It's a new model with better ballistic properties and designed to be worn on the outside. It passes for a winter jacket, but it'll stop most rifle-caliber rounds outside a hundred yards," he said. "Not tremendously comfortable, mind you, but who cares, right?"

"Thanks, Dwayne. I appreciate it."

Once she was alone again in her office, Ella sat back in her chair and closed her eyes. Her stomach was still in knots. That had been a very close call tonight and, despite Blalock's intent, no vest could stop a high-velocity fifty-caliber bullet—at least none she'd ever seen. And if it was a head shot . . .

Ella took a deep breath, then let it out again, staring down at her hands and willing them not to tremble. Now that she was a mom, incidents like tonight's shook her up more than ever. Yet leaving the department was not an option. Despite her responsibility to her daughter, she also had a debt of honor to pay the tribe who'd financed her education and her training. The tribe needed its cops, and Ella knew she was exactly where she belonged.

Dawn deserved to grow up proud of her mother and to know that she'd always stood for the right. It would be testimony enough of a life well spent, and would speak for her long after she was gone, and serve as an example of courage to her daughter.

As the phone rang, Ella focused back on the job. It was Big Ed, calling from home. He'd been notified about the shooting by the watch commander, and wanted to know all about it. Ella began to go over the evening events, minute by minute, with her boss. A time for work and a time for family, that was the way to walk in beauty.

FOUR
✗ ✗ ✗

Despite the late hour, Ella got busy at her computer terminal checking through police data files and the federal crime base for a hit on a sporting goods store, or a collector. Very large bore target rifles weren't in great demand, so it wasn't long before she found a likely connection to the sniper attack.

Hunter's Emporium in Farmington had reported the theft of a fifty-caliber telescope-equipped target rifle, a night scope, and fifty rounds of match ammunition. The video camera at the establishment had captured the fleeting image of a tall, slender man wearing a mask, but no ID was possible. A second parking lot camera showed the thief leaving in a metallic gray late-model pickup. The vehicle tags had been stolen as well.

Justine came in a moment later. "I retrieved the file on Artie Manyfarms. He still has a lot of relatives in this area, including his mom in Gallup. I also read that he and his brother have years of experience in hunting and competitive shooting. Artie was the better shot of the two." She paused. "Ella, for what it's worth, my money's on this guy."

"Contact the Gallup police and the McKinley County Sheriff's Department. We need to put Mrs. Manyfarms under surveillance," Ella said.

"She's remarried now, her name is Sanchez."

"Make sure she's watched twenty-four/seven," Ella said, standing up to stretch and yawn. "After that, go home. We need to get at least a few hours' sleep. We have to report to work early in the morning."

"Deal."

About a half hour later, Ella walked out of her office. She was dead tired and, to make matters worse, she was getting that odd sick feeling at the pit of her stomach— the kind that usually meant things at work were going to turn to complete and utter crap soon.

The way Ella figured it, by tomorrow morning Rose would know all about what had happened. It was inevitable, even if she didn't notice the extra patrols Big Ed had ordered around their home. On the Rez, secrets were as rare as hen's teeth. After that, Ella could expect Rose to be furious with her for at least a week. The risks associated with police work always affected her deeply, and anger was Rose's way of dealing with it.

Trying to push back the gloominess she felt, Ella allowed her thoughts to turn to Harry. She'd invite him for dinner the first chance she got. At least it would help put her mother in a better mood.

"Harry, come soon. You're my only hope," Ella whispered as a cold wind blew around her. Realizing that she was talking to herself, and convinced she'd lost her mind, Ella got into her unit and drove home.

Ella woke up with a start as a pan, then another, clattered to the floor. She could hear the radio blasting in the kitchen, giving the weather report with the same old forecast—cold and dry. Ella squinted against the first rays of sunlight, trying to orient herself. The clock on her bedstand said it was 6:45.

With a groan, she placed the pillow over her head and tried to go back to sleep. Within seconds, another pan clattered loudly to the floor.

Dawn came into the bedroom holding her stuffed dinosaur. *"Shimasání* angry," she whispered.

"What happened? Did you do something?" Ella muttered sleepily, her eyes semiclosed.

Dawn shook her head.

"Sweetie, let me sleep a while longer," Ella begged, curling up beneath the covers.

The radio in the kitchen changed stations and suddenly country music blasted down the hall. Ella groaned. Who was she trying to kid? She wouldn't get any sleep. This was Rose's revenge. "Mom!"

There was no answer.

Accepting her fate, Ella got out of bed wearing her ancient Shiprock Chieftains sweatshirt and wool socks. The wood-and-coal stove in the living room, one they'd added to supplement the butane heater, already had a fire going inside and the house was warming up slowly.

Ella padded into the kitchen while Dawn remained in the living room to play with her toys.

"Mom, show some mercy," Ella pleaded.

"Oh, are you up?" Rose had to speak loudly to be heard over the radio.

Ella turned the music down, then sat, lowering her head to the kitchen table, using her folded arms as a pillow. "Mom, I didn't get to bed till after three," she croaked. "What are you doing to me?"

"Your daughter gets up at six-thirty in the morning. I was taking care of her," Rose snapped, making scrambled eggs in the old iron skillet.

"Fine. Then if you have everything under control, I'll go back to bed."

Rose scraped the scrambled eggs out of the skillet onto a plate with a large metal spoon, banging the spoon against the skillet to dislodge a few chunks of egg. It sounded like the stamping machines at a steel mill. Ella stopped at the door and groaned loudly. "Mom, I swear, just one more loud noise, and I'm going to arrest you for disturbing the peace."

Rose glowered at her. "You may be a cop, but I'm your mother. I outrank you. Now explain why you never bothered to tell me that someone was trying to kill you!"

Ella rubbed her eyes. Rose must have heard about the sniper incident already. It had to be a new Rez record.

The only thing she could figure was that there'd been early news reports on the radio or a piece in the Farmington paper. "If you're talking about the sniper—"

Rose glared at her. "If you're not even sure what I'm talking about, there must be a lot more going on you haven't told me."

Ella returned to the table and plopped back down in her chair. This was going to be a long morning. "Mom, what did you expect me to do, wake you up at three in the morning to give you a full report? I'm sure you would have slept real well after hearing that. Come to think about it, maybe *I* would have managed to sleep late. We could have had this fight then."

Ella was fully awake now, glaring at her mother.

Rose shrugged. "I see your point, but that doesn't mean I have to like hearing about you being in danger. Do you have any idea who did this?"

Ella wondered why she hadn't taken a firmer stand on this issue years ago. Maybe it was because she'd been raised not to fight with her parents. "We're still trying to find out what happened. Someone took a shot at me, and then I learned that one of the twins from that conspiracy last year has broken out of prison. It's very possible that he's the one who came after me."

Rose sat across the table from Ella and studied her daughter's expression. "But you have your doubts about that, don't you?"

Ella nodded. Her mother read her like a book. "From a logical standpoint, he's a really good suspect. He's got a motive—revenge—and had enough time to have stolen a weapon and come looking for me."

"Your intuition is more reliable than your logic. It's your gift."

Ella knew what her mother meant. It was all tied to her family's past and the strange legacy that had been handed down through the generations. Her brother, Clifford, was said to have inherited leadership qualities and a remarkable gift for healing. Ella's special ability was said to be intuition. But those who believed in that legacy never took into account the years of study Clifford had dedicated to becoming a medicine man, nor all the training Ella had obtained as an FBI agent, then as a cop. The legacy held more appeal because there was nothing either glamorous or magical about hard work.

"I don't know, Mom. I just have the strong feeling that we need to work slowly and not accept any of the easy answers that present themselves."

"In the meantime, will you be wearing that heavy armored vest I saw in the living room?"

Ella nodded, vaguely remembering leaving it there last night as she'd made her way through the house in the dark. "It's a loaner from FB-Eyes."

"Oh, I nearly forgot. I think you should know that early this morning at around five, an officer drove by, stopped, and aimed his searchlight all over. He took a good long look at our house before driving on," Rose commented.

Ella looked up at her in surprise. "I slept right through it. My boss ordered extra patrols just to make sure there's no trouble."

Ella finished breakfast with Dawn on her lap, glad to be with her girl for a little longer today even if it had cost her some extra sleep. She had a feeling that she'd be putting in some very long hours during the next few weeks.

Leaving Dawn with her juice cup in front of the television to watch a children's program on the educational channel, Ella showered and dressed. By the time she walked down the hall, ready to go to work, she heard her mother in the den. Ella went to find her.

Rose was standing at the window, lost in thought, a piece of paper in her hand. Hearing footsteps, she turned her head and smiled at Ella. "I came across your brother's baptismal certificate in the back of a drawer this morning," she said, and smiled sadly. "I still remember that day as if it were yesterday. Your father wanted your brother baptized and he wouldn't take no for an answer, so I eventually gave in. But I hated it."

Rose looked down at her hands. "That was so many years ago, but the time between then and now seems like nothing more than the passing of a few hours."

"Do you miss Dad?" Ella asked softly.

Rose nodded and sighed. "I liked knowing that he needed me to take care of him, whether he admitted it or not."

Ella was suddenly aware of how lonely her mother was. It should have occurred to her before now that having her daughter and granddaughter around wouldn't be enough all by itself for Rose, but she'd never stopped to think about it. "Mom, you need to start going out and meeting new people."

She shook her head. "I can't. It just doesn't seem right. Even when Bizaadii asked me to go have dinner with him at the Totah Café, I said no."

She recognized the nickname. It meant "the gabby one" and it had been given as a joke to Herman Cloud, who was known for being a man of few words. Herman was also Philip and Michael Cloud's uncle, and a long-time family friend.

"But why? You two have known each other practically forever and you're both traditionalists, so you have a lot in common. Why don't you reconsider his invitation?"

Rose smiled knowingly. "Think it through, daughter. How would you really feel seeing your mother in the company of a man who is not your father?"

Ella wanted to deny that it would bother her, and open that door for her mother, but experience told her that Rose would see through any attempt she made to hide the truth. "It would probably make me feel strangely at first, but I'd get over it. You've helped me out so much, Mom. You take care of my daughter and I can never thank you enough for that. But you're entitled to a life of your own as well.

"And your friend has been close to me and my brother for a long time," Ella added. "Remember how he helped me when I returned to the Rez, and how many times he's helped protect us from our enemies? That man is very special to me. You couldn't have picked a better companion."

Rose nodded slowly and thoughtfully, then looked at Ella. "And what about you? I worry more about your future, daughter. You're still young, but instead of having a busy social life, all you do is work. Our people believe we have a right to remarry when we lose our mates, and on this I agree, as long as those left behind show respect by waiting a few years before seeking a new companion. What are you waiting for?"

"I don't like to date coworkers, you know that, and meeting men outside the department is difficult." She stopped, then in a thoughtful voice added, "But now maybe things will be different. . . ." Ella realized what she'd said, and silently cursed herself for her own stupidity. Rose wouldn't let this go now.

"So there *is* someone!"

"No, not really." Ella knew that denying anything was pointless. She was only postponing the matter. The subject would keep cropping up in every conversation until Rose finally got the answer she was looking for.

Well, at least it had distracted her. Ella stopped by the front door, then glanced back, trying to look casual. "Oh, Mom, my friend the deputy federal marshal is coming back into town as part of an investigation. I may ask him over for dinner."

As Ella bent down to kiss Dawn good-bye, she heard her mother chuckling.

It was eight-thirty by the time she walked through the side door of the station. Lucas Payestewa, the young Hopi FBI agent, greeted her, holding a cup of coffee in each hand. " 'Morning."

Ella smiled at him, accepting the offered cup. It was hard not to like the chubby little fed most of the cops now called Paycheck. "Good morning, and thanks for the brew. Is Blalock already in?"

"He's with Big Ed, so we should probably head over there and join the council."

A few moments later, both FBI agents, Ella, and the Special Investigations team composed of Justine, Officer Tache, and Sergeant Neskahi were sitting or standing around Big Ed's desk.

"Now that we're all here," Big Ed said, "Officer Tache can start his report. Ralph?"

"I finally recovered the bullet this morning. I went out there at around five-thirty after the sky was starting to lighten up, looked around, and resighted the trajectory. That's when I found it. The round had lodged in a telephone pole after ricocheting off the sidewalk."

"Was it a fifty-caliber like I thought?" Ella asked.

"You were right on the money with that one."

"The bullet is pretty banged up," Justine said, taking over for Ralph as they reached her area of expertise. "We probably won't be able to positively link it to a particular weapon, but we should have enough points of similarity to disqualify some makes and models."

Justine glanced over at Ella. "I also followed up on the report you left on my desk and spoke to the owner of the sporting goods store in Farmington that was robbed. He verified that the ammunition stolen is manufactured by PMC, and consists of full-metal-jacketed rounds of six-sixty grains." Justine paused. "Those are elephant-hunting-size slugs, equal to more than four of the bullets you use in your nine-millimeter pistol, Ella."

Big Ed cleared his throat and watched the people in the room for a minute or two before speaking. No one said a word. They all knew him well enough to wait, knowing when he had something to say.

"We have a deadly situation on our hands, people. Every officer in the Four Corner states is on the lookout for Artie Manyfarms and that special target rifle. But they have other things to do, too, so we can't count on anyone else solving our problems. This is now our top priority. I want this sniper, people. I have a gut feeling he's still on our land."

"Chief, pardon me for saying so, but the police are stretched pretty thin all over the Rez right now," Blalock said. "No one in this room slept more than a few hours last night. You need help. Is there a chance you can import talent from other PDs or the BIA?"

"I'd rather not bring in anyone who doesn't know the area or the people here, and a lot of the Bureau of Indian Affairs officers are from other tribes." Big Ed stood and began to pace. "But it's more than that. Our people need to believe in *us*, and bringing in outsiders isn't going to help. The vandalism episodes we've been having have really undermined us, and have taken a huge toll on morale. If it looks like we can't make an arrest without outsiders on our team, it'll lower this department's credibility to zero."

"Catching the perps is going to take a combination of hard work and luck, Chief. There's nothing we can do without more cops," Ella said. "The only tactic that's worked as a deterrent is increasing our patrols, but just as soon as they're scaled back, it all starts up again. That's the way it's been since last October, off and on."

"To catch this sniper we're going to have to work with the community and encourage people to tip us off if they hear something, like who the next target might be," Big Ed said. "But unless we stop the vandals nobody will be very anxious to help us."

"I'm going to get a map of the area, post it on the bulletin board in my office, then start indicating with colored pins where the incidents occurred, and when. There might be a pattern if we look at it long enough," Justine suggested. "That could help with placing our manpower."

"Chief, maybe we should take a closer look at what Lieutenant Manuelito is doing in the Window Rock area.

Petty crime has gone down significantly in that district," Tache said.

Ella bristled. Manuelito was a hard line cop who had never given her anything but grief. It was no secret that there was bad blood between them. But, in all fairness, he'd come through for all of them last year when his help had been sorely needed. That particular operation had earned him a promotion and a transfer.

"I know what he's been doing," Big Ed said. "He's set up random, variable-intensity patrols on a grid system. They tried the same thing over at To'hajiilee, but it didn't work nearly as well."

Ella couldn't help wondering if Manuelito had simply driven the bad guys toward easier pickings in the more populous Shiprock area, or maybe gone on the take and tipped them off to vulnerable locations. She tried to push back the thought, almost sure that her intense dislike of the man was playing a big part in her suspicions.

"These vandals always seem to be one step ahead of us," Ella said. "I figure that they must have police scanners and know when our officers are responding to calls. That would explain why the community crime watch hasn't been more effective in helping us catch these guys in the act. The suspects almost always clear the area before we arrive."

"Do you have a recommendation?" Big Ed asked, knowing she did.

"Let's get encrypted cell phones and use them instead of our radios. We can't ask our officers to lay out their own money for this, Chief, but this happens to be something we really need to gain the upper hand."

"There's no way I can squeeze the funds for this from our current budget," Big Ed answered. "But there may be another way. Maybe community business leaders will come forward with a grant if we can convince them it'll help put a stop to this crime wave, which seems to be focused on our area. Let me work on it from that angle and see how it goes."

"I'll find out if the bureau can help you," Blalock said.

"We have to keep up the pressure on whoever's responsible for the wave of petty crimes, now more than ever," Big Ed continued. "But I want the SI team's top priority to be finding this sniper. Clear?"

All of the Navajo cops nodded.

Ella stood, and as she did everyone's attention shifted to her. "First, I want to thank Agent Blalock for the use of the new-model FBI vest. But I'd also like to request that the FBI loan us similar vests for everyone in the SI team. If I'm the target, those who work beside me will also be in the line of fire at a crime scene."

"I'll make the request formal," Big Ed said.

"And I'll push from my end, too." Blalock looked around the room, reading the expressions of his fellow cops. "In the meantime, let me bring everyone up to date. We've traced the serial number of the explosive used to blow up the Dumpster outside the Totah Café. That stick came from a road construction site over by Navajo Lake, where they lost a whole case of high explosives. ATF stands ready to lend a hand if they're needed."

Payestewa spoke slowly. "What we need is a motive for all these low-budget, harassing petty crimes. This is too organized to be as random as it appears at first glance."

Big Ed and Ella exchanged a quick look, but neither said anything, wanting to protect their only source—Coyote.

The Hopi agent continued. "What bothers me is that no one's claiming responsibility. Usually a variety of groups are eager to take the credit, especially when local youth gangs are involved. If nothing else, we should have heard some gossip, and that's the really weird thing about this. Until now, I never believed it was possible to keep secrets on the Rez."

"People are distracted these days," Big Ed said, leaning back in his chair. "They're fighting for survival."

Big Ed's secretary came in holding a police report and handed it silently to her boss.

The chief studied it, then expelled his breath through clenched teeth. "Joe Wallace's outhouse was blown up. He's mad as hell and wants officers out there right now." He glanced at Ella. "I want you to handle this personally, Shorty, and see if you can unruffle his feathers. I shouldn't have to remind you that his brother is one of the new members of the Tribal Council."

When the meeting ended, Ella walked to her office with Justine alongside her.

"I appreciate you asking for extra vests," Justine said. "My family worries about me on the job more than ever now."

"I don't like the idea of getting special treatment," Ella answered.

"If there's only one vest, then it's right you should get it. The sniper is gunning for you. Besides, you have a young daughter to worry about." Justine paused, then added, "Not that you're getting any extra sympathy from me on that count. I think you're lucky to have a little girl like Dawn."

Ella looked at her in surprise. "Since when are you into kids? And, just so you know, there are days when I'd cheerfully give her away to the first person who comes to the door."

Justine smiled. "Yeah, yeah. You're tough, Ella. And, to answer your question, I've always liked kids, though I doubt I'll ever have any. Time's passing, and all that."

Before Ella could reply, she heard the phone in her office ringing. Jogging ahead, she grabbed it after the third ring.

"Investigator Clah," Ella snapped as she reached for the phone, but whoever it was had already hung up.

Ella muttered a curse. "I hate it when that happens." Suddenly her cell phone began to ring. A sick feeling spread over her. Whoever it was sure was trying hard to track her down.

She flipped the unit open with one hand. "Ella Clah," she answered.

"Ella, it's me, Kevin. I've got some bad news. Your mom is in the emergency room at the hospital."

FIVE
—— ✕ ✕ ✕ ——

Ella felt her stomach plummet. For a moment she couldn't breathe, or speak.

"Ella, did you hear what I said?"

Through sheer force of will she managed to answer. "What happened? Where's Dawn?" Ella asked all in the same breath.

"Dawn is safe. She's with me," Kevin answered.

Knowing that her daughter was safe and her mother in a place where she was getting help gave Ella time to gather her wits. "What happened?"

"I'd just turned down the gravel road leading home when I spotted Rose driving in my direction, toward the highway. She was all over the road, but she pulled over when I honked the horn and she saw me trying to get her attention. It turns out she'd cut her hand and was trying to drive herself to the hospital. There was blood everywhere, but you would have been proud of Dawn. She handled it really well. She kept telling Rose 'That's okay, that's okay.' "

Ella smiled, a touch of pride weaving through her. "Dawn's not an ordinary kid, you know." Even as she said it, she knew that all moms felt the same about their kids. But Dawn *was* special. "How's my mother doing now?"

"She's getting stitched up and should be fine. But listen, Ella, although I was happy to give your mom a ride here, I have a problem. I can't stay at the hospital any longer with Dawn and I can't take her to work with me either. I have an important meeting in less than an hour."

"I'll be there in ten minutes or so."

"Thanks."

"No problem."

After quickly explaining the problem to Justine, who agreed to handle the Joe Wallace incident and inform Big Ed, Ella ran out the side door of the station and hopped into her unit.

The situation had unnerved her more than she cared to admit. The thought of her mother injured, and trying to drive herself to the hospital while she had Dawn with her, was disturbing.

Rose should have called her. She would have gone home double-time or called the EMTs. But Ella knew precisely why her mother hadn't done that. Being independent was everything to Rose. To admit she needed help went against everything she was. The fact that she'd accepted Kevin's help was enough to tell Ella how serious the situation had been.

Ella's worries continued to grow as she raced to the hospital. Rose was never an easy patient. Feeling her insides tying themselves into knots, Ella forced herself to remain calm. She'd need a cool head to deal with her mother's situation.

Ella entered the waiting area of the ER a short time later and found Kevin across the lobby, holding a wriggly Dawn in his arms.

Seeing Ella, Kevin gave her a tight-lipped smile. "Finally! Dawn's pretty fussy right now. It must be all the excitement."

Ella took Dawn and then set her down on the floor, keeping a tight hold on her hand. "She just hates to be carried most of the time."

"It was the only way I could think of to keep her from running up and down the halls."

Ella stared at him, wondering why a man who could sway a skeptical jury of twelve adults and cower a hostile witness in zero flat couldn't deal with a two-year-old. "Where's my mom?"

"Through those doors," he said, gesturing by pursing his lips.

Ella heard someone come into the lobby behind her. Turning, she recognized Kevin's young assistant, Jefferson Blueeyes. The slender, well-dressed Navajo had the eyes of a hawk. She'd only met him a few times before, but he was well educated, had almost no accent, and seemed even more ambitious than Kevin, if such a thing were possible.

Jefferson nodded coldly to Ella, and then to Kevin. "We have to get going. You can't afford to be late to this meeting," he said cryptically.

Kevin checked his watch. "I've got to go. I'll call you later."

Kevin strode out of the door before she could even say good-bye or thank him. For a moment, Ella remained in the hall wanting to see Rose, but wondering whether she'd be able to take Dawn inside the ER. Then she heard someone call out her name. Ella glanced up and saw Dr. Carolyn Roanhorse-Lavery coming in through the same door Kevin had just passed through. Ella smiled, glad to see her.

Based on an understanding of the high price tribal beliefs often exacted on those who had to walk the line between traditional and modern cultures, their friendship had stood the test of time. Ella had been as much of an outsider once as Carolyn was, so she understood better than most the hard road Carolyn traveled. As the head pathologist and medical examiner for the tribe, people avoided contact with her as much as possible. No Navajo wanted to be around someone who worked with dead bodies for a living.

Fortunately, things were a lot easier for Carolyn these days. Now that she was married to an Anglo physician in her own field, Carolyn's loneliness was no longer as acute. Yet, despite the different roads their personal lives had taken, Ella and Carolyn had remained close.

"I haven't been in to see your mom for obvious reasons," Carolyn told Ella. "Being around me might have frightened her right now. But I was able to check with the nurse and Dr. Martinez. Rose apparently damaged some tendons and may need surgery later."

Carolyn looked down at Dawn. "Hey, short stuff. Want to go with me to look for some ice cream?"

"Yes!" Dawn looked up at Ella with a pathetic, pleading expression, a tactic she'd only recently perfected. "*Shimá*, please?"

"All right. You can go if you promise to be good." Ella gave Carolyn a grateful smile.

"In case you're wondering why I didn't offer to help the gentleman," she said, deliberately avoiding mentioning Kevin so that Dawn wouldn't catch on, "it was because I figured he needed to play single parent at a time of confusion. It was good for his education."

"Tell me the truth. Was she awful to him?" Ella asked, bracing herself.

"Awful? Nah. Active, yes. But she was just trying to get him off the cell phone so he'd pay more attention to her."

"I get the picture. Thanks." She looked at Dawn and in a stern voice added, "You do whatever Aunt Carolyn tells you to do. Is that clear?" Carolyn was no relation to Ella or Dawn, but her friend had insisted upon the honorary title.

Dawn nodded somberly.

Holding Dawn's hand, Carolyn gave Ella a smile and the two walked off. "Take your time. We'll be in the cafeteria when you're ready."

Ella went through the ER doors and, after asking the nurse at the desk, proceeded to one of the small curtained partitions that doubled as a room. From what she could tell, most of the other partitions were also currently occupied with patients.

Ella found her mother a moment later. Rose looked as pale as the white muslin sheets on the hospital bed. Ella swallowed before speaking, determined not to let

Rose know how much seeing her like this had affected her. The last time her mother had been in the hospital, she was barely alive after the accident with a drunk driver. Though her mother looked a thousand times better than that now, it still wasn't any easier seeing the woman who'd raised her looking so vulnerable.

"Mom, what happened?" Ella asked, fighting to keep her voice steady.

"Oh, daughter, I'm sorry about this. It was just a stupid, careless accident."

"Why didn't you call me when it happened, or call the paramedics?"

"I figured it would be faster for me to drive myself to the hospital than wait for help. My hand was really bleeding."

"What happened?"

"I was boning a chicken and listening to the news on the radio when I bumped into the counter and knocked off the butcher knife. I automatically grabbed for it without thinking and I got the blade instead of the handle. I put some herbs on the cut immediately to stop the flow of blood and wrapped my hand in a towel, but it wasn't enough. I knew I had to come to the hospital, so I got into the pickup with my granddaughter. Long before I reached the highway, I realized I'd made a mistake. I was just too dizzy. About then your child's father came by and gave me a ride."

"Good thing he was there."

Rose nodded, but her lips were pursed tightly.

Ella suppressed a sigh. It was no secret that her mother didn't like Kevin, but that situation had grown steadily worse in the last few months. Rose simply didn't approve of the way Kevin's priorities seldom included spending time with his daughter though that neglect was, traditionally, the custom of Navajo fathers. The fact that Dawn wanted to see him and Kevin seldom visited was enough to irritate Rose.

"Is he still out there taking care of my granddaughter?"

"No, he's gone to a meeting," she said before thinking, then wished she'd dodged the question.

"Then who has my granddaughter?" Rose asked quickly, trying to sit up and look past the curtains surrounding the bed.

"She's with my friend," Ella said, guiding Rose back down onto her pillow.

Rose nodded slowly. "Bijishii."

Ella recognized the name her mother had given Carolyn. It meant the one with a medicine bag. As Carolyn herself had said, it could have been a lot worse, considering her medical specialty.

"She's a good woman, Mom."

"I know," Rose said quietly. "She cares for my granddaughter. But I wish . . ."

"Her profession is her profession," Ella said firmly. "And what she does is sorely needed, no matter how unpleasant it seems to you."

"I'm not against her, daughter. I know life isn't easy for . . . that kind of doctor."

"No, it's not. She needs friends, and we need her."

Rose sat up, then tried to get off the bed, but wavered badly. Ella forced her to stay where she was. "Mom, what do you think you're doing? You still have an IV in your arm."

"I've had enough. It's time for me to go home. My hand feels better now. I don't need to see the doctor anymore. I know what I have to do."

"You can't leave now, Mom. That's not the way it works." Seeing the spark of defiance in her mother's eyes, Ella shook her head firmly. "No, Mother. We're staying until the doctor says you're ready to leave."

"What exactly are we waiting for? The bleeding's stopped, and now the healing has to begin. It's time for a *hataalii* to take over," Rose insisted.

Ella knew she'd lose the argument in another minute.

She had to do something quickly. "I'll call my brother for you, then. He'll be glad to come here."

"Well, if you're sure . . ." Rose lay back down, and Ella made sure the IV wasn't being crimped.

She knew that the speed with which her mother had given in was directly proportional to how ill she really felt. "I'll be right back."

Ella stepped out into the hall and saw a doctor striding toward her. The name tag on his white coat said Dr. Martinez. At a glance, she suspected Dr. Martinez had Navajo blood, but was also partly Hispanic. Right now he seemed in a hurry and was probably overworked, like most of the doctors at the hospital these days. The police department wasn't the only public service experiencing financial cutbacks.

"I'm Ella Clah, Rose Destea's daughter. Were you looking for me?"

He nodded, but didn't offer to shake hands. "I wanted to speak to you first, then ask you to convey this information to the rest of her family. Your mother will need to take very special care of her hand. I've stitched her up, but I'll need her back in a week, earlier if she experiences any problems. Most important of all, she's not to put any stress at all on her hand. She could rip out the stitches and cause even more damage." He paused, then added, "She's right-handed, and I understand that she uses a cane."

"Yes, from time to time. Her legs were badly injured in an automobile accident a few years ago."

"If she normally holds the cane in her right hand, switching to the left may take some practice, or may not be much help at all. But it's imperative she doesn't put any pressure on her injured hand until she's fully recovered."

"Will she need surgery?"

"Tendons on three fingers were badly cut. If I see that her hand isn't healing well and her dexterity is impaired, surgery might be indicated. But, right now, I just want to give those stitches and her own body a chance."

"Understood." Ella realized that under the circumstances she had only one option. She'd have to find someone to take care of Rose and Dawn during the day. The only problem, of course, was how to tell her mother. Rose would hate even the thought of having anyone looking after her or her granddaughter.

Dr. Martinez gave her a wry smile. "From what I've seen of your mother, I don't think she'll appreciate taking a vacation from her normal routine."

"That's an understatement, Doc. I'll just have to be insistent. How long will it be before you can release her?"

"A few more hours. I need to see how she reacts to some of the painkillers and antibiotics we've given her."

"All right. Thank you." As the doctor moved away, Ella went farther out into the lobby. Cell phones weren't allowed inside certain areas of the building and the ER was one of them. She'd call Clifford from the lobby.

As she reached the reception area, Ella pulled out the phone, but before she had a chance to dial, she saw Clifford walking into the hospital.

He hurried over. "I just found out Mom was injured. One of my patients saw your daughter's father bringing Mom into the emergency room and came to tell me. How is she?"

"Asking for you," Ella said and filled him in on the accident.

Clifford winced the second he learned that Rose would need someone to help at home. "You're planning to tell her, right?"

"I was hoping maybe we could both tell her."

"She might take the news better from you," Clifford said a little too quickly.

"Nice try, brother. But you're not getting out of this so easily. I need you to back me up."

"Yeah, okay," Clifford said with a sigh. "But it's going to be almost impossible to talk Mom into this."

"We have to remind her that it's only temporary, and that having extra help will speed up the healing process. We'll point out that her granddaughter needs her to get well quickly. The way I see it, pitching it that way is our only chance."

"And it's a slim one." Clifford looked at her hopefully and added, "Are you sure you don't want to handle this alone—woman to woman?"

Ella glowered at him. "You're *not* chickening out."

"Okay, okay."

Ella and Clifford went to where Rose was, but the minute they stepped into her small enclosure Rose braced herself for a fight. Maybe it was seeing both of them coming in that tipped her off, but Rose had a set look on her face that meant trouble. Ella explained what the doctor had told her, trying not to be affected by the way her mother was glowering at her.

"He's a doctor, but he doesn't know *everything*." Rose stared at Clifford. "You should know that better than anyone. You're a *hataalii*!"

"Mom, we're only trying to make things a little easier for you," Clifford said, and looked at Ella in desperation.

Ella resisted the urge to roll her eyes. He'd always been such a pushover. "Mom, we need you to get well. My daughter needs you," Ella began, knowing she was in for an argument.

Rose heard Ella out, then shook her head immediately. "No. That's not acceptable. I can take care of myself and my granddaughter with one hand tied behind my back."

When both Clifford and Ella continued to hold their ground, Rose's eyes grew wet with tears, accusing them of seeing her as *xa'asti*, ancient and beginning to disintegrate.

Ella saw Clifford go pale. Any minute now, he'd surrender.

"Will you go take care of my daughter?" Ella abruptly asked him. "She's with my doctor friend in the cafeteria.

It looks like I'm going to be here for a while." Clifford's relief was so evident she nearly laughed.

"I'll take her home with me," he said. "She can play there. Visit all you want."

Ella watched as Clifford practically fled the room. Her brother could battle skinwalkers with iron courage but he was utterly lost in a debate with his own mother.

Ella turned her attention back to Rose. "Okay, Mom, there's no more need for tears. You upset my brother, but I'm not going to let it get to me so easily. Your age is not the factor here, and you know it," she said in a brisk no-nonsense style. "You simply have an injury and you need time to heal. To do that, you can't use your hand, so you're going to need help around the house. I'll find someone to come in during the day, and you're just going to have to do your best to cooperate with her."

"How could you show me such disrespect? I raised you better than this!"

"Quit trying to put me on the defensive so you can avoid the issue. It won't work."

Rose sighed. "You're a very stubborn daughter."

As Ella looked at Rose, she realized that her mother's feelings hadn't really been hurt at all. It had been an act to manipulate them into letting her have her own way. Ella bit the corner of her mouth to keep from laughing. "You can be such a stinker, Mom."

"I really *don't* want a stranger in my house, daughter," Rose said in a quiet but determined voice.

"Then I'll try to find a Navajo woman you know to come in and help you."

"You'd better find someone with a lot of energy if you expect her to take care of my granddaughter."

"I know," Ella said, glad that her mother was becoming part of the solution now, and not the problem.

"And someone who can cook a decent meal—that is, if I'm not going to be allowed to cook either."

"You're not. So tell me, any idea who we can get?"

"None at all," Rose said firmly.

Ella exhaled softly, realizing Rose was trying to set another trap. "I didn't think so."

Time dragged on, and Rose tried Ella's patience mercilessly. Ella came up with names of people both her mother and she knew, ones who might be willing to take on the job, and each time Rose vetoed her suggestions.

And so it continued until it was finally time to take Rose home. As Ella went out to the lobby to sign the release papers, Carolyn came up to her.

"I walked by a few times and heard you two arguing. Did you settle on a companion for Rose?"

Ella shook her head. "We need someone by tomorrow, but she's turned down everyone I suggested."

"I have an idea. Gloria Washburn is looking for work. She's a practical nurse who's going back to night school. Why don't you give her a try?"

"Can you contact Gloria for me? I'm going to have my hands full."

"Consider it done. If for some reason she can't be there bright and early tomorrow, I'll call you back tonight."

Ella finished signing the release forms, then went back to get her mother. Before long, they were on their way home in Ella's Jeep.

"Tomorrow a nurse Bijishii recommended will stay with you and my daughter, at least until I get home," Ella said using Carolyn's nickname. "Let's see how she works out. And, Mom, *try* to be nice to her, okay?"

"I know you have important work to do. We won't bother you at the office," Rose said simply.

"Mom, its okay to bother me, just don't make her crazy, okay? For your granddaughter's sake keep things peaceful at home."

Rose smiled but said nothing, and Ella bit her lip to suppress a groan.

When they finally arrived at the house, Rose had become subdued and it was clear to Ella that her mother was exhausted from today's ordeal. She helped Rose change into her nightclothes and get into bed, then walked to the bedroom door. "Good night, Mom. I'll be back soon. I'm just going to get my daughter."

"Drive carefully," she muttered, but by the time Ella had her jacket on again and peeked into the bedroom, Rose was already asleep.

Ella drove to her brother's home and, as she pulled up, saw that only one vehicle was there. Loretta's small sedan was gone. Ella went up to the house and knocked.

Clifford opened the door and Dawn rushed up and threw her arms around Ella.

"*Shimasání* better?"

"Yes, but you'll have to be very quiet when we get home. She's already gone to bed. And I need you to be very, very good tomorrow. Your grandmother is sick and needs time to get well."

Dawn nodded somberly.

Ella glanced around as Clifford motioned her inside, but it appeared that Clifford was the only one home. "Where's your family?"

"My wife took our son to her mother's for a few days."

Dawn wriggled free and Ella set her down, allowing her to return to the toys she had scattered on the floor. "Is there trouble between you two again?" Ella asked, keeping her voice soft.

"No, it's not like that." He waved her to a couch. "I'll explain some other time. There's something else I need to talk to you about now. Have a seat. Remember when you asked me to find out anything I could about the vandalism that's been going on?" Seeing her nod, he continued. "Well, I've spoken to some of the Fierce Ones, and there's speculation that the trouble is being caused by outsiders."

"What makes them think that?" Ella asked. The Fierce Ones was a group of traditionalists that often behaved as behind-the-scene vigilantes to control criminal behavior. They put pressure on those believed responsible, and on their families. Clifford had joined the group, hoping to temper their sometimes extreme measures.

"Some are convinced that one of them would have heard something by now if it had been the work of anyone in our tribe."

Ella nodded. "Makes sense. If you hear anything more, let me know right away."

"I will." Clifford nodded.

Ella glanced over at Dawn, who seemed happy to be playing with her cousin's toys. "And thanks for taking care of her for me."

"She's no trouble. To be honest, right now, without my wife and son, the house feels empty."

She nodded and waited for him to say more. If Clifford wanted to talk she'd listen, but she wouldn't push.

At last he continued. "I've been looking into the possibility of moving closer to Gallup, near my wife's family. She really misses them. The problem is that most of my patients are in the Shiprock area."

Clifford drew in a breath, then let it out slowly. "But that's not the only thing that's holding me back. The truth is I don't want to live any closer to my mother-in-law and her family. I think they would undermine our marriage. They've never really approved of me and they're constantly making little comments that stir up trouble. Yet, it's done in such a way that if I respond to their words, I come across as the bad guy."

"In-laws can be a problem," Ella said, silently acknowledging that she didn't particularly like Loretta or her family, and didn't blame her brother for wanting to keep his distance.

Looking over at Dawn, Ella realized that her daughter had been listening a little too intently. Cautioning Clifford with a look, she helped Dawn put away the alphabet blocks she'd been playing with, and then helped her put on her coat.

"Take care of yourself and, if you need anything, just

let me know," Ella said, picking Dawn up and moving to the door.

Clifford gave the little girl a pat on the cheek. "Bring her back anytime."

As Ella drove home, she speculated on what would happen next on the Rez. Instinct and experience told her that things would continue to escalate, and that the police in her corner of the Navajo Nation would be in crisis before long.

Glancing back in the rearview mirror at her daughter, she saw Dawn had already fallen asleep in her child seat. Ella felt the hard edge she used to keep the world at bay melting away as she gazed at her child. Just looking at Dawn made all her other worries fade into the background. The love she felt for Dawn simply put everything in a new light. "Sleep, little one," she whispered. "I won't let you or the tribe down."

When they reached home, Ella fixed a light supper for Dawn, who was half-asleep, and a quick sandwich for herself, though she wasn't at all hungry tonight. Hearing Rose stirring in her bedroom, Ella knocked at her door. Her mother stood by the chest of drawers looking at a photo of Ella's father.

"Mom, are you okay?"

Rose looked at her, and nodded. "It's at times like this when I miss your father the most."

"Is your hand hurting? Should I go get your pills?"

Rose shook her head. "It's not that." She lapsed into a thoughtful silence before speaking again. "It's just that we depended on each other for so many years. I'll never understand how I could fall in love with a Christian preacher, a man so different from myself. But I still miss our endless arguments over Christianity and the Navajo Way. You appreciate your traditions much more when you have to explain and justify them to someone else," she said with a sad smile.

Ella thought about that for a moment. "I think you've got something there, Mom. Our modernists and traditionalists may be constantly at each other's throats but, deep down, they're all *Dineh* and they know it. The Anglos have it a lot worse. Many of them have no ethnic identity. They wander in the world, tribeless, trying to connect to something—a church, a social club, a career, anything that will give them a sense of belonging. That's much harder when they don't really have any roots like we do here on the Rez."

Rose gave her a gentle smile. "That observation sure took its time reaching your heart. Maybe you *are* learning."

Ella laughed. "Yeah, Mom, I'm slow, but I eventually get things right."

As Ella helped her mother into the kitchen, they passed Dawn in the living room, and saw that she'd curled up on the couch and had fallen asleep.

Rose stopped to watch her grandchild for a minute. "Put her to bed first, then you can help me out. She deserves her sleep. She was very brave today."

"She'll be fine for a little bit longer," Ella whispered as she gently placed a crocheted blanket over her child. "Let me fix you some soup first."

Ella helped her mother to a seat in the kitchen and then, while Rose ate some warmed-up mutton stew and tortillas, went back to the living room. Before she could pick up Dawn, a soft knock sounded at the door and she hurried to answer it.

It was Justine, who slipped in quickly to get out of the cold. "Hey, cousin," she whispered, seeing Dawn asleep on the sofa. "I thought I'd stop by after my shift and see if there was anything I could do to help out. How's Rose?"

"She's in the kitchen. Why don't you keep Mom company for a few minutes while I put Dawn to bed?" she asked.

Dawn stirred groggily as Ella picked her up. For the first time in weeks Dawn went to bed without a protest. Ella kissed her daughter's forehead, then made sure she was warm, with plenty of blankets. Closing the child gate but leaving the door open, Ella walked back to the kitchen.

By the time Ella joined her mother, Justine and Rose were talking easily. Ella pulled up a chair and as she listened to their conversation realized that Rose and Justine now had something in common. Part of Justine's finger had been lost, costing her a certain amount of dexterity. Rose was now facing a similar situation, and that had created a new understanding between them.

"The pain was difficult at first, but the worst of it came later when I had to accept it and adapt," Justine said.

"What worries me most is the doctor's unwillingness to say much about the extent of the damage."

Hearing another knock at the door, Rose's face brightened considerably. It suddenly occurred to Ella that having a houseful of people was just what her outgoing mother needed most to keep her mind off her current troubles.

Ella saw Abigail Yellowhair, the widow of State Senator Yellowhair, standing at the door with a large bouquet of roses. Knowing Abigail's political aspirations, she wondered if this was her way of campaigning.

"Come in," Ella said. "It's freezing outside now with the wind."

Taking Abigail's coat, she gave the woman a smile. "My mother's going to love these flowers. Why don't you take them to her? She's in the kitchen. I'll go find a vase."

In the few moments it took for Ella to find the vase and take the flowers from her mother's hands, Rose's mood had already improved by leaps and bounds. She was the center of attention and loving every second of it.

"We're looking for a homemaker's helper," Ella said, fixing coffee for everyone. "Preferably someone who can stay here until I get home, which may be quite late sometimes. If any of you hear of someone who might be interested, let us know."

"We need a traditionalist," Rose said flatly.

Abigail considered it for a moment, then spoke. "Do you know the head of the Plant Watchers?"

"Yes, she and I are good friends," Rose said. Lena Clani and she had known each other most of their adult lives.

"Her granddaughter is looking for work," Abigail continued. "She's young, around nineteen. I, unfortunately, didn't have a job I could offer her but, if you give her a call, you might be able to work something out with her."

"That's a great suggestion!" Ella said. "Thanks."

Rose stood up unsteadily. "I better take my dog outside one last time tonight before the wind gets any colder."

"I'll take Two out, Mom," Ella said, noticing the mutt sitting anxiously by the door.

Rose shook her head. "I can still take a few steps without your help, daughter. Take care of our guests." Rose grabbed her coat from the hook, wrapped it around her like a cloak, turned on the porch light, and went outside with Two.

Ella kept an eye on her mother from the kitchen window. "She's as stubborn as a mule," Ella muttered. "I love her, but she's going to make me crazy someday."

Abigail laughed. "That's the way it is with families, dear. With one hand you want to hug them to you, and with the other you want to push them out the door."

Ella and Justine laughed. "Well, it does make life interesting," Ella agreed, walking back to the kitchen table.

Seeing the glow of headlights on the wall, Ella stepped into the living room and took a look out the front window. "I think that's Wilson Joe's car."

"He's probably looking for me," Justine said, glancing at her watch. "I didn't mean to stay this long. He was going to meet me at home and then take me to a dance on campus tonight."

Ella smiled, glad that the two were dating. Wilson would always be her friend, but they would never be anything more. There just hadn't been any spark between them, though Wilson, at one time, would have cheerfully argued the point.

"Can you let him in?" Ella asked Justine. "I'm going to get Mom and bring her back inside the kitchen before she freezes to death waiting for the dog to do his business."

"Sure."

Ella reached for her coat and put it on as she walked through the kitchen. By the time she joined her mother outside, Wilson had come around to the back with Justine to join Rose and the dog.

Rose, seemingly unaffected by the frigid temperatures that had the rest of them shivering, looked at Ella casually. "You shouldn't be out here, daughter. It's much too cold, and we still have a guest. Let's go back inside."

After saying good-bye to Justine and Wilson, Ella silently followed her mother and Two inside. Sometimes it didn't pay to argue.

It was seven-thirty the following morning when Gloria Washburn arrived.

When Rose saw Gloria in her nurse's uniform, she gave the young woman a look of pure disdain. "I do *not* need a nurse," she said, then motioned Ella into the kitchen for a private word. "I would rather have my friend's granddaughter here," Rose hissed.

"I'll talk to her as soon as I can, but for today, at least, you'll have to accept the nurse's help." Ella grabbed a homemade tortilla from the refrigerator and smeared butter on it. Just as she took a bite, the phone rang.

"It's for you," Rose said with disapproval, not moving

from her chair. "Calls this early always are."

Ella picked up the receiver, hurriedly swallowing, and heard Big Ed on the other end. "I want you and the crime-scene team to head over to Frank Goldman's place. Someone blew up the pump to his well last night. Since he's a vet, he needs to have plenty of water available for the sick animals he's tending." He lowered his voice. "And my wife's horse is over there right now, recovering from surgery, so I'm taking a real dim view of this latest act of vandalism. Catch 'em, Shorty. I've just about had it with this crap."

Ella could hear the barely controlled anger in the chief's voice. "Okay. I'll see what I can do to get some evidence against these perps. Shall I check on Claire's mare while I'm there?"

"Yeah, please. Claire's really upset over this."

As Ella hung up, she saw the worried look Rose gave her. "It's another instance of vandalism," Ella told her. "No one's hurt, but it's tricky," Ella added, then explained.

"Are you leaving now? Maybe the nurse can fix you something more for breakfast than just a tortilla." Rose glanced at Gloria.

"I'd be happy to," Gloria said. "It won't take long."

"Thanks, but I better be going," Ella said, and kissed her mother good-bye.

Leaving the kitchen, she stepped into the living room and found Dawn wrapped in a down comforter watching cartoons. Ella gave her a quick hug and kiss, then walked out across the frozen ground to her Jeep.

Things were okay at home for the moment but, knowing Rose, there was no telling how long that peace would last, especially today.

SIX

— ✕ ✕ ✕ —

Within twenty minutes Ella and the crime-scene team were at the vet's place. The clinic was off the highway close to Hogback, and between two low hills. Goldman lived on the Rez despite the fact that he was white and therefore Anglo, so she supposed he made a good living doing what he did.

While the team gathered evidence around the rubble of the shattered cinder-block pump house, Ella went to talk to Goldman. He saw a lot of people during the week. Maybe he had some idea who'd done this to his pump.

"Hey, Doc," Ella said as she went to meet him on the porch.

Frank Goldman was rail thin, with a ruddy complexion, and well over six feet tall. He usually wore an easy smile, but today his expression was glum.

"Are you any closer to catching whoever's been doing this kind of thing around the Rez?" he asked.

"Not yet. The truth is we could use a little help."

"Just tell me what I can do."

"You see quite a few people every day, Doc. Have you heard any rumors about who could be responsible for all this?"

Well bundled up against the cold in a down jacket, he sat down on the old wooden chair on his porch, and a golden retriever trotted up and sat beside him. "I'm a Jewish *bilagáana*, and although I live here, I'm still considered an outsider. I'm tolerated because I'm needed, but not many tell me anything beyond their problems with their animals."

She let the silence stretch out.

"If you see Big Ed, would you tell him that his mare is doing fine now, and his wife should pick her up as soon as she can? I'm not going to be able to keep any large animals overnight unless they're in serious condition. It looks like I'm going to be hauling in water for a while."

"How long will it take you to replace the pump?"

"I'm having someone come by later today to take a look. If they can't make a hookup to the old well casing, they'll have to drill another well." He paused. "To be honest with you, it might get expensive and, all things considered, I may end up cutting my losses and move on. I've been thinking of opening a practice in Farmington. The Rez isn't that hospitable to strangers, you know."

She nodded. "Better than most," Ella said, remembering how it had been for her when she'd returned after living in Los Angeles. People had called her L.A. Woman and would barely acknowledge her presence. "But your services are needed here."

He shrugged. "There are several competent vets in Farmington. People will just have to transport their animals a bit farther, or pay for a home visit."

Ella looked at him, knowing that most local farmers couldn't afford to pay any more for a veterinarian. "Wouldn't you rather stand up to these punks?"

"I came here to make a difference, not go to war. But more and more I've been seeing the Rez dividing into factions who are constantly at odds with one another. Progress, no matter how anyone defines it, is going to come at a cost here. And people who belong to neither the traditionalists nor the modernists are going to be caught in the crossfire."

Ella nodded slowly. She had a feeling he was right, though she still hated to see the only vet in the area leave the Rez. "Things will settle down, Doc. Just don't go making any rash decisions."

Frank nodded, then stood and went back inside the house, taking his dog with him.

Ella checked on the others who were busy collecting evidence. Although there was plenty of debris to pick up, nothing looked as if it would provide them with conclusive answers.

"I was hoping we'd find a nice set of prints on the door to the pump house that weren't blown to smithereens," Justine said, "but we struck out, just like yesterday at the Wallace place. And they left no tools behind. They moved fast, used a fuse and the same type blasting-cap detonator as with the Dumpster and the outhouse, then boogied out. All I have is another pin to place on my map of vandalism incidents, which, except for their concentration in our area, appear more or less random."

"I thought that might be how it would look. But here's an idea. If you get a call from the press, tell them we found something we think will lead us to the perps. I want to make the guys behind all this worry a bit. So far they've held all the cards, so maybe it's time we played a few mind games with them."

Justine smiled. "Right, boss."

As Ella started walking back to the SUV, her cell phone rang. "Ella, it's Harry."

"Hey, I was told you'd be coming back," she said, glad to hear his voice. "Did you just fly in?"

"I drove in from Albuquerque, and I've been on the Rez for about six hours following a lead. Right now I'm about two hundred yards downwind from a 'killed' hogan north of Beclabito. I've got reason to believe Many-farms may be in there, but I'm going to need backup before I go in to check it out. I don't want to risk letting him get away."

Ella suppressed a shudder of aversion. The purely instinctive response surprised her, because she didn't consider herself a traditionalist. One hogan should have been as good as any other. Yet it wasn't. A "killed" hogan was one where a hole had been made in the north or west wall to remove the body of a person who'd died inside. The dwelling was then abandoned and left to the ghost of the dead.

"I'll bring a team along with me," Ella said. She wasn't thrilled about going there, but she'd do her job.

"No. Come alone. If he sees the cavalry he'll go into fight mode. What I'm hoping to do is catch him before he knows we're there."

"All right. I'll head over now. Be very careful, Harry. We have reason to believe he may be armed with a fifty-caliber sniper rifle."

"Good to know."

After they'd agreed on where to meet, Ella quickly told Justine what was going on, then pulled back onto the highway, heading west at a fast clip. Despite the circumstances, she was looking forward to seeing Harry again. He'd occupied her thoughts often since the last time they'd seen each other.

She'd never really believed in things like chemistry but, around Harry, all bets were off. He really appealed to her on almost every possible level. Although she'd never thought about him romantically when they'd worked together, after he'd left New Mexico and re-turned months later as a federal deputy marshal, he'd seemed like a new man—especially to her.

With a sigh, she brought her thoughts back to the business at hand. What she respected most about Harry and what she liked most about herself, was that they were both seasoned, professional law enforcement officers. Attraction had no place in that equation, at least while they were on the job.

It wasn't long before Ella arrived at the rendezvous point, a low spot in a shallow ravine beside the highway and south of the hogan, which wasn't visible from the road. It was already past noon, yet the ground was still frozen in the shade, and the breeze that flowed off the Carizzo Mountains to the west still went right through her, chilling her to the bone despite her gloves, leather jacket, and wool sweater underneath.

As Ella looked around, walking away from the SUV, Harry stepped out from behind the embankment of the ravine where it passed beneath the highway, and smiled.

"Hey. We sure do meet in the oddest places, woman," he teased.

"And we're usually armed. Does that make us kinky?"

"Yeah." He grinned, climbing up to where she stood, but, like her keeping below the road level to avoid presenting a silhouetted target to anyone hiding among the junipers or brush.

Harry was Ella's height, and had put on a few more pounds of muscle since the last time she'd seen him. It was obvious that he'd continued to work out. Right now he was wearing a military surplus olive drab parka over a black turtleneck sweater, close-fitting jeans, and lace-up boots. He looked like an honest-to-goodness soldier of fortune.

Ella wondered if any of the vividly lecherous thoughts she'd entertained briefly had shown on her face. Harry was extremely observant but hard to read, and the tiny grin on his face told her nothing. Uncomfortable all of a sudden, she turned quickly back to business.

"What's the situation here now?" she asked, looking warily down the arroyo Harry had emerged from seconds ago.

"I was given a tip that Manyfarms would be there," he said, cocking his head toward the north. "I've circled the area and studied the several-hour-old boot prints I've found, but I haven't seen Manyfarms. Someone drove up a while ago in an old gray pickup, an Indian I couldn't quite make out because of his low-brimmed hat. He took in a cardboard box of something, stayed about an hour, then drove off. It wasn't Manyfarms, so I didn't make a move."

Harry led the way, cautioning her to remain silent, and they hiked up the arroyo a quarter mile or so until he motioned for her to stop. Pulling out a small pair of binoculars from his coat pocket, Harry peered cautiously over the rim of the narrow wash, here no wider than his outstretched arms. Ella followed his gaze, making sure she was looking through a thin shrub along the edge of the embankment. Two hundred yards away was an old, weather-beaten, hexagonal fitted-log hogan with a clay sealed roof.

"Notice the smoke coming from the smoke hole in the center of the roof?" he said. "Either someone's still in there, or the guy who was here earlier is wasting fire-wood."

"Making a direct approach now is probably a bad idea. We have no cover, except some low brush, and no idea what we're up against. On top of it all, we can't assume they don't already know we're here."

"Yeah, but you've got to consider the fact that who-ever's inside may not be Manyfarms. It's quite possible that the tip I got is way off base. This may be just a waste of time."

She took another look at the terrain, considering their options. "I'll tell you what. By crawling up the narrow tributary to this wash, we can go a little closer to the hogan and get a better look. Once we're there, we can decide what to do next."

"Fair enough."

They went up the little channel, an empty, erosion-carved ditch that ran closer to the side and rear of the hogan, with Ella leading the way. Then, about fifty yards from the hogan she saw another much deeper arroyo concealing a silver pickup. It was almost completely covered with gray and brown tumbleweeds, and blended in well with the vegetation. They might have missed it completely if they hadn't been able to get so close.

The tailgate was facing their direction, and Ella wrote down the license plate number in a small notebook she'd pulled from her pocket. The vehicle fit the description of the truck that had been seen racing away after the sniper incident.

Ella motioned for Harry to return to the larger arroyo where they'd been earlier. Once they'd put more distance between them and the hogan, she filled him in quickly. "Sorry, Harry. We're not doing this solo. I'm calling for backup now. The sniper who shot at me was driving a silver pickup. He was a very good marksman, too, who only narrowly missed his target though he was nearly a thousand yards away, and in a crosswind. And from what I can see there's only one quick way into that hogan—the doorway. The side has been punched out, according to custom, but the hole isn't big enough for either of us to crawl through quickly. If we go in after him, whoever takes point is dead, and at point-blank range, that fifty-caliber rifle could penetrate both our vests, front and back. We're going to need special tactics on this one."

Harry nodded. "Yeah, under the circumstances, I think you're right. There are probably enough unchinked gaps between the logs of that old hogan to allow anyone inside to see in every direction. All it would take is a little bad luck and he'd spot us sneaking up. So call it in. But make sure your people stay out of sight and sound until we're ready to make a move. I'm still not sure how many people are in the hogan, or even if Manyfarms is there at all. Keep in mind that most Navajos would assume that anyone entering a killed hogan is a skinwalker. Many people around here would happily provide us with a false tip in hopes we'd shoot first and ask questions later."

"Good point," Ella acknowledged, then relayed instructions to Justine via her handheld radio.

Next, Ella borrowed Harry's binoculars and studied the blue tarp that had been draped over the front entrance. "Whoever's in there has got the entrance covered up well. Better than with a blanket, I'll give him that."

"I suppose we can just sit tight until he comes out,"

Harry said. "Beats getting anyone's head blown off."

"Yeah, that's what I was thinking, too," Ella answered. "Or if he spots us and refuses to budge, we could toss a tear gas grenade through the smoke hole."

"We'd have to get in pretty close to do that, and avoid being spotted coming up."

"Yeah, but with enough cover fire from our team, he'd have to stay low until we lobbed it off."

"How much backup do you think we'll have?"

"Justine is rounding up the forces. She'll contact Blalock and Payestewa, the new Hopi agent. Ralph Tache is on call, and Sergeant Neskahi will be coming with him, probably."

Less than thirty minutes later Ella met the local officers in the arroyo beside the highway. Harry had stayed behind, maintaining his surveillance of the hogan.

Ella filled them in quickly. "The problem is that the suspect only has to cover one entrance. Face-to-face, we won't be able to use our superior firepower and numbers."

"Sooner or later he'll have to come out," Blalock said. "Then he's ours."

"So you vote to wait, too?" Ella asked.

"Yeah. We can zip up our jackets and hunker down for as long as it takes."

They positioned themselves in key points around the hogan, maintaining watch without breaking cover. Soon the trail of smoke from the hogan stopped completely.

Her radio crackled softly. "Ella, there's something we really should have considered," Harry said. "It's possible that the fire was left burning, and the guy I saw was just dropping off supplies for later. There might not be anyone in there at all now."

"Or he may be waiting us out, hoping we'll go in for a closer look," Blalock interjected. "The best snipers have more patience than their targets."

"Yeah, there's that possibility as well," Harry agreed.

Blalock came back on the air. "I vote we continue waiting."

No one argued.

Hours passed slowly and the temperature dropped even more as the sun got low in the sky, disappearing behind the nearby mountains. But it didn't get truly miserable until the wind picked up. Even when crouched below ground level in the arroyo, the cold was merciless because the earth had remained in the shade all day long, frozen, and provided neither warmth nor much shelter.

"After this is over, I'm going to stay beneath my electric blanket for the rest of the winter," Justine whispered into her radio.

"Toughen up, lady," Blalock growled back.

"Great, now it looks like we're going to get snow," Payestewa said as clouds began rolling in from the west, further darkening the sky.

"No, that would mean we'd finally be getting some moisture, and that ain't gonna happen, boys and girls," Blalock muttered.

Minutes ticked by slowly as the temperature continued to drop and silence stretched out between them.

"I think it's time I went in for a look," Harry said at last. His position in the ditch made him the closest one to the hogan. "I can move silently."

"You peek through that doorway or the hole in the side, and you're liable to lose a lot of body heat through the hole in your chest," Blalock said.

"Yeah. I know," Harry replied. "That's why I was thinking of doing what he doesn't expect. Now that the wind is coming up, it's probably whistling though the hogan, making some noise. He won't be able to hear what's going on around him very well so I figure I'll take the homemade ladder that's resting on the ground beside the west side of the hogan and climb up onto the top. Even if he hears me, which is unlikely, the roof is thick and he'd have to fire blind. But if all goes as I plan, that situation will never come up. I'll get a quick look inside and be out of there before he ever figures out he had company."

"If the guy is quick with his trigger, you could catch a bullet in the forehead. That's just too risky," Ella said.

"Actually, we're running low on options," Harry responded. "We have less than an hour of daylight left, and no night scopes. If he has a night-vision device, he could crawl out of that hogan in the dark and pick us off one by one."

"It's your operation, Deputy," Blalock said, "but I'd recommend we wait until twilight to make our move. We'll still be able to see each other, and he won't have any advantage with a night device."

"Sounds reasonable," Ella agreed.

"All right," Harry added.

Another half hour passed. None of them had had anything to eat or drink for a while and the cold was beginning to numb their skin. Blalock had sent Payestewa for hot coffee earlier, and everyone was grateful for the gesture, though the liquid, stored only in foam cups, was lukewarm by the time they got to drink it.

"Quick, somebody remind me why I became a cop," Justine said over the radio.

"You wanted excitement in your life," Neskahi answered. "And you liked working outdoors."

"Hang on, people. Stay sharp," Blalock grumbled.

Ella didn't argue. She knew that the chatter helped morale and kept them focused, but Blalock was still a by-the-book sort when the chips were down, and his motives were good.

Restless and cold, Ella tried to shove her gloved hands deeper into her pockets, but nothing was working now. The cold was biting into her fingertips, and her toes felt frozen. She'd always had cold feet and even the thick wool socks she wore in the winter weren't doing much good out here. She promised to stuff herself with warm food when she got home, put on two layers of socks, and wear fuzzy slippers until morning.

As Ella thought of home, she began to wonder how things were going back there. She hoped Rose was getting along with Gloria. Her mom could be impossible when she chose to be. Sometimes Ella just wasn't sure what would drive her crazy first—Rose, Dawn, or her job.

Her teeth began to chatter uncontrollably. "People, if we don't do something soon, I'm going to be shaking too hard to shoot straight," Ella said. "We're just not equipped to pull an all-nighter."

"What she said," Neskahi added.

"I never knew you were a wuss, Ella," Payestewa teased.

"Meet me at the gym sometime. We'll compare wuss factors," she shot back.

"Okay, boys and girls. It's time to make our move," Blalock said, his voice shaky from the cold. "But I'd reconsider that ladder if I were you, Ute. I've checked it out with my binoculars, and it looks like it's been outside in the elements for a long, long time. I'm not sure it'll hold that extra weight you've put on lately."

"I'll go up instead," Ella said. "Harry outweighs me by fifty pounds or more, and I'm lighter on my feet." Which had probably frozen and fallen off during their extended surveillance, Ella realized. She just hadn't gotten around to noticing yet.

"You might have a point," Harry said, conceding. "Okay, we'll both go, Ella, and I'll cover your back."

"Give the rest of us a chance to move in close enough to cover you first," Blalock said. "If he starts blasting, we want to be able to take him down immediately."

"I'm for that," Ella said, adjusting the bulletproof vest she now wore whenever she was out. The additional warmth it provided had been very welcome today.

"All right. We're going in, low and slow, everyone at once. I'll let you know as soon as we're in position," Blalock said.

Ella flexed her hands, trying to get the blood rushing

through them again, then took off her gloves and placed them in her pockets. She'd want the extra dexterity, just in case shooting began.

"Okay, Ella, Harry, go!" Blalock muttered into the radio once the rest of them had crawled closer to the hogan.

Ella slipped her radio onto her belt as she crouched, then moved quickly and silently across the frozen earth, reaching the west side of the hogan a few steps ahead of Harry. Grabbing the wooden ladder, she yanked it off the ground and swung it upright. With only a quick glance toward the entrance of the hogan, she propped the ladder up against the side of the hogan at a safe angle.

Harry was there now, pistol out. He held the ladder for her with his other hand, and nodded.

Ella stepped onto the ladder and climbed up, trying to ignore the creak of the wood. Clambering onto the clay-covered roof, she inched up on hands and knees toward the charcoal-rimmed smoke hole in the center, listening for any sounds within.

The wind was whistling around her now and she was being pelted by blowing sand. She held her breath as she approached the opening. Her heart hammered against her sides as she considered the possibility that he was waiting for her, and she'd get a bullet right between the eyes.

But if she looked quickly and ducked back, by the time his brain registered her presence and sent the message to his trigger finger, she'd be out of sight again. At least that was the theory. But what if he were already squeezing the trigger?

Images of Dawn came unbidden into her thoughts. Swallowing back her fear, Ella peeked inside, then ducked away.

It had been pretty dim inside the hogan, but the dwelling had appeared empty except for a slight warmth and the glow of coals directly below. But she'd caught a glimpse of an object close to the entrance.

She moved back for a closer look, and still no gunfire came. As her eyes adjusted to the light, she was able to confirm her suspicions about the doorway.

"No one's in the hogan," she said in a normal voice, turning to look at Harry, who was at the top of the ladder. "But had we tried to rush the door, we would have been history. There's a trip wire, and enough explosives in a box by the entrance to blow us all to kingdom come."

She heard Harry advise Blalock on the radio, but something else held her attention now. She leaned over the opening and stuck her head farther in, using the flashlight she'd taken from her pocket. "At least there's some good news. There's no fuse this time. The bomb is set on a timer."

"How much time's left?"

"I don't know. It's too small to see clearly. But there are at least four digits."

Her radio crackled at the same time Harry's did. "Get off of there, you two," Blalock advised. "And don't touch a thing. I'm calling your bomb-disposal unit. If they can't handle it, then the ATF or county people will."

"Dwayne, don't you remember? Our bomb-disposal unit is made up of one guy, Sam Pete," Ella said. "And I can tell you he hasn't done anything this complicated in a long time—if ever. Wires and detonators and other devices are tied together down there. It looks like a high school science project. If I were you, I'd get on the phone to the ATF."

Rose Destea stood at the window, watching the moon rise in the east, bathing the hills that had stood as their guardians since their clan first moved to this land generations ago. There was an odd stirring in her soul tonight. Even the mountains and the gray clouds billowing from their heights looked troubled. Something was wrong, and she could feel it. A mother knew things about her children without ever having to be told. It was an instinct nearly as old as the four sacred hills that surrounded them.

Ella was in danger somewhere out there on this cold night. Rose could feel it with every breath she took. She glanced over at Dawn, who was playing quietly on the living room floor. She was usually an active child but, tonight, she was as moody as her grandmother. Though she didn't dare ask, Rose could have sworn that the child sensed the same thing she did.

Gloria Washburn placed a gentle hand on Rose's shoulder. "Are you all right?"

Rose gritted her teeth. It bothered her having a stranger touch her, and, as a Navajo, the young woman should have known better. But the newer generations seldom spared a thought to the old traditions of their culture. "I'm fine, thank you," Rose said, moving away and going toward the hall.

"I wish you would let me do something for you, like fix you a bite to eat," Gloria called out. "Are you sure you're not hungry?"

"You have taken care of my granddaughter's meals, and that's enough for now. I'll eat later when my daughter returns."

Gloria exhaled softly, then sat down on the floor to play with Dawn.

Rose looked around what had once been her husband's study. It was now part office, part sewing room, but it still felt like John's domain. Sitting down on one of the upholstered chairs, she looked down at her hands. Even without the injury, they still belonged to an old woman. She'd always made it a point to hide her age from her children, but in another two months she would turn sixty-six.

Rose stood before the mirror. The soft wrinkles on her face spoke of more than years, they reflected a life often punctuated by harshness. Yet, inside, she still clung to her hopes and dreams, waiting for the right time to act on them, just like when she'd been twenty.

Rose reached into her pocket and brought out a photo taken at the Chapter House party a few months ago. Herman Cloud stood beside her, close but not touching. After John's death, she'd thought she'd never fall in love again. She'd thought herself too old for that nonsense. But she knew now that she had feelings for Herman. He saw the world with the same weary eyes that she did and yet, like her, he burned with the same need to protect the legacy of the *Dineh*.

She placed the photo back in her pocket. Some things were better kept from one's children.

Feeling a tug of her long skirt, Rose looked down and smiled at her granddaughter. "What is it, *hatsói*, my daughter's child?"

"*Shimá* coming home now," Dawn said in a very certain voice.

Rose looked at her granddaughter. All the women in their family had received the gift of intuition, and Dawn seemed to have gotten an early start.

"She'll be here, soon," Rose said.

Dawn nodded. "Coming home," she repeated firmly, then returned to her toys.

Rose smiled. At least her granddaughter wasn't boring. So much of life these days was. That was one of the main reasons she'd become so involved in trying to keep gambling off the Rez. Even at her age, Rose knew she still had a lot to offer the tribe. She loved taking care of her daughter and granddaughter, but she now wanted more out of her life than that.

SEVEN
✖ ✖ ✖

Ella crouched beside Sam Pete on the roof of the old hogan, a bit warmer now that she'd borrowed an extra coat from the bomb squad officer. ATF would not be able to respond for another hour, so Sam was all they had.

Sam hadn't been able to examine the bomb layout inside through the smoke hole without using heavy binoculars and a large, powerful flashlight. He'd had trouble aiming both at the precise spot simultaneously, so Ella had volunteered to hold the light for him.

Since both the entrance and hole in the side had been crossed with trip wires that would set off the detonator, Sam's plan was to use the ladder to climb down through the smoke hole and disarm the bomb.

"Shine the light on that timer now, so I can see exactly how many minutes I'm going to have to disarm the device," Sam asked.

Ella moved the beam of light toward the small black timer, not much larger than a wristwatch display, which lay on top of a mass of duct tape, sticks of explosives, batteries, wires, and pieces of cardboard. Without the binoculars, she couldn't read the numbers on the timer, though she was less than ten feet above the bomb.

"It looks like I have fifteen minutes left," Sam called to Ella loud enough for the others, at a safe distance away, to hear. "That's enough time for me to disarm it by disconnecting the batteries leading to the detonator."

Together, they pulled the narrow ladder up onto the domed roof of the hogan, and lowered it inside through the smoke hole, maneuvering it carefully so it didn't make contact with any wires or portion of the bomb. While Ella lit his way with the flashlight, Sam squeezed himself carefully through the narrow opening and went down.

Crouched beside the bomb, Sam looked at it more closely. "This is more complicated than I thought," he said, taking at least another five minutes to examine the device without touching anything. At long last, he reached into his jacket pockets and brought out two wire cutters.

"We've still got a few minutes, but I don't dare move anything because I just don't know what's underneath all that duct tape—maybe a mercury switch that will set it off if I jiggle things. The best bet is still to simultaneously cut the two wires leading to the batteries. Ella, you'd better put some distance between you and the hogan. I'm making an educated guess here, that's all," Sam said, looking up at her.

"Who's going to hold the light? You need both hands to cut the wires at the same time. You're stuck with me, Sam," Ella replied, giving him a thumbs-up.

"Okay, then," he said with a nod. "Here goes."

He knelt down and positioned both cutters on the wires leading to the batteries, then holding his breath, snipped both at once. The only sound either one of them could hear was the wind whistling through the cracks in the hogan walls.

"Oh-oh," Sam said. "These batteries must be dummies. The real ones are probably somewhere inside all that duct tape." He paused, then shouted. "It's started a twenty second countdown! Get out of here, Ella."

Sam virtually ran up the ladder, and Ella grabbed hold of his arms and yanked him onto the roof.

Sliding down on her behind, Ella dropped off the roof without even considering the distance. She hit the frozen ground hard, rolled from the impact, then took off running. "Head for the ditch," she yelled at Sam, who was a few seconds behind her.

"Fire in the hole!" Sam yelled as he sprinted up even with her. He reached out to grab her hand, then tripped over a clump of brush and fell flat on his face.

"Keep going!" Sam yelled, scrambling to stand, but Ella turned back and yanked him to his feet.

"Now we'll go!" Ella saw the ditch ahead and jumped down into it, Sam beside her.

"Cover your ears," Sam said, ducking down.

Time seemed to stand still. Ella didn't know how many seconds had gone by, but nothing happened.

"Well, is it going off, or not?" she asked.

"It's cold. Maybe the batteries—" Sam's words were drowned out as a deafening roar shook the earth around them, blowing chunks of log and earth over their heads. The wave of heat that enveloped them was almost a welcome relief from the bitter cold, but the shock wave left her ears ringing. Debris rained all around them.

As she turned her head, she saw Sam Pete. He was smiling, though his face was covered with dust and grime. "You say something?"

Ella stood by the SUV, now closer to the blasted ruins of the hogan, with Blalock beside her. "This was a real well planned setup," she said, still brushing off the dirt and dust. "If anyone had tried to crawl in through the side hole or the entrance, they would have died in the explosion. And the timer was set to go off as soon as it got dark, around the time anyone staking out the place might have decided to make their move. I have a feeling that Manyfarms let himself be seen by someone he knew would recognize him just to draw us here, hoping some of us would be caught by the bomb delivered by the Indian with the hat. I'm sure Artie Manyfarms knows Harry's on his tail, and would ask for backup from someone he knew and trusted."

"Agreed. But that doesn't bring us any closer to finding him," Blalock answered, "or whoever the guy was who prepared the surprise."

"I owe you big-time, Ella," Sam Pete said, joining them.

She accepted the cup of coffee he was offering her from his thermos bottle. "Don't give it another thought," she said, her voice still unsteady. "Helping each other is part of the job."

Sam shook his head. "I won't forget that you stuck with me. That took balls, Ella."

"Er . . . thanks, I think. But, to be honest, I really felt we'd both reach the ditch with a few seconds to spare." Had she considered it at length, and weighed the odds more carefully, she wasn't sure she would have still stayed back to haul Sam to his feet. She owed herself and her family more than that. And one look at Blalock's face told her that he thought she'd been recklessly loyal or stupid. She couldn't tell which.

"Okay. Let's move on," she said, taking a sip of the coffee, which was surprisingly warm.

"I'll gather up all the pieces and reconstruct the device. As soon as I have something, I'll let you know," Sam said.

Ella saw the anger and determination on his face, and didn't doubt his resolve for a minute. Sam would do his best to come through for her.

"Let's start searching," Ella said. "With this wind, we may lose bits of crucial evidence if we wait until morning."

"I'll get a lantern from the back of my car," Blalock said.

Neskahi joined them at the tail end of the discussion. "I'll take Ralph Tache back for the crime-scene van. It has floodlights and a generator."

They spent the next three hours searching the carefully marked off perimeter with methodical precision. Due to the harsh weather and wide debris field, Tache used a video camera equipped with flood lamps to physically record the crime scene. Every shred of material—plastic, metal, or paper—that might have been part of the device was filmed, coded by site location, and photographed in place before being bagged and tagged.

At long last everyone gathered by Blalock's sedan. "Okay. What do we have?"

Sam Pete was the first one to speak. "The explosives look like the same type and brand as those used in the random bombings we've been having, except that this one had a timer and electrical detonator instead of a nonelectrical blasting cap and fuse."

"Then we've already uncovered something important," Ella said. "Manyfarms must have made contact with the people responsible for the bombings, and one of them placed the bomb for him."

"I managed to lift some prints from the silver pickup we suspect was used in the sniper incident," Justine added. "I'll process them tonight before I call it a day."

"Look, we're all half-frozen," Ella said. "And it's been a long night. Let's head home and get an early start tomorrow."

Justine shook her head. "First, those prints, then I'll crash."

"I'm with you, Ella," Blalock said, and Neskahi concurred. "Better to get a fresh start in the morning than work when we're so tired we could miss something important."

Payestewa remained uncharacteristically quiet. "Is something bothering you, Lucas?" Ella asked at last.

He considered his answer carefully. "It appears to me that we were set up by a group of people, not just one or two. That means we, meaning the Bureau, need to get more actively involved in the vandalism investigations the Tribal PD have been handling exclusively till now, particularly in this area. The lesser crimes appear to be linked to the major ones."

Ella said nothing. She hated the thought of feds crawling around the Rez handling their case, but it could have been worse. Blalock and Payestewa's connections would be helpful. And Harry . . . well, at least he was Navajo.

As everyone got ready to leave, Ella smiled when she saw Harry putting his rifle on the rack in the back of his pickup. The habit was shared by most on the reservation. He may be a deputy federal marshal now, but he belonged to the Rez and the Rez to him.

"Hey, Harry. Why don't you come by tonight? Mom would love to see you."

"Does the invitation include dinner? I'm starving," he said with a grin.

"Yeah, but I'll have to do the cooking."

"Oh."

Ella laughed. "Try not to look as if you think that means a serving of ptomaine with a side dish of salmonella, will ya?"

"It's not that. I just remember that your idea of breakfast is a tortilla with butter. I'd like my meals more substantial. I'm a growing boy."

"Hey, now it's a matter of pride. Ya gotta come."

Harry laughed. "Okay. Let's see what you can whip up, lady."

As Harry followed her home in his truck, Ella tried to quiet her conscience. The truth was that she'd had an ulterior motive for inviting Harry over tonight. She'd been gone all day and she had no idea how Gloria and Rose had gotten along. If there had been trouble, Ella knew Rose would keep a lid on it until after Harry left, and she could face an argument with her mom a lot better on a full stomach.

She arrived forty-five minutes later. Knowing Harry was not far behind her, Ella hurried from her car. She could at least warn her mother and postpone any major problems. As Ella opened the front door, Gloria met her. The young woman had the wary look of someone just coming out of combat.

"Was it that bad?" Ella asked softly, already suspecting the answer.

Gloria gave her a wan smile. "Your mother, I think, will be better off with someone else. I'm no traditionalist, Ella, and I forget things like not using proper names. I just wasn't raised with the old ways."

With only those few words Gloria had given Ella an accurate picture of how the day had gone. "Do me a favor?" Seeing her nod, Ella looked at her watch. "It's not too late. Call Jennifer Clani and ask if she can take your place tomorrow. I'll pay her whatever she asks. If she agrees, you're off the hook."

"I'll get her to come if I have to pay her myself." Grabbing her coat, Gloria whispered good-bye and slipped out the door.

Rose came out of the kitchen, anger putting a spark in her eyes. "You've been gone since early morning, daughter. For a modernist, you've never heard of a telephone?"

Suddenly a man's heavy footsteps sounded on the porch and, hoping for the best, Ella opened the door. Rose's expression changed in the blink of an eye.

"You're back, Deputy Marshal!" Rose said with a bright smile. "And you've come to visit. That's wonderful!"

"Your daughter promised to cook dinner for me. I'm used to danger, so I accepted," Harry teased.

Rose looked at her daughter, a bemused expression on her face. "What do you plan to fix?"

"Hot dogs?" Ella joked. "I wouldn't want our guest to think I'm too domestic."

"Don't worry, Investigator. Your image as a tough cop will remain safe," Harry said. "But I thought we had a deal. You were going to cook something more substantial. Caving in already?"

"Well, okay. I suppose a deal's a deal. Let me see what we have in the cupboard. I can heat up a can of beans with the best of them."

Rose groaned. "Don't worry," she said, giving Harry

a despairing look. "She *can* cook—with someone looking over her shoulder. I'll supervise, and, providing she can follow a recipe, we may live through this meal."

"Hey, you two, you're giving me a serious inferiority complex," Ella protested.

Harry burst out laughing. "You don't have an insecure bone in your body."

"Yeah, yeah," she said with a grin. Little did he know. "Keep each other company for a minute, okay? I'm going to go check on my kid."

Rose glanced back at Ella. "Be careful not to wake her. She hasn't been herself today."

"Is she sick?"

"No, I think she was just worried."

Sensing her mother didn't want to discuss it further, Ella let it drop for now. She went to Dawn's bedroom and tiptoed in. Her sleeping daughter looked completely at peace. Grateful that the craziness of her world had never touched her child, she brushed a gentle kiss on Dawn's forehead, then tiptoed back out of the room.

When Ella entered the kitchen a moment later, she saw Rose had brought a package of chicken patties out of the refrigerator. "You can pan fry these, make mashed potatoes and gravy, and heat up a can of green beans. Those are things you can fix."

"I'll give it a go."

A half hour later, they sat around the kitchen table eating chicken cutlets smothered in green chile with mashed potatoes on the side. They'd all decided to forgo the gravy, which had showed a remarkable resemblance to gray cottage cheese.

Rose took a small bite of the chicken. "You *had* to put olives in the chile sauce, didn't you? Sometimes I wonder about my daughter," she added, glancing at Harry. "She'd put olives in everything if I didn't complain. I've even seen her opening a jar of those giant black olives and snacking on them late at night as she plays on her computer."

"We all have our vices," Ella admitted. "I love olives. Green or black. I'm not really choosy, except I hate those stuffed with pimentos."

"This isn't half bad," Harry said as he took another bite. He was already on his second helping of chicken and potatoes.

"I slave away at the stove after a hard day at the stakeout, and that's the best compliment you can come up with?"

"Hey, I know you pretty well by now. If I gave you too much of a compliment, you'd think I was lying."

Ella laughed. "Well, you still could have tried a little harder."

After everyone finished, Ella began to gather the plates. Rose stood, wanting to help, but Ella shook her head. "You're not getting near the dishes, Mom."

"I'm used to picking up after myself. I can help." Harry stood and started gathering the silverware.

"In that case, I'm going to watch the late news and weather, and leave you two alone," Rose said, walking out of the kitchen.

"Can you believe that she's never let me buy her a dishwasher?" Ella said as Harry helped her clear the rest of the table.

"It's not her way. Rose has lived all her life without one, and probably to her it would just be a waste of money."

"Yeah," Ella agreed. "Mom always says she won't pay for what she can do herself."

Ella washed while Harry dried and, all in all, it was a good arrangement, because it kept them close but physically out of contact. Ella wasn't sure if she was going crazy or not, but the awareness between them was definitely growing, and the weeks they'd been apart only made his presence more exciting to her. She wanted to touch him, to have him touch her. She'd lived all her life being separate, but that's not the way she wanted things to be between Harry and her right now.

"Ella," he said, his voice low. "I've been thinking—"

He never got a chance to continue. His cell phone rang and he answered it. Excusing himself, Harry stepped across the kitchen, listened for a moment, then said something in reply and ended the connection. "That was Blalock, Ella. I'll help you finish here, but then I've got to go. One of the people who live in the general vicinity of the hogan called the PD after the explosion. He saw a green van that he didn't recognize racing away from the area. Big Ed had an officer follow up on it, and about an hour later a San Juan County deputy found an abandoned vehicle matching that description over in Aztec. The engine was still warm. I need to go over and check it out. Sheriff Taylor will meet me there with his crime-scene team. Why don't you come with me?"

She shook her head. "That's out of my jurisdiction. Although I've worked with Sheriff Taylor before, I don't think he'd like it if I horned in, so I better stay here."

"Are you sure?"

"Very." Ella dried her hands, and walked him to the door. "What were you going to say before?" she asked, stepping outside onto the porch with him.

Harry stopped, then stared at the ground for a moment. "Just that I've missed . . . New Mexico. I'm trying to get assigned a bit closer to home." Harry leaned over and gave her a light kiss on the cheek. "You better go back inside before you catch pneumonia."

Ella stood there for a moment as he drove away. Too many thoughts and feelings suddenly crowded her mind. Hearing Rose moving around in the kitchen, she came back inside, scarcely aware of the cold.

"He likes you, daughter," Rose said.

"Mom, were you watching?"

"I may have noticed you two outside."

"Mom!" Ella pretended to be offended, then walked off. At least this was one way to avoid a lengthy discussion with her mother right now, one she definitely wasn't prepared to have.

It was nearly eleven when a car pulled up in the driveway. Rose, who had been watching as Ella finished straightening the kitchen, walked to the window and peered out. "It's your child's father. I hope he doesn't think he's going to see her now."

Ella slipped on her jacket and shook her head. "I'll go out to meet him."

Kevin was waiting by his sedan holding a package as she opened the door and stepped out onto the porch. Someone else was driving, probably Jefferson Blueeyes. The two were like twins attached at the hip these days.

At least Kevin had shown enough good sense and manners to respect Navajo customs and not come up to the door uninvited, particularly at this late hour. Ella waved at him to come inside. She'd initially planned on talking to him outside on the porch, but it was just too cold.

"Where's your mother?" Kevin asked, following her in. He was as good-looking as always, but he looked tired. His tie was loosened at his neck, and his eyes were bloodshot.

"Probably in bed," Ella said pointedly.

"I know it's terribly late," he said, "but I brought a present for Dawn, and I thought you could give it to her when she wakes up tomorrow. I meant to be here hours ago, but things got crazy. It's been a long week."

Ella took the brightly wrapped package from him. "What did you get her?"

"It's a new stuffed dinosaur. The one she's been carrying around is faded and practically falling apart."

Ella fought the urge to roll her eyes. "The reason it's in that condition is because she carries it around everywhere. It's her pal. I'll give her your new one, but don't expect her to discard the old one for the new. She's not like that."

Kevin didn't pursue it. "I also came by to talk to you,"

he said quietly, looking her up and down from head to foot. "I heard about the bomb at the abandoned hogan. Are you all right?"

"Of course. Don't I look okay?" she asked rhetorically.

"I was worried, Ella. I sure wish you'd settle on a little less dangerous job, or else take a staff position." He paused then added, "Why don't you come work for me?"

Ella stared at him in confusion. "As what?"

"I'm sure the Tribal Council could find some use for your talents. Maybe conducting background checks on tribal employees, or serving as police consultant for the council. It could be a job you work eight to five, with weekends off."

"Kevin, let's get one thing straight. I don't want you to find me a job, or create one for me. I'm happy where I am."

"You've had an inordinate amount of good luck, Ella. But things are different now, and someday your luck may run low. Our child needs you alive and healthy."

"She *has* me, on both counts. I'm here for her. And, just so you know, very few cops actually get killed in the line of duty."

"But a lot of them get shot at, or shot."

"More Navajos die in traffic accidents. You want me to get a horse?"

He shook his head. "Try a mule. You'd have more in common."

"If you're trying to sweet talk me into doing what you want, you're not getting anywhere."

He met her gaze. "If I *could* sweet talk you, I would. But I'd have better luck persuading a brick wall to sing a song. When you're convinced you're doing the right thing, nothing ever sways you."

"Is that so bad?" Ella asked softly.

Kevin thought about it. "In this case, it is, because

you're wrong this time, Ella. You really are. You owe your child more than this."

Ella tried to bite back her anger, but was only partially successful. "Now you're crossing the line into the part of my life that's none of your business. My daughter has the best I can give her. I'm in an important, satisfying job that pays the bills and often even lets us get a few extras. I provide for my family, Kevin. I've never asked you for a dime—which is a good thing, since months go by sometimes before you remember to send some money to contribute to your daughter's expenses. But I don't mind, I really don't. Just don't spout this stuff about the responsibilities of motherhood to me. I'm here for her on a daily basis, which is far more than anyone can say about you."

"I'm working for the tribe now, representing the People. I have serious responsibilities."

"And what am I doing? Serving fry bread at the Totah Café? You know more than most people what I do for the tribe, so I'm surprised you'd even dare to make a comparison. Leave, Kevin. It's late and I'm in no mood for this."

Kevin stood his ground. "I have to tell you something else first. I'm going off to To'hajiilee on tribal business in the morning. I want to talk to everyone on the Rez about the gaming issue and get their feelings on the issue before I vote. That means I'll be on the road a lot and I won't be stopping by as often."

Ella shook her head. "You mean from 'hardly ever' to 'almost never'?"

"Tell Dawn, okay? Make her understand."

Rose came in then, wearing her robe and warm slippers. "Would you like some coffee?"

The invitation surprised Kevin, but not as much as it did Ella.

"I'm sorry, Rose. I can't stay. I've got my assistant in the car waiting for me."

Rose nodded curtly. "Before you vote on the question

of gambling, remember that nearly all of the traditionalists are opposed to it. For every good thing gaming will bring, it will take away something we value. We already have alcoholism to deal with, but the casinos will bring in a new addiction—the illness which comes when people think they can get rich overnight. There are many poor people here who will be tempted to spend what little they have on the slot machines. Then they'll pawn everything they own to raise a few more dollars to gamble. After that, they'll have nothing."

"With the money gaming will bring in, we can put programs in place to help those poor people," Kevin argued. "There are families who don't even have a working woodstove, and it gets below zero a lot in the winter. The tribe needs to have a plan—and the funds—to help them. There's also something else to consider. The casinos would create many new jobs for our people. The *Dineh* wouldn't have to leave the reservation just to find work. I'd really like people to understand exactly what they stand to gain, so they can make an informed decision."

"I'm not saying that there aren't advantages. I'm saying that the disadvantages, in the long run, will outweigh the benefits. The council has to consider both sides of that issue *very* carefully," Rose countered.

"We are. That's why I'm going to visit many different communities. I want to see how they feel about things, and get an idea of what the People would like. The council works for all the tribe, not for themselves."

"When we've had referendums before, the People have always said no to gambling," Rose reminded him.

"Yes, but I want to see how people feel now, especially after such a hard year. Adversity often changes people's minds. Then I'll vote according to what I perceive is the will of the majority."

He checked his watch. "I've got to go now." He glanced at Ella. "Take care of our daughter and tell her I came by."

"You don't have to worry about her," Rose said. "I've always said that she needed a father figure who'd be around more, but my granddaughter has already become friends with her mother's marshal friend. He was here again for dinner tonight."

Ella stared at her mother as she ambled away slowly. At that moment, she could have cheerfully throttled her.

"Harry Ute's been dropping by?" Kevin asked as soon as they were alone.

"Yeah. One way or another we always seem to end up working together," Ella said with a shrug.

"But how often can that be? He's not assigned to this area."

"Not yet, but he soon could be," Ella answered.

Kevin held her eyes. "And you plan on dating him?"

"Look, Kevin, your aide is probably frozen by now. You better go."

"Answer me."

"It's really none of your business; but, yes, I intend to see him when he's around."

Kevin's eyes narrowed, and he gave her a curt nod, then left.

Ella instantly regretted having given Kevin any information about Harry. Kevin knew how to pull strings. Hopefully he wouldn't be able to interfere with Harry's intentions to relocate closer to home. From now on, she'd watch what she told Kevin.

"Don't worry, daughter. He can't hurt your friend in any way," Rose said, returning to the room and reading Ella's expression. "He'd be risking his career if he tried to block a Navajo from getting reassigned to this area and anyone found out."

Ella exhaled softly. "Mom, you shouldn't have said anything."

"I was only trying to motivate him to visit my granddaughter more often. She's so happy when he comes," Rose said.

"He loves her in his own way, Mom, and no matter

how aggravating things get between us, he's my daughter's father. Our relationship may not have worked out, but what came of it is beyond price," she said gesturing toward Dawn's room.

Rose nodded thoughtfully. "But not all relationships lead to disillusionment, daughter. You should settle down and marry your marshal friend. You'd make each other happy because you understand one another so well." She paused. "But maybe you need a little help."

"Mother, don't you dare talk to my friend about this. Don't even hint!" Ella said walking down the hall with her.

Rose didn't answer. Instead, she walked into her room and closed the door behind her.

As Ella trailed off to her bedroom, the sound of her mother's soft laughter followed her, making her worry even more.

EIGHT
✖ ✖ ✖

It was a few minutes before seven the next morning when a vehicle pulled up outside. Dawn, watching cartoons, remained glued to the spot. Rose's admonitions about not opening the door to strangers had apparently worked. Ella, in the kitchen fixing coffee, went to see who it was.

A young Navajo woman with long black hair tied back in a ponytail, bundled up warmly in a wool coat, stood outside her vehicle waiting to be invited into the house. Two came out to the porch with Ella and watched closely, though he didn't bark or growl.

Ella waved, inviting her to come in, suspecting this was Jennifer Clani. A traditionalist would never come up to the door without permission. Sure that her mother had noticed it, Ella breathed a sigh of relief. Maybe Jennifer would work out.

"*Yáat'ééh,*" the young woman greeted, using the Navajo word for hello. "I'm the granddaughter of your mother's friend. The nurse who was helping your mother told me to be here at seven."

Ella smiled as Jennifer, followed by Two, came into the living room. From what she could see Jennifer was just perfect. Ella took her coat and saw she was wearing a long velvet skirt, a thick knitted wool sweater, a wool shawl, and leather boots.

Rose came out of the hall, saw Jennifer, and smiled. "You're my friend's granddaughter."

Jennifer nodded. "I'm here to help you around the house and do whatever you need. Grandmother told me to assure you that I'm not here to interfere, just to lend a helping hand until yours heals." She looked at the bandage on Rose's hand to emphasize the point.

Rose nodded and smiled. There was no doubt in Ella's mind that having Jennifer rather than Gloria around the house would be easier for Rose to handle. Best of all, Rose would take it easy on her out of respect for her close friend Lena Clani.

Ella took Rose aside while Jennifer spoke to Dawn, who'd come up to talk to her. "I suspect that you antagonized Gloria to the point where she wouldn't come back, but I know you'll be nicer to this girl. Please try to make sure everything goes smoothly."

"I'll take good care of her."

"No, Mom. She's here to help *you.*"

"Daughter, you worry too much."

Ella picked up her buttered tortilla from the counter and turned to Jennifer, who'd followed them into the kitchen. "I'll need you to start by helping fix Mom's and my daughter's breakfast. I have to take a shower and get to work."

"My daughter is always rushing," Rose said sadly. "So much like an Anglo." She gave Jennifer a long look and, as Jennifer nodded sympathetically, Rose brightened. "You look just like your grandmother described you. She talks about you a lot."

Jennifer smiled. "I'll get started fixing scrambled eggs, toast, and bacon if you have it. How's that, Aunt?" she asked, using the term out of respect.

Rose beamed. "That would be very nice, and more sensible than cold cereal," she said, making a face at Ella.

Ella, following the dictum that said discretion was the better part of valor, fled the kitchen.

By the time Ella was out of the shower and dressed, her daughter and mother were in the kitchen eating a full breakfast. There was toast, butter, eggs, oatmeal and fresh bacon on the table. It smelled wonderful, especially the bacon, and Ella grabbed a piece for herself.

To her surprise, Dawn was ignoring her juice cup and actually eating her oatmeal. Knowing that her daughter *hated* oatmeal, she looked at Jennifer. "What did you do? That's nothing short of a miracle," she said, gesturing casually to Dawn's efforts with the cereal.

"Brown sugar and bits of apple works with my nephew. I thought your daughter might like it that way too."

"Great idea." Ella kissed Dawn and her mother goodbye. "I'm off to work. Call if you need anything," Ella told Jennifer. "My mom has my office and cell number."

As Ella walked out of the house, she felt really optimistic about the arrangement. With luck, this would work out for everyone. Even Rose was happy—at least for the moment.

After scraping off the frost from her car windows while the engine warmed up, she left for the station. Her only worry today was that Dawn might prove to be more of a handful than Jennifer had expected. Though her little girl was generally good, Dawn was extremely active. Taking care of Dawn *and* Rose would require the patience of a diplomat and the stamina of a cross-country runner.

Today, she'd make it a point to call Jennifer and make sure things were going all right. If she had to, Ella was prepared to stop by home and read Rose and her daughter the riot act.

Ella had just sat down at her desk with a cup of coffee when Justine came into her office. "Hey, you're in early," Ella said looking up at her.

"You usually beat me, I know, but today I had so much work waiting, I came in at seven." She placed a file folder on Ella's desk. "That's my report on the car vandalism we investigated at the Riverside neighborhood."

"Anything interesting?"

"One thing—and it's something we should go check out," Justine said.

"Give me the Reader's Digest version," Ella said, not bothering to read the report at the moment.

"I split the work with Neskahi and we made it a point to go back and talk to everyone on that street. As it turns out, this incident may not be related to the others. Ranelle Francisco is the manager at the First Trust Bank, and she said she's been having a lot of problems with one of the tellers, Lea Tsosie. There was a problem with her cash drawer, and Ranelle told Lea that she would have to make up the missing money or the police would be called in. Lea apparently threatened to get even with her."

"And Ranelle thinks Lea and a friend vandalized every car parked on that street just to get back at her?" Ella asked incredulously.

"Ranelle says that it would be very difficult for the tellers to get hold of her address but, apparently, Lea followed her into the neighborhood a few nights prior to that incident. Ranelle didn't know if she was in danger or not, but when a cop car drove by, Lea headed back to the highway and left the area."

"Lea could have been in that neighborhood for any number of reasons," Ella said.

"That's what I thought, too, so I checked it out. When I dropped by Lea's home, she wasn't there, but I spoke to her parents. I found out from them that she didn't come home the night the cars were vandalized."

"Okay, so we need to see if she has an alibi and access to a pickup like the one we chased." Ella glanced at her watch. "It's still early. Let's go. We may be able to catch Lea at home."

Justine drove and Ella gazed out the window, gathering her thoughts. Even when events seemed to be random they seldom were. "It's a matter of finding the pattern, then we'll have answers," she said under her breath.

"Now you're sounding like your brother, the *hataalii*," Justine teased.

Ella smiled. "Sometimes the old ways make a heckuva lot of sense. Right now we're being pulled in every direction following up on all these petty crimes and trying to find our sniper. We need to stay centered and focused, and the way I found to do that was to lean on what my mother taught me about 'walking in beauty.' The Navajo Way teaches that everything in life is interrelated, and only by seeing the pattern can one reach harmony. That's what I'm going to do on this case—I'm going to concentrate on seeing the whole picture and then try to figure out where everything fits."

Justine drove down a gravel lane that led up to a white-and-blue mobile home. It had been well maintained and a simple wooden porch had been built beside the front door. On the right was a small area fenced in by chicken wire that was apparently used to grow vegetables in the summer, but now it stood barren except for the brown stalks of a few dead plants. The shaded ground still glistened with frost.

Ella zipped up her jacket, stepped out of the vehicle, and waited. This wasn't a traditionalist area, but a little - courtesy couldn't hurt. A moment later, an elderly woman came to the door and waved for them to come in.

"Hurry. It's freezing outside," Ruth Tsosie said. "It's not very warm inside either, but it's better than out there."

Ella noticed immediately how cool the interior of the trailer home was. It had to be around sixty.

"We're low on LP gas," she said. "The company that supplies us hasn't stopped by yet. We pay our bills, but it's been such a cold winter, supply is low, and they're having trouble getting around to all their rural customers."

"How about electric heaters?" Ella suggested.

"We have one of those in the bedroom." She paused, pulling her heavy cardigan tightly around her. "So tell me, what can I do for you?"

"Is your daughter home?" Ella asked.

Ruth nodded, then asked, "Is this about the problem at the bank? My daughter would *never* steal money."

Lea appeared from down the hall, and apparently having heard the conversation, added, "I really think that Ranelle or someone else is messing with my cash drawer. No matter how careful I am, I always seem to come out short."

Ella sat down as Ruth waved to the couch, but she didn't take off her jacket. Justine sat in the chair opposite Ruth. "Do you think Ranelle's out to get you?" Ella pressed.

"She sent you here, didn't she?" Lea didn't wait for an answer from Ella. "But I told her I'd sue her for harassment, or false injury, or whatever the lawyers could dream up." She smirked. "The problem is that she knows I can't prove anything, so she's not really worried."

"Do you know where she lives by any chance?" Ella asked, keeping her tone casual.

Lea thought about it. "Somewhere up on the mesa, I think. West of the highway would be my guess, but I'm not sure. I saw her there not long ago when I dropped Henry off one night."

"Henry?"

Lea's eyes widened. "Never mind. He's got nothing to do with this."

"Let me be the judge of that," Ella answered. "Right now I need to get a feel for what's going on at the bank. Does Henry work there too?"

"Will you tell Ranelle what I tell you?"

"Not unless it involves a crime against the bank or her specifically."

Lea thought about it, then nodded. "Okay, I'll trust you. Henry Yabeni works at the bank as a loan officer, and he and I have gone out a few times. Ranelle would go ballistic if she found out. She hates me, and Henry is a member of her clan."

As Ella began to question her about her whereabouts on the night the cars had been vandalized, Lea began to fidget nervously.

"I can't remember where I was."

Lea's mother stared hard at her. "They asked me the same question earlier, but all I know is that you didn't come home that night."

Lea looked at the floor, her lips pursed.

"It would be a lot easier for you if you just answer the question," Justine said.

Lea exhaled loudly. "I was at Cecelia Yazzie's, okay? She's been teaching me about weaving."

"All night?"

"Yeah. It got late, so I just slept over instead of driving home half-asleep."

Ruth gave her daughter an incredulous look, but didn't say a word.

Ella watched Lea looking everywhere but at her mother. The young woman was lying and doing a really bad job of it. "You sure?"

"Yeah."

Ruth looked at her daughter, then at Ella. "What's this all about? I get the feeling this isn't about the cash drawer."

"I'm not at liberty to say anything more at this point," Ella said, "but if Lea's alibi checks out, she'll have nothing to worry about." Ella looked at the young woman, but Lea was staring at the turquoise ring on her finger. She looked as though she were about to be ill.

Ella and Justine walked back to the SUV. Once they were both inside, Ella glanced at Justine. "Did you see the look on her face when I told her we'd be checking out her alibi? She's terrified."

"It's almost a waste of time to check with Cecelia Yazzie. I'm virtually certain she won't back up Lea's story."

"Unless Lea gets to her first. But I've got to tell you, Lea doesn't strike me as the kind to go around bashing cars like that, but there were two people involved. Maybe she drove and someone else tossed the bricks."

"Where to next?" Justine said as they reached the highway. "The Yazzie home?"

"Right. I know where Cecelia lives. She sometimes hosts the Weaver's Society meetings that my mother attends."

They arrived ten minutes later at an old cinder-block house north of Shiprock along the Cortez highway. Smoke was coming out the chimney, and a ramshackle pickup was parked in front of the house. There were no trees and only native grasses and brush around. Out here, nothing was around to stop the cold wind when it blew. Off to the north were tall mesas and isolated rock formations that reminded Ella of Monument Valley.

Justine parked in view of the front window, and before long someone waved at them from the front door. "Quick. I don't want to open the door for one second longer than necessary."

Cecelia was in her midforties and lived alone in the two- or three-room house. Ella saw the cordless telephone and a half-filled cup of coffee beside it on the dining table. She had a feeling that Lea had already called her.

"Sit down, please. I have something to explain to both of you. I supposed you're here about Lea?"

Ella nodded, and Justine silently took out her pocket notebook.

"She just called me. She feels terrible about this, but she didn't want her mother to know where she really had been that night, so she had to make up a story. Lea's been spending some time with Henry, her boyfriend. But her mother, Ruth, wants her to marry Wilbert Vigil. You see, Henry works for a relatively low salary at the bank, but Wilbert Vigil owns his own business." She shrugged. "Ruth wants financial security for her daughter, but Lea has her eye on Henry instead."

"Maybe she's in love," Justine said with a tiny smile.

"Love?" Cecelia shook her head. "That's Anglo thinking, girl. Romantic love is nothing more than hormones. When two people commit to each other and look to the future together, that becomes a love that can endure. The other fizzles out as fast as an open can of cola on a hot day."

Ella nodded slowly. Romantic love usually played no part in Navajo thinking. But both she and Justine had seen too much of the Anglo world not to be affected by it. Ella knew she wanted both, and she had a feeling that Justine did too.

Ella stood, thanked Cecelia, then added, "We better go speak with Henry. Think he'll be at the bank already?"

"Lea figured you'd want to check with him, and told me to let you know that Henry is supposed to be helping his father gather firewood today out near their home by Narbona Pass. John and Claudia Yabeni are traditionalists and all their heating comes from a woodstove."

Ella glanced at Justine. "We need to find out exactly where the Yabenis live and head up there. If they're out cutting wood, we'll find out where or wait for them to return. But we better get going. It's a two-hour ride from here provided the roads are in good condition."

"If you locate Henry you might want to take the time to really talk to him. He's a gossip, but an informed one. That guy knows a lot of people in the area."

"Thanks for the tip," Ella said.

Justine settled behind the wheel as Ella fastened her seat belt. "Are you sure you want to go all the way out there?"

"We need to verify the stories, and the sooner the better," Ella said. "But let's go back to the station and get my vehicle. The jeep is better off-road, and I have a feeling we're going to need some heavy-duty traction if there's any snow in the woodcutting area up there."

As they drove back to the station, Ella wondered why it always seemed she had to travel long distances whenever there was a crisis at home. The last thing she wanted to do on Jennifer Clani's first day on the job was to go on a long road trip.

"How are things going with your mom?" Justine asked as if reading her mind.

Ella filled her in. "I think, or maybe I should say, I'm *hoping*, Jennifer will work out."

"Do you mind a suggestion?" Seeing Ella shake her head, Justine continued. "Invite Harry over to dinner as often as possible while he's here. It'll keep Rose distracted and on good behavior."

Ella burst out laughing. "Harry might have something to say about that."

"I doubt it. Harry loves to eat, and I bet he's always up for a dinner invitation. It's a wonder he used to be so thin. In fact, if you want his undying loyalty, serve chocolate cake. The gooier the better."

Ella gave her a quick look. "And you're so knowledgeable because? . . ."

Justine laughed out loud. "My older sister Jayne had a thing for him years ago. She found out everything she could about him."

"I didn't know they'd dated."

"Please, Jayne? I think she's dated everyone on the Rez at one time or another."

"If you recall anything else like that about him, fill me in."

Justine smiled. "I thought you'd say that."

Ella said nothing.

"Of course, you've already got a huge head start," Justine said.

"Huh?"

"Harry always liked you."

"What's this 'always'?"

"Yeah, it's true. Ask Ralph Tache. You just never noticed until recently." Justine paused. "Of course, I can see what's caught your eye. Harry's changed since he joined the Marshal's Service. He's more confident—and his body's looking real buff, too, now that he's put on about thirty pounds."

Ella burst out laughing. "Well, hands off, cousin. At least until further notice."

It took nearly two hours to find John and Claudia Yabeni's house. Henry's mother then gave them directions to the designated area where the men had gone to gather firewood. Her directions had sounded good, but when it came time to actually carry them through, they realized how many dirt tracks wandered through the Chuska Mountains. Turn west on the main path, then north before you get to the canyon left a lot of room for interpretation when all the tracks looked the same and the canyons ran nearly side by side for miles between the ridges coming off the mountains.

They got lost twice. Finally, as they drove through a meadow surrounded by tall pines, they heard the distinctive roar of a chain saw up ahead.

"If we have any luck at all, that'll be them," Ella said.

They parked at a clearing about twenty yards from an elderly man and a younger one who were busy cutting down a gnarly old pine.

Seeing Ella's vehicle, the men stopped their work and turned off the chain saw, waiting for them to approach.

"This is legal, Officers," the elderly man said, obviously noting the weapons at Ella and Justine's waists. "The tribal forestry people set this area for people gathering firewood. We're just not allowed to take young, healthy trees."

"And I have a Forestry Department permit for a full pickup load," the younger man added, coming up to Ella and reaching into his jacket pocket.

Seeing that the elder man had remained behind, Ella felt free to use proper names.

"Henry?" Ella asked softly.

He nodded. "Your partner looks familiar, but do I know you?"

"No, we've never met," she said. "I'm Investigator Clah. I spoke to Lea earlier today."

"Is she okay? Is something wrong?" he asked quickly.

"Not that I know of. I just need you to verify a few things concerning Lea and some stories we've been hearing about the bank."

"It's been like a war zone there lately," he mumbled.

Henry's father, John Yabeni, joined them a moment later. "If you don't mind, Officer, may I continue my work while you're speaking with my son?"

"Go right ahead."

Justine watched the elder Yabeni for a moment as he walked back to the now fallen tree. "Why don't I give him a hand?" she asked Ella. "He doesn't seem very comfortable with that chain saw."

"He's not. That was my idea so we could finish faster."

"Go help him," Ella said. One-to-one questioning always worked better for her anyway. She walked a safe distance away from where they'd been sawing, and Henry followed. First, Ella had him verify Lea's alibi.

"Yeah, I remember that. It was my birthday and we went to one of the pueblo casinos near Bernalillo to celebrate. We didn't get back to the Rez until early the next morning."

Ella glanced over at Justine and saw she'd taken the chain saw from John and was helping him cut up the tree trunk.

"Does Ranelle have a problem with anyone else at the bank?"

"Not that I've seen. Normally, she gets along with everyone. But for some reason, Ranelle took a dislike to Lea from day one." Henry paused giving her a long, thoughtful look. "But you're not really worried about the bank. I bet what you're really investigating is the incident that left her precious car without a windshield."

"Yes, and I need to see if there's a connection between that instance of vandalism and some of the other
incidents we've had," Ella said.

"Well, if there is, Lea's no part of it. She's just not
like that. If she has a problem, she'll stew about it for a
while, then get into somebody's face, that's all."

Ella allowed the silence to stretch out between them
and watched Justine sawing off the branches before tack-
ling the tree trunk. John Yabeni was hauling the
branches to the truck.

"If what you want are the guys who've been stirring
up trouble around here," Henry said slowly, "you're
looking in the wrong direction. You're thinking it's a
disgruntled worker, someone working out his anger. But
I don't believe that's what it's all about. I listen to people
talking all the time, and my guess is that you should be
keeping an eye out for a group of troublemakers who
have decided to wage war on the tribe. It's the type of
thing one would assume modernists might do, as opposed to the traditionalists, but that doesn't make sense
either because the modernists have been the targets, by
and large."

"Any idea why someone would want to wage war on
the tribe?" Ella pressed, curious to find out more of what
he'd learned.

"See, that's just what makes it tricky. Considering the
targets, it would be easy to blame a traditionalist group
like the Fierce Ones, but this isn't their doing because
they wouldn't use these methods. So that leaves us with
the modernists. But, as I said, that makes even less sense.
Maybe it's some Anglos."

Ella was about to comment when the chain saw made
a strange, labored, high-pitched squeal, then snapped. As
she turned her head, she saw John Yabeni stagger back,
blood pouring down his chest, then fall to the ground.

"Dad!" Henry ran toward him, then looked at Justine
in confusion. "What happened?"

"The chain hit something real hard and just snapped

before I could pull it loose," Justine stammered, dropping the saw, which had stopped running.

John moaned as Ella lifted his sweater. A piece of metal chain was imbedded in his chest. There was so much blood already she couldn't tell if he was injured anywhere else, but that was enough for her to know he was in trouble.

Henry took off his jacket and placed it over his father. "We need an emergency medical team out here."

Ella shook her head. "It would take them forever to find us, even in the helicopter. We'll transport him to a location where they can meet us and pick him up." She knew that before long, John Yabeni would go into shock.

"Justine, make as much room as you can in the back of our Jeep. Flip down the backseat." She then looked at Henry. "You'll need to keep your father as calm and motionless as possible."

Using a blanket as a stretcher, they carried the injured man to the Jeep. As they walked past the tree they'd been cutting into sections Ella saw the cause of the accident clearly. A section of the saw's cutting chain had snagged on a large nail that had been pounded into the trunk at an angle.

For a moment her mind went back to an incident she'd heard about during her days with the FBI in California. An environmentalist group had used a similar tactic when they'd tried to prevent a logging company from clear-cutting a grove of old-growth forest. But why was this happening here? It didn't make sense.

A few minutes later, they were on their way. Henry was beside his father in the back, comforting him as best as he could, and Justine was at the wheel. Ella, sitting beside her, noted that Justine's hands were shaking.

"Do you want me to drive?" Ella asked.

"No, let me do this. I know it's your unit, but I need to do something right now."

Ella didn't argue. "You're not blaming yourself, are you?" she asked quietly.

"Don't, it wasn't your fault," Henry added, hearing what Ella had said. "I'd been warned that somebody was spiking trees out here, but I forgot to tell you and Dad when you took over for me and started cutting up the trunk. The truth is I got distracted and he paid the price."

"This has happened before?" Ella asked surprised.

"Twice, that I know of, not counting now," Henry replied. "The first was when old man Benally was out chopping firewood, but he was using an ax so all he got was a nicked blade and a shoulder ache. The next time was with Wallace Curtis, the high school principal. He was in this area gathering wood, using a chain saw like us. He grazed a huge nail, but all it did was dull the chain."

"Didn't anyone report this?"

Henry shrugged. "Most of those who've been gathering firewood heard about it, and the forestry department told everyone who applied for a cutting permit. Apparently Mr. Curtis reported it right away."

Ella suppressed her frustration. If the forestry people didn't notify the police, there was no way to look for suspects unless a ranger just happened to catch someone in the act. The lack of communication between tribal agencies was nothing new, and it wasn't something that required funding to improve.

Ella tried the radio and managed to reach the station, relaying the emergency to the hospital.

Ella glanced back at Henry. "How's your father?"

Henry looked down at his father. "I don't think he can hear us, but he's breathing," he said, fear making his voice shake.

"He may be in shock. Keep the blanket and jacket over him," Ella said, then glanced at Justine. "We need to make it to Sheep Springs. The medivac helicopter won't be able to find us among these canyons, but they're going to meet us there."

Ella took out a geological survey map from the glove compartment, searching for shortcuts. "But first we need to find the fastest way to the paved road. Any ideas?" Ella looked back at the young man.

"No. Dad always insisted on driving around here, and I never paid much attention to which direction we were going."

"Call it in and let Dispatch find someone who knows this area," Justine suggested. "I don't dare try going as the crow flies because it'll just be too rough a ride."

As Ella looked back at John, she saw that he was either asleep or unconscious now. They had to move fast. His life depended on it. Snow flurries began to fall as Ella called in for help. Based on their current surroundings and her map, she gave Dispatch her approximate location and direction of travel.

Ella waited as Dispatch called on area experts. Finally, Big Ed came on the radio. "Shorty, my uncle Raymond lives in Crystal. He thinks he knows where you're at, and is going to meet you. Just stay with the road you're on now, and keep heading south. He knows a shortcut to the highway."

"Ten-four, Chief."

A thick, heavy silence fell over them as they kept an eye out for Raymond Atcitty's truck. Less than five minutes later, Justine spotted the gunmetal gray truck coming their direction. "Wherever that old truck can go, we can follow," Justine said flatly.

Justine kept pace with the chief's uncle, following less than a hundred yards behind him. Raymond had found an old fire break, a clear-cut area between stands of trees, that wound downhill quickly.

Aware that they hadn't heard a sound from John for at least five minutes, Justine turned her head for a quick look. The sight didn't do much to calm her.

"Stay focused on your driving," Ella ordered.

Justine nodded once, but she looked physically ill.

Following Raymond's lead, they managed to reach the paved road, Highway 134, in fifteen minutes. Five minutes later, heading east at a fast clip, they encountered the helicopter coming west to meet them. John and Henry were airborne within two minutes, and quickly disappeared into the northern sky.

Forty minutes later Ella and Justine arrived at the hospital. By then, every single muscle in Ella's body was cramping with nervous tension, and Justine looked about to explode.

They found Henry, who was pacing in the ER lobby. Seeing them, he shrugged. "Still no news, but he was alive when we arrived."

"We'll catch whoever did this, Henry," Justine said.

Henry nodded absently, but his gaze remained glued on the ER doors, and it was easy to see that his thoughts were only on his father.

"We'll check back later," Ella said.

Justine followed Ella outside. "You realize that this is the coldest winter the Rez has had since we were kids. People need firewood more than ever. If there are other trees . . ."

"I know," Ella answered. "Stop by the tribal newspaper offices. I want to talk to Jaime Beyale. She'll help us spread the warning."

"Leaking the news might create more trouble. It's going to shake people's confidence in the authorities even more."

"They've forced our hand, Justine. We don't have a choice. We have to warn as many people as we can of the danger. Our first duty is to the tribe. If we fail at that, then we deserve all the barbs aimed our way."

NINE
✕ ✕ ✕

They arrived at the tribal newspaper's offices in Window Rock about an hour and a half later. The threat of snow had ended as quickly as it had begun, and the rough, red sandstone mesas were bathed in late afternoon sunshine. Ella went into the newsroom while Justine stopped by the vending machines in the lobby for something to eat.

As Ella knocked on Jaime's open office door, Jaime looked up. She'd cut her hair short since Ella had last seen her, and wore thick reading glasses that made her look like an intellectual. Seeing it was Ella, she smiled. "Hey, Ella, come on in. What's up?"

"I need your help. I'd like the paper to run a story warning the *Dineh* of a problem," she said, then filled her in on the spiked trees and the accidents.

"We already heard about the two earlier instances you mentioned, and we ran a short piece you probably missed," Jaime said. "But I'll tell you what. This time I'll make sure it makes the front page. There's supposed to be a big polar air mass dropping down from the north in few days, and I know people will be out there trying to top off their woodpiles. I hear that even the LP gas trucks are getting behind on their Rez deliveries."

"Times are tougher for the *Dineh* than they've ever been."

"Yet at a time when money's scarce, we have people driving around, wasting gas, and creating problems for the tribe. How do you account for all the vandalism that's been going on, Jaime? Have you heard any rumors?"

Jaime took a deep breath. "I'm working on a story right now, Ella. You can read it in the next edition of the paper."

"I'd rather not be surprised," Ella said seriously. "Would you cut me some slack this time and fill me in on your conclusions."

Jaime met her gaze with a level one of her own. "I don't *have* to do that, you know."

"Yeah, but I'm still asking."

"You'll owe me, Ella. Understood?" Seeing Ella nod, she continued. "I have a source who claims that most of the incidents around the Shiprock area are directed toward one goal. Someone hates Chief Ed Atcitty, and wants him replaced. They're trying to make him look incompetent so enough pressure will be put on the council to have him fired as Shiprock police chief."

Though the news had taken her by surprise, Ella tried not to let it show. "How good is your source?"

"Truthfully? I'm not sure. But I won't run the story until I can confirm it with two independent sources. Otherwise, it'll seem as if I'm trying to make excuses for Big Ed and cover for his incompetence. But I have to tell you, from my initial research, I think this story's on target. When Big Ed was appointed, he beat out another candidate for the job—Carl Benjamin, from the BIA. Remember him?"

"Sure, but he passed away from a heart attack last year, didn't he?"

"True, but his brother, Arthur, is lobbying for the job on the basis that he's better qualified than Big Ed to handle the current crisis."

"What are his credentials—besides ego?"

Jaime grinned. "He's got a degree in criminology from the University of New Mexico and he worked for the state police for fifteen years. Ten of those, by the way, were at a desk job, with no great responsibility."

"And someone claims Arthur Benjamin is behind all this?"

"No, the talk is that someone is trying to make it easy for him by discrediting Big Ed."

"Who?"

"Rumor is it's some of the backroom boys from the progaming faction. Arthur is a strong advocate for gaming, unlike Big Ed."

Ella nodded. "Politics and big money have always been friends. If you hear anything we can use, will you call me?"

"I'm a reporter, Ella. I don't work for the Tribal Police."

"If you have knowledge of a specific crime—"

Jaime held up her hand. "You know I don't." She paused. "But I will tell you this much. Even if someone *is* working actively to make Big Ed and the police look like fools, you have the power to stop it. Catch whoever's behind the vandalism and now the problem with the trees, and Big Ed could be off the hook."

"We need a name. Who's your source?"

"I can't tell you that."

"How do you know this isn't just someone's active imagination, or another troublemaker?"

"Instinct."

Ella nodded. She couldn't argue with that. Intuition and instinct had been her most faithful guides throughout her years in law enforcement. "Just remember, Jaime, if you pursue this story and it's true, you'll be challenging some dangerous people when you go to press. You may even be risking your life."

"I'll be careful, and you do the same."

"You can bank on it."

As soon as they reached the station, Ella hurried to her office, shut the door, and called home. Jennifer answered immediately.

The first observation that hit her was that Jennifer actually sounded cheerful. Or maybe, by now, Jennifer was delirious. "How are things over there?" Ella asked her quickly.

"Fine. It has been quiet all day. Right now your daughter and your mother are in the living room playing see-and-say. I've been catching up on the laundry."

Ella wanted to let out a cheer.

"Oh, your mother asked me to say hello to you. She knew it was you when the phone rang. She said that you have a tendency to worry too much."

Ella almost choked. "Tell Mom and my daughter I'll be home as soon as I can."

"Don't worry if you're a little late. I can stay as long as I'm needed."

"You're wonderful," Ella told her, totally relieved.

Ella hung up and stretched out in her chair, relaxing for the first time in hours.

"Hey, boss," Justine said, walking in. "I've got some good news."

"What's up?"

"John Yabeni's going to be fine. He'll have to stay in the hospital for a few days while they watch him for signs of infection, but they think he should be able to recover completely."

"That is great news."

"I'd like your permission to personally follow up on this incident and see if the others who were victimized can give us any more information. Also, I'd like to talk to people who live in the Narbona Pass area and see if anyone knows anything."

"Go for it. This is a deadly game, and it has to stop before somebody is killed or maimed."

Ella glanced up as Big Ed walked into her office. "Chief, can I help you?"

"Shorty, you and I have to attend a Chapter House meeting tonight. I understand they're discussing the police department's failure to put a stop to the crime wave we're experiencing. From now on, I want to make sure the PD is present at any meetings where this is on the agenda. I don't want anyone to think we're afraid to confront the issues head on."

"I'll be there," Ella answered, "but I sure wish we had something concrete to share with those people tonight."

"We can only tell them what we've tried—the extra patrols, the concentrated sweeps in targeted neighborhoods at night, and that we're following leads now that may point the way to whoever's responsible," Big Ed said. "But we'll have to keep any specifics to ourselves. For all we know, the perps will be sitting in the front row taking notes."

"The only thing most people are interested in are results," Ella warned quietly.

"I know, but we need to confront this issue or we're going to lose even more credibility." He paused, then continued after a moment. "Also, I'm getting a lot of pressure from the Tribal Council to make sure this department remains high profile. They think that even if we don't catch the criminals, we need to show people that we're out doing something."

"I'll be there, Chief," Ella said. Maybe she could prevail on Jennifer to stay a little longer tonight.

As Big Ed walked out, Justine's gaze stayed on her. "If you need a baby-sitter, Ella, I can take care of Dawn tonight."

Ella smiled. "We really have become great partners if you can read my mind that easily."

Justine laughed. "Oh, I've been doing that for a long time."

"Cocky, aren't you?" Ella teased as she placed several folders back into the file cabinet. "And thanks for your offer to baby-sit, but I think I've got Dawn covered tonight. I'm going to try and get Jennifer to stay a while longer. But, if she can't, I'm sure Mom can take care of her for a few hours."

Hearing approaching footsteps, Ella looked past Justine's shoulder and saw Harry. "Hey, how's it going?"

she asked, wondering if her voice sounded just a little too eager.

Justine stood. "Well, I better get back to my office. I've got reports stacked miles high."

Harry strode in and smiled at her. He was dressed in dark blue slacks and a tan pullover sweater. It was a far cry from the man who used to live in blue jeans when he'd worked for her.

Ella watched him sit down in the chair Justine had vacated. "Bad news on the green van," he said. "It was wiped clean. And the plate on the pickup used by the guy who made a delivery to the hogan turned out to be stolen."

Ella looked down at the report on her desk. It was Sam Pete's paperwork on the explosion at the hogan. She remained quiet for a long moment, analyzing, probing, and weighing the information. "From what I see here, there's nothing particularly noteworthy about what we recovered around the hogan. But Sam's getting some tests run on the explosives residue." She slid the report across the desk to him.

"I know you're facing multiple problems on the Rez now, Ella, and I heard you and Justine have already had a long, rough day. I sure wish I could lend you a hand," he said while scanning the report.

"Catch Manyfarms and that'll take one big load off my mind. I'd like to lose this thick FBI vest I'm supposed to wear all the time now."

"I'll catch him, Ella," he said in a deep, sure voice. "You can count on that."

Ella saw the gleam of determination in his eyes. "You've always been very good at your job, Harry. I could really use you back on the SI team, you know."

He shook his head. "Being a U.S. marshal suits me. I have more responsibility, and I like the respect I get wherever I go."

Ella remembered her days in the Bureau. She felt proud flashing her gold badge and seeing the awareness in people's eyes. "Yes, I understand what you mean. But do you feel you're part of a team? Among your own people that was never a question."

He considered it for a long moment before replying. "I maintain a little distance from the others, but it's something I've always done—here or in the Marshal's Service."

Ella nodded slowly, remembering how it had been when he'd worked with her. Harry had always been friendly enough, but he kept to himself, and rarely socialized with other cops outside the job.

"In that one respect, we're very different. I don't like feeling separate from my team or being perceived as different, and that's the way it was for me a lot of the time at the Bureau."

"Your problem is that you analyze everything too much and you never give your instincts as a cop a rest," he said with a grin.

Ella laughed. "This from another cop? Get real. There's no such thing as an eight-to-five cop. The job becomes part of who we are and we carry it with us even after we go home. Don't tell me you're not the same way."

"I am," he admitted. "But it gets to be a problem at times."

"Yes, it does."

"I've heard talk about the Chapter House meeting tonight. It could bring out a lot of bad feelings toward the PD."

"Big Ed and I will be there. Maybe that'll help defuse the anger," she said, not really believing it. Ella stood up and grabbed her keys. "I was going to invite you for dinner, but what I plan to do is pick up a pizza and take it home. Mom will have apoplexy, but Dawn loves pizza, and so do I."

He walked her to the side doors. "Normally, I'd love sharing some pizza, but I've got a meeting with Blalock. I've had a tough time hooking up with him today, but he's agreed to meet me at the Totah Café in a half hour."

"In that case, we both better get going."

Ella phoned home to let them know not to cook supper, then picked up a pizza on the way. The smell of pepperoni and melted cheese made her mouth water. Her mother usually avoided these kind of meals. She was convinced that half the problems on the Rez could be fixed by banning the sale of all fast food, even fried chicken. Nothing encased in cardboard appealed to her in the slightest.

As Ella walked in the door, Dawn let out a squeal and ran toward her in her half-stumbling fashion. "*Shimá*, pizza!" Dawn carefully took the big box from Ella and with Jennifer's help carried it to the kitchen.

Ella smiled at Jennifer. "Gee, I think I'm running second place to pizza these days."

"You realize that kind of food isn't good for her," Rose said, glowering at Ella.

"It's just one meal," Ella protested, placing a slice on Dawn's plate, cutting it up into tiny pieces, then allowing her to eat it in front of the television set.

As soon as her daughter settled down, Ella joined Jennifer and Rose in the kitchen. "I need to talk to you both," she said. "I have to attend the Chapter House meeting tonight," she explained. "I'd like you to stay a while longer," Ella added, looking at Jennifer. "Can you manage it?"

Rose chuckled. "I've already asked her to stay."

Ella looked at Rose, surprised. "Did you know I'd be going?"

Rose gave her an exasperated look. "No, daughter, but *I* intended to go to the meeting, and I wasn't sure when you'd be home."

"Why are you going?" Ella asked, still trying to figure it all out. "You usually skip them unless there's a question that affects us directly."

"The issues that will be discussed there tonight *will* affect all of us, daughter. I'm going. I intend to keep up with what's happening on our land. A friend will be picking me up in an hour."

"Who?"

"Bizaadii," she answered.

Ella recognized Herman Cloud's nickname.

"Oh, well, good for you," she said lamely.

Her mother was going on a date. The news shouldn't have taken her by surprise, but despite the fact that she knew Herman was perfect for Rose, she just wasn't ready for this on an emotional level, not just yet. Ella took three slices of pizza and placed them on her plate, encouraging her mother and Jennifer to help themselves.

The world around her was going insane, but it wouldn't benefit any of them to meet it on an empty stomach.

Ella left shortly after dinner, knowing she'd arrive before the meeting began. She told herself that the reason she was leaving home early was to gather information. She wanted to hang around and eavesdrop on the unguarded conversations of people when they first arrived.

But deep down she knew she was lying to herself. The truth was that she would feel strange seeing her mother driving off with Herman for the evening, and she was determined to hide her feelings from Rose until she learned to cope with it. Her mother deserved to start living her own life again. She'd remained alone for too many years already.

As Ella got out of her unit, she saw Cecelia Yazzie waving at her.

"I'm surprised to see you here tonight, Ella," she said coming over to join her. "Your mother comes once in a while, but I don't remember the last time you were here."

"I was told that police protection was going to be discussed, and the chief felt that we should be here to explain what we've been doing."

"That's a really good idea, but you might have a fight on your hands. I don't think the police will have many friends here tonight."

Seeing another acquaintance drive up, Cecelia waved at the other woman and with a quick good-bye to Ella, hurried away. Ella noted the relief on Cecelia's face as she left, and suspected she'd been happy for an excuse to put some distance between them if the department was going to be on the hot seat.

As Ella approached the group of people clustered by the front door, no one said hello, made eye contact, or even nodded, though she was well known in the community. She realized then that her first impression had been right on target. People were intent on avoiding her. It was irritating to have the public treating her like the plague, but she kept to herself, not speaking to anyone and, instead, listened to the snatches of conversations going on around her.

It wasn't until nearly everyone was inside and seated that she saw Mrs. Yellowhair, the late senator's wife. Ella looked around for Big Ed, and spotted him slipping in a few minutes later. He gave her a nod as he took one of the few remaining seats in the back.

The meeting opened with the Pledge of Allegiance, with everyone standing and participating. Ella was reminded again how patriotic the *Dineh* were, especially the elders, but there were a lot of modernists in the gathering tonight, and they were equal participants.

The Navajo equivalent of a town meeting evolved into a report and discussion of the latest incidents of vandalism and the rising cost of auto repairs and insurance as a result of those events. With many Navajos unable to afford insurance, the price of a new windshield seemed astronomical.

Ella noted that the speakers, taking their turns, spoke English, mostly, and probably considered themselves nontraditionalists. As talk shifted to the role of the police the discussion grew heated, and people began interrupting each other, a form of behavior usually not present on the Rez except when emotions ran high.

Then one man stood up and the room fell silent. He had a presence that commanded the attention of everyone. Ella recognized Rudy Brownhat as a member of the Fierce Ones, the traditionalist group that, until recently, had held a lot of power on this part of the Rez.

As he looked around the room before speaking, the silence was nearly absolute. "This entire crisis has tested us," he began. "But instead of banding together to identify these criminals, we've allowed the incidents to divide us. That has weakened us far more than the actual crimes ever could. The *Dineh* have survived through the generations by working together as one and that's what we need to do now."

Cecelia Yazzie stood. "I don't think the problem has anything to do with a lack of unity. Most of us have day jobs and, at night when we're tired, that's when the vandals hit. What we need is a strong police force, but the protection we've been given so far is weak and ineffective."

Ruth Tsosie stood up then, taking the floor. "I think our police department needs new leadership—someone like Lieutenant Manuelito, perhaps. My niece lives over in Window Rock and she tells me that he's found ways to stop the lawlessness. His district is quiet and peaceful. No one dares stir up trouble there. Although other places on the Rez are having problems, the Shiprock district is, by far, the worst."

Ella hadn't planned on speaking, but she couldn't let this slide. Big Ed didn't deserve to be shown so little respect. Manuelito was a grade A jerk and if he'd had success curbing crime around Window Rock, it was mostly due to luck, and because communities in that part of the Rez were totally different from theirs. Shiprock was a much bigger population center.

As Ella stood up she felt everyone's gaze shift to her. "Everyone here has been quick to complain, but it's time to set the record straight. Our local officers have all been working double shifts, putting in long hours because we just don't have enough manpower to deal with everything that's been happening. We've given up time with our families and done our duty because it's our job. But we need—and deserve—community support. We want people to keep their eyes open and report suspicious vehicles and individuals. If we work together, we can stop what's been happening."

"We've called you," one woman challenged, "but by the time the officers show up, it's all over."

"Our police department is on a shoestring budget, and because we don't have as many officers as we need, we're spread too thin sometimes. That's why we're asking the public to take a more active role," Ella answered. "Try to get descriptions of the vehicles and the drivers, so that when an officer arrives, they have something tangible to go on."

"So the heart of the problem is that there aren't enough police officers, and that's due to lack of funds?" Brownhat asked.

"That's it in a nutshell," Big Ed said, standing. His deep, resonant voice commanded respect, and the room grew silent. "We'll do the best we can with what we've got, but we need the support of the *Dineh*. The way things are now we can't do it alone."

Mrs. Yellowhair stood up and, in the cool, calculating manner of a politician, waited, looking over the crowd and making eye contact. "What Chief Atcitty has just told you is a hard fact we all have to face. The tribe has had to cut the budgets of nearly every branch of government. No one needs to be reminded that this has been a hard year and many of our people have needed help with food and heat for their homes. Those efforts have depleted our treasury to the point where, now more than ever, the basic needs of the *Dineh* are not being met. That's what finally convinced me that we need a new source of income, and that it's time to institute tribal gaming. Until we do, we're going to be facing one crisis after another."

Ella saw the exchanged glances and nods people gave each other. If there was one thing that could be said for Abigail Yellowhair, it was that she knew how to work a room.

"With the additional funds well-managed gaming would provide," Mrs. Yellowhair continued, "we'd have enough money to hire more officers and give them better equipment and training."

"Throwing money at the problem is an Anglo way of thinking," Brownhat said.

"We need additional police officers and firemen, but we can't hire them. Money—or more specifically, the lack of it—*is* the real problem," Mrs. Yellowhair argued. "We expect miracles from our police officers but they're human beings and no one can be at their best when they're outnumbered and exhausted."

Rose stood up and Ella stared at her mother in surprise, not having seen her come in earlier. "Gaming could bring in more money for the police force—a very good thing, since they'll need even more officers to combat the rise in crime that accompanies casinos and one-armed bandits," Rose said, her voice strong and insistent. "Some *will* get rich—and our tribe may have bigger bank accounts, but it will be at the expense of others—some who will lose everything pursuing their get-rich-quick dream. That's not living in harmony. How can anyone walk in beauty knowing that's the path our tribe will be walking down?"

As her mother continued speaking, Ella saw a side of Rose she'd always been too close to notice before. Ella knew how much others respected her mom, but it was clear that Rose was a force to be reckoned with. No one seemed inclined to argue with her—a sentiment Ella sympathized with enormously.

"It's true that we need to find money to meet the needs of the *Dineh*," Rose continued. "But let's not do that by destroying the very people we're trying to protect." She looked at Mrs. Yellowhair squarely. "Our tribe can find other ways to get the funds we need. There are federal programs, grants, and loans available if we choose to ask for help—programs supported by the taxes we all pay. But, in the long run, part of the answer lies in demanding a greater share of the profits from the fuels and natural resources that leave the *Dinetah*. And if the outside companies mining our land refuse, then we have to take over those businesses and run them ourselves."

When Rose finally sat down, it was quiet for some time. At length Mrs. Yellowhair stood up again. "Okay, Chief. Talk to us. How bad is the situation in the police department and what kind of financial support do you need right now?"

"We believe that the vandals are monitoring police radios, so we need to raise money so our officers can be given scrambled cell phones. This *will* give us an edge— one we need very badly."

"All right. One way or another, I'll see that you get them."

Ella wondered if it would just turn out to be another wannabe politician's empty promise. Yet, as she studied Mrs. Yellowhair's expression, she came to the conclusion that if it didn't happen, it wouldn't be for lack of trying on her part. The woman had made some powerful friends as the wife of a former state senator.

Ella stood up to speak again, but before she could open her mouth an explosion rocked the room, rattling the windows so hard some of them cracked. Excited voices rose and filled the room as chaos ensued.

Ella worked her way to one of the windows, aware of the scent of burning fuel that now filled the air. A large fire lit up the parking lot and grounds outside.

Weaving through the panicked crowd, Ella left the building and drew closer to the source of the explosion. Through the black cloud of billowing smoke, Ella could see Big Ed's brand-new white pickup engulfed in flames.

TEN

✖ ✖ ✖

As Big Ed rushed past her carrying a fire extinguisher, Ella ran to stop him. It was already too late to salvage the truck. Flames reaching the gas tank had caused the explosion. Two broken beer bottles on the gravel and a familiar scent told her exactly what had happened. Bottles filled with kerosene and plugged with rags set on fire had been hurled against the truck.

Realizing how hopeless the situation was, Big Ed never activated the extinguisher. Instead, he turned and moved to help her keep people away from the fire. His face was drawn and his eyes glittered with anger. "Don't worry about the truck now, Shorty. Just help me keep everyone back."

Ella knew that this incident had been calculated to produce the most damage—not only to the vehicle but to Big Ed's reputation as well.

The chief suddenly glanced at her, then looked around quickly. "Shorty, go back inside right now," he yelled over the increasing roar of the fire. "This might be a diversion to draw you out into the open. You're illuminated right now and a sitting duck for the sniper."

"I understand, but first, we've got to get people to move their vehicles to safety so the fire can't spread. And, after that, you're going to need help to make sure nobody disturbs any evidence around the truck. I've got my vest on, and I'll keep moving, but I'm needed out here right now."

Big Ed held her gaze, then nodded. "All right, but stay sharp." After finding the nervous owners of the vehicles on both sides of the burning truck, the two officers drove their cars away to a safe distance.

Justine showed up ten minutes later. The fire department had been called, but they were even less funded than the police, and were still on route with their ancient equipment. "I heard the call over the radio," Justine said. "I was on my way home, but I figured I might be needed here."

"You figured right," Ella said. "Let's start questioning people. I want to know if anyone saw anything, or if they remember someone leaving early. I was too preoccupied with what was being said during the meeting to notice much of anything going on outside, and no one around me left early. Big Ed was closer to the windows, so talk to him first."

Justine glanced around, spotting the chief talking to people coming forward for a look at his burning truck. "Did Big Ed get someone at the meeting especially ticked off tonight?"

Ella considered it. "I don't think so. He defended his viewpoint well, but he didn't go on a verbal offensive, or make any accusations. But that's a good angle. Stay on that and ask around. Maybe someone else will have a different take on that."

As they began to question onlookers Rose approached Ella. "I'd like to go home. Do you need me to stay?"

Ella noticed that her mother was clinging to Herman's arm for support. Getting around was difficult for Rose without her cane. Maybe it should have bothered her, but for some reason it didn't. It seemed so natural, and despite the fact that Herman wasn't her father, Ella realized it wasn't so bad seeing her mom with him after all. Maybe adjusting to her mother's suitor wasn't going to be as hard as she thought. Knowing that either way, it was her mother's business who she choose to see, Ella tried to put her mind on the problem at hand. "Do you remember anyone around you leaving early?"

"No, in fact, I'm sure no one did," Rose said. "With

the seating up to capacity, everyone would have noticed something like that."

"Did you see or hear anything that looked suspicious?" Ella pressed.

Herman and Rose both shook their heads.

"This was calculated to make the chief look as bad as possible tonight," Ella said wearily, glancing back at his truck. "If they're trying to discredit him, they're doing a great job."

Rose placed her hand on Ella's arm. "Your chief made his point well, daughter," she said softly. "Despite what happened, it was a good thing he came tonight. Maybe the politician's wife," Rose said referring to Abigail Yellowhair, "will finally realize how serious the situation is at the police department right now. She's one of the very few people in a position to help you."

"She does have a lot of connections," Ella agreed.

"May I take your mother home?" Herman asked.

Ella nodded, seeing traces of exhaustion on her mother's face. "I wish you hadn't come. I know your injured hand is bothering you. But I have to say that you sure held everyone's attention when you spoke," Ella added, a touch of pride in her voice.

"I've walked through time longer than you and most of the people here," Rose said, alluding to her age in the Navajo way.

"Many look up to your mother. It was right for her to take a more active role in what's been happening," Herman said.

"It's time I allowed myself to be more than just your mother, daughter," Rose said quietly.

Ella understood. Women had always wielded the real power in the tribe. Unlike the way it was in the Anglo culture, where "traditional" often meant a stay-at-home mom, in the Navajo culture, the word had a deeper meaning. To the *Dineh*, it signified a way of life defined and sustained by religious beliefs and cultural practices. It meant a basis for thought and action, but it did not confine a person's boundaries. If anything, it expanded them.

Women on the Rez often played many different roles. She did so herself on a daily basis, and that was part of what made her life such a fulfilling one. She should have recognized the same need in her mother long before now but, somehow, she hadn't. Rose had always been just "Mom."

"I'll talk to you when I get home, if you're still up," Ella said.

As Rose and Herman walked away, Justine joined her. "I'm getting nowhere, and the chief's mood is worsening every second. Not that I blame him. His truck is completely toasted."

"Here comes the fire department now," Ella said, gesturing.

Ella watched the firemen setting up, trying to coax a stream of water out of the secondhand equipment. The hose had been repaired in several places, and the pump was barely working. "If this doesn't prove to those still here that, without funds, we're all fighting an impossible battle, I don't know what will," Ella said quietly.

While the firemen worked, Ella questioned the people still hanging around, but after ninety minutes of negative responses all she had to show for her efforts was a great deal of frustration.

At long last, out of water and with no hydrant nearby, the firemen began putting away their equipment. Justine then began sorting through what little evidence there was from around the burned truck.

Ella saw Big Ed standing by the building, a scowl on his face, and walked over, intending to offer him a ride home. Before she could reach him, the chief's wife, Claire, pulled up in her old four-wheel-drive SUV.

Big Ed saw Ella approaching and went to meet her. "Shorty, I'm going home. I'll send a wrecker over tomorrow morning to haul what's left of my truck to the junkyard. Let me know what you and your assistant find out after you review the evidence."

"We'll have a report on your desk sometime tomorrow," she said.

Big Ed gave her a tight-lipped nod and strode off. The next few days at the station would be hell. There was no way he'd forget or allow them to forget the vandals who'd publicly humiliated him, not until they had the perp in jail.

"I'm taking what little evidence I've gathered back to the station," Justine said, joining Ella, "then I'll head home. What about you?"

"I'm going to check out businesses around here that might sell kerosene. Let's see if anyone remembers who their last few customers were. At this time of night, I figure it'll be only a handful of gas stations. After that, I'll head home too."

"Good luck."

Ella got into her unit and drove back to the highway. Sometimes she wondered what it would have been like to have an eight-to-five job where she could leave her work at the office every evening. Often, after putting in twelve hours like today, she ended the shift feeling far more frustrated than satisfied.

Of course everyone in law enforcement felt the same way at times. And dealing with a public who didn't always understand or appreciate what the police were doing—or the cost it exacted on their personal lives—made it a lot tougher.

As she arrived at the first gas station on the way into Shiprock, Wilbert Jones, the young Navajo night attendant, glanced up and nodded. Ella parked near the entrance to the old-fashioned facility, which also provided simple auto repairs and brake jobs.

Having recognized Ella, Wilbert came out to meet her. "What's going on? I heard the fire truck going by and saw lights flashing all over the place. Did the Chapter House burn down?"

Ella explained, then got to the reason for her visit, pointing to the hand-lettered sign that read Kerosene propped up on the windowsill. "Do you remember who bought kerosene from you in the past day or two?"

"No one bought any from me tonight, but we have some regular customers. A lot of traditionalists use kerosene lanterns, and some of those who work construction use kerosene heaters this time of year. Your brother buys from me several times a year. I think he has a lantern in his medicine hogan."

She remembered Clifford's lantern. She'd always cautioned him not to store a lot of the highly flammable liquid. Yet, in reality, fires caused by those lanterns were few and far between.

"Who else carries kerosene?"

"Jeez, Ella, almost any gas station, trading post, or hardware store around here. Paint stores too. Pick one and they probably have it."

Ella saw the hope of getting a fast lead on the arsonist disappear before her eyes. With effort, she pushed back her disappointment.

"Okay, thanks." Ella said good-bye to Wilbert, then made two more stops, but she learned nothing new.

Deciding to delegate the rest of the checks that would need to be done on the retail stores tomorrow, she finally went home. She needed to get some rest. Tomorrow would be a busy day. In the morning, when Big Ed was in a marginally better mood, she'd tell him what Jaime Beyale had said about Arthur Benjamin being out for his job. Maybe Big Ed would be able to tell her who might be inclined to help Arthur's chances by discrediting the department and the chief in particular. But right now, all she wanted to do was see Dawn, check her e-mail for a chance message from Coyote, and then go to bed.

Ella noticed the lights were all out inside the house when she got home. As she opened the front door and walked in, only Two came to the door to greet her. Ella bent down and scratched the shaggy dog's head. "What are you doing up, boy?"

Moving quietly through the house, she stopped by the fridge, picked out a slice of cold pizza, and, holding it with a paper towel, went to her room.

Two followed her in. "Is this love, or are you after my pizza, mutt?"

Two licked his chops.

"Forget it, dog. No chance."

Ella stripped out of her work clothes, glad to be free of the bulky vest, then wearing a long T-shirt, sat in front of her computer and switched it on. Messages from Coyote came at odd times, as if the man were familiar with her crazy hours. Tonight, there was nothing, not even e-mail waiting for her. Though Wilson Joe and she often kept in touch via e-mail because of their schedules, lately she hadn't heard from him at all. She knew he was dating Justine and, although she was glad they'd found each other, she still missed his letters.

She glanced down at Two, who was still eyeing her pizza. "Hey, dog, how come everyone lately is finding romance, but the train keeps passing me by?" The dog looked at her pizza, then back at her.

She gave him a piece of crust, then consumed the rest while Two was occupied with the more resistant fare.

Ella waited on-line a bit longer, wondering if Coyote would eventually show, but nothing happened and, reluctantly, she shut the computer down. As she started to climb into bed, Two raised up on his hind legs and leaned against the windowpane. His throaty growl made a prickle race up her spine.

Ella grabbed her pistol from the top shelf, where she kept the weapon so Dawn wouldn't be able to reach it. Inserting the clip, she stood to one side of the window, peering out as she operated the slide, feeding a round into the chamber. There was nothing outside that she could see, yet as she glanced down at the dog, she saw his hackles were raised and that he meant business.

Ella set the pistol down, slipped on her jeans and shoes, then grabbed her weapon again. As she passed through the darkened living room, she reached for her bullet-resistant vest and wiggled into it as she moved.

Ella opened the back door and slipped out, using a silent, palms-up gesture to order Two to wait. There was a figure up ahead, moving beside the woodpile. As she inched closer, Ella realized from the strong smell that he was dousing the firewood with kerosene.

"I'm a police officer and I have a gun. Don't move." Ella ordered, wishing she'd brought a flashlight.

Startled, the man took off running.

"Damn!" Ella brought her pistol down and took off after him. She wouldn't shoot someone for vandalism, no matter how tempted she was.

Hearing the back door open, she turned her head and saw Two getting out. Though she was running at top speed, Two shot past her, closing the gap between him and the perp like a wolf after a rabbit.

The running man was approaching a parked car up the driveway when the porch lights behind them went on, illuminating the area somewhat. As he turned his head, Ella realized the vandal was wearing a ski mask. Two suddenly lunged forward, trying to bite him in the leg, but catching only a portion of the man's baggy trousers.

The car door opened and the man dove inside, simultaneously throwing something at the dog. Two dodged, and barely missed being caught in the slamming door.

As the driver stepped on the accelerator, Two shot after the car, running parallel to the vehicle to avoid the spray of dust and gravel flying back from the spinning tires, but the vehicle quickly outran the dog.

Ella whistled for Two, who reluctantly gave up the chase, then trotted back to her.

"Good boy! You may be old, but you can really do the job when you have to," she said, patting the excited animal.

Ella searched the ground for whatever the man had

tossed at Two and found the plastic water bottle he'd been using to douse the firewood with kerosene. It was still half-full. With luck, it would also have prints she could match up.

Ella was jogging back to the house to call it in when she saw Rose standing by the back door, speaking into Ella's cell phone. "Did you call the PD?"

Rose nodded, handing the phone to Ella. "The officer is still on the line."

"Thanks, Mom. Go back inside. I'm going after them. Check Two and make sure he's okay. And stay away from the woodpile. It's been soaked in kerosene."

Ella made a quick report as she ran to her unit. She hadn't seen the perp's license plate, but she knew it was a dark-colored old four-door sedan. She asked Dispatch to have the patrols be on the lookout, and to approach the two inside with caution. They hadn't fired at her, but there was no way to know for sure if they were armed.

Spewing gravel and sand behind her tires, Ella sped after them and, within a few minutes, spotted the fleeing vehicle less than a mile ahead. They'd turned on their lights, and were going as fast as the gravel road would allow, throwing up enormous clouds of dust.

Ella had always been proud of being a good cop, one who never acted out of anger, but when they attacked her family's home, the rules changed. She was going to catch up to those suckers this time.

Knowing that a patrol unit would be dispatched to her house and that Rose and Dawn would be protected gave her the confidence to continue her pursuit. She floored the accelerator and felt the souped-up engine respond. As she reached the top of the next rise, she saw the sedan swerve out onto the highway, turning north toward Shiprock.

Her cell phone rang, and she picked it up without taking her eyes off the road. "Hey, Ella, this is Justine. I'm at the intersection of Five-oh-four, heading south down Six-sixty-six."

"Excellent. I'm in pursuit of a dark sedan coming your direction," she explained, giving her partner the highlights.

"I'll block the road a quarter mile below the top of the last hill coming into the west side of town. They won't see me until the last minute," Justine advised.

"Stay sharp, and avoid a collision. They're flying right now."

Ella thought about calling for more backup, but knew that it was up to her and Justine. If the perps were monitoring police radio frequencies, she didn't want to let these guys know what she was planning to do next.

A moment later, coming out of a low spot in the road, she caught sight of the pair in the dark-colored sedan a quarter mile away. They were just about to crest the long hill leading down into Shiprock's southwest quadrant.

Slowing down, then topping the hill ten seconds behind them, Ella had her foot off the gas and was prepared to brake quickly if necessary. Several hundred yards below she saw Justine's unit blocking the center of the highway, emergency lights flashing. The driver in the dark sedan slammed on the brakes, spinning around and coming up on two wheels as the driver barely prevented the car from rolling. He did nearly a 180-degree turn, tires squealing.

The sedan came to rest in a cloud of dust and burning rubber less than ten feet from Justine's unit.

Ella had slowed already, and came up close before slamming on the brakes, blocking the suspects with her Jeep. Jumping out and steadying her aim by resting her arms upon the top of the hood, she trained her weapon on the driver.

"Get out with your hands up!"

ELEVEN

—— ✖ ✖ ✖ ——

Justine directed the spotlight of her vehicle on the car's interior.

A few seconds later, the pair came out slowly. Neither were wearing the ski masks now, but she could see one dangling out of the driver's jacket pocket.

"Lie down on the pavement, facedown," Ella ordered, moving around behind the suspects' vehicle to take a quick glance inside. She wanted to make sure there wasn't another perp hiding in there.

While Ella kept watch, Justine handcuffed the two Anglo men, then frisked them thoroughly, removing their wallets for identification purposes. Ella kept her weapon trained on them throughout, then helped her partner lead the prisoners to the backseat of Justine's unit, locking them inside.

Ella watched the two Anglos through the glass. They were out of their element here, and from the frightened look on their faces, they knew they'd been lucky avoiding an accident during the pursuit.

"Get their vehicle off the road, then search it," Ella told Justine as Officer Philip Cloud pulled up in his squad car from the direction of Shiprock.

Philip came out to join her, then glanced at the two suspects. "You caught them. Good job. I'll take care of traffic." Removing flares and orange traffic cones from his vehicle's trunk, Officer Cloud put out the warning signals in both directions for oncoming traffic. It was so late, few vehicles would be on the highway, but it was procedure. Borrowing Ella's keys, he moved her Jeep off the highway, clearing one lane.

"They've got one unopened bottle left from a six-pack of beer and close to two gallons of kerosene in the back," Justine called out after a few minutes. "There are several old dish cloths torn in half as well. Looks to me like they intended on making more Molotov cocktails tonight. The beer is the same brand as the bottles found at the Chapter House."

"I've also got another piece of evidence back at the house—a water bottle partially filled with kerosene. The passenger was getting ready to set fire to my mother's woodpile when I interrupted him," Ella said. Then, opening the driver's door to Justine's unit, she looked inside at the suspects, reading them their rights.

"You guys are going down, you know that, right?" she added, getting into the driver's seat and watching the men through the wire grid separating the prisoners from the front as she drove Justine's unit off the highway, parking behind her own Jeep.

The driver of the sedan laughed nervously. "Don't make such a big deal out of this. We were just playing a prank. We didn't hurt anyone."

"Your idea of fun is trashing other people's property, right?" Ella pressed. "Smashing mailboxes, breaking windshields, and blowing up things?"

"Hey, the insurance pays for it anyway, right?" the second man said with a shrug, his voice slurred from the alcohol. "What's the problem?"

"Shut up, man," the one who'd been driving ordered, poking his partner with an elbow. He glanced at Ella, his eyes as cold as the night air. "I didn't do a thing, and this idiot has had way too many beers tonight." He gestured toward the passenger, who smelled of beer even from the front seat. "He doesn't even know where he is anymore."

Justine came up behind Ella and examined the wallets she'd confiscated. "The driver of the vehicle is Eric Smith, and his buddy is James Little," she told Ella.

"Why are you two smashing windows and blowing up

private property here on the Rez?" Ella prodded.

"We needed the money." James, the man Two had chased and nearly caught, shrugged, then burped loudly. "It wasn't our idea, and we don't have anything personal against Navajos. Actually, the guy who hired us is one of your own."

"Our own?" Ella repeated, hoping she could keep the guy talking. Any new information, even from a drunk, could help open up this investigation to a new level.

"I told you to shut up," Eric said, jabbing James with his elbow again. "I was just out for a drive, that's all."

James gagged, and for a moment she thought the man was going to throw up in Justine's unit.

Ella gestured for Justine to take Eric to Officer Cloud's vehicle. They needed to separate the pair if they were going to get anywhere with them.

Ignoring his protests, Justine took the driver over to Philip, who was watching for traffic. Once Eric was secure in Philip's patrol car, Ella focused on James. His eyes seemed to be glazed over, and she had a feeling Eric had been right about James having consumed most of those beers.

"Look, if you help me now, I'll be able to tell the judge you cooperated," Ella urged. "Later, if Eric tries to make a deal by testifying against you, he'll be too late."

"You don't understand what's going on," James said, speaking slowly now, trying not to slur his words. "We both got laid off last summer, and money's been really tight. Even construction jobs have been just a few days here, a few days there. Then this Indian in a suit and expensive snakeskin boots came up to us outside the union hall one night, asking what we'd be willing to do for a handful of easy money. We told him we didn't go in for stealing stuff or shaking people down, but that wasn't what he was looking to hire us for anyway. All he wanted was for us to stir up a little trouble and run the stupid tribal cops ragged." James grinned, then his jaw fell. "That was him talking, not me. No offense, ma'am."

Ella tried not to smile. "None taken, James. You were saying . . ."

"Well, this Indian guy was going to provide us with whatever we needed and he'd pay us a couple hundred after each raid. It was too sweet a deal to pass up, and we never hurt nobody that I know of."

Ella decided not to point out Charlie's nearly fatal heart attack at the Totah Café bombing, or John Yabeni's accident with the chain saw. "Who was this well-dressed Indian? Can you tell me his name?"

"He never said, and we never asked." James shrugged. "He just told us to meet him later that night at the Palomino Bar. That's when Eric gave him our phone number, and, after that, he called whenever he needed us."

"How did you get paid?"

"The first time it was half the cash up front and half when the job was done. After that, it was always after the job was done."

Justine came up and handed Ella a computer printout. "This was under James's seat, along with a radio scanner and all the hookups needed." Ella glanced at the paper and realized that it was a list of addresses. Most of the places already hit had been crossed off, but it was clear from the latter portion of the page that they'd caught the men before they'd finished tonight's work.

Ella studied the page. The Chapter House was listed and next to it was the license number and make of Big Ed's pickup. Her mother's home wasn't listed by address, but there was a brief but accurate set of travel directions, along with the exact location of where she normally parked her unit at home—behind the trees by the side of the house.

"You were supposed to go to all these places tonight?" Ella asked.

"Nah. We could split it up any way we wanted. But we wouldn't get paid until the job was finished," he said.

"Look, I've got a two-year-old kid and a wife. I've helped you, so how about cutting me some slack with the charges?"

"I'll see what I can do," Ella replied, happy that for once, a drunk had proved to be an asset to her job. "The DA will know you cooperated." Ella walked away, then stopped and turned back. "Oh, one more thing, James. You used the scanner so you'd know when the police were out looking for you, right?"

"Right. But we never heard about the roadblock tonight. Don't know why."

Ella gave him a confused look, wanting to keep him wondering. Sooner or later, when he was sober again, the use of cell phones would occur to James. Or maybe not. The man didn't seem too bright.

Leaving the prisoner, James, secure in the backseat, Ella walked over to Justine, who was loading the bagged and tagged evidence into her unit. "Thanks for the backup, partner. I would have probably lost them if you hadn't come along. And that was a smart move using the cell phone."

"Thanks. I was glad to help. I was having coffee with Wilson when I got the call. They couldn't reach me on the radio because I'd just gone off duty and had left my handheld in my unit. Remembering what you'd said about someone monitoring our radio calls, I decided to stick with the cell phone. Now I'm glad I did."

Philip came over then, forcing Ella's thoughts back on business. "I called in a tow truck for the perp's car."

"Good," Ella said.

"Do you want to keep the pair apart all the way to the station?" he added.

"I think that's our best move right now," Ella answered.

"Agreed," Justine said. "I'll take the one I have, you can keep Eric, Philip," Justine added, then glanced over at Ella. "I can finish this up, if you want to go home.

Don't look now, but you're not wearing much, and your lips are turning blue."

"I grabbed a coat, but I'm only wearing the T-shirt I wear to bed underneath," Ella said, suddenly very much aware of the numbing cold that had spread all over her body. At least she'd been able to question the perp from Justine's car where she'd been next to the heater. "I think I will go home. Let me know if there are any problems, and make sure you have that scanner checked out to verify it can pick up our radio calls. I'm especially interested in seeing if it's been modified to monitor our tactical frequencies."

Ella headed back home with the heat inside her department vehicle turned up to blast furnace. She felt warmer now, but all she wanted to do was crawl under the covers. When she got home, Rose was waiting and met her in the living room with a cup of hot chocolate.

"I figured you'd need this when you got home."

Ella sipped the steaming liquid slowly, grateful for the warmth that seeped through her. "Thanks, Mom."

"Did you catch him?"

She nodded. "I'll tell you more about it as soon as I can."

"Most of that cord of firewood out back is ruined," Rose said. "With that much kerosene soaked into it, it's a hazard."

"I figured that," Ella answered. "Did all the commotion wake my daughter up?"

Rose shook her head. "Children sleep soundly. She feels secure and loved and the confusion that often touches our family doesn't reach her. It's her innocence that protects her."

"I'm grateful for that."

"But it won't always be that way. Children grow up quickly. Soon enough she'll learn what it's like to be afraid. It's inevitable when her mother's a cop."

"I'll deal with that when it comes." Ella was too tired to tread over that old ground again.

As Ella drank her hot chocolate she brought out the list that Justine had given her. It had been bagged in clear plastic and tagged, but she'd forgotten to give it back to her. She'd have to sign the bag and record the date and time now to keep the chain of evidence intact.

As she read the addresses again it became clear to her that someone had been watching and gathering information about people in their community. The chief's truck had been described in detail down to the license plate. But most significant of all was that the address listed beside it was that of the Chapter House. They'd known where the chief would be.

"Do you know why we were hit?" Rose asked.

"I have a few ideas." Ella looked at her mother carefully. "Do you have a theory?"

Rose nodded slowly. "It might have been in retaliation for my public stand against gambling, something I've gone on record about and made clear long before tonight. Some people, like your daughter's father, don't approve of my speaking out. My opinion carries weight among the traditionalists and they know that." Rose stood up slowly. "I'm going to bed, daughter. I'm too tired to stay up, and my hand aches from the cold. We'll talk more about this tomorrow."

"Feel better, Mom."

Ella continued staring at the list and trying to create a picture in her mind. Finally, too tired to think anymore, she walked to her room. Two was lying in the hallway. "You were a good dog tonight," she said patting him on the head. "Glad to see you're safe, mutt."

Ella peeked in on Dawn, making sure her blankets were in place but not entangling. Then she crept across the hall into her own room.

As Ella crawled into bed, Two followed, positioning himself beside her, snuggling against her legs. Appreciating the warmth, Ella turned off the lamp on her nightstand and fell asleep almost as soon as her head hit the pillow.

The next morning Ella arrived at work early. Yet, despite the early hour, Justine was already there ahead of her again.

"Good morning, boss," Justine said as Ella passed by the vending machines where she was standing.

Ella eyed the stash of candy bars in Justine's hands, but didn't criticize her eating habits after Justine offered her one.

Ella opened the chocolate crunch bar and took a bite. A tortilla smeared with butter and peach jam, a cup of coffee, and now a chocolate bar—that was some breakfast. She made a mental note to pick up some vitamins one of these days.

"I thought I'd be the only one here this early," Ella said, stifling a yawn.

"It's definitely a coffee-by-the-gallon morning. But I figured you'd want me to run a make on the perps and try to lift prints off that bottle you found at the house."

"I've got the list you found too," Ella said, handing her the plastic bag, sealed, signed, and labeled.

"Thanks. The rap sheet on the suspects is already on your desk. This morning I'll also try to match the tire prints at your place to those of their vehicle. With luck, I'll have everything ready for you before the end of today."

"Thanks."

Ella stopped by her office first. Then, as she passed the briefing room on her way to the holding cells, she saw Sergeant Neskahi and asked him to join her. While they walked toward the lockup area, she briefed him on the two suspects they'd brought in the night before. "I need to question the pair a little more and push them for answers. James was the only one who cooperated last night. What I'd like you to do is help me out in there and jump in whenever you want, especially with Eric, the die-hard."

"Wanna play good cop/bad cop?"

"No, not with these two. They've probably seen it before. Let's try to make them feel as disoriented as possible since they're on the Rez and away from their turf. I think that'll work to our advantage."

Ella led the way to an interrogation room, then asked the jailer to bring one of the suspects in. She'd begin with the one who'd cooperated the evening before.

This morning, however, James had an industrial-sized hangover and was in no mood to be helpful. After getting only curt replies and statements contradicting the answers he'd given them last night, Ella tried another tactic. "James, you told me yesterday that you had a family who needed you, and that you wanted to cut a deal by cooperating. I *will* help you, but not if you clam up on me now and start changing your story," Ella said.

"I've decided to wait for my attorney. The courts provide one and I was told he'd be here today."

"You have the right to have an attorney present, I told you that last night, but also remember that you want something from me. Cooperate, and I'll make sure you get the best break possible."

"I've already told you everything I know," he grumbled.

"Let's concentrate on the Indian who hired you."

"As I said before—I only saw him twice and both times it was at night, outside."

"Tell me about that second meeting, then, not the one near the union hall. You didn't describe it last night."

"We were walking from Eric's car toward the bar, expecting to catch up with him inside, when he stepped out between two pickups and blocked our way. Eric almost took a swing at him, thinking we'd been set up to be robbed. But that didn't make sense, because he already knew we were out of work. Anyway, the guy was spruced up in a nice suit and spoke real polite, you know?" he added with a shrug.

"No, we don't know," Neskahi said. "Polite how?"

"His English, man. It showed respect. He kept calling us 'gentlemen.' "

Neskahi glanced at Ella with raised eyebrows. "What else?" he pressed.

"He reminded us that we'd told him we were interested in picking up some quick cash. Then he pulled out a roll of fifties. That got our attention."

"What did he look like?" Ella asked.

"I don't really remember details, you know? Hell, to be honest, I'd been powering down beers all day, and all I can really tell you for sure is that he was wearing a cowboy hat and had a dark mustache. His face was pockmarked, too," he added.

"Anything else?" Ella asked.

"I never saw his eyes. I remember that. His cowboy hat had a wide brim and it hid most of his face. It made me uneasy."

"Then why did you take the job?"

"The money, man. Why else? But I've got to tell you, this guy had thought of everything. He left us a different car or pickup each time, and got us the police scanner the girl cop found under the seat. He wanted us to know what you guys were doing so we could stay ahead of you."

"How were the targets selected?" Ella prodded.

"I don't know. All I can tell you is that he would make up a list of instructions on what he wanted done, along with addresses and directions, and leave them in the car or pickup each time. He also left the materials—the bombs, and whatever else we needed—for us. The bombs already had blasting caps and fuses, so all we had to do was stick them somewhere, light the fuse, and haul ass. It was mostly local stuff except for one time when he had us roaming around the mountains driving nails into all those trees. But even that was in the general area of Shiprock. It was a place where folks around here would go to get their firewood. That time he even provided us with a forestry map, two hammers, and a sack of nails."

He paused, then added, "But I'm really sorry that old man got cut the other day. We just figured we'd ruin a few chain saws."

Again Ella tried not to let her anger show, recalling the nightmare the victim had gone through, and how Justine had beat herself up feeling guilty. Wanting desperately to know who was sponsoring all this, she considered finding a copy of the Navajo newspaper and showing him a photo of Arthur Benjamin, but knew that would be thrown out of court. Still, if she did manage to get a photo of Benjamin and place it among others in a photo array . . .

"How about that hogan? Did you set off the timer using a remote?" Ella knew that the person who planted the bomb was probably the Indian Harry had seen carrying in the box, but she wanted to check now to see how the two Anglos fit in.

James looked genuinely puzzled. "What hogan? We just blew up things like that pump house and the garbage container. Oh, and that outhouse. Blew the crap out of it, I guess. The bombs we got were just sticks of explosives with blasting caps and fuses. I wouldn't know how to use a timer anyway. I just work as a framer. Never did any wiring."

Ella stared at him, trying her best to look skeptical. Although she believed he was telling the truth, anything more he could add would just sweeten the pot.

"Why did this 'Indian' choose you and James, and know where to find you?" Ella asked. "Did you see him talking to anyone else?"

"I didn't notice him with any of the other guys who came to the union hall looking for work. I guess we were just lucky. Or maybe not, now that I think about it. Look, I'm trying to cooperate because I want out of here, but that's all I know. Really," James insisted.

Ella reached into her pocket and took out her small

notebook. She tore out several blank pages, then handed them to James, along with a stubby pencil.

"What's this for? A written confession?"

"No. We can get all the formal writing done when your lawyer is present. Just write down the times and places where you did a job for that Indian, and what you remember about each time. If you run out of paper, ask for more. The more incidents we know about, the more we can clear up and the better it will look for you in court. Anything you can add that will keep people from getting hurt cutting down those trees will also go a long ways in helping you avoid a negligent homicide charge."

Ella looked at Neskahi, and added, "Sergeant, will you stay with James while he writes? I'm going to talk to Eric now." Ella stood.

Neskahi nodded, bringing out his own small notebook. "I've got more paper, James."

The prisoner looked up. "Do you happen to have a pocket calendar?" he asked Neskahi.

Ella slipped out and tried to interview James's partner in his cell, but Eric simply sat there and glowered at her, even though Ella urged him to tell his side of the story.

Neskahi joined her a short time later and tried his luck next, but got no further.

An hour and a half later, Neskahi walked with Ella back to her office. "Things are going pretty well now, for a change. We're making progress and it looks like we'll clear up a lot of the open cases with these two, including the tree spiking. So why are you so quiet? What's bothering you?"

"I'm not sure. For now, keep what we've learned from the prisoner to yourself. I want to play this real close until I'm ready to make a move on the person who's behind this. These guys aren't very bright, but they were sure getting good intelligence from someone."

"You've got it. Let me know how else I can help."

"I will."

Ella made out a report of everything she'd learned,

but placed it in a limited distributions folder. For now, she would give it only to Big Ed, Justine, and the rest of her team, including Blalock. There was much she hadn't put down in the report—but theories based on gut feelings had no place in the official document.

After proofreading it, she walked to Big Ed's office and found him there, already working.

Ella went inside, then filled him in quickly, opening the file to the spot that contained a duplicate of the list they'd found in the men's car. "The real problem is what the list implies."

He studied it. "This is bad, Shorty. They knew I'd be at the Chapter House, and even that you park your unit behind the trees near the side of your house. That means that someone's keeping tabs on us. And if these guys are telling the truth, we still don't have a suspect for the blast at the hogan that almost killed two cops."

"I wanted you to see the file right away because there's something else I need to talk to you about. It's hearsay, so it's not in a report." Ella told him about Arthur Benjamin. "I have no proof. All I know is what Jaime over at the newspaper office told me in confidence. But I want to look into this. The problem is that I'm going to ruffle feathers if I do, and it could all blow up in my face."

Big Ed leaned back in his seat, lips pressed tightly together, and rocked back and forth in his chair—a regular habit—allowing the silence to stretch between them as he considered the matter.

Ella didn't interrupt but, after a while, impatience began to gnaw at her, and the rocking started to get on her nerves.

"This disturbs me a great deal," he said at last. "At one time both Arthur and Carl were friends of mine. Of course that all ended when I got the job of chief instead of Carl. After he died, his family came to the conclusion that losing the post to me was what killed him. I couldn't do a thing against that belief."

"Should I start looking into Arthur's background and that of his associates and see if there's any connection to the trouble we've been having? Almost all the major problems have been limited to the Shiprock district."

He nodded. "Do it, but I'm willing to bet that you'll find nothing. Arthur is a smart cookie. If he wants my job, he'll play rough. But whether he'd actually risk lives—that I'm not so sure about. One thing I can tell you is that Carl was too soft on people and played by too many rules. But Arthur told me once that had he been the one competing with me for the post of police chief, he wouldn't have lost."

Big Ed paused, lost in thought. "But the reason Carl didn't get the job wasn't because of anything he did or didn't do. It was because his heart condition showed up when he took the physical. It pretty much disqualified him as a police officer at any rank."

"Does Arthur believe that?"

"Probably. He's no one's fool. But he still has an ax to grind. The real problem with Arthur is that he spent his entire life trying to prove he was smarter and better than his brother, but nearly everyone still preferred Carl."

"So what you're saying is that Arthur probably doesn't really want your job—he just wants to accomplish what his brother couldn't—become Shiprock's police chief?"

"That's my guess. It's a complicated situation, Shorty. I've known that family almost all of my life. Carl was just another one of the guys, but Arthur never fit in anywhere. Admittedly, it was his own fault. He always held himself apart. Even now, he goes around dressed like an Anglo, wearing a silk tie and suit. He calls it having standards that define him and thinks he's making an image for himself. But what he doesn't realize—though he certainly should—is that around here what he's doing is not a plus."

"Suits?" Ella looked at the chief, then shook her head.

She didn't know any Navajos who wore suits and a cloth tie to work. Even Kevin dressed casually unless he was going to court or meeting with tribal officials.

"Western-cut suits, mind you, but never a bolo tie. And he must polish his boots twice a day! He's never late, he's never early. He arrives on the dot. Every time. Around here, we're all on Indian time except for Arthur. But I've got to admit he can get the Anglos and the federal government's attention with his role-playing tactics. He's managed to get grants and programs for the tribe that none of our politicians could, and *that's* what has made him friends here on the Rez."

"Okay, I'll let you know if I dig up anything interesting on him," Ella said. "But I'll keep a low profile."

"I'll alert the other districts on the Rez who've had sporadic trouble with vandalism to be on the watch for Anglos, not Navajos. We've had the worst of it here in the Shiprock district, but everyone needs to be apprised. Also, make sure your team realizes that whoever hired these two could hire another pair to replace them. Without catching the man behind it, this is just a temporary fix."

Justine was waiting in Ella's office when she returned. "What's up?" Ella could see the frustration on her partner's face.

"I checked out the radio scanner in the car the two Anglos were driving. It can monitor all our frequencies, those of the forestry department, and even those FB-Eyes uses. That requires special refinements and parts that aren't available to the public. I looked for the serial number in hopes I could track down the buyer, but the numbers had been filed off. It's not in the original case, anyway. I think it was probably stolen from a federal vehicle originally, but I doubt it can be traced."

Ella filled her in on the description of Eric and James's Indian "employer."

"There are some Navajos with mustaches, but not

many," Justine said slowly, "and a rough complexion could describe a lot of men."

"It's still too general a description, but at least it's a start," Ella said, then added, "Do you know Arthur Benjamin?"

"I know *of* him, but I don't know him personally. Why?"

"I'd really like to know if he's sporting a mustache these days."

"I'll check around and get back to you on that," Justine said.

"Also, see if there are any other Indians, doesn't matter which tribe, hanging around the *Dinetah* who fit that description."

"Good call. To a lot of Anglos, an Indian is an Indian— one size fits all."

"Yeah, you know what they say, we all look alike," she joked.

As Justine left her office, Ella picked up the phone and called her brother's home. Clifford spoke to a lot of people during the course of a day. Maybe he could get a lead for her on the Indian man who'd hired the Anglos. People were far more likely to talk to him freely than they would a cop.

After a quick conversation with Clifford, she hung up. He'd help if he could, but now it was a matter of waiting. She was getting ready to catch up on her paperwork when FB-Eyes, Agent Blalock, walked in.

"Tell me about the two Anglos you've got in the holding pen downstairs," he said, dispensing with the small talk.

"They're small-time, but the guy who apparently hired them is another matter," she said, describing the list of targets, their Indian employer, and the altered police scanner.

"I'll have Payestewa check out the pair's phone records and their backgrounds. If we can figure out how this mystery guy chose them, we may find a lead we can use. I have a feeling they weren't picked at random outside a union hall."

"Me, too." Ella rubbed her eyes. "But I don't think we'll find any easy trails. Nothing about this case seems to be simple."

TWELVE
✕ ✕ ✕

Rose glanced down at her bandaged hand. It throbbed every time Herman hit a bump in the road, but she wouldn't complain. This morning she'd been really worried about being able to replace the ruined wood. Most of it had been contaminated with kerosene. Although the house was heated by LP gas, there were rooms like the den that got very little heat from the ducting system. Without the woodstove, some rooms in the house would become intolerably cold.

"I'm glad you decided to come with me," Herman said quietly. "I like having the company."

"My daughter expects me to stay home until my hand heals, but I can't do that. I do avoid using it, but I won't let this injury rule my life."

"Your daughter is a police investigator with many responsibilities. She's used to taking charge of others, and it's natural for her to try to do the same with you."

Rose nodded thoughtfully. "I love her, but I wish she'd chosen another profession. To make things even worse, she's so dedicated she gives it everything she has. What she doesn't realize is that her career will be a poor companion if that's the only thing that defines her by the time she reaches my age."

"What do you see when you look back on your own life?" Herman asked quietly.

Rose thought about his question, gently touching the moments and memories that had made up her past. "I see a life of great joys and great sorrows. All in all, a life well spent. But it's the future that interests me more these days. There's still a lot left for me to do," she added. "And you, old friend, what do you see of your years and for the future?"

Herman kept his eyes focused on the road ahead. "I see a life that has been hard. Very hard." He thought of the son he'd lost in Vietnam and the daughter that had never made it past her eighth summer, a victim of lung disease. His wife had died many years ago, and with his only living son working in California he was now alone. Families no longer represented a unit that couldn't be broken. "Some people fear dying," Herman said. "But dying is easy. It's the living that's hard."

A long silence born of understanding descended between them as the miles stretched out. Finally Rose spoke.

"And now here we both are, going to gather firewood, taking care of the business of living."

Herman smiled at her. "That we are, old woman," he said with a twinkle in his eyes. "And your daughter is going to kill me when she finds out that I took you with me for this."

"My hand is hurt, but my arms still work. I *can* help carry the firewood back to the truck. All you have to do is load me up."

Herman shook his head. "You're not a wheelbarrow. That's for me to do."

"I'll do as much as I can," she said firmly. "You'll just have to trust that I know when to stop."

"Just don't get too tired out there. Your daughter's a great shot," he teased, "and she *always* carries a gun."

They reached the forest site that had been designated for firewood gathering about an hour later. Herman got out and, working together, they selected several dried-out pines that had been marked with an orange spot by foresters for cutting. They would be easy to cut down and still give them a good supply of firewood.

"Keep a sharp eye out for any spikes or nails, or other kinds of vandalism," Herman warned, telling her about those who'd been injured using saws.

"At least all we have is an ax and a handsaw. There's a limit to the harm that can be done to that or us if you strike a nail."

They'd been working for about ninety minutes, Rose only carrying light loads back to the truck, when Victor Charlie, the tribal newspaper's young cartoonist, came by. He had his own load of firewood in the back of his truck.

Victor pulled up besides Herman's pickup and got out, greeting Rose and helping Herman cut up the last of the wood he'd selected. Victor wore a buzz cut hairdo, and had on a faded green olive drab military jacket with the original user's black name tag still on it—Mortensen.

A perpetual teenager, though the man was in his twenties, Victor wore blue earmuffs that covered a set of headphones. Electric cords from each ear led through the neck of his jacket to a radio or CD player nested in an inside pocket.

"So how are things with you?" Victor asked Rose, apparently having turned off his music for the moment. "I heard about what happened at your home the other night. You must have been frightened."

"Angry is more like it. I think those thugs were sent to scare me because I oppose gambling on our land. They fight like cowards, ruining an old woman's firewood so she and her family won't have a way to stay warm. They're acting like those gangland hoodlums you see on TV."

Hearing her comments, Herman put the last of the wood in the back of his truck, stowing away the ax and handsaw, then helped Rose into the passenger's seat. "Well, good luck to you, nephew," he said, slipping behind the wheel. "We have to get going."

As soon as they were away from there, Herman glanced over at Rose. "He works for the newspaper. Did you know that?"

Rose shrugged. "So? What did I say that wasn't true?"

Herman exhaled softly. "I hope you have a lot of influence over your daughter."

"Why?"

"Because she's going to want to kill me now for sure—after she finishes with you, of course."

It was late in the afternoon when Ella went to visit Arthur Benjamin. His home, west of the town of Shiprock in the farmland just south of the river, was a very un-Navajo-like building. The large one-story ranch-style dwelling was constructed in the shape of a U with an east and west wing. The courtyard in the center, enclosed at the mouth of the U by a tall wrought-iron fence, was barren except for a terra-cotta frog planter.

Ella knocked on the right side of the double doors at the end of the flagstone walk, and was shown inside by a polite Navajo man in his late twenties. He was wearing a white dress shirt and blue slacks and she assumed he was Arthur's butler, assistant, or whatever.

Ella looked around the foyer, peering into the rooms beyond through the open doorways. The house was decorated like the pages of a magazine advertising southwestern decor—not the everyday kind, but the type actors and movie stars usually opted for. Painted cow skulls were mounted on the whitewashed walls, and a lamp fashioned from horseshoes stood next to an uncomfortable-looking leather-and-pine chair embossed with a cowboy cattle drive scene.

Asked to wait in what was apparently the den, Ella walked around the large room, trying to get a feel for Arthur Benjamin. Among some of the Santa Fe upscale art was a painting by a well-known New Mexican artist. It depicted a hogan and a herd of sheep on a solitary mesa, surrounded by windswept piñons that reminded her of bonsai plants on steroids.

Ella studied the painting, trying to figure out how Arthur Benjamin viewed it. Did he see the setting as the ideal, an old lifestyle to be overcome, or simply another aspect of Navajo life?

Hearing footsteps in the doorway to her left, Ella turned her head.

"I'm Arthur Benjamin," he said. Glancing at the painting she'd been studying, he added, "That's a classic, isn't it, Investigator Clah?"

Benjamin was a tall, slender Navajo man in his late forties with a thin, dark mustache. Since Navajos weren't known for thick facial hair, it wasn't particularly attractive. To her, it looked like Arthur had been sniffing charcoal.

"It's one of my favorites," Arthur continued, crossing his arms across his chest. He was wearing an expensive wool sweater and gray slacks. "The artist depicts our past realistically, but in a modern medium. He uses acrylic pigments exclusively."

Ella nodded slowly, still unable to get a handle on the man. "Are you a new traditionalist, then?" No other faction on the Rez straddled lines the way they did. They incorporated the old into the modern. They claimed to believe in the old ways—at least in spirit—yet lived more like Anglos and used technology like radio, television, and the Internet to spread their message of Navajo pride and increase their foothold on reservation life. She'd seen traditionally shaped hogans made of stucco, heated with natural gas, and with tiled or plush carpet floors, but still used for worship. It was a peculiar blend of old and New Age, but it seemed to be gaining more advocates every year.

Arthur shrugged. "I don't like labels, but if I had to choose one, I'd say I was a realist." He waved to the couch, the only comfortable-looking seat in the room. "Why don't you sit down?"

The cushions were too soft. Ella had to fight the feeling that she was resting on quicksand, and would be unable to extract herself before being sucked out of sight.

"So what brings you here, Investigator Clah?"

Ella knew that she had to phrase things very carefully. Arthur Benjamin had powerful friends and the last thing Big Ed needed was more people breathing down his neck.

"I'm aware of your experience in law enforcement and your interest in our police department, and I was wondering if you would share your thoughts with me about the current situation? The police department, particularly the Shiprock district, is under siege from vandals. But it's not youth gangs this time. We're facing what seems to be an organized campaign to make us look foolish."

"I would have said incompetent," he answered with a vaguely mocking tone. "But surely you didn't come here just for an old cop's opinion."

"You're not currently involved with law enforcement, I believe, but you're in contact with both our people and our leaders. I thought your insight might prove useful to me as I continue my investigation."

"The biggest problem facing our tribe is the police's inability to cope with the current situation, which has hit almost everywhere on the Rez, though, as you pointed out, the incidents of vandalism are far greater in this district. None of it is the department's fault, mind you—they just don't have the funding for enough officers. That's why I believe your chief is being irresponsible taking a stand against gaming. With the extra money that would provide, we'd finally have the resources the department needs to get ahead of the criminals."

"Do you think the increase in crime is being engineered by those wanting the adoption of gambling on the Rez?"

He smiled mirthlessly. "I've heard the gossip you're referring to, that I'm somehow responsible for this crime wave because of my ambition. But you can check out my activities on the nights in question. I've been making appearances at Chapter House meetings all around the Rez and visiting with our leadership nearly every evening lately. When they're at home and away from their offices, the current officials have more time to discuss the issues the tribe is facing."

"Is it true, then, that you're hoping to step in as chief of police in Shiprock if there's a change in leadership?"

He gave her a cold smile. "*If* there's a change?" He shook his head. "I think that's a foregone conclusion. Most people will readily admit that the need for radical changes on the Rez has arrived, especially in this area." He paused, then added, "Now tell me something. Did you come to verify the rumors so you could protect your own interests, or did someone send you to check up on me?"

Like most ambitious men, Arthur assumed others plotted and schemed as he did. "Neither. I came because a man of influence will overhear many things and I was hoping to get your help."

"I'll certainly let you know if I hear who's behind these crimes."

Arthur stood, his way of ending the interview, when the young man she'd assumed was his employee entered from an adjoining room. With the door open, Ella saw what could have only been a fifty-caliber rifle displayed in a glass case on the opposite wall of a game room. Without waiting for an invitation, Ella stepped past him to take a closer look at the weapon.

Almost as long as the nearby pool table was wide, the enormous telescope-equipped bolt-action weapon had an adjustable synthetic stock with a hole at the hand grip, and was resting on a sturdy bipod attached to the forward end of the stock. At the muzzle of the long, heavy barrel was a massive muzzle brake.

"It's a beauty, isn't it?" the younger man said, coming up beside her. He offered his hand. "I'm Robert Benjamin, Uncle Arthur's nephew." He smiled. "I was a gunner on an APC while in the army. Of course, the fifty-caliber weapon I used then was a Browning machine gun."

She studied the long-range target rifle, wishing she had a court order so she could have it test fired and a ballistic comparison done. "What do you use a weapon like that for these days?"

"Special competitions held by the Four Corners Gun Club. It's for ultra-long-range targets, out a thousand yards or more."

She nodded, and looked closely, trying to spot any indication that it had been fired recently. The weapon looked pristine, with few signs of handling beyond some vague scuff marks on the stock.

"Would you like to take a closer look at it?"

"Yes, if you don't mind," Ella answered.

He unlocked the cabinet and carefully lifted it out with both hands. As she took it from him, she realized it weighed more than thirty pounds. "Wow, this is some weapon."

"Have you ever fired one?"

She laughed. "No, this kind of firearm was not included in my law enforcement training."

"It's fun to shoot. I'll be glad to take you to the gun club sometime and let you give it a try."

Ella checked the action and receiver, but the weapon was spotless. If it *had* been fired recently, it had also been thoroughly cleaned and lubricated since.

"Even assuming you fire from benches or prone, and that the muzzle brake brings the recoil down to a manageable kick, how accurate can anyone be with something this heavy and cumbersome?" she asked.

"You're correct about the technique and mechanism," he said. "But to answer your question, I've won my last three shoots at a thousand yards."

"How much competition is there around here for such a specialized sport?"

"More than you'd think, though fifty-caliber weapons are generally too expensive and intimidating for most shooters. Right now I've been meeting up with three other regulars, all Anglos from the Farmington/Bloomfield area. They're all ex-military, like me."

Ella considered asking for their names, but she wasn't quite ready to tip her hand yet. She glanced at Arthur, who was eyeing her with renewed curiosity. It was impossible to tell exactly what he was thinking.

"Your interest in this particular weapon," he said. "Is it professional or personal?"

"Both," she answered honestly. How much more personal could it get than having someone try to blow her head off?

"I've seen my nephew shoot. He never misses what he's aiming for," he said with a smile.

It wasn't family pride etched on his face. It was something else, but Ella couldn't quite put her finger on the emotion.

"Well, I'm sure that we've taken up enough of your time, Investigator Clah. We don't want to keep you," Arthur said.

Ella nodded. It would be a pleasure serving this guy with a search warrant.

Ella was driving toward the station ten minutes later when her cell phone rang. It was Justine.

"I thought you'd appreciate a heads-up. Brace yourself," Justine said.

"Now what?" Ella asked, feeling every muscle in her body tensing up.

"Keep an eye out for the tribal paper today. A friend of mine works in production, and called to tell me that Victor Charlie brought in a cartoon everyone thought was so hilarious they put it in today's edition in place of one he'd already done. It features the image of a woman some say resembles your mother, though it has the usual disclaimer to avoid lawsuits."

She felt a sinking feeling at the pit of her stomach. "Any idea what the cartoon's about?"

"No, she told me that she wouldn't scoop her own

paper, but that you'd be very interested. And Jaime Beyale also wrote an editorial based on whatever it was Rose said to Victor. Apparently, he spoke with her earlier today. My understanding is that the editorial and the cartoon will run together."

Every instinct Ella possessed told her she wasn't going to like this. Her mother had always been a quiet person, but these days it was like living with a stranger with a familiar face. She just wasn't sure who Rose Destea was anymore. And that bothered her more than she would have ever dreamed possible.

THIRTEEN
✖ ✖ ✖

Ella drove to Clifford's home. She needed to talk to him about their mother. She had a feeling he'd appreciate some advance warning on what was going on, too. The truth was that right now, she could use his insight. He'd always been closer to their mother and she just wasn't sure how to deal with Rose anymore. Ella was certain that if Rose kept taking on the progaming factions, she'd soon find herself in way over her head. Yet Ella just didn't know whether she had the right to say anything about it to her mother or not.

When Ella arrived at her brother's place she saw him standing outside the entrance to his medicine hogan talking to a patient. She waited in her unit, not wanting to interrupt him, but a moment later his patient left and Clifford waved for her to approach.

It was ice cold inside the medicine hogan and she longed for the warmth of the house, but she didn't say anything as he put away the herbs and the bowls he'd used to prepare infusions.

"I'm glad you stopped by, sister. We need to talk," he said.

Ella wondered if he'd heard about Rose, too. "What's up?"

"I was very disturbed by the news you shared with me when you called earlier today. I don't like the idea of Anglos being hired to come in and disrupt us here on our own land. Then, finding out that an Indian hired them . . ." Clifford shook his head in disgust. "To me, that's the worst kind of betrayal."

"I agree with you. Even if we find out that he's not a member of our tribe, he shouldn't turn on other Indians."

"I've spoken to several people this morning trying to learn something you can use without betraying what you told me in confidence. There's plenty of talk about what's going on, but I'm not sure how reliable it is. Some believe that traditionalists are now facing a carefully orchestrated effort meant to undermine our influence over the tribe."

"What do *you* think?"

"That our people desperately need someone to blame and when they find out the Anglos responsible were hired by an Indian, all the factions here will start blaming each other. That's going to end up creating even more division and confusion."

"I wish there was a way to bring about a solution. What our people need now is a real leader," she said.

"Our mother is being seen as one of the traditionalist leaders. Did you know that? People admire her for holding on to her beliefs even though she married a Navajo who followed Anglo ways."

"She was always her own person. But tell me, what do you think of her outspokenness lately?" Ella asked.

"I'm not really sure what to think," Clifford answered slowly. "It's her right to do and say whatever she pleases, but I've always seen her as our mother, not an activist. It's hard for me to switch gears on that now. And, to be honest, I worry about her safety. I'm not sure if she realizes what she's stirring up, and the danger that may put her in."

Ella said nothing for several long moments. "I believe Mom knows exactly what she's doing, but I don't think she fully understands what the price could be." Ella exhaled softly. "I hate this. I want our old mom back."

Clifford smiled sadly. "That's not going to happen. For years she kept a low profile because it was the easiest way for her to live with our dad. But with both of us grown, this is her time, and she intends to follow her own heart now. You've noticed that she's been spending some time with our old family friend. I think it's good for her, too."

Ella nodded, thinking of Herman Cloud. He and Clifford, both traditionalists, had great respect for each other, so it seemed only natural that he would be more likely than she to approve of Rose's growing friendship with the man.

They remained quiet for a few minutes, then Ella brought the conversation back to business. "How do the other Fierce Ones feel about all the petty crimes we've been having around the Rez? Have you heard anything from them?"

"We're no longer the strong force we used to be on the *Dinetah*," he said sadly. "Too many of us have been hit by hard times. When people have to struggle to stay warm and put food on the table, everything else becomes less important. Several of the Fierce Ones have had to move away to get jobs, even off the Rez. Others are simply too busy with second jobs, trying to make ends meet, and taking care of their families. Though many traditionalists feel like traitors for even thinking about it, some are starting to consider the advantages gaming could offer the tribe. Face it, sister. When your stomach is so empty it hurts, and you're cold, you learn to make compromises and accept second choices."

"I know," she said quietly. "But I really resent people like the late senator's wife," she said referring to Abigail Yellowhair. "She's using the tribe's hard times to push her own agenda."

"You're judging her too harshly. Like her husband did, she thinks strictly in practical terms."

Ella thought of the conspiracy that Coyote had mentioned. It was possible that Abigail was playing a role in that. Until she knew more, she couldn't afford to rule out anything or anyone.

"Oh, I nearly forgot to tell you," Clifford added. "Your marshal friend stopped by. He asked for my help in getting word out to the traditionalists that a fugitive, that Manyfarms boy," he said using the name of an enemy freely, "is in our area." He paused. "He's also very concerned about you. I could hear it in his voice."

Ella looked at her brother and suppressed a smile. Clifford was fishing. He wanted to know what her relationship with Harry was. "I worry about him, too. He's a good friend."

"But one no longer living on our land," her brother said, looking at her carefully. "He comes and stays until his business is done, but his path is out there—away from us."

"He lives his life the way he sees fit," Ella said, trying to sound logical instead of emotional. "We all do."

Clifford said nothing for several moments. "Be careful, little sister. Heartache can come in many forms."

Lost in thought, Ella didn't reply right away. As her gaze fell on a Navajo rug her mother had woven years ago for Clifford, she suddenly realized that she hadn't mentioned the newspaper article yet. "Mom's going to be the subject of a cartoon and editorial," she said, telling him what she knew.

Clifford cringed. "This evening's edition?" Seeing Ella nod, he added, "What's it all about?"

"I don't know. Our second cousin—my partner—got a tip but there wasn't much in the way of details. That's what worries me."

Clifford smiled. "Because when it comes to Mom, you're beginning to hate surprises?"

"You've got it." Ella took a deep breath. "I better go. Today's edition should be out by now."

"Let me know what you find?"

"Sure."

Ella left her brother's hogan and drove to the closest convenience store. The paper had just been delivered. Ella sat in her unit, scanning the issue, and it took just a few seconds for her to find what she was looking for.

What caught her eye first was the cartoon drawn by

Victor Charlie that was at the top of the editorial page. In a parody of a wagon train being attacked by Indians, he'd sketched Anglos in stereotypical mafia suits riding SUVs around a hogan and shooting flaming arrows. A caricature resembling Rose was in the center, rushing around with a bucket of water trying to put out the arrows that had struck. The cartoon caption read, "The gaming issue heats up."

Ella closed her eyes, then opened them again slowly. Unfortunately, the cartoon was still there. Farther down the page was an editorial by Jaime. In it, she cited an "unnamed source" who'd speculated that the gaming question had spawned an Indian mafia. The editorial then explained the recent lawlessness on the Rez from that basis. Jaime ended her article by stating that the cops were at a loss because they were outmatched—the twins of poverty and crime had banded together, becoming a formidable force.

Ella stared at the short piece, knowing in her heart where Jaime had gotten the information about an Indian syndicate. Rose must have inadvertently leaked information pertaining to the case. She'd taken the rare bits and pieces she'd learned from Ella at home, formulated her own theories to explain what was happening on the Rez, then used that to support her antigaming stand.

Blaming herself more than her mother, Ella drove directly home. This time, they'd have to talk. Rose had the right to say whatever she wished but, as the mother of a high-ranking cop, she had to use more discretion.

When Ella arrived, Rose was in the kitchen helping Jennifer compile a list of the grocery items they'd need the following day.

Ella's expression must have spoken volumes, because Dawn, who'd come in to say hello, gave her a fast hug and retreated to the living room. Jennifer excused herself just as quickly and went to take care of Dawn.

Ella plopped the newspaper down on the table, opened to the page with the cartoon. "Mother, explain. Your name isn't mentioned anywhere, but this cartoon figure sure looks a lot like you."

Rose looked up at her. "I do *not* have to explain myself to you, daughter."

Ella exhaled softly. "Mom, there's something you have to understand. Because you're the mother of a cop, your opinion will be seen as a mirror of what the police are thinking. In this case, today's article suggesting that there's an organized force battling against Navajo interests could end up jeopardizing the life of a contact of mine, probably another law enforcement officer."

Ella had expected to see contrition on her mother's face, but although there was a touch of regret, Rose's reaction surprised her.

"I said nothing about your contact and you know it. On the rare occasions I've spoken to your reporter friend, I've stated my own opinions, nothing more, and I won't stop having an opinion simply because my daughter's a cop. It's time you realize that I have a life separate from yours and that I'm entitled to that. You have no right to ask me to put your career ahead of the things I have to do."

Ella stared at her mother in surprise. Everything she'd said was true and, maybe because of that, she had no idea how to answer.

"And just so you know, my belief that there's a unified force battling those of us who are against gambling isn't something I got from you. I've seen evidence of that myself, and I've heard many others talking about it."

Ella didn't want to ask, but she had to do it. "Exactly what have you heard?"

"There's been talk among my friends that outsiders—members of the progaming factions from other tribes—are coming to the reservation. Some people say that they've been meeting with our leaders, trying to influence them."

"Mom, gossip is notoriously unreliable. What probably happened is that someone in tribal government was seen talking to a member of another tribe, someone who's also involved in the gambling operations on that reservation or pueblo. That's all it takes to start a rumor."

"It's more than that, daughter. A friend of mine has seen outsiders meeting with some of our politicians. She won't give me names, but I know her information can be trusted." She held her hand up, stopping Ella before she could speak. "No, I won't tell you who she is. She spoke to me in confidence and that's how it'll stay."

Ella suspected Rose meant Lena, but there was no way she'd know for sure if Rose refused to say more.

"I'm tired. I'm going to watch TV, then go to bed," Rose said, then walked out of the room.

Ella stared at the empty chair her mother had occupied. The one constant she'd always had in her life had been the sense of security that had come from the same familiar routines at home, and Rose had been at the heart of that. But now, the things she'd taken for granted were changing, and nothing in her life would ever be the same again.

The kitchen phone started ringing at precisely 7:12 the following morning. Assuming it was for her, Ella picked it up.

"This is Ron Sanchez," a man's voice said, then proceeded to identify himself as a reporter for the largest newspaper in the state. "I'd like to speak to Rose Destea. Is she available?"

Rose walked inside the kitchen and took the phone her daughter handed her. She listened for a moment, then answered. "I have never represented myself as a leader of the traditionalists," she said firmly. "Some may refer to me that way, but it's only because they happen to agree with what I'm saying."

Rose paused, and seeing Ella staring at her, deliberately turned her back. "Yes, I believe that there's an organized criminal element working against us, hoping that we'll open casinos and institute gaming. That's one reason many of us are opposed to it."

Ella glanced at Jennifer, who was getting Dawn's breakfast ready, then back at Rose. There had been a time when all early morning phone calls had been about police work. She suddenly found herself wishing for those good old days.

Dawn ate from Ella's lap, and holding her little girl and actually having time to play and feed her felt like heaven. But the pleasure of the moment ended way too soon. There was a knock at the door, and, when Ella went to answer it, she found a reporter from the tribal newspaper. By the time she called Rose to the door, Big Ed, who'd been unable to get through on her home number, called Ella on her cell phone. Ella gave him a quick update on her visit with Arthur Benjamin, then agreed to meet him later. She'd tell him about the editorial then.

Ella showered and dressed quickly. She envied the women who were able to stay at home with their kids until they were in school. Seeing her daughter grow and change right before her eyes made her realize how fleeting her daughter's childhood would be and how she'd have to take special care to treasure the moments. "Be very, very good for me today," she told Dawn when she returned to the living room.

Dawn threw her arms around her and gave her a kiss. "I'm a big girl. I take care of *Shimasáni.*"

She smiled at her daughter then, giving her one last hug, left the house.

Ella drove north, passing the stark volcanic neck of Ship Rock on the left as she headed to the station. Around here, the land was cold and dry, even more barren than usual in the depths of winter.

Ten minutes later Ella entered the station and went directly to Big Ed's office.

He finished the report he'd been writing longhand as

she took a seat, then looked up. "You want to tell me about Jaime's editorial?"

Ella winced. "Then you've seen it?"

He nodded. "But I don't hold you accountable. We can't control the press."

Ella exhaled softly. "I've done my best to protect Coyote, Chief, but that story may cost him dearly. There's something else you have to know. The information Jaime alluded to in the editorial may end up being attributed to information Rose got from me, but that's not the case," Ella said, and explained what Rose had told her.

"Things are heating up, Shorty," Big Ed said. "I think it's time we held a meeting and let the FBI and others on your team know that we may be fighting an Indian mafia, not just isolated instances of vandalism and crime. It's time to spell it out in black and white. We have a sniper to track down, that's still critical. But that case is going to have to share our priorities now."

"I think you're right."

"Then call everyone in and set up a meeting in my office."

"I'll do that right away. One more thing. I'm thinking about getting a search warrant." She told Big Ed about the fifty-caliber rifle at the Benjamin's home.

"That's interesting, Shorty, but if that's the weapon the sniper used to take a shot at you, I'll eat my boots. Arthur Benjamin would *never* be that sloppy. Were they toying with you, you think?"

Ella considered the possibility. "Maybe Arthur was, but not the nephew. I'm sure he didn't have a clue."

"I'll support whatever you decide, but tread carefully."

An hour later, Ella, Justine, Tache, Neskahi, Paycheck, and Blalock came together for a formal meeting in Big Ed's office.

Ella opened the discussion. "We have reason to believe there's an intertribal syndicate working on the Rez.

Their goal is to get gaming passed by whatever means are necessary and then make sure their people are in key positions so they can rake a percentage off the operations."

"Like the old days in Nevada," Neskahi said slowly and quietly. "I've heard those rumors. From that angle, the reason for all the crimes we've been experiencing is simple to explain—the more distracted the police are, the less likely we are to notice what they're doing."

"That makes sense," Justine said.

Neskahi shrugged. "But there are others who believe that it's the traditionalists who are spreading the rumor about a syndicate to make people afraid—that it's all propaganda generated by antigaming forces to manipulate the People."

"There's holes in that theory," Ella said. "The traditionalists don't want gaming, that's true, but they're not working against the tribe. They value order and harmony most of all, and spreading rumors promotes neither."

"Ella, I think everyone saw the newspaper cartoon focusing on the gambling issue, and it can't be a mistake that the woman depicted there bears a striking resemblance to your mother. I know Rose hasn't been letting her position on gaming remain a secret, but what does the newspaper know that we don't? I'm getting vibes that maybe you're holding back on us," Justine said slowly. "But we're a team, and we deserve your trust. How did you find out about this Indian mafia?"

Ella hesitated. Everyone here deserved her trust. Justine was right about that. "I've been working with an informant. I can't say anything more specific about this person except that both Big Ed and I trust the information that's been passed on to me. This source warned me that there's a major conspiracy unfolding. A Native American syndicate is working covertly to take over gambling operations on tribal lands all across the nation. They're focusing on us now, the largest tribe in the country."

"You're in touch with a fed, then?" Blalock said, and shook his head. "Never mind. Don't answer that."

"Their plan has several steps," Ella continued. "The first part of their strategy is to discredit the existing tribal government and the police, creating a general lack of confidence in government. That opens the door to radical change."

"If that information is accurate, then we have a huge problem on our hands," Tache said.

"Nothing I'm telling you now is to leave this room, understood? My source is apparently on the inside, and one wrong move could cost him his life." Seeing everyone nod, Ella continued. "This syndicate is said to be willing to back any politician, honest or dishonest, who's in favor of gaming. I've been warned that they'll use whatever methods are necessary—blackmail, intimidation, or worse—to force those they can't defeat politically to vote for gaming when it comes before the Tribal Council."

"Just how long have they been in operation here on the Rez?" Neskahi asked.

"I'm not sure, but I can tell you that last fall the syndicate, organized in small, autonomous units like terrorist cells, was responsible for framing me for Justine's supposed murder. They wanted to destroy our Special Investigations Unit and perhaps bring down Big Ed as well. You all came through for me and we took that group down." She paused. "But now another cell, with new people and tactics, is operating on or near the Rez. Their goal, from what we've seen, is to manipulate public opinion."

"But you have no hard physical evidence that this Indian syndicate even exists, do you?" Blalock asked slowly.

"No, I don't, but there are comments made on the record by one of those arrested last year that support the existence of the Indian mafia, and we also have circumstantial and anecdotal indications of it."

"The problem gathering evidence is that, to date, all we've done is arrest the bit players," Big Ed said. "The ones pulling the strings have always eluded us."

"Like now. The two Anglos we caught don't even know who they're working for," Justine said.

Neskahi leaned forward in his chair, elbows resting on his knees. "Here's a thought. Abigail Yellowhair is very much progaming, and we know her husband was on the take for a long time. If she's playing by his rules and is on the take as well, we may be able to use her to lead us to the others."

"She was an unsuccessful candidate for her husband's office. Why would they bother to try and enlist her?" Justine said.

"She may be of use to them in other ways," Ella said, knowing Justine was a friend of the Yellowhairs and suspecting that would cloud her judgment. "But we have no proof she's dirty, and we can't judge her on her husband's actions. The most we can do is keep an eye on her."

"That woman is a politician through and through," Big Ed said. "If we're seen to be making a move against her, we can expect her to retaliate—hard. Tread carefully, people."

"So we'll have to be very subtle," Ella said.

Neskahi scowled. "We can't work a case if we're afraid to muddy the waters."

"Agreed, but we don't want to tip our hand either," Ella said firmly, "not until we're ready to make our move."

Once the meeting ended, people began leaving, but Big Ed signaled for Ella to wait. As soon as they were alone, he gestured to a chair. "You told them more than I expected you to, Shorty," he said.

"I had no other choice. I just wish I could have told them more about Coyote. Everything I know about him so far tells me that he's an undercover fed. I thought for a while that he was my old FBI partner, but there's no way he could have infiltrated a group of Native Americans. Joe was very, very Anglo looking. My old supervisor, Henry Estrada is a better choice, but even as good as he is, he'd need months of work in order to manage such a ruse."

"If you figure out who Coyote is, Shorty, I want to know."

"You've got it."

Ella went back to her office and found Payestewa waiting for her. "I've got something for you, Ella. Checking with the phone company, I've learned that the Indian who hired the two Anglo suspects called them from a cloned cell phone each time he made contact. We can't trace him to any number, name, or residence."

"Great. More good news to add to my totally crappy day."

Blalock joined them a moment later, and Payestewa closed the door behind him.

"We need to tell you something that you'll have to keep confidential for now," Payestewa said.

"Of course, you're free to tell Big Ed," Blalock added.

"All right. What's up?"

The young Hopi agent cleared his throat. "Originally, I was sent here by the Bureau to keep tabs on the Indian syndicate you're trying to get a handle on now. They felt, after assimilating all the available intel, that the syndicate would concentrate on the Navajo Rez next. They were right, but I still haven't been able to identify the players yet, except those we caught last fall who set you up for Officer Goodluck's apparent death."

"Do you have any suspects at all?" Ella asked, wondering if *he* was Coyote, then nixing the idea. Payestewa was no undercover operative walking the line. He was already becoming well known in the area, and couldn't be in two places at the same time.

"All I know is that there are two key individuals in the area—each working independently of the other—which implies two independent cells controlled from the outside. There's also reason to believe that neither knows the identity of the other, which is consistent with the strategy of cells. If you don't know who the other players are, you can't rat them out."

Ella looked over at Blalock. He was a man who didn't like to ask anyone for anything. Having the Bureau send in a second team must have stung. "How long have you known about Paycheck's real assignment here?"

"He couldn't tell me right away. I only found out about it a few days after Justine was rescued. I was mad as hell when I heard about it, too. I don't like the Bureau playing games behind my back on my turf."

"And until now you were under orders not to tell me?" Ella asked Blalock.

"I couldn't even say anything to Big Ed. I was ordered to keep my mouth shut until the Bureau was sure which local Navajo cops could be trusted."

"We're sure that Big Ed, you, and your team can be trusted, Ella," Payestewa said, "but outside that, we can't tell the good guys from the bad. There are people we suspect, of course, but we've got nothing on them."

"Like who?" Ella asked.

"George Branch, the radio talk show rabble-rouser, for one. He's very much progaming but, like it is with Mrs. Yellowhair, it's hard to say if he's acting out of conviction or something more sinister."

"Remember that about a year ago we saw some Native Americans meeting with Branch in a sweat lodge in the middle of nowhere," Blalock said. "We've yet to identify those guys, though one of the men warned your officer Tache off with gunfire."

"Branch is a hard case. You can forget getting anything out of him. And Mrs. Yellowhair, like most of the progaming big names here, has a lot of clout in the community. Investigating them without a lot of grief is going to be impossible."

"There's another Navajo who bears looking into, and

you're the person in the best position to do it," Blalock said.

"You mean Kevin," Ella said, guessing where he was going.

Blalock nodded. "Some people believe that the progaming forces practically paid for his election."

"That's probably true," Ella conceded, "but now that he's in office, Kevin has apparently backpedaled on them. He's leaning toward another public referendum. That's something that progaming factions are fighting because the Navajo Nation has voted it down every time it's come up. If anything, Kevin's their enemy now."

"He may be on his way to becoming that, but the progaming people aren't giving up on him yet. A good source tells me Jefferson Blueeyes has been putting a lot of pressure on Kevin to return to his original position and not alienate his supporters," Payestewa pointed out.

Ella gave Payestewa a respectful look. "Your sources are good."

"Even though I'm a Hopi, right?" He finished her thought with a chuckle.

Ella laughed. "Yeah, but I didn't say it, you did." She glanced at Blalock, who shrugged. "I know about Blueeyes, but I also know that when it comes down to it, Kevin makes up his own mind."

"Blueeyes is Navajo, but he was raised off the Rez," Payestewa said. "I also know for a fact that he has close ties to the activists on the Arizona side of the Navajo Nation. He bears watching."

Ella looked at Payestewa closely. She'd always suspected there was more to him than met the eye, but it irritated her to know that the Hopi agent was more informed than she was on this. She'd do better from now on. "Okay, I'll take it from here. If there's a problem we should all be aware of, I'll let you know."

FOURTEEN
✖ ✖ ✖

As soon as Payestewa and Blalock left her office, Ella called Justine. "Get me absolutely everything you can on Jefferson Blueeyes—Kevin Tolino's aide."

"How soon do you need it?"

"Yesterday."

Ella pulled up the files the tribe had on both Kevin and Blueeyes and studied them carefully. She was familiar with most of what it contained about Kevin, but Jefferson Blueeyes was another matter. She knew practically nothing about him.

His file, however, was of little help. It listed his education, his date of birth, and other factual and career data she could have found almost anywhere. The information looked like résumé filler, which was probably where it came from.

Justine came in a moment later. "I figured you'd pull up that file yourself, so I didn't bother," she said, looking at Ella's screen. "What I do have is a bit more anecdotal, but my informant is good as gold."

Ella looked at Justine and smiled. She should have known that there'd be no substitute for her cousin's contacts in the community. Justine came from a big family. "Okay, give."

"Blueeyes is a bit of a enigma around tribal government offices. He makes friends easily, but apparently he's not close to anyone, at least openly. He's single, reasonably good-looking, and makes a good income, so a lot of the women have set their sights on him. But nobody local has made any headway, not even a date beyond coffee. Some thought he might be gay, but that talk died down when one of the secretaries at his office saw him with a dark-haired woman in a bar in Farmington. The way they were acting left no doubt that he's partial to the female sex."

"Was she Indian?"

"Yes, but not Navajo. I heard that she looked like she was from one of the pueblos. The woman who saw them didn't recognize her."

"Anything else?"

"Blueeyes sometimes annoys the hell out of Kevin. They've been overheard having some shouting matches."

"Over what?"

"Blueeyes apparently oversteps his own authority and makes decisions for Kevin, sometimes even reversing what Kevin has told him to do. That invariably makes Kevin spitting mad, but Blueeyes keeps on doing it."

"I'd like Blueeyes watched every waking hour for a few days. But we've got to make sure he never finds out what we're doing. That would not only tip him off if he's tainted, it could also bring Kevin and the Tribal Council down on the department. We don't need that right now."

"Then we can't use anyone in the SI team. He's seen all of us at one time or the other since he works with Kevin."

"Who can we pull in from the department? We need someone we can trust completely, someone with top-notch skills. Any suggestions?"

Justine thought about it and then nodded. "How about Jimmy Frank? He's been a patrolman for twelve years, and has mentioned to me several times that if there's an opening in our unit, he'd like a shot at it. Why don't we give him a chance?"

Ella knew Jimmy. He was a good cop. "Is he on duty now?"

"Yeah, in fact, he's here at the station now. He had

to bring in a couple of kids who'd cut school and were driving down the highway half-drunk," Justine said.

"Ask him discreetly to come to my office," Ella said as her phone began to ring.

As Justine left, Ella picked up the receiver and was surprised to hear Jaime Beyale at the other end of the line.

"I need to know if Rose's theory about an Indian mafia is one shared by the police department. Is there an ongoing investigation and, if so, is there anything you can tell me about it?"

Ella gripped the phone so tightly that her knuckles turned white. "My mother's opinions are her own. Ask her. She'll tell you the same thing," Ella said coldly.

"Is Rose working with the police—however remotely?"

"We don't recruit people in their sixties."

Jaime laughed. "That's a great quote. Hope it looks as good to you tomorrow when you read it in my column."

Ella slammed the phone down. Dealing with the press wasn't her strong suit. She'd always thought that the founding fathers had been playing a joke on the public when they came up with the notion of freedom of the press.

Jimmy Frank knocked at her door and Ella, glad to take her mind off Jaime, waved him to a chair. He'd acquired a slight potbelly since the last time she'd seen him and what hair he had left was longer than regulation length and combed over. In white clothes and an apron, Jimmy would have looked more like a short-order cook than a cop.

"Jimmy, I have a surveillance assignment for you, but it's a touchy one and it's up to you whether to accept or decline. No one can know about it, and it's imperative that the subject doesn't see you tailing him. Do you think you're up to something like this?"

Jimmy grinned from ear to ear. "You bet I am. I've

stalked deer and elk with my brothers since I was six—not for hunting, just for fun. We used to make a game out of seeing how close we could get before they spooked."

"You're going to be stalking something far more dangerous, and you can't ever let him suspect the police are watching," Ella warned. "The person I've got in mind is cunning and may be dangerous."

Jimmy grew serious. "I've been hoping to get into your unit for a long time, so I've been taking the specialized law enforcement courses the feds offer each year. I've learned how to keep someone under surveillance in an urban environment. Here I've found it's even easier for me. I look just like every other citizen, and people usually don't notice me unless I want them to. Tell me, who's the target?"

"Jefferson Blueeyes. I need to know who he sees, what he does after hours, what his routines are—anything and everything you can get me. But keep your distance. If he sees what you're doing, it'll warn him off and we'll get nothing from then on that will be of any use."

"Why is he a suspect?"

"I can't tell you that yet, but I have reason to believe he's playing a dangerous game, so be extremely careful."

"Why aren't you using someone from your own team?"

"Blueeyes knows all of them because of his association with Kevin Tolino. I need to use someone he won't be watching for."

"You're safe on that score. He and I have never met. Do you want a twenty-four/seven on him?"

"No, you'd need backup to do that right and I have no one I can spare. So you're clear once you're convinced he's gone to bed for the night. But I want you back on duty as soon as he gets up in the morning." Ella pulled a file photo and handed it to Jimmy. "Do this for three days, then report back to me. If he does anything you think is unusual or obviously illegal, get back to me ASAP. And don't use your police radio. We have reason to believe someone's listening in on our frequencies."

"No problem. I carry a cell phone because my wife has a health problem and can't drive."

"Great. About the cell phone, that is. Here's my cell number." Ella jotted it down on the back of one of her business cards, then handed it to Jimmy.

"I'm just about set, then. But what about my patrols?"

"I'll arrange to have someone cover for you. It's only three days, so I'm sure I can get someone to put in some overtime, or maybe extend the patrol area of someone working your shift."

As Jimmy left, Ella went to talk to Big Ed. She knew he would go along with this, despite the officer shortage. They needed a break on this case, and the sooner they found something the better it would be for everyone.

Big Ed listened as she filled him in. "It's risky. Tolino is a powerful man and if Frank gets caught . . ."

"I trust Jimmy to do the job," Ella said. "And you've seen him, Chief. He *does* blend in. Jimmy's an excellent cop, but he's not exactly a walking recruitment poster for the department. Out of uniform, he certainly doesn't fit the image. That will work to our advantage."

He mulled it over, rocking back and forth in his chair, then finally sat forward and nodded. "All right." He leaned back in his chair again. "Just do one thing, Shorty."

"Name it."

"Start thinking of a cover story in case this one blows up in our faces."

"I don't think it will, but if we get caught, I'll say that it was a training exercise for Jimmy, who wants to join our unit."

"Blueeyes and Tolino will never believe it, but I'll back you up. As a matter of fact, I'm going to write it out just as you described and make it an order. I'll put a copy in all our files. That way, we'll have a paper trail that precedes this if we need it."

"Good idea."

"One more thing. Abigail Yellowhair came through for us. She got several local businesses to pony up the money, and a Farmington electronics outlet is setting up the account and programming the equipment for free. Everyone on your team is now being issued a cell phone and a list of everyone else's numbers, and there were two left over. I'm taking one. You can give Jimmy the other."

"Great. He has one of his own already, but this will save him some money."

Ella left the chief's office, called Jimmy, and left the phone for him with the desk sergeant. She was now feeling more positive about things than she had in days. Action. There was no better prescription for what ailed her.

Ella was at the soda machine in the lobby when Justine ran up to her.

"We've got to get rolling. Betty Nez was just found dead in her home. She's an office temp for the tribe. Her daughter Millie called it in, and she's hysterical. Dispatch couldn't get anything except the victim and location. Tache is loading up the crime-scene van now, and Neskahi will meet us there."

"Let's go. If it's a homicide, we'll have our work cut out for us."

While Justine tried to question Millie in the living room, Ella surveyed the kitchen where the body was located, keeping out of the viewing field while Tache took the necessary photos.

She'd never seen so much Elvis memorabilia in her entire life. The living room had been a virtual shrine, and the kitchen was nearly the same. There were Elvis dish towels, and even an Elvis sponge that featured a grainy image of the King holding a guitar. It looked like something out of a horror flick. The salt and pepper shakers on the table were miniature images of the rock and roll legend in blue or white sequined jumpsuits, and two of the walls held posters of the King—one of them of the young Elvis, and the other of the singer at his best looking—in tight, black leather.

Ella crouched next to the body. Betty Nez was lying prone on the ceramic tile floor inches away from a tipped-over step stool, her neck twisted in an unnatural angle. One of the cupboard doors above the counter was open. At first glance, it appeared that she'd climbed up on the step stool to get something from the cupboard, then fallen off and broken her neck. But experience told her to withhold judgment. Betty worked for the tribe in an office with the tribal chairman, and with a conspiracy going on, that raised questions in Ella's mind that made everything worthy of a closer look.

Looking at the kitchen table, Ella saw that it was slightly out of alignment with the counter. Bending down to table level, she noted there were a few scattered grains of salt indicating the salt shaker had possibly been knocked over when the table was knocked out of position. But who had set the salt shaker back up again, and why?

"Where's Carolyn?" Ella asked Tache after asking him to get a shot of the table's position and the spilled salt. "She's been called, right?"

"Yep, and I'm right here," Carolyn said, stepping into the kitchen. She'd put on weight recently and Ella guessed her good friend now weighed in at well over two hundred pounds. For a large woman, however, she had an inexhaustible supply of energy. Dr. Roanhorse-Lavery was arguably the best medical examiner in the state, and virtually the only one still operating outside the State Medical Investigators Office based in Albuquerque.

"Hey, give the doctor some room to work," she muttered, turning sideways to pass between the table and where Ella stood. "Not everyone is a bean pole, bones."

"Yeah, yeah," Ella said with a tiny grin. No matter what Carolyn's mood, the Navajo doctor was one of the most loyal friends anyone could ever hope to have.

"Man, this Elvis decor is a gag fest." Carolyn glanced around, but once her attention shifted to the corpse, she was all business.

Ella knew the pathologist would miss nothing, but Carolyn hated to have anyone looking over her shoulder while she worked. Ella backed off. One time when she'd hovered, Carolyn had taken off one of the plastic gloves she'd been wearing as she inspected the body and snapped it at Ella like a rubber band. Even the memory made her shudder.

Carolyn had just been teasing, of course, knowing that it wasn't the sting that would annoy Ella but the physical contact itself. Like Ella and all the Navajo officers, Carolyn wore a second set of gloves beneath to avoid direct contact with the body, which was a big taboo for Navajos.

Ella picked her way around the small house, studying everything. Betty Nez was an immaculate housekeeper, and the only room that appeared to have been disturbed was the kitchen. Satisfied for now, she went to join Justine, who was still questioning the victim's daughter.

"I can't imagine what happened. Mom shouldn't even have been home. I bet she came back to be with *him*."

Justine looked at Ella. "Betty was divorced, and recently she'd started dating again."

"Who?"

"Millie doesn't know."

"I never met her boyfriend," Millie said. "Mom was trying to keep the whole thing a secret. My sister and I suspected that she was dating a married man, probably someone at work, since she very rarely went out on her own." Millie paused and swallowed, big tears falling down her cheeks.

"Is there anyone your mother might have confided in, perhaps another woman she worked with?" Ella asked. "We need to track this man down in case he was here when she died."

"Mom didn't confide in people easily, but I imagine her co-workers knew," Millie said. "It's hard to keep things like that secret for long around here."

Aware, from the absence of the flash, that Tache had stopped taking photos, Ella let Justine continue questioning Millie and made her way back into the kitchen.

Ella crouched by Carolyn. "So what do you think?" she asked in a low voice. "Do we have a case here, or is it accidental?"

"Someone was trying hard to make you believe it was a simple accident, but that's not what the evidence tells me. All I've got is preliminary, mind you, but there are bruises on her upper arms, around her neck, and loose hair on the back of her head that indicates she fought with her attacker. I've already bagged her hands, and will be scraping her fingernails in case she managed to scratch whoever came after her. I'm thinking that this person grabbed her, she pulled free, but he yanked her back by the hair. She fell, which would explain the bruise on her knee, and then her attacker slammed her head against the floor. The first time he did it, she would have gone out like a light. After that, it would have been easy for him to complete the job. I put her time of death at between ten and eleven this morning."

Ella, working along with her team, took the house apart, searching for prints, for tracks outside, and signs of forced entry. As she worked, Ella found herself wishing Betty hadn't been such a good housekeeper. She needed something—one clue—that would lead her to Betty's lover.

Ella took a long look around the bedroom while Sergeant Neskahi and Officer Tache examined the rest of the house. The Elvis lamp on the nightstand had a velvet lampshade with images of Elvis lining the bottom near the red fringe. The bedspread had an image of Elvis in the center, with eyes that appeared to wink depending on the angle of the viewer.

Ella tore her gaze from it and checked the nightstand, then the floor, looking for anything that would point to the identity of Betty's lover. But the room was clean, too much so. It looked like a good hotel room after housekeeping had finished. Did anyone really clean this thoroughly, or had someone made a concerted effort to remove any traces of evidence? Even the wastebasket in the bathroom, which fortunately held no Elvis-inspired items at all, was empty. The vacuum cleaner in a hall closet had a new, unused bag installed.

She went back into the living room and approached Millie. "Did you touch anything in the kitchen before or after you found the body?"

"No. When I got to the kitchen and I saw the body I just couldn't move. I could tell Mom was dead from the way her neck . . . you know. Finally I just ran to the phone." Millie shook her head slowly, tears flowing again.

"I'm sorry, but one more question. Would you say that your mother was a really good housekeeper?"

"Yeah," Millie managed a brief smile. "She was proud of her Elvis memorabilia, and she liked everything perfect so she could show it all off. She was constantly adjusting furniture and such to make everything look just right." Millie wiped her tears with a tissue, then continued. "When one of your detectives asked me about the two glasses in the drain rack by the sink, I realized Mom must have come home to meet her boyfriend, but then something happened. Mom *always* dried glasses and plates off immediately and put them into the cupboard. No way she'd have left anything just sitting there like that."

Giving Justine a nod, Ella went back to the kitchen. Carolyn was bringing out the body bag to contain the corpse.

"You through?" Ella asked.

"Yeah, but I'll need some help putting the body away and loading the bag into the back of my van."

Though Tache and Neskahi were within hearing distance, both of them vanished instantly.

Carolyn looked at Ella. "I'm not moving and neither is this body until I get help. Get Neskahi. I think he was the one who went out into the backyard."

"I can help you," Ella offered.

Carolyn glowered at her. *"I said, get Neskahi."*

"But why?" Ella asked, puzzled.

Carolyn gave her a smug smile. "Because he made a crack about my weight."

"Oh, well, since you have a good reason like that," Ella said with a tiny smile, "it's hard for me to refuse." Ella went to the back door and signaled for the sergeant to come back in.

Neskahi's face fell and he walked back slowly, shoulders slumped, head down. "That's what I get for asking if she'd already searched the refrigerator," he muttered as he moved past Ella.

Once the body had been taken away and only the masking tape outline remained, Ella tagged and bagged the salt shaker.

She then sat down on the kitchen floor and turned over the trash basket onto a layer of paper towels. Except for two empty cola cans and a copy of yesterday's tribal paper, there was nothing of interest, not even a used vacuum bag. Then she noticed a piece of gum stuck to the newspaper. Ella picked up the paper with the gum still attached, then bagged and tagged it, along with both empty cola cans. With luck they'd get fingerprints off the cans, and be able to link the DNA on the gum to a suspect—if she ever narrowed it down to anyone.

Ella took one last look around and stared at the tape outline pensively. Whoever had been there had been careful. There were no signs of a struggle except for a few grains of salt and the slightly out-of-position table. A crime of passion? Not this well planned.

They left the crime scene nearly two hours later. The closest neighbors had been questioned, but houses here were at least a quarter of a mile apart and no one had seen or heard anything. The trash pickup had been the afternoon before, they learned, and nothing was in the trash can outside the house.

"She was a real pretty woman," Justine said. "I wonder why someone like her would get mixed up with a married guy?"

"She wasn't getting any younger, cousin. Maybe she didn't have a lot of choices and she was lonely."

"But there are plenty of men around, no matter what age you are."

Ella laughed. "Yeah, but a lot of women have trouble connecting with them after they pass a certain age. And some of the leftover men have been leftover for a good reason."

"I know, Ella. But if I were looking for a guy, I'd go to places where I could meet single men and just take my chances. And if I didn't meet anyone I liked, I'd go it alone instead of settling. I can't imagine picking a married guy just 'cause he was the only one interested." She shuddered. "I guess I'm not wired that way."

"Not many women cops would be likely to fall for the tired lines these guys come up with. We deal too much in reality and have few illusions about human nature."

"Which also makes it hard for us to sustain relationships, doesn't it?" Justine observed.

"Yeah, that, too." She gave Justine a concerned look. "Are you and Wilson having problems?"

She nodded. "He wants to move things along at a faster pace than I'm comfortable with," Justine said. "Right now I'm trying to cope with what happened to my hand, and I'm working really hard to make sure I can qualify on the firing range. That's my first priority— well, that, and keeping up with my caseload. Yet he's talking about our future together and how he wants to settle down. He's even started mentioning marriage." Justine shook her head. "I just can't deal with all that right now."

"You have to do what's right for you, but be careful," Ella said thoughtfully. "I've learned that life goes on whether we're ready or not, and the right person can slip through our fingers before we even realize it," Ella said, thinking about Harry.

Justine glanced over at her. "Is that what happened between Wilson and you?"

Ella shook her head. "Wilson and I have always been such good friends that people believed there was more going on than there was. Wilson got wrapped up in that too for a while, before he finally accepted the fact that I just didn't love him in that way. Then he got involved with Lisa and, in time, that turned out to be an even bigger disaster for him. I think the reason he's rushing you now is because he's afraid that things will go wrong again and he'll lose you."

Justine nodded. "I thought that, too, so I offered to move in with him and see how it went, but he said no. He told me he's not even remotely interested in halfway commitments."

"Consider the relationships he's had and you'll understand where he's coming from."

"What about you?" Justine asked. "Don't you ever think of settling down with a man, particularly now that you've got Dawn? It would be good for her to have a full-time daddy in her life."

"It's precisely because I've got Dawn that I have to be careful. I don't want her to be hurt. She's my first responsibility. But to answer your question, yes, I would like to find the right man and settle down."

"Do you think Harry could be the right guy?" Justine pressed.

Ella laughed. Justine's instincts were right on target, as usual. "I don't know. We understand each other's responsibilities very well, so that's a start. What happens in the future is anyone's guess."

"But it's always that way, isn't it?" Justine said, looking down at what was left of her right forefinger.

"Yes, I guess it is," Ella said, wishing life came with a really good set of instructions.

Rose watched her granddaughter playing in her room with Jennifer. It bothered her to have a stranger practically living here, but what really annoyed her was seeing how easily Dawn had accepted this new person.

Turning away, Rose walked to what had once been her husband's study. The room was divided in two these days—half was Ella's office and the other half was her sewing and weaving room.

Rose searched for a novel Ella had given her last year. It was the story of a Navajo man who'd been turned into a vampire, but he was subject only to the beliefs of the *Dineh*. Prayer sticks accomplished what crosses could not. Ella had found the novel entertaining and had recommended it to her.

Finding the book on the shelf, Rose sat down on the sofa and began reading, but soon she was forced to give up. No matter how hard she tried to concentrate, her thoughts seemed to drift back to Herman. It had been nice having a man her own age to talk to yesterday, someone who remembered the good times and the bad times on the Rez as she did.

With a sigh, she tried to focus back on the book, but to no avail. Finally, hearing a car driving up, she stood. A knock sounded at her door shortly thereafter. "I'll get it," Rose called out.

A man she recognized, a member of the Tribal Council, stood on her porch. Ronald Etcitty was one of the leaders of the progaming faction pushing for the council's approval.

"Can I help you?" she asked.

"I understand that you speak for many of the traditionalists who are opposed to gaming, and I'd like a chance to talk to you about our position," he said.

"If you know I'm a traditionalist, you should have also shown me the courtesy of waiting outside and not approaching my door without an invitation," Rose said softly, but clearly.

"I would have, but my heater won't work very well unless the car is moving, and I didn't know if you'd even heard me drive up. Won't you forgive the lapse?" He flashed her a wide smile.

To Rose, a smile from a politician served the same function as the noisy tail of a rattlesnake. "Come in, then. We'll talk."

Jennifer peered out from Dawn's room and, receiving a nod from Rose, returned to play with the little girl. Two was sitting in the doorway, watching the stranger.

Rose gestured to him to have a seat. "All right. You have my complete attention, Councilman."

Ronald Etcitty kept his voice low. "Your daughter is a well-respected policewoman for the tribe, but she's in a precarious position right now. Did you know that?"

"What do you mean?" Rose asked. She didn't like where he was heading. Tension gripped her, but she tried to remain outwardly calm.

"Our tribe's finances are almost completely depleted. Officers, I'm sure you've noticed, are being overworked to the point of exhaustion. Crime is on the rise and yet their ability to do their job well is being compromised. What's worse, their lives are more at risk than ever before because of the impossible demands being made on them." He paused, obviously for effect, then continued. "By working against gaming, you're opposing the opportunity to practically guarantee a safer working environment for your daughter."

Rose held herself perfectly still. She was furious, but she wouldn't give him the satisfaction of knowing he'd pushed the right buttons. "My daughter would be in even more danger if casinos opened on our land. A flood of professional gamblers, organized crime, and alcohol can't result in anything good for our people."

"Are you aware that as things stand right now, if your daughter needed backup from other officers, she probably wouldn't get it for a half hour or more? Without the funds to hire new officers, we're going to be facing a real crisis very soon. Of course, one solution we've been considering is redistributing our current officers to cover more ground. Your daughter's unit would undoubtedly be disbanded and she could be sent to Window Rock, for example, or way over to Tuba City." He looked through the doorway to where Dawn was playing. "The tribe has a day-care center in Tuba City, so your granddaughter would be looked after—though I suspect they've had some staff cuts too, so she wouldn't get the attention you can give her here."

"This almost sounds like a threat." Rose commented pleasantly. He'd succeeded in scaring her, but she was determined not to let him know it.

"Oh, no, not at all," he said smoothly. "I simply came to provide you with more information. I thought that if you could understand the realities of our tribe's situation, you'd be able to explain these things to others who have also opposed gaming."

"In that case, I'm afraid you've wasted your trip." Rose stood. "I agree with the council that we need funds desperately. But gaming is not the answer."

His eyes flashed with a trace of anger. "And what solutions do your antigaming group propose? Do they have any idea at all how we can ease the tribe's financial crisis?"

"I'll think more about it and discuss the matter with

other people. For now, the only thing I can say is that you don't fix one problem by adding another one."

As the man left, Jennifer came out to join Rose. "I only heard a little of what you said, but I think you really handled that well."

But it hadn't been good enough. Rose knew she was making enemies and, sooner or later, they would rally against her. She could only hope that when the challenge came, she'd be able to meet it with courage and dignity.

FIFTEEN
✖ ✖ ✖

Ella and Justine spent most of the afternoon at the local tribal offices questioning Betty Nez's coworkers inside an empty conference room. Betty had been well liked, and from what Ella could see the entire secretarial pool was mourning the passing of a friend. As they questioned the group, one by one, a picture of the murdered woman began to emerge.

"Everyone knows each other here," Lea Benally, a young receptionist in her midtwenties, explained. "We don't always get along, mind you, and there are times when we'd cheerfully choke each other, but the truth is we're all in the same situation and we know it. We have jobs, and we want to keep them. Our friend always worked hard and helped whoever was running behind. She'll be missed."

Ella noticed that no one wanted to mention Betty by name. Even among these modernists, not many were willing to tempt fate by inadvertently summoning the *chindi*.

"Who was she going out with?" Justine asked pointedly.

Lea squirmed. "We all knew she was seeing *someone*, but she was careful never to say who he was."

"But you still had a good idea, right?" Ella pressed.

"We made a guess, but we don't really know for sure," Lea said with a shrug.

"Tell me who you think it was," Ella prodded.

Lea hesitated. "He had nothing to do with what happened to her. I'm certain of it."

"Then we'll be able to prove that right away," Justine answered.

There was a knock at the door and a Navajo woman in her early fifties wearing a gray wool suit peered inside. "I'm sorry to interrupt, Officers, but should I ask one of our tribal attorneys to be present?"

Ella looked at Rita Zahnes, the office supervisor, and was surprised to see the trace of fear in her eyes.

"Why would you think that's necessary?" Ella asked. "Our questioning is routine at this point. We're just getting background information."

"I spoke to some of my people, and I understand that you've been asking them to speculate on who our co-worker was dating. Speculation like that could get them into serious trouble." She shifted her gaze to Lea. "I wouldn't want anyone to face slander charges or a reprimand."

Lea's eyes grew wide, and she turned to Ella. "I honestly don't know anything. She and I were friendly to each other here at work, but we were always focused on our jobs. There's not much time to just chitchat."

Ella looked at Rita. "We asked all of you not to discuss the deceased until we'd spoken with everyone here, but it looks like you didn't respect that request. So I'd like to talk to you next. If you feel you need an attorney, by all means call one right now."

"I don't *need* an attorney," Rita said, instantly on the defensive.

"We're glad to hear that you've got nothing to hide," Justine said.

Excusing Lea, Ella gestured for Rita to have a seat. "We already know that the deceased was seeing a married man, and we have an idea of who that person is," Ella bluffed. "I don't think you want to be charged with obstruction of justice, and I do believe you'd like to see whoever killed your friend put in jail. Why don't you just tell us what you know and let us do our job?"

Rita looked down at her hands and bit her bottom lip.

"Look, this is very awkward for all of us. Sure, there's been gossip about who she was seeing, but the way it started . . . I just don't know if any of it is true."

"Tell me what you heard," Ella said.

"The gossip all started when Lea saw the woman who worked here," she said avoiding the name, "with a guy who looked like Andrew Talk."

"The Tribal Council member." Justine verified with a casual nod as if she'd already known about this.

"Yeah, but Lea was in a bar in Farmington at the time and the room was dark. Lea said that she got up to go say hello to her, but, before she could get across the room, her coworker ducked out with the guy."

"All right. Send Lea back in, and this time *don't* discuss this with anyone."

"You don't even have to ask," Rita said, moving quickly to the door as if fleeing from a rabid dog.

Lea came in a moment later. "Look, I really don't have anything to say—"

"Lea, relax," Ella said. "Whatever you tell us will be kept confidential."

Lea's eyes narrowed and she looked at Ella thoughtfully. "You already know, don't you? That's why you're pressing me. You need to hear it directly from me?"

Ella nodded. "That's it in a nutshell."

"The truth is I never got close enough to our friend to say for sure who she was with. That place was really dark, but from the glimpse I got, I think it was my boss, Andrew Talk. I wanted to go say hi to them, but one of the guys there suddenly grabbed me and asked me to dance. By the time I got free, they were gone."

"Lea, I want you to think really hard. You say that you never got close, and you couldn't see the guy really well. So what is it that made you think it was Andrew Talk?"

"To be honest, the only clear look I had of him was when he was hurrying away, but I saw the back of his belt and that's when I knew who it was. I suppose it might have been someone with the same name, but . . ." she said with a shrug.

"Now you've lost me. What do you mean 'the same name'?" Ella asked.

"The guy I saw was wearing a hand-tooled leather belt. As he walked away, the spotlight on the dance floor caught it and I saw the name Andrew tooled in outline on the back. You've seen those belts, haven't you? The high school kids make them all the time."

"And that convinced you that it was Andrew Talk?" Justine asked.

"Well, that, and the fact that Andrew has a belt like that. I've also seen the way he would look at her when he thought no one else in the office was watching. He really liked her."

When Lea left the room Justine glanced at Ella. "I probably see two or more of those belts every day. Even some of our cops wear them off duty."

"I say we pay Mr. Talk a visit," Ella said.

"Okay. His office is at the other end of the hall," Justine said. "I remember seeing his name on the door when we walked down here."

"Let's go."

The office was empty, and one of the men working across the hall came out. "If you're looking for Mr. Talk, he's been out since yesterday."

"Do you have his address?" Ella asked, flashing her badge.

Before long, they were under way, but Justine was uncharacteristically quiet.

"What's on your mind?" Ella asked.

Justine exhaled softly. "I don't know the Talks personally, but I've seen his wife a few times. She's a good-looking woman, and they have two beautiful daughters—twins. It's a shame that he's playing around and screwing up his family. I've seen how hard that kind of thing is on the children. It takes a toll on everyone."

Ella lapsed into a thoughtful silence. Situations like the Talks' only helped remind her how good her own life was. Being a single mom was tough and, at times, lonely, but it was better to be alone than living with a mate who didn't understand or respect the meaning of family.

When they arrived at the councilman's home, Lorraine Talk, Andrew's wife, greeted them at the door. Two raven-haired seven-year-olds were playing behind her in the living room.

Ella flashed her badge. "We need to talk to Andrew."

Lorraine turned her head. "Go to your room, girls."

As the girls raced off down the hall, Lorraine invited Ella and Justine inside.

Ella looked around the large living room. Everything was tasteful but not ostentatious. The tiled terra cotta floors were beautiful and elegant. The furnishings, mostly plush leather and wood, gave the room a homey feel.

Ella studied the Navajo rugs hung by wooden rods upon the pale yellow walls. She could tell by looking that those were antiques, woven on large wooden looms according to the time-honored ways. The Two Gray Hills pattern on one, made with handspun wool in shades of black, brown, and white, was exquisite and she knew it would have fetched a handsome price off the reservation.

"Sit down." Lorraine gestured to the rich chocolate brown leather couch.

Ella took a seat and studied the athletic, attractive woman in her early thirties. Justine remained standing near the hall, watching intently in case Talk was somewhere in the back of the house. Her only hope, Ella realized, was to catch a glimpse of Talk if he was there, because there was no chance she'd be able to hear anything over the shrieks and laughter coming from the twins.

"The girls are really excited today. You'll have to forgive them. They just came back from an overnight field trip. They traveled to see the Albuquerque Biological Park. Now tell me, what can I help you with?"

"I need to talk to your husband," Ella repeated.

"Oh, I thought you wanted to talk to me *about* my husband." She gave Ella an apologetic look. "I'm sorry, but Andrew moved out."

"I just came from his office, and this is the address we were given," Ella said.

"Andrew hasn't discussed any of this with the people at the office. I don't think he wants them to know that we've been having marital problems," she answered, her voice low.

"What happened between you two, may I ask?"

Lorraine stood and walked around the room nervously. "The problems between my husband and me are personal, and strictly between the two of us."

"I hate to press you on the issue, but it's crucial to a case I'm working on. Was Andrew seeing someone else?"

Lorraine stopped in midstride, put her hands on her hips, and looked directly at Ella. "I have no idea and, to be honest, I really don't care. I kicked him out because I couldn't stand his drinking. And, more importantly, I didn't want to expose the girls to that kind of behavior."

"Was he ever violent?" Justine asked matter-of-factly.

"Andrew had fits of temper, but he never touched me. He knew better. I'm in better shape than he is. If he ever raised his hand to me, I'd break it off at the wrist and hand it back to him. I'm a brown belt in karate, and I'm working on my next level."

Justine smiled. "I wish more women had your attitude."

Lorraine shrugged, dismissing the compliment. "There are some things a woman should never allow." She went to a table in the far corner, pulled open a drawer, and brought out a pad of paper and a pen, talking as she wrote. "This is his new address. I've never even seen the place, so I can't tell you how to get there. But I think he said it was just south of the old high school—which is now an elementary school, of course."

"Thanks," Ella said taking the slip of paper.

Minutes later, after they were back on the road, Justine glanced at Ella. "She's holding something back. She didn't react at all when we mentioned that we were investigating a crime that might involve her husband."

"Yeah, I noticed that, too. She wasn't in the least bit curious about it, which indicates that she already knows."

"I wonder what's going on? Judging by the way she spoke about Andrew, my guess is that if she's holding out on us, it's to protect herself and the girls, not him."

"Let's see what we can get from Andrew," Ella said. "I intend to push him pretty hard now that we know about him and the dead woman." Ella realized that she too had avoided using Betty's name. Even though she didn't believe in the *chindi*, some habits died hard.

"Both Betty and Lorraine are meticulous housekeepers," Justine commented, apparently not noticing how Ella had avoided saying the dead woman's name.

"Maybe Andrew likes the domestic type. I guess that means you and I are in no danger of catching Mr. Talk's roaming eye," Ella joked.

"Thank fate for small mercies," Justine said, laughing.

The difference between the tiny stucco-and-wood frame house that Andrew rented and the one where his wife and daughters lived was like night and day. The exterior of this place was falling apart, with cracked plaster and faded paint. The shingles on the roof curled up at the ends, and several were missing. But then again, for the roof to leak New Mexico would need rain or snow, so Talk was in no immediate danger.

Ella knocked and a moment later Andrew Talk appeared at the door. He was her height, and wearing jeans and an open shirt despite the cold. She could smell whiskey on him and automatically took a step back. Justine caught her eye, having detected the alcohol as well. They were both on their guard now, watching him carefully.

"Mr. Talk, we need a few minutes of your time," Ella said, flashing her badge. Justine brought hers out as well.

He waved them in, slammed the door noisily behind them, and then walked slowly and unsteadily to the worn living room couch across the threadbare carpet. "What can I do for you?"

Though his eyes were bloodshot and the bottle on the small coffee table was nearly empty, his speech was clear. Ella, acting on experience, remained on her guard and was glad to see that Justine was standing near the door, her coat open to reveal her weapon. If he made an aggressive move, both would be in position to counter it.

"I need to know about your relationship with Betty Nez," Ella said, looking around the small room, trying to figure out where an odd smell was coming from. It reminded her of rotting leaves.

"My . . . what?" He'd started to slouch, but the name caught his attention and he sat up straight.

"We understand that you two were having an affair," Ella said.

For a moment he didn't answer, he simply stared at her. Then he glanced at Justine, who simply nodded.

Andrew recovered after a beat and leaned back, his gesture overly casual. "I have no idea what you're talking about. Betty does keyboard entry and clerical work at the tribal offices, and I work with her. She and I see each other every day, but it's strictly professional. Did my wife send you?" he added with a sneer.

"No, she didn't need to. But we did speak with her. That's how we found out where you're staying," Ella said.

He sat up, nodded, then leaned forward, resting his forearms on his knees as he spoke. "Then you probably know that my wife and I have some serious problems.

She kept the house, as is customary among the tribe, but maintaining her and my daughters there is taking every cent I make. I live here because it's all I can afford."

He pointed to the dirty wall. Tack holes and lighter rectangular outlines showed where posters had hung before. They were now replaced by two small, expensive-looking oak frames that looked completely out of place. "Those are my diplomas. I have two university degrees. The tribe paid for my schooling and I took the opportunity to attend Stanford and earn my MBA. I have a lot to offer this tribe, and I work every day to prove it. If Lorraine says that I'm a threat to the kids or something . . ."

Ella heard the barely concealed anger growing from his words, and saw his fists clench. She sat up and unbuttoned her coat. If she had to reach for her weapon, she wanted to be ready. "Just take it easy—relax." She smiled. "I told you, we're not here because of your wife. We want to know everything you can tell us about Betty."

"Why? Is there some trouble at work?" His eyes narrowed as if he were trying to focus carefully on what she was saying despite the cloud of alcohol numbing his senses.

"She was murdered."

"What?" He started to stand, bumped his knees against the coffee table, and knocked over the bottle. It fell to the carpet, unnoticed, spilling most of the whiskey still inside. Andrew sagged back onto the couch, scratching his head as tears started to form in his eyes. "No, that can't be right. I was just . . ."

"With her?" Ella finished for him.

Talk's face turned a sick gray color, and for a moment or two she could have sworn he was going to be throw up right then and there. If it was an act, he deserved the Academy Award.

He took several deep breaths, wiped the moisture from his eyes with the back of his hand, then managed to answer her, clearing his throat as he spoke. "Look, this puts a whole new slant on things. I wouldn't have said anything—for Betty's sake, not my own—but murder . . . How? Where? Are you sure?"

Ella nodded, not wanting to digress in order to get his story unrehearsed. "We already know you were having an affair with her, Mr. Talk," Ella said. "What I need to know now is did you see her earlier today, and when?"

"I was planning to. We'd both taken off work so we could go for a drive and talk. I'd intended to break up with her today, but I wanted to let her down easy, if I could. Betty is . . . was . . . a lonely woman. She was older than me by several years, and wanted more for herself than I could give her."

"Marriage?" Ella asked.

"Yeah. Lorraine and I have an understanding, kind of an open marriage without saying so. The difference is that in the past she never knew for sure if I was stepping out on her, and she would never ask. But this time, through no fault of mine, she found out about Betty."

Ella stared at him with the same interest she would have reserved for an insect that had crawled out from under a rock. She noticed Justine's scowl all the way across the room. "Did Betty tell her?"

"No, it's much worse than that." Andrew was quiet for several moments, staring at a wet spot on the carpet, not realizing or maybe not caring it was spilled whiskey. "Although I didn't know it at the time, someone had been tailing Betty and me—not Lorraine—and had taken some pretty revealing photos."

Talk looked around for the bottle, discovered it was on the floor, then picked it up without trying to pour himself a drink. "Whoever it is has been blackmailing me for weeks. I first got a call at work from a Navajo guy, at least that's what he sounded like. He told me that unless I did as I was told he would make sure my wife received some photos of Betty and me together in bed. He then described a few things to let me know he meant business."

He paused, ran a hand through his hair, then continued. "Betty and I . . . well, we did a lot of things that Lorraine would think of as perverted. If Lorraine saw those photos, I knew she'd never let me near our girls again. I asked the guy how much money it would take, but he just said he'd be in touch, then hung up. I heard from him again two days later."

"Wait a second. He called and told you he'd seen you and Betty, I get that. But how did you know that the guy actually had photos? Did you ask him for a sample?" Justine asked.

"He was kind enough to send me one," Talk said sarcastically. "I found it at the office on my desk in a plain brown envelope right before he called the second time." Andrew pressed his lips together tightly.

"It was a color shot and focused enough to show exactly who we were, and what was going on. My first thought was that Betty had set me up. After all, the photo was taken while we were at her house. But when I showed it to her, she almost passed out. She wasn't faking either. I don't think she'd ever seen a graphic photo like that in her life. Once she calmed down, we figured out that the man must have gotten up right next to the back window and used a telephoto lens." His hands clenched into tight fists. "I wanted to kill the slimeball."

"What did the blackmailer ask for the next time he called?" Ella asked.

"He still didn't want any money, and that took me by surprise. He said for me to wait, remember what he had on me, and that he'd be in touch just before the gaming issue came before the council. He said he'd instruct me how to vote at that time. If I didn't vote the way he wanted me to, then my wife would receive the photos."

"What did you do?" Ella prodded.

"I'm not stupid. I knew that if I gave in, he'd never stop blackmailing me, and I couldn't live that way." He stared soulfully at the empty glass on the coffee table by the bottle. "I thought about it, then went home that night and told my wife about the affair, hoping she'd forgive me. But she didn't." He paused for several minutes. "My marriage is wrecked, but they have no hold over me anymore."

"What about the photos?" Ella asked.

"Lorraine promised me that if she got them, she'd throw them away without looking at them—providing I don't contest the divorce. She'll get the house, and full custody of the girls. Everything."

"They could send the photos to the press," Ella said.

"They won't be able to print them. Admittedly, the story alone would damage my career, but it wouldn't destroy it. Many other politicians have survived scandal. But I don't think the blackmailer will go that route. The point has been made. I won't knuckle under and I'll vote the way I want on gaming. I'm even prepared to resign, if it comes to that."

"Where were you earlier this morning, say between eight and eleven?" Ella asked.

"I was driving around. I was supposed to meet with Betty, like I said, but I needed time to myself first so I could figure out what to say to her."

"Can anyone corroborate where you were? Did you stop at a coffee shop, or at a gas station, for instance?" Ella asked. "A liquor store or bar?"

He stared at her in surprise. "You can't seriously think I killed Betty!"

"Why not?" Ella countered calmly.

"I got rid of the blackmailer even though it cost me my marriage. Why on earth would I kill Betty after that?"

Ella looked directly at him. "Revenge for all the trouble the relationship created for you."

SIXTEEN
✕ ✕ ✕

Rose sat with Lena Clani at the kitchen table while her friend sipped herbal tea. The years had left a mark on both of them, but together they'd shared the joys and heartbreaks of life, and the bond of friendship had remained strong between them.

"You and I have been friends for many, many years," Lena said. "I know when something's troubling you. Let's talk it through like we always do."

"It's nothing. I'm just feeling old and tired tonight," Rose said slowly. Instinct and the experience that came with age told her that discussing what was bothering her with Lena would only end up putting her friend in danger, too.

Lena looked down at the tiny leaves at the bottom of her tea cup. "I understand not wanting to talk about a problem. Words have power and speaking of something can sometimes bring it to pass. But you're my friend and I want to help you."

"I'm facing some serious trouble, old friend. If I tell you what's going on, the people after me will come after you, too."

Lena reached out and patted Rose's hand. "No one has to know you said a word to me. It'll stay between the two of us."

Rose considered Lena's offer. She desperately wanted someone to talk to besides Ella, whose opinions seldom matched her own. "You'll have to be careful not to let on that you know any of this."

"That's not a problem. Now, tell me what's bothering you so much. It won't make your problems go away, but maybe they'll be easier to bear if the two of us shoulder the load."

Rose looked at Lena. Some friendships were beyond price. Lena was a stubborn, proud woman and maybe that was why they understood each other so well. They'd both spent their lives on the reservation, and their hearts were part of this land. Yet, with their children grown and husbands long gone, both had reached a crossroads. Being mothers and grandmothers was no longer enough to define them, to center their days, or even give them that elusive sense of purpose they both needed so much.

"I've angered some powerful people, old friend," Rose said slowly, and told her about the politician's visit and the controversy she'd stirred up.

Lena heard Rose's account without interrupting. When Rose finally stopped, Lena gave her a worried look. "So what do you plan to do now that you've got everyone's attention?"

"I won't back off—that much I know. In fact, if anything, I intend to be more vocal and public about my opinions. No one has the right to threaten me and think they can get away with it."

Lena gave her a long look, studying her expression, before responding. "Are you afraid?"

Rose hesitated, then nodded. "My enemies know that the way to hurt me is through my family. I'm willing to stand up to them, but I don't know how to protect my family and still do what needs to be done."

"Your daughter can protect herself. You know that. And she likes a good fight. She'll stand with you. And that's the way it should be. You'll always love your daughter, but you wouldn't respect her if you didn't think she was as strong as you are."

Rose smiled at Lena and nodded. "You know me so well. It's easy to talk to you. You see things in the same way I do. Most important of all, you understand what I'm fighting for. If we don't protect the Navajo way of life, it'll simply disappear."

Lena smiled slowly. "That's true enough, but that's not why you won't let this matter drop. There's a personal reason, too." Lena gave her friend a long, knowing look. "You won't back down from this fight because you're afraid that, if you do, it'll prove that old age means you're no longer useful, and that courage belongs only to the young."

"I won't deny what you've said, but there's more at stake here than my pride," Rose said. "I really believe that allowing gaming on the Rez is a huge mistake. The way we're going, the Navajo way of life will become like those plastic plants people put in their homes and on graves. A bad copy that just isn't the same—without roots and incapable of growth."

"So what will you do next?"

Rose smiled slowly. "I told you about the warning the politician gave me. Now I intend to send them one of my own."

"You're going to go stir up even more trouble, aren't you?" Lena leaned forward. "Okay, count me in. What's your plan?"

Rose's smile widened. "I'm going to wear traditional clothing—my long skirt, velvet blouse, and my silver-and-turquoise jewelry—then go to the fund-raiser the modernists are having at the old high school to launch their campaign promoting gaming on the reservation. I'm not going to contribute to their cause, mind you, but I want to be there for their business meeting."

"But you won't get anywhere with them if you go dressed like a traditionalist. In fact, you'll stick out like a sore thumb," Lena said, then stopped. "And, of course, that's exactly what you want."

"I don't intend to go so I can pick a fight. My being there will be statement enough. It'll make them think of what they're doing—and what they'll be giving up."

"But how will you get there? You can't grasp the steering wheel with your injured hand and driving with one hand is dangerous, especially on our bad roads."

"I was hoping you'd join me."

Lena smiled. "I have a little bit of a problem seeing clearly at night these days, but if you help me watch the road, we'll be okay."

"Then we're set. Come on. You can wear some of my things. We're still the same size."

Once they were dressed, Rose left Dawn with Jennifer, and set out with Lena. Although it was only six in the evening it was completely dark outside this time of year.

They drove slowly toward the main highway, Rose guiding her friend carefully.

"Stay in the middle of the road. There are several holes up ahead on my side," Rose said.

Lena managed to hit them all with unerring precision anyway, and Rose groaned as they bounced around. "Try to surprise me by missing a few of these ruts."

Lena muttered under her breath. "Be quiet, old woman."

"What's with the 'old woman'? I'm exactly your age."

"Yes, but I'm not the one complaining," Lena answered. "You do realize that you're going to make some of them very angry tonight. Are you sure you're prepared to deal with the fallout from that?"

"Sure I am." Rose laughed nervously when Lena gave her one of her skeptical looks. "I didn't say I wasn't scared. I said I could deal with it."

"Now I know where your daughter gets her courage—and her stubbornness," Lena said.

"That's the real curse in our family," Rose said with a wry grin.

Rose made sure the door slammed loudly behind her as she and Lena walked into the auxiliary gym now filled with at least two hundred men, women, and children. Everyone automatically looked back to see who'd just come in and a small rumble of disapproval went through the room as Rose's presence was noted. Even the speaker stopped.

Rose nodded to the speaker, who cleared his throat and continued. Although the crowd grew silent again, many were still watching the newcomers.

Rose had brought her cane—a reminder to people there of the accident a drunken driver had caused—and stood silently against the wall. Lena remained beside her, tall and proud.

A well-rounded Navajo man wearing a sports coat got out of his metal folding chair in the front row and approached them hesitantly. He had on a name tag that identified him as a host. "We're having a fund-raising meeting here," he whispered. "Are you lost?"

"No. Not at all," Rose said, her voice soft and sure.

"I think you must be," he insisted, this time his whisper a bit louder. "This is a meeting for those of us working to bring gaming to the Navajo Nation. I've heard that you're an opponent of gaming."

"I understood that this was a public meeting, and this is certainly a public building. I'm here to listen to what your people have to say." Rose matched his voice level with her own.

"They're here to spy," someone sitting close by hissed.

Rose couldn't see who'd spoken. It could have been any of a dozen sitting near that side of the gym. Instead of replying, she said nothing and remained standing where she was.

The speaker at the front stepped away from the podium, and waited. The meeting had come to a stop.

"I'm sorry, but you're disrupting our meeting," the man in the sports coat said, all thought of subtlety lost. "Would you please leave."

Rose felt no need to whisper either. "I've only spoken when spoken to first. Are you and the speaker so uncertain of your position and yourselves that you won't allow two old Navajo women to watch and listen?"

The man expelled his breath in a long whoosh, then looked at the speaker and shrugged.

"She has no business here," a woman near the front row said, standing and glancing toward Rose. "We can't speak freely with the opposition standing here listening."

Rose gave her a sad smile. "And that's the problem. You see me as 'opposition' instead of as another member of our tribe. Whether we stand for gaming or against it, we're all *Dineh*, and that puts us on the same side when in council."

"We are Navajos, as you say, but we're divided on this issue. Refusing to acknowledge that is pointless," Atsidi Benally said.

Rose recognized the white-haired man in the jeans and flannel shirt immediately. He taught the Navajo language at the college and until that very moment, she had believed he was a traditionalist.

As if reading her thoughts, he said, "I *am* a traditionalist, but necessity forces me to accept change."

Rose shook her head slowly. "We will lose more than we gain." To emphasize her point, she took a step forward, leaning awkwardly on her cane, using her uninjured hand.

"For the record, not all nontraditionalists want gaming," another woman said, standing up in the middle of the second row and turning to face the majority of those attending. "Quite honestly, I don't think bringing casinos and liquor onto the Rez is a good idea. There are too many drunk-driving accidents here already." She glanced at Rose. "I know you need a cane to help you walk because of what a drunken driver did to you. My own cousin was hit by a drunken driver while he was crossing the street in front of his own home. He was in the hospital for weeks. Like you, I came tonight for a chance to demonstrate my opposition."

The speaker called for order as a heated argument began between Atsidi and the last woman to speak over whether alcohol service was to be a part of the gaming proposal.

As the argument escalated, Rose glanced at Lena, nodded, and together they headed for the door quietly. "I've done what I came to do," Rose said as they began walking back to Lena's car. "They'll now have to consider the alcohol issue along with gaming, and their debate won't just ignore the facts that they don't want to face."

The car was a distance away and they walked slowly, but the night air was bitterly cold and by the time they reached Lena's old sedan they were both looking forward to the warmth of the heater. Lena opened the door for Rose, but they suddenly both jumped back. The seats were covered with what appeared to be ashes.

Lena shuddered, then forced herself to take a closer look. "This isn't skinwalker magic. These ashes aren't from bones or a body. It's just a nasty prank." As she brushed the black debris out onto the asphalt of the parking lot, she added, "It came from somebody's fireplace. There are pieces of wood still in it, and what looks like charred newspaper."

"Whoever it was probably didn't know enough about traditional beliefs," Rose said slowly, clearing away the black, sooty flakes with her handkerchief. "Had it been daytime, spilling ashes here would leave a trail for Poverty to find us. But by putting them out at night, ashes will help us scatter any evil."

"Let's get this off the seats and go home," Lena said. "I've had enough for one day."

"Me, too. But at least it ended well for us," Rose said, thinking about Ella and wondering how she was doing tonight.

Ella stood and walked casually around the dingy living room in Andrew Talk's rental house while he went to the bathroom.

"We're almost done here," she said, glancing over at Justine. "I just want to make sure we get all the information we can out of him before we leave."

"He's so scared I don't think he's holding anything back."

Andrew came back into the room, having washed his face, combed his hair, and tucked in his shirt so that he looked like a neat drunk rather than a sloppy one. Ella focused on him.

He stood tall, attempting to restore some lost dignity. "If I'd had something to do with Betty's death, I would have been smart enough to get myself a really good alibi. I wouldn't have left myself open like this. Give me credit for some intelligence."

"There are crimes of passion."

He waved his hand in the air, disgusted. "That's not my style. Talk to people who know me."

"Rest assured, I will," Ella said.

"What you really need to do is find out who was blackmailing me. Maybe Betty found out who he was and he killed her, or maybe he killed her to get revenge because I took away his hold on me. Or maybe he's trying to scare me into doing what he wants by letting me know I'm in danger now." Even as he said it, he looked over to the window, his voice starting to shake slightly. "Do you think I'm going to need police protection?"

"Unless you can prove you're in direct and immediate danger we can't give it to you. You should know from your position on the Tribal Council that we just don't have the manpower. But you shouldn't assume you're in danger—at least not yet. There's just not enough evidence to support it."

"That's easy for you to say. It's not your neck on the chopping block." He dropped down on the couch again, loosening his collar, which he had only buttoned a few minutes earlier. "Are you sure the police can't protect me?"

"We can step up the patrols around this area until we get a big call, but if you want a bodyguard you'll have to hire one yourself."

Concluding with Talk, who locked the door immediately behind them as they left, Ella and Justine walked out to their unmarked police unit. "We have to go back and question his wife again."

"Tonight?"

"Yeah. Did you have other plans?"

Justine shrugged. "I was supposed to meet Wilson, but he'll understand," she said flatly. "Do you think Lorraine did it?"

"I don't know, but she's high on my list of suspects right now. She's in good shape and is trained in martial arts. What I need to find out now is if this murder is simply the outcome of a domestic problem, or something greater."

"You think the circumstances were engineered to produce results?"

"Let's say I'm open to the possibility." Ella glanced at her watch. It was almost eight. She'd have given anything to call it a day and go home, but there was still work to do.

They drove back to Lorraine Talk's home in silence. Ella's thoughts were on Dawn when her cell phone rang, interrupting her musings. Ella picked it up and heard Kevin's voice.

"I've got a little free time this evening, and I'd like to come by and visit my daughter. Is that going to be a problem?"

"When?"

"I can arrive around eight-thirty. How about it?"

"Yeah, that's fine. I should be home by then and, with luck, she'll still be awake. But don't get her too excited playing, or she'll never go to sleep later."

"Okay." Kevin paused, then added, "I understand your mother caused quite a stir a little earlier tonight."

"Huh?" The comment took Ella by complete surprise.

She'd assumed Rose was at home. "What happened? What are you talking about?"

"You haven't heard? A patrolman had to go to the valley elementary school—the old high school—to quiet things down. One of the programing groups rented the auxiliary gym for a fund-raiser, and your mother showed up."

Had he told her that Rose had become a magazine centerfold, he couldn't have surprised her more. "My mother went *where*?"

"You heard me right. Oh, she didn't get arrested or really start anything. Apparently she brought up a few issues, people started arguing, and she left. People are saying that she must have cast some Navajo magic on them."

"Oh, please."

"I thought you knew about this already, Ella."

"I've been out working a case, Kevin. I don't keep up with every call from Dispatch," she said, then muttering a quick good-bye, broke the connection.

"What was that all about?"

She told Justine what Kevin had said.

"Your mother? Rabble-rousing? No way."

"I know, it threw me for a moment too. But if Mom did that, it was just to make them think. I'll never believe that she went there just to cause trouble." Yet even as she said it, she wondered what her mother's reasons had really been, and if she'd ever find out.

When they arrived at Lorraine Talk's house, the woman answered the door while talking to someone on a cordless phone. Lorraine gestured for them to come inside, then hung up quickly.

"We've just come from talking to your husband," Ella said.

"I know. That was him on the phone."

"You lied to us, Lorraine," Ella said flatly. "That's not a very smart thing to do."

Lorraine sat on the couch, tucking her legs under her. "I didn't lie to you."

"You said you didn't know if there was another woman."

"She's not a woman—she's a filthy slut."

Ella held her gaze. "Whatever you think about her, you're still a liar. Giving a false statement to a police officer during a capital investigation is a crime. We can take you to court, or jail."

"Even if I was just trying not to incriminate my children's father?"

Silence stretched out between them, but Ella waited. Justine sat back on the easy chair, stretching out as if she were just about to watch a movie on TV.

Lorraine stood, glanced down the hall toward the girls' room, then came back. "Look, I'll level with you," she whispered, returning to the couch. "Andrew had affairs from time to time. I've suspected it for years, but it didn't really matter to me because I knew he'd never leave me and his daughters. But this mess with the blackmailer . . . That's something else. I didn't want my daughters and me dragged through the mud."

"Do you think Andrew killed her?"

Her eyes widened. "You're not serious!"

Ella said nothing. She simply stared at the woman until she answered.

"That's absurd. It's one thing to have an affair—his male colleagues would consider that a plus or at least not a minus—but killing someone? No way. He loves status, and he loves his position on the Tribal Council. He wouldn't risk it over a woman—any woman."

"Exactly," Ella answered. "But what if Betty threatened to embarrass him publicly?"

"By showing the photos around?" She shrugged. "It would have hurt her more than him. His friends would have injured themselves trying to pat him on the back. Admittedly, it would have cost him some votes eventually—but he would have been working on what spin to put on it to make himself seem to be the unfortunate victim, instead of wasting his time with that woman."

"What about the embarrassment it might cause *you*? How do you feel about that?"

"I think Andrew should have kept his pants zipped," Lorraine snapped, "and it *is* an embarrassment to me, but I'll get my revenge when we go through divorce proceedings. Count on it."

"What were you doing this morning at around ten-thirty?"

"Now you think *I* did it?" She stared at Ella in disgust. "From ten to eleven I was meeting with the principal at my girls' elementary school, straightening out their health records, which the school nurse screwed up completely." Lorraine shook her head. "You're looking in the wrong direction. Any woman who has wild monkey sex with a married man and has someone else taking blackmail pictures of it is mixed up with some pretty sick people. If I were you, I'd find out who that woman was associating with."

"You don't think she was an innocent victim?" Justine observed.

"Innocent? Give me a break. An innocent woman doesn't have an affair with a man who's married and has two little girls. She was in on it from the beginning."

"You're that sure?"

Lorraine rolled her eyes. "If someone was outside your window taking photos, wouldn't you know it? I would, that's for sure."

"Maybe not if you were . . . distracted," Ella said diplomatically.

"Andrew's not that distracting. Believe me."

Ella saw Justine was biting her lip trying not to laugh, but mercifully Lorraine couldn't see her face. Ella stared at the carpet, forcing herself not to even crack a smile. "You're not planning to leave town anytime soon, are you?" she asked at last.

"What if I am?"

"If you do, then please check in at the station before you leave and let us know where you can be reached."

"Am I a suspect?" Lorraine challenged.

Ella met her gaze. "Yes."

SEVENTEEN

✖ ✖ ✖

By the time Ella got home she was exhausted, but as she walked through the door her daughter let out a shriek.

"Mommy!"

That one word energized her instantly. Although up to now Dawn had only used the Navajo word for *mother*, hours watching a children's educational show each morning had obviously taught her more Anglo words.

Rose gave Dawn a mild disapproving look, but Ella scooped up her child in her arms, and sat down on the couch, holding Dawn in her lap as Jennifer said good-bye, put on her coat, and left.

"So tell me what you did today!" Ella said, giving Dawn her full attention.

Her little girl was a bundle of squirming energy tonight. She gestured with her arms and spoke about Jennifer and playing ball, and all the little things that attested to an active day.

As Ella held her daughter, the job and all her worries about the investigation faded away. Being with her daughter soothed her soul. It was the best part of any day.

Ella got on the floor to play with Dawn's blocks and, distracted, forgot to tell Rose that Kevin was planning to drop by later on. At a quarter to nine they heard a car drive up and Ella quickly told Rose.

A moment later, he was at the door holding a huge present for Dawn. Seeing him, Dawn ran up to Kevin, arms open.

Kevin scooped her up with one hand and held her,

shutting the door behind him. "Hey, little pumpkin!"

"For me?" Dawn said, reaching for the box.

"It's a present. Do you want to see what's inside?" Kevin teased, holding it out of her grasp.

"Yes!"

Kevin set her down and gave her the box. Inside was a large set of interlocking Lego blocks with a barnyard theme. Ella studied the label, which said the pieces were for children from toddler to preschool age. She was glad to see that they were large and nothing her daughter could put in her mouth easily. "You really shouldn't bring her expensive presents so often. She has to accept you as her father, not as a Navajo Santa Claus."

"It makes me happy to buy her things." Kevin shrugged.

Ella sat down on the floor with Dawn, showing her how to fit the pieces together to make a corral for the pigs and cows, and a cart pulled by a pony.

Kevin sat on the couch, watching and offering encouragement and advice from a distance, like the county extension agent. Ella knew that children made him nervous, and when Dawn was active and happy as she was now, he didn't seem to know what to do with her. She wondered if maybe he considered child's play beneath his dignity.

Rose ambled off to the kitchen, annoyed that Kevin had showed up so close to Dawn's bedtime and mumbling about having all those pieces underfoot to trip on.

After she left, Kevin looked at Ella and exhaled softly. "Your mother doesn't think much of me, does she?"

"Do you want the truth?" Ella asked with a half grin.

"Never mind."

Dawn spent some time taking some of the smaller animals in and out of a red wagon pulled by a tractor, then started putting the pieces back into the storage box, one at a time, with a thunk. It was evident that Dawn was sleepy, and she knew she was supposed to pick up her toys before bed.

"I'm going to put her to bed," Ella said softly, lifting Dawn into her arms. The little girl fussed a little as Ella carried her to the room, but settled down when Ella brought over the stuffed dinosaur Dawn liked to sleep with.

Kevin had followed Ella to Dawn's room and seeing the mattress on the floor, scowled with disapproval. "I can't believe you haven't bought her a small bed of her own."

"Mother is a traditionalist. She didn't believe in cribs, either, and in this case she and I are in agreement. And Dawn is so active, I worry about her trying to climb out of bed in the morning when she wakes up before I do. Here she's safe. We have a childproof gate for her so she'll stay put at night. The rest of the room is safe as well," she said softly.

"She's going to live in a modern world, for heaven's sake, Ella, not sleep on the dirt floor of a hogan."

Ella shot him a cold look. "I know what's best for my daughter."

Kevin shook his head and watched as she tucked Dawn in and gave her a good-night kiss.

Ella glanced back, thinking Kevin would want to give his daughter a good-night kiss, too, but he remained at the doorway. Although she said nothing to him, it bothered her to think that he wasn't comfortable around his own child. Yet, what surprised her most was Dawn's quiet acceptance of her father's attitude. She hadn't expected nor asked for a kiss from him.

Ella led Kevin back down the hall. "She's a pretty cool kid, Kevin. You'd feel less awkward if you gave yourself and her a chance and lightened up a little."

"I've never been around kids much, even those of my relatives. I was the youngest in my family and even my cousins were older than me. But I'm getting better. Dawn and I get along fine."

Kevin followed her back into the living room, then

sat on the sofa. "I need to talk to you about something else for a few minutes."

"I'm listening," she said, sitting across from him in a comfortable stuffed chair. All the furniture was comfortable in her family's house, it occurred to her.

"I heard about the murder Councilman Talk's been implicated in," he said. "Word was going around after you visited his wife."

"And?"

"He's a key player in the gaming issue, Ella. So far he's straddled the fence, but the way things are shaping up it's possible he could end up with the swing vote. It's going to be close, and nobody knows if he's going to vote for or against tribal gaming."

"I don't understand what you're worried about. Are you afraid he'll get arrested and lose his place on the council before the vote comes up?" she asked.

"No, that's not it." He paused for a very long time. "The truth is that I don't think he had anything to do with what happened to Betty Nez," he said softly. "I think that they tried to blackmail him, and then killed his girlfriend when he wouldn't knuckle under. And what's even worse is that I have this feeling that the murder may have been committed by the same people who've been trying to intimidate me. I've been getting some veiled threats over E-mail and the phone."

"Who's threatening you, and why?" Ella asked, surprised that Kevin was opening up to her now.

He took a deep breath and then let it out slowly. "I've made some enemies, Ella, powerful ones. The progaming people are really angry with me because I'm suggesting one more referendum to let the entire tribe decide the fate of gaming on the Rez."

"You accepted financial support from the progaming people to help get elected. They expected your loyalty and your vote. Politics works that way, I'm told."

"They didn't buy me, Ella. They made a contribution because I was listening to their concerns and proposals.

But I have the right—the responsibility—to change my mind if I see fit."

He paused. "But in trying to evaluate all sides of this question fairly, I've created some major trouble for myself. The pressure is really coming down on me. Even my aide, Jefferson Blueeyes, is trying to get me to return to my original position on the issue."

"If you want a tribal referendum, and think it's best for the tribe, then stick to your guns," Ella concluded.

"The problem is that I'm still unsure of what the right thing is for the tribe. That's why I want to keep my options open. But the way things are now, if I ultimately decide that gaming *is* the way the tribe should go, the people who've been trying to intimidate me will conclude that their pressure tactics worked. That'll mean that every time they want something from me, they'll turn up the heat and make my life a living hell."

"I hate to state the obvious, but it's your own ambition that got you into this mess, Kevin. Organized crime and gambling are old friends. You should have expected a problem like this to crop up." She studied his expression carefully to see if he knew or had heard anything about the Indian mafia. When he didn't react, she added, "I'll try to help you out. As a cop, it's my duty."

"Thanks." He met her gaze. "You just can't understand what getting elected meant to me. I had to compromise and become a player to get where I wanted to be. It was the only way, Ella." He shook his head, looking away. "Your life is much simpler because the most you've ever aspired to is being a cop."

"And my being a cop is exactly what's put me in a position to help you. Ironic, isn't it, how we little people can also make a difference sometimes." She didn't wait for his answer. "Tell me something. Just how much do you know about Blueeyes? Could he be behind the threats?"

"I don't think so. He does his job, and tries to help me do mine. That's it."

"But you said he's progaming?"

"Yeah, he honestly believes our tribe is too poor not to take advantage of this opportunity. On a personal level, I agree with him."

"I don't get it. Then why did you change your position?"

"Because I represent the People, not myself. Anything that's going to impact on the reservation as much as a casino will should have the support of the majority of the tribe. A lot of my colleagues believe that once people see the money rolling in, everything will fall into place." He paused. "But I'm not sure."

"Are you just worried that you'll be voted out of office if gaming turns out to be plagued with skimming and corruption?" Ella pressed.

"This isn't about me, Ella. I honestly want to work for the good of the *entire* tribe, not just the businessmen or the unemployed. I know you think I'm in politics to make a name for myself and because I enjoy the power and prestige, and that's partly true. But there's more to it than that."

Ella wished she could ask him more directly about Blueeyes and his affiliations, but Kevin was smart and she couldn't take the chance. Until she was certain that he could be trusted, she just couldn't risk giving Kevin information that might be leaked to the wrong people.

"I'll do what I can for you, Kevin. The first thing I'm going to need is evidence of these threats so I'll have something to work with."

"None exists. I didn't record any of the phone calls, and I deleted the E-mails. The thing is, Ella, I don't want any of this to became public. It'll raise questions about certain contributions that'll just put some very powerful people in a bad light. I confided in you because I felt you should know in case things get . . . more serious." He met her gaze and held it.

"You're tying my hands, Kevin."

"Do your best. And just so you know, I don't expect

you to give it priority. I'm aware that you've got problems of your own right now with that sniper out gunning for you. A fifty-caliber bullet won't just put you in the hospital."

"I know. That's why I'm wearing special armor these days. Don't worry. Harry is searching for Manyfarms and he's a good man. I have no doubt he'll get the job done."

Kevin's eyes narrowed when she mentioned Harry. "Will he be leaving after that?"

"Yes, probably, but I don't really know what his plans are," Ella said.

There was a flicker of relief in Kevin's eyes. "Let me know if there's anything I can do from my end of things to help you. I'll be there for you, Ella, if you need me."

He sounded sincere, but Kevin had become the ultimate politician. Almost everything he said sounded heartfelt, whether it was or not.

Ella led him to the door. "I'm beat. Do you mind if we call it a night?"

"No problem." Kevin stopped by the door and, for a moment, Ella thought he was thinking of kissing her.

She stepped back. " 'Night."

As he stepped off the porch Ella closed the door. Kevin never ceased to surprise her, but renewing their relationship was the furthest thing from her mind.

After locking the doors, Ella went to her room. Two was asleep in the hall and Rose was already in bed. The house was quiet and she was exhausted. Ella glanced at the computer. She just didn't have the energy for it tonight. Crawling into bed and snuggling deep under the covers, she fell asleep minutes after her head hit the pillow.

Ella woke up shortly after sunrise, rested, and ready to face the new day. The sun was creeping over the horizon and the faint early morning rays filtered through the curtains. After showering and dressing, she sat down in front of her computer, and switched it on. She hadn't heard from Coyote recently and she was starting to worry about him.

Ella answered E-mail from friends out of state, then as she was about to log off, an instant message flashed onto the screen.

"I was hoping you'd be there early this morning. You didn't log on last night," Coyote wrote.

"Long day yesterday," she typed back. "Do you have any news for me?"

"I'm close to identifying some of the Indian mafia who are working from inside the Rez. Hope to have something for you soon."

She answered quickly. "Some of our politicians are being strong-armed. Things are getting worse. Can you give me anything I can use now?"

There was a long pause before an answer flashed on the screen. "I have reason to believe that Manyfarms may have obtained the support of the Indian syndicate since you're a threat to them as well as him. But if Manyfarms fails, they will probably hire a second person to come after you."

Ella felt a touch of fear creeping up her spine. Times were tough and it wouldn't be hard to find someone willing to kill a cop if the payoff was big enough.

Suddenly Dawn rushed into the room, Rose right behind her. "She's up early today and she wants to play with you."

"Give me one more minute, okay, short stuff?" she asked her daughter.

Dawn made a pouty face, and her lower lip shot out. That meant tears would begin to flow any second now and Ella recanted.

"Okay, little monster, sit on my lap then, but be very quiet until I finish my work. Agreed?"

Dawn nodded somberly and Ella knew she'd do her best, but asking a two-year-old to be still was asking for a miracle.

As Dawn settled on her lap, and Ella took another

look at the last message Coyote had sent, she shuddered involuntarily.

Feeling it, Dawn looked up at her, concerned.

Ella smiled to reassure her that everything was okay, then shook her head. "Shhh." Concentrating on the keyboard, she answered Coyote.

"Your warning is a wake-up call for me," she typed. "I'll be on the lookout."

"One more thing. The murder of the councilman's girlfriend is their handiwork. I'm trying to get proof right now."

Ella stared at the screen, holding her little girl against her with one hand and trying to type with the other.

"Get me what you can, and I'll move on it."

"Be careful," Coyote wrote, signing off.

Ella toggled the print command, and then placed the sheet of paper that came from the printer into a folder. She'd take it to Big Ed. Maybe together they could come up with a viable strategy. One thing was clear. She couldn't take Dawn anywhere outside the house with her. It would only expose her child to the same danger she was facing.

Dawn, as if sensing something was wrong, shifted slightly and laid her head against her mother's breast. "*Shimá* sad?"

"No, sweetie, I'm just worried about work."

Jennifer walked into the room after knocking on the open door. "Shall I take her now for breakfast?"

"Please," Ella said, her mind still on Coyote's warning.

Dawn slid down her legs and rushed to Jennifer. "Pick up!"

Jennifer laughed and scooped Dawn up in her arms. As they walked out of the room, Ella watched. Her daughter obviously enjoyed Jennifer's company. She felt a twinge of jealousy, but before she had the luxury to indulge the feeling, Rose came back in.

"Your daughter is getting too fond of my friend's

granddaughter," Rose complained. "Maybe you should say something. Your daughter shouldn't be so quick to trust strangers."

"Mom, she's two years old. The entire world is her friend unless they do something to hurt her feelings."

"I just don't like this," Rose said in a whisper. "A week ago, I was the person she turned to when you weren't home. Now it seems your daughter prefers that girl over both of us."

"We need her here, Mom. We should be grateful we have her, and that my little pumpkin is happy."

Rose nodded reluctantly and left her daughter's room. Alone, Ella picked up the phone, checked her notebook for Jimmy Frank's cell phone number, then dialed it. He answered on the first ring.

"I don't mean to rush things, but do you have anything on Blueeyes yet?"

"I've been with him from dawn till late night, but from what I've seen, this guy is a straight arrow. He arrives at work early and stays until late. So far, his meetings have been all business and Kevin's usually along—well, except for last night. The subject spent a grand total of ten minutes in an East Main bar in Farmington. I followed him in, he talked to a dark-haired woman long enough to have a half a beer, then he left and went home to his trailer house alone."

"Any idea who the woman was?"

"No. I asked around as casually as I could, but I couldn't find out anything, even from the waitress who'd served them. She looked Indian to me, but I'm certain she's not Navajo."

"Stay on the job today and tomorrow and keep me posted," Ella said, then hung up.

"Hurry, or you won't have time for breakfast," Rose said, returning to check on Ella.

"Mom, I need to talk to you alone for a second. Exactly what happened last night before I got home?"

"What do you mean?" Rose asked innocently.

"Mother, don't," Ella said. "Why did you go to that meeting? You caused a lot of trouble. A patrolman was called out because people got ugly after you left. People are now saying that you did some kind of magic to make them turn on one another. That type of talk is the last thing I need right now."

"I won't stop doing what I see as my responsibility to our tribe just to avoid silly gossip. I wouldn't expect that of you, daughter, so please don't expect it from me."

"Just tell me what happened," Ella said, mollified.

Rose did, then ended by telling her about the ashes they'd found in Lena's car.

"That must have really surprised both of you," Ella said.

"It did, but it wasn't a big deal, not like—" Rose looked away.

Ella eyes narrowed. "Like what? Finish it, Mom."

Rose stared at an indeterminate spot across the room. "Never mind."

"No, Mom, I have to know."

Rose sighed, then told her about tribal councilman Ronald Etcitty's visit. "It was unpleasant. He wanted to frighten me, but he wasn't openly hostile or threatening. It was more like he was explaining the facts in the most negative way possible."

Ella battled the anger that threatened to erupt inside her. There was no way she'd allow anyone to come to her home and try to intimidate her family. Yet, she'd have to tread carefully. Everything he'd said was true— the only thing really open to question was his intent. "I'm going to pay that councilman a visit, Mom. I'll handle this."

"Don't you dare," Rose said. "This is *my* fight, and I won't have you interfering. He will not get what he wants, and that's enough. Your job is to make sure his predictions don't come true."

Ella stared at Rose in surprise. She couldn't remember

the last time her mother had raised her voice. "Mom, I can't allow him to—"

"*You* are not involved." Rose paused and took a deep breath. "This politician told me the truth as he saw it. Granted, it was worded in a way intended to scare me, but he made no illegal threats. How I respond to him is up to me."

The phone rang and Ella started to reach for it, but Rose shook her head. "It's for me."

Ella stared in amazement at her mother, then slowly smiled. Rose had come into her own, and no one was going to stand in her way, certainly not her own daughter.

Proud of her mother, Ella closed the door, giving Rose her privacy. At work, Ella was a woman with a certain amount of authority, but at home she was just Rose's daughter and Dawn's mom. And for now, all she needed to think about was having breakfast with her daughter.

Ella sat in Big Ed's office as he read the printout of her exchange with Coyote earlier that morning. His concentration was evident in the fact that he wasn't rocking back and forth in his chair.

"You could come under fire without any warning, at any time, indoors and out. I don't like this, Shorty."

"Cops are always targets, that's nothing really new. And there's nothing we can do about it except stay on our toes. But I'm going to warn Justine and the others and let them know what's going on."

"Good idea. Your partner, in particular, needs to know. I know she's been looking out for you, but this will put her on guard everywhere you go together. At least Blalock and the FBI finally came up with those special vests. Every member of the SI team will be picking one up when they report for duty today." He paused. "On another matter, have you seen Farmington's morning paper?"

"No, not yet." She braced herself, thinking he was probably referring to another article about her mother.

"Andrew Talk resigned his Tribal Council position. He made a statement to the press explaining that he was being blackmailed to vote a particular way on the gaming issue, and he would not allow himself to be put in that situation. He assured the tribe that he'd never cast any previous votes while under coercion and would never do so. He also blamed the typist's death on the blackmailer."

"Did he reveal why he was being blackmailed?"

"He called it a 'momentary indiscretion' and said that one mistake wouldn't compel him to make an even greater one." Big Ed paused. "He'll probably come out of this okay politically, and maybe pick up a few supporters because of his honesty."

"I should go talk to him. If he resigned, maybe it was the blackmailer's idea, not his. I'd like to know exactly why he did this now."

"He's in Farmington at the moment. He called me this morning to say that he was afraid they'd go after his wife and daughters next, so he rented a condo for them in one of those gated communities. He'll be there all day with his family, but he asked that you don't divulge his family's whereabouts and, if you have to speak with him, that you be careful no one follows you." Big Ed slipped her a piece of paper with the address and telephone number.

"I wonder if he resigned because he wanted to put a different spin on things, or because he was really afraid for his family?" Ella asked as an afterthought.

"Find out, Shorty. But now we have a new problem. The shady people trying to lean on our politicians have suddenly had a spotlight shined on them. They may retaliate in some way and we've got to be ready for that. The stakes just got higher."

"I know. Those vests couldn't have come at a better time." Ella stood. "I'll get to Farmington and see if Talk has anything to tell me."

"Keep me posted."

Ella stopped by her office, and seconds after she sat down, Justine came in, displaying the special vest like a model on a fashion show runway. "Well, what do you think of the new winter look for plainclothes cops?" Justine teased.

"It's so *you*." Ella nodded enthusiastically. "Just don't leave home without it. Do you have anything new on Betty Nez's murder yet?" Ella grew serious.

"No. The formal autopsy report hasn't come in yet, and the only prints we found in her house were her own, her daughter's, and Talk'g. The salt shaker we took from the table had been wiped clean."

"Talk still has no alibi, so he remains a suspect. Did any of the neighbors report seeing anyone at the Nez house that morning?"

"No, and we've now had a chance to speak to everyone in that area. The problem is that most of them work and were gone. It was too early for someone coming home for lunch to see anything."

"Perfect timing for our killer."

Justine nodded. "Big Ed just buzzed and said you wanted to talk to me."

Ella smiled. The chief knew how to motivate her without saying a word. "Yeah. We've got problems." She told Justine about the increased danger of attack.

"I'll keep my eyes wide open, Ella, wherever we are. Just remember to keep wearing your own vest."

The look that passed between them spoke volumes. They both knew that bulletproof vests . . . weren't.

"Come on, I want to go talk to Lorraine and Andrew Talk again. I'll fill you in on the way," Ella said, grabbing her keys and tossing them to Justine.

As they drove to Farmington, Ella telephoned Andrew using the number the chief had given her. "We're coming to speak with you again."

"Fine, but don't come to the . . . here," he said quickly. "This is my wife's home now and I want it to be a safe place for her and the girls. If someone follows you . . ."

"No one will."

"I can't take that chance," he said flatly. "I'll meet you at the coffee shop in the mall on West Main."

"All right."

Ella passed the information on to Justine. "I want to find out why he gave that statement to the press. It was my impression he wasn't going to resign unless he had no other alternative. If the blackmailer contacted him again we need to know."

"Do you think that's what happened?"

Ella shook her head. "I have a feeling he's playing us—and the voters."

"What he pulled was pretty convenient for him," Justine agreed. "Let's see what he has to say about it."

By the time they arrived at the coffee shop, Andrew Talk was already there. He was wearing a baseball cap that shaded his face, and he'd traded his office clothes for a nylon ski jacket and jeans. He waved at them from a corner booth as they came in the front door.

"I'm glad you picked a booth where we can have some privacy," Ella said, sitting down and ordering some coffee from the waitress. "And I notice you're dressing down."

"And you two must shop at the same store." He noted their matching dark blue vests, which outwardly looked like casual winter garb.

Talk waited until the waitress had refilled his cup and taken their order for coffee before he continued. "I figured you'd want to talk to me after you heard the news. That's why I told Big Ed where I'd be."

"We appreciate that. Now tell me what happened. What prompted your sudden resignation?"

Talk expelled his breath in a soft whoosh. "There was no new threat, but the more I thought about it, the more I realized I had to do something positive. My priority is the tribe, and I felt that the public needed to know the kinds of people involved in this divisive issue. If they tried to blackmail me, you can bet they're doing the same thing to some of the others, too. The *Dineh* needed to know that. Maybe this will force the weasels who are trying these strong-arm tactics to back off. If it does, then it was worth the cost."

"You speak of 'they.' What makes you think that there are others involved in the blackmail, and not just one guy with a camera?" Ella asked.

Talk hesitated. "I'm not at liberty to say."

"You've spoken to some of the other council members, haven't you?" Ella's gaze grew hard. "Don't you dare pull this 'honor the good-ole-boy network' bull. I'm investigating extortion, murder, and now political corruption. If you insist on playing games with me, you're going to be slapped with obstruction of justice. Am I making myself very clear?"

"Extremely," Andrew said coldly. He paused, considering his words carefully. "I have reason to believe that there's at least one more member of the council who's being blackmailed. I don't have any evidence to prove it, but I've heard a rumor that a pueblo woman has been passing the threats along to the councilman via meetings with his aide. These meetings are short and usually clandestine."

Ella knew Andrew was talking about Blueeyes and Kevin. Nevertheless, she went through the motions. "Who's the councilman?"

"The rumors haven't been specific about that."

"Then tell me who you suspect. Is it someone local, or are we talking about a councilman from the Arizona side of the Rez?"

He shook his head. "It's your job to uncover what's going on. I've helped you all I can." Andrew stood up and tossed several bills on the table. "And from now on, stay away from my family."

"I may still have to talk to your wife."

"Then meet with her at our attorney's office," he said

flatly, then looked through his wallet, picked out a business card, and threw it on the table. "She told me the kind of questions you asked her. I won't have you talking to her again unless an attorney is present."

"Why are you so worried—if you have nothing to hide?"

"I'm a politician. I've learned never to underestimate the danger someone bucking for promotion can pose and the depths to which they can sink."

Talk strode off before Ella could answer.

Justine looked at Ella. "You really pissed him off."

"That I did."

"But you know what, boss? I don't think he killed Betty Nez. On the other hand, it's pretty obvious he's playing games. His resignation seems to be more political maneuvering than anything else. He's probably hoping that after all's said and done, he'll come out looking like the tribe's savior, and his constituents will be begging for him to run for office."

Ella smiled. "What a cynic. I didn't think you had it in you, cousin."

"One of the first things you learn as a cop is that if you assume the worst, you'll probably be right." Justine stopped and added, "Of course, you also learn other useful things, like placing a gun back in the holster with your finger on the trigger will cause you to walk with a limp."

Ella laughed and stood, ready to leave. Then, out of the corner of her eye, she saw three men entering the coffee shop. She smiled immediately, recognizing the man leading the way. It was her old boss from L.A., Special-Agent-in-Charge Henry Estrada. She stepped in his direction, then stopped and turned away as she realized that the two Indian men with him weren't Navajos or people she recognized.

"What's up?" Justine asked softly.

Ella shook her head and walked to the cash register, trying to come across as casual. Henry had avoided looking directly at her, yet he knew she was there. The answer to his strange behavior came to her suddenly, making her heart pound frantically and her palms break out in sweat. Henry Estrada was Coyote.

As she stood at the cash register, Ella looked around the room indifferently, careful not to let her excitement show in any way. She wanted to identify the men with Henry, but one had his back to her and the other wore a cowboy hat that cast a shadow over his features. The only part of his face she could see clearly, his cheek, showed deep pockmarks. Henry was keeping watch while the other two men talked, behaving as if he were providing security.

As soon as they stepped outside, Justine looked at Ella. "What's up? Is there something I should know about the three who came in just as we were leaving the booth?"

She didn't want to tell Justine what she knew about Coyote yet, so she answered cautiously. "I couldn't see them clearly, but I saw enough to know that the one wearing the jeans, a leather sport coat, and expensive cowboy hat had pockmarks on his face. All in all he fits the description of the man who hired the two Anglos we arrested. Remember my report?"

Justine nodded. "Let me go back inside. I can get a closer look as I pretend to leave a better tip at our table."

Ella shook her head. She knew it would be too risky with Henry inside. "They may have seen our weapons and made us as cops. I've got a better plan. Let's drive a little farther away, then stake out the shop. We'll get their license plates as soon as they return to their vehicle or vehicles. Then we'll follow the guy with the pock-marked face."

EIGHTEEN

✖ ✖ ✖

They waited for nearly an hour, but their patience finally paid off. Seeing all three men get into the same gray vehicle, Ella called in the license plate.

"The vehicle belongs to Four Corners Rental," Dispatch told her within two minutes.

"Ten-four." Ella glanced around the street, but there was very little traffic. "Follow them, Justine, but hang way back. There aren't that many cars around to blend in with."

"If I stay back, we may lose them."

"We have to take the chance," Ella advised. "We can't risk getting any closer, not without having them make us. But it looks as though they're heading for Shiprock, and there's only one direct route. We may have gotten lucky."

They drove out from the edge of the city on the main highway, heading west toward the Rez. Justine hung back, and Ella kept her eyes glued on the sedan a half mile or more ahead, determined to get a lead without compromising Coyote.

For the next ten minutes they kept at least one vehicle between them and the sedan, but then Justine had to hit the brakes and almost come to a stop to avoid a gasoline truck pulling out in front of them at Kirtland, a farming community east of Shiprock. As they waited for a chance to get around the slowly accelerating truck, with a plodding van in the passing lane, the sedan disappeared over the next hill.

By the time Justine reached the crest of the hill, the

sedan was gone. Realizing the vehicle must have turned off onto one of the side roads, they headed south and drove into a residential area along the old two-lane highway.

"They couldn't have made us," Justine said, unable to spot the sedan anywhere. "We were too far behind."

"They may have suspected we were here," Ella said, "or normally take circuitous routes and backtrack to throw off any potential tails. We underestimated them." She wondered if Henry, worried that she'd compromise him, had tipped them off. He may have noticed the tribal unit behind them despite its being unmarked. He never missed much, as she recalled, and he was driving the other two.

"Do you realize where we are?" Justine asked suddenly.

Ella glanced around and smiled. "We're near George Branch's house. Now, this is an interesting turn of events. Let's make a pass by his place."

"We're still out of our jurisdiction," Justine warned.

"Do it anyway."

They passed by the small farmhouse just east of the reservation line a short time later, but although the flashy SUV the radio personality drove was there, the sedan they'd been following was nowhere in sight.

"Drive back toward Kirtland on the old road along the river valley," Ella said, frustrated. "Maybe we'll get lucky."

Though they were thorough, the search proved futile, and by the time they were on their way back to the Rez both of them had lapsed into a heavy silence that continued until they arrived at the station.

It was two o'clock in the afternoon, and having skipped lunch, Ella stopped by the machines in the lobby and got a prepackaged sandwich. Although they always tasted like the cellophane they came wrapped in, it was better than nothing.

Back at her desk, Ella checked with the car rental

company and learned that they didn't own a gray sedan the make and model she described, only white ones. The rental sticker and the license plate turned out to have been stolen from one of their vehicles. The news didn't surprise her. Somehow she'd expected them to throw her a curveball.

Justine came in a moment later and Ella filled her in.

"Figures," Justine muttered. "Talk about a useless lead. Should we put out a bulletin on the car?"

Ella shook her head. "Try it, but only by word of mouth, land line, or cell phone, even if it takes a while. They've probably already changed the tags again, or dumped the vehicle. And make sure our officers don't move in if they do find these guys. We want more on them than auto theft."

Ella leaned back in her chair, mulling over the morning's events as Justine put out the report. As soon as Justine was finished, Ella glanced at her. "You came to tell me something. What's up?"

"I wanted to let you know that I'll be away for a few hours."

"How come?"

"I'm going to the pistol range and see if I can qualify with my weapon."

Ella nodded. "Have you had any time to practice?"

"Some," she said. "And I've been doing a lot of dry firing to get comfortable with my new grip. But if I don't feel ready after I get there, or I have a bad day, Sergeant Hobson will let me try again in a few weeks."

"Just do your best, Justine. I know you can do it. Just let your natural confidence take over."

Ten minutes later, Ella was working at her desk when a call came in through her cell phone.

"You know who this is, right?" a man's voice asked.

"Coyote," she said, instantly recognizing Henry's voice, but not wanting to use his name in case he was using an unsecured phone.

"Exactly. Thanks for not tipping my hand today."

"It was one heck of a surprise," she said honestly. Now she knew for sure how Coyote had known so much about her past and her days in the FBI, and also how he knew her unlisted cell number. "Have you got something new for me?"

"Not yet. But I need you to back off. Don't try to find me. Things are tense right now, and one slip is all it'll take to get me killed. In fact—" There was a long pause, then a hurried, "Gotta go."

Ella heard the sudden change in his voice, but there was no time to ask him what was wrong before he hung up. Telling herself that he knew where to find her, and that he was smart enough to request emergency backup if he needed it, she forced herself to try to relax.

Henry—Coyote—probably didn't know the real names of the men he was with, and they obviously didn't know his. Her guess was that he'd put himself in a position to be recruited as a bodyguard and muscle, which explained both his behavior in the coffee shop and his lack of specific knowledge about their plans.

In the meantime, she had a job to do. Ella drove to Agent Blalock's new office. Now that the tribe had given him a suite in the tribal offices building, he was easier to reach.

He sat behind his desk, sorting through a stack of files at least two feet tall.

"Why don't you file some of those, Dwayne? You'd be able to track down the ones you need a lot faster."

He looked up and gave her a grin. "They *were* filed, but I'm trying to put a crime report together for the Bureau. These reports are a pain in the butt. They want statistics that I never have just so some bean counter can put the data into a computer, then hide it in an obscure file no one will ever read."

She sat down across his desk. "At least the Bureau gave you a fancy new office to work in."

"Yeah, but you didn't come to compliment the decor," he said, watching her. "What's going on?"

She met his gaze and held it. "I wish I'd only come to thank you for getting the vests for my team, but I didn't. I just experienced something that made me realize that you and Paycheck have been holding back on me. Paycheck's not here now, so how about giving me some information off the record?"

"What do you need?"

"You're being passed information by the same guy who's been helping me, right?"

Blalock regarded her thoughtfully. "I wondered how long it would take before you asked me that."

Ella watched him wrestling between Bureau procedures and his own instincts. It was a familiar battle. All cops, federal and local, were buried under a ton of rules and regulations but, in some cases, bending the rules became critical to a favorable outcome.

"What I tell you stays strictly between us, clear? Someone's neck is on the line, and he's been given a long leash so backup can't be there to help him out if he's made."

Ella nodded.

"Our contact goes by the name of Trickster."

"I know him as Coyote. Same thing, really, at least if you ask a Navajo."

"I know his identity, and I can tell you that he's a good man, but he's in pretty deep on this case. He's been offered the chance to bail a few times already but he didn't take it, and now I'm afraid that his luck may be about to run out."

"I know who he is, too," Ella said. "I saw him today by accident. At least I didn't give him away."

Blalock nodded slowly. "He wants to dig up details on the latest scam the syndicate is brewing before he breaks cover. Apparently they've decided to pull out all the stops. No more penny-ante outhouse explosions or busting windshields. They intend to kick something into motion that will make the scandal Talk laid out in the paper seem like a wedgie by comparison."

Ella sat up. "Does he have any idea what it is?"

"Not yet. Apparently the people he's dealing with suspect that they've got a traitor in their midst and they're all watching each other now, waiting for a slipup."

"Coyote's definitely playing a dangerous game," Ella said, still protecting him as had Blalock by never mentioning his name.

Blalock nodded. "I'm expecting to hear from him again soon, but there's no way of knowing how much advance notice we'll have to stop whatever's going to happen. That's why I've stuck real close to my desk and my computer lately."

"If you hear before I do, pass the word to me as soon as you can."

"Count on it. And vice versa, Ella. You know you've got backup here, not just thicker vests."

"Thanks."

Blalock looked at her as she stood. "Where are you headed now?"

"I'm not going to wait for Coyote to get in touch. I'm going to try and figure out what the syndicate's next move is going to be. If it's that big, there should be telltale rumblings somewhere."

Ella went out to her unit, lost in thought. There was only one person she was certain would know if something was brewing that involved Navajos. Without hesitation, she switched on the ignition and drove to her brother, Clifford's, house.

The sun had already set and the moon was bright in the clear deep purple sky as she drove south down Highway 666, occasionally gazing at the mountains off to the west beyond Shiprock. She'd never thought about them much when she'd been a kid living on the Rez; they'd always been there, hazy blue in the summer and a cold gray-green in the winter.

But these days she could feel the comfort that living within the shadow of the sacred mountains brought to her people. Even in times of trouble, their heights were a sign of strength and things that endure. The tall peaks and long ridges were a part of the *Dineh*, who carried their soil in medicine bundles and offered prayers to them.

As she drove up the narrow trail that led to her brother's house and medicine hogan, she caught sight of the white cloud rising from the hogan's smoke hole, and saw a saddled horse tied up to the simple hitching post not far away.

Ella parked the SUV so that it was visible from the entrance and waited. Soon she saw her brother emerge, and a man she guessed was his patient unfastened the rope that tethered the horse, slipped easily onto the saddle, then rode away as if glued to the animal.

Seeing Clifford waving for her to enter, she climbed out of the unit and went inside.

"I couldn't see his face, but from the way he got on that horse the man had to be of the Red House Clan," Ella said with a smile. "Families from that outfit," Ella said, using the word Navajos preferred when referring to neighboring family groups, "always seem to do well at the rodeos."

"They do have a way with horses," Clifford agreed with a nod. "And you're right. It was one of them, the grandfather who lives over by Big Gap," he added. "Age hasn't affected him much. He's just as active as any of his sons or grandsons."

Ella sat down on the sheepskin rug. "There's always an incredible sense of peace in your medicine hogan," she said quietly, staring at the fire.

He sat across from her. "Then rest here awhile. You live and work in a very troubled world."

"So do you, *hataalii.*"

"Yes, but peace always surrounds my work. I don't think you can say that about yours."

"No, I can't," Ella admitted. For a long time she said nothing and Clifford didn't interrupt her thoughts. "I'm in trouble, brother," she said at last.

"How can I help?"

"The tribe's enemies have something in the works and, unless I find out what it is and who the players are, I won't be able to stop them."

"I've felt the stirrings around me. Even the Fierce Ones can't control or influence what's been happening."

"What's going on since I talked to you last? You have all been silent for months."

"There's been a serious split. I could see it coming, and that's the main reason I stayed with them. The Fierce Ones started out as a vigilante group that would enforce traditional laws and codes of conduct—like forcing adults to keep better track of their kids. Now there's a group within the group who believe it's time for the Fierce Ones to accept a new mandate. They support gaming as a way to ease the Navajo people's financial crisis—but they want to make sure they're in a position to oversee everything so that corruption doesn't get a foothold. This new agenda has really divided us, and as long as we're fighting among ourselves, we aren't much good to anyone else."

"Tell me something—do you think this new agenda was something the splinter group adopted because of outside influences?" Ella asked.

"You mean were they manipulated or pressured into accepting gaming?" Clifford shrugged. "Yes, but only by the times. People need to find answers that'll put food on their tables and keep their houses warm."

"I'm beginning to think that gaming's our only short-term option. I can't think of another way to stop this cycle of poverty, can you?" Ella mused, not really expecting an answer.

"Our mother brought up a suggestion," he said.

"At a meeting of the Fierce Ones?" She'd really thought that nothing her mother could do would surprise her anymore. Now she realized she'd been wrong.

Clifford laughed. "No, she's not a member of the

Fierce Ones. She mentioned it to me, and I passed on the suggestion to the others."

Ella breathed easier. "What was it?"

"She wants to set up a vast Internet site."

"Mom said *that*?"

Clifford laughed. "Yeah, it surprised me, too. But apparently she'd been watching you go on-line and surf the waves or whatever they call it."

Ella chuckled. "This conversation seems really strange, considering our surroundings," she said, glancing around the hogan.

Clifford nodded. "Keeping the old, but embracing the new. That's what we're all going to have to do, it seems. I shudder to think that the new traditionalists may have stumbled on the right path for the tribe to take."

"I wouldn't go that far yet. So tell me about the Internet idea."

"Mom thinks the tribe should operate it and provide Navajo artists and craftsmen with a worldwide outlet for their work. In return, a percentage of everything that was sold would go back to the tribe."

"I don't think that'll bring in enough revenue."

"She also suggested we take tribal treasures, like our best jewelry, art, and historical items and have some of our people accompany them on a worldwide tour of museums at every major city. The admission would also create revenue for the tribe."

"I'm impressed. Mom's really been thinking things through."

"Wait, there's more." Clifford looked at his sister. "Brace yourself. It suggests that our mother is not one hundred percent traditionalist after all."

Ella looked at him with an expectant grin.

"She read that the Russian air force is raising money to pay their bills by allowing people to come and ride in their war planes and charging them incredible sums of money. That gave her an idea. She wants to charge substantial fees and invite people to come in and see what it's like to live in a hogan for a day or two, cleanse themselves in sweat lodges, or go visit a sacred site, or even be allowed to attend a three- or four-day Sing, following all the ritual precautions, of course.

"Then she said that she learned this is actually being done on the Arizona side of the Rez, at least by a few Navajos. Mom said that as long as the guests are required to follow our customs during their visit, that at least the outsiders are getting an education for their money. They'll be learning instead of simply losing their money to gambling."

Ella stared at her brother, as surprised as if he'd told her that Rose had decided to spike her hair and dye it pink. "Okay. Promoting tourism? That settles it. Our mother was abducted by aliens. The woman posing as her is an imposter. We need to take her back to Roswell and make the exchange."

Clifford laughed. "For years she spent all her time taking care of Dad and of us, but did you know that as a young woman she was always active in tribal business? Not politics, no, but teaching others how to treat certain illnesses with Native herbs, helping to train midwives, and making sure that the companies that tore up our land, like the uranium companies, restored what they'd destroyed? Of course the damage from that is something we're all still paying for. Many Navajos have become ill as a result of radiation poisoning from the waste that contaminated our waters. But Mom and others like her fought hard to get them to clean up some of the damage."

"She never mentioned any of that before." Ella paused. "Of course, in all fairness, I never asked, either. She was always just Mom."

"I know. It was the same for me. But, apparently, she needs more in her life now."

Ella nodded. "I've got to tell you, I really miss the mom I grew up with."

Clifford laughed. "Because she always catered to you."

"What are you talking about? She didn't always cater to me. *You* were her favorite because you and she think alike."

"Yes, but you were the one who gave her the biggest headaches, and problem children always get special treatment," Clifford retorted smoothly. "One of the reasons they become problem children, I think."

"You're nuts. I was—" Ella stopped speaking and smiled. "My world is coming apart at the seams and we're talking about who Mom liked best."

Clifford laughed. "Some habits die hard."

"Tell me more about this splinter group that came from the ranks of the Fierce Ones. What did they think of Mom's suggestions?"

"They like them, but they also want faster action. They're looking for the quickest way to ease the crisis, not just the best long-term solution."

"That's what I was worried about. Would they take matters into their own hands and create trouble just to put pressure on the rest of the tribe?"

"Possibly."

"Do they have anything cooked up right now?"

"I couldn't tell you. These people will never speak freely around me because they know I'm not in sympathy with them. Though they're still part of the Fierce Ones, they really don't share their plans with the rest of us. We've allowed them to continue calling themselves Fierce Ones because this is the best chance we have of keeping tabs on them."

Ella nodded. "Okay. Just know that there's something brewing on the Rez that may or may not be connected with what you've been telling me, and it's going to hit the fan soon. So tell me if you hear about anything going down."

"You've got it." Clifford paused, then after a moment

added, "You know, Mom may be of more use to you on this than I am."

"How so?"

"You know her group of herbalists, the Plant Watchers, is made up mostly of elderly people. Their age often tends to make them all but invisible to the younger ones, who'll speak freely around them without giving them a second thought. You may find Mom's group quite valuable to you now."

"Come to think of it, they've been helpful before. And it's not like I'm asking them to become spies, I just want to know if they've overheard anything helpful. Thanks for the reminder."

Ella drove home quickly. One way or another, she intended to find out what the Indian syndicate was going to do next.

When she arrived home, Ella saw Justine's unit parked there and, fearing trouble, ran inside. Her mother was supervising Jennifer with dinner while Dawn played alone with her new log set in the living room. Everything was quiet, though Justine was nowhere in sight.

Looking up and seeing Ella, Dawn held out her arms. *"Shimá!"*

Not "Mommy" this time. She knew that Rose had undoubtedly spoken to Dawn about that. Ella smiled, picked up her daughter, and gave her a hug.

"I missed you," Ella said.

"Butterfly kiss!" Dawn said.

Ella fluttered her lashes against Dawn's cheek, then allowed her daughter to do the same to her.

"I'm hungry," Dawn said.

Rose came out of the kitchen and smiled at her daughter and granddaughter.

"Where's my cousin?" Ella asked quickly, meaning Justine.

"She asked to use your computer while she was waiting for you to get home."

Ella felt the tingle at the base of her spine that always

signaled trouble. "Oh, okay. Let me go find her."

Ella hurried down the hall to her room. If Justine had logged on to the service she used, Coyote would assume it was her. With luck she wouldn't be too late, and all Justine was doing was checking out the new computer game she'd given Ella for Christmas.

As Ella walked inside and saw her partner at the computer, her heart started beating again. Justine was playing the game.

Justine turned around and gave her an easy smile. "I hope you don't mind. I couldn't resist."

"No problem." Ella walked over and sat down on the bed beside Justine's chair. "But we need to have a talk, and I hope it won't make you angry."

NINETEEN
✖ ✖ ✖

Justine stood and stared at Ella, her mouth open. "I'm sorry I didn't ask permission first, cousin. I just thought—"

"No, that isn't it. There's something you should know, and I've been putting it off for security reasons. But you're my partner, and we face danger together too much to keep this from you any longer. It's time I took you into confidence about my contact." Ella sighed.

She explained briefly what she knew for certain about Henry Estrada—Coyote—and how important it was to keep his code name and method of contact a secret from everyone.

Justine thought about it a while, then finally spoke. "I wish I'd been trusted earlier with this information, but I appreciate you telling me about Coyote now. I'll keep it to myself, you can count on me. Who else knows?"

"I had to tell Big Ed, and I recently discovered that our local FBI agents know of him by another code name. That's it, except, unfortunately, for one other person who discovered him by accident."

"Your mom?" Justine smiled. "It's hard to keep a secret from her anyway. It's like she reads minds sometimes."

"You're right about that. Anyway, now that you know, hopefully you'll understand where I've been coming from when I've made some of these speculations about our cases." Ella stood. "Just don't ever discuss Coyote's existence with anyone. He's undercover and playing for his life."

"I figured that."

"Maybe he'll contact me while you're here. I was hoping for something soon. Coyote always seems to know when I'm home. But enough about that. Tell me what brought you here tonight."

"In the cosmic scheme of things, I suppose it's not really important. Wilson and I had a fight, and I didn't want to go home 'cause I expect he'll be stopping by. He gets along well with my mother, and she's all for my getting more serious about him. Mom points out that Wilson is, well, who and what he is, a nice, decent man with a good job and the respect of the community," Justine shrugged. "And he's not a cop."

"But? There must be one of those in there somewhere," Ella speculated. "You know I think Wilson would be good for you too. What do *you* want? That's what is important here."

"Ella, I've been through so much the last year, including being manipulated into nearly messing up our friendship, my job, and my whole life. Except for that damn problem with my pistol qualification, I really am getting my act together again, and thinking of getting my own apartment, finally. With my job back on track, I'm not sure I want to add total commitment to Wilson into the picture right now. And I'm certain that is what Wilson wants." Justine looked around the room, not making eye contact for a while, tears beginning to form in her eyes.

"Then don't rush into anything, if my life example is any help for you at all. If Wilson really cares that much about you, and you about him, he'll realize that and give you more time." Ella reached over and grabbed her cousin's hand, giving it a gentle squeeze.

Just then a small bell rang on the computer, and a synthesized voice announced that E-mail was incoming. Justine rose from the chair, and waved Ella into the seat.

Ella sat down in front of the computer, reading Coyote's message.

"Large-scale sabotage of some sort is being planned.

Haven't gotten details yet. Hope to get more info soon."

Ella glanced up at Justine, then typed a response. "How can I help?"

The reply came quickly. "Someone out there must know something. The Indian mafia tries to recruit from the tribe. Keep your eyes and ears open."

Before Ella could thank him, Coyote was gone. Ella switched on the printer, then printed out the latest exchange.

"I need you to work with me and help me dig up something we can use to counter the syndicate's plans."

"Of course." Justine sat down on the edge of Ella's bed. "Where do you want to begin?"

"To tell you the truth, I don't know yet," Ella said.

Justine shook her head. "Me neither. Let's come up with a game plan so we can stop whatever the syndicate's brewing up."

"We'll both have to think about it for a bit," Ella said, leading her out into the hall. "Why don't we have some dinner with the family while we mull things over."

Justine shook her head. "No, I think your advice about taking my time, and asking Wilson to do the same, might be the best way to go. I'm going home, and if he's there, maybe I'll talk about it tonight with him if he's cooled off. If not, I'll just play it by ear. The drive home will help clear my thinking. If I come up with any ideas about that game plan with the syndicate, I'll call."

"Do that."

"And Ella, thanks again for trusting me. I know there was a time last year when it would have been dangerous for you to take this step."

"It wasn't your fault, Justine. There were other forces at work then. Let's don't talk about it anymore. We've moved on, and now we're a real good team again."

"We've always been a good team, boss. Now we're better." Justine laughed, and walked into the hall. "I'll say good-bye to your mom, then go see what I can do about Wilson."

A few minutes later, Ella went into the kitchen. Jennifer had gone home, and Rose was stirring a pot of beef stew simmering on the stove.

"Mom, I need to talk to you," Ella said, starting to set the table.

"Not about my antigaming stand again, daughter. I've had a long day."

"It's not about that." Ella told her mother about the conversation she'd had with Clifford, and his suggestion that Rose and the Plant Watchers might be able to help. "Something's brewing out there, Mom. I've received a tip that some big disaster is about to go down, and I need to find out what it is before it happens. What's the latest gossip at the Plant Watchers meetings?"

Rose sighed. "Nothing new, I'm afraid. The people my age aren't scared. They know that we've gone through trying times before, and we'll survive. It's the ones your age and younger who seem to want the path cleared for gaming because the lure of prosperity is hard for them to resist. That's creating tension in many families."

"I've heard some of your proposals," Ella said.

"They could work, but they'd need time to catch on. Most of all, they need the tribe's support." Rose paused. "I gave another interview to the news people today—actually, television reporters from Albuquerque."

"Okay," Ella said slowly. "Give the highlights."

"I detailed my proposals and asked the public to get in touch with our leaders if they found the idea of exploring our Navajo way of life appealing and would be interested in looking into the possibilities. I was 'test marketing,' you know?"

Ella chuckled. "Okay. Thanks for the advance warning." She still couldn't quite get used to the idea of her mother as an activist.

"There's more," Rose said.

Ella groaned. "I had a feeling—" Seeing her mother's

eyes narrowing, she stopped, throwing up her hands in mock surrender. "Okay, tell me."

"I got a call a while ago from an Albuquerque station. The story has been picked up by their national bureau, and they expect it will be on the network news."

Ella stared at her mother, but no words would come.

"Well, say something. Silence isn't your style, daughter."

Ella swallowed. "Mom, I'm very proud that you have the courage to speak your mind, but I have to be honest with you. I'm really afraid that you're making some big enemies right now."

"Yes, but there are people—friends—watching over us, too, daughter."

Ella knew that once before, when trouble had struck, Herman Cloud and other traditionalists had joined forces to watch over them here at home. "That's good, but I'll see if we can increase police patrols in this area, too."

"You don't have to, you know. We *are* well protected."

Ella didn't argue the point. "One more thing, Mom. Just so you know, I won't be taking my daughter anywhere outside this house with me for a while. I can handle the fact that I'm a sniper's target, but I don't want to put her in that kind of danger."

Rose nodded somberly. "All right. Do you have any objections if I take her out?"

"No. I don't think your enemies are as direct as mine," Ella said.

"Good. By the way, if you have a moment, there's something else I need to talk to you about." Seeing Ella nod, she continued. "I went to the doctor this morning and learned that my hand isn't mending properly. The surgeon feels that he can correct the problem with a minor procedure, so I've consented. The good news, of course, is that once my hand has finally healed and I can use it again, we won't need to have my friend's granddaughter here every day like we do now."

"Mom, with you so involved with the gaming issue, we'll probably need a homemaker's helper even after you recuperate."

"I'm not saying that we won't need her some of the time, but she won't have to be here every single moment, daughter. After all, she's not a relative and it's not good for your daughter to get too used to her."

Ella smiled, suddenly understanding. Rose was jealous of the attention Dawn was giving Jennifer. "Mom, she's an asset to both of us right now. Let's wait and talk more about this after your surgery, okay? When do you have to go in?"

"Tomorrow around ten. I already have a ride to the hospital, so you don't have to worry. I'll be out in two days, maybe earlier if things go well. In the meantime, my friend's granddaughter will stay with your daughter until you get home each night."

"Who did you get to take you to the hospital?"

"Bizaadii." Rose used her nickname for Herman.

Ella smiled, hoping her mother hadn't noticed. That hope, of course, was as futile as wishing the sky to turn bright yellow.

"He's a good friend, daughter. I know you might have problems accepting a man in my life, but he's good for me. And he treats me well, too."

"Very true," Ella said, trying to sound understanding but not really wanting to encourage her mother either. She still had mixed emotions, despite her own respect for Herman.

"Your father is always in my memories, daughter. But we have to move on with our lives."

Ella nodded. Her mother was right, but still . . . "I know what you're saying, and your friend is my friend too. I just feel a little odd, sometimes. Just give me a while, Mother. I'll adjust," Ella asked.

"All right."

Dinner was quiet, and Dawn seemed more interested in watching her favorite video about a cartoon bear's adventures than in anything else, so Ella excused her early. After clearing up the kitchen, she went to play with Dawn. Tonight, however, Dawn wasn't interested in playing after her short video ended. She was tired and cranky, and when Ella finally put her to bed she only fussed for a short time before drifting off to sleep.

Ella watched the second half of a mindless television movie, then after Rose went to bed, decided to do the same.

Ella walked to her room and started to turn on her computer, more out of habit than anything else, but then decided against it. She'd already communicated with Coyote tonight, so there was no need for her to log on again.

Wearing a long, ratty sweatshirt she'd owned since high school, she crawled in between the sheets and fell promptly asleep.

The next morning, by the time Ella emerged from the shower and dressed, Dawn still hadn't come into her room. Worried, she started down the hall and heard Dawn and Jennifer playing in the living room.

Ella checked her watch. Jennifer was early. As Ella went into the living room, Dawn looked up and said hi, but continued playing with Jennifer, who pretended to grab her and then chase her around the couch. "She's already had breakfast," Jennifer said. "We're going to make a farm with her Legos next. Would you like to join us?"

Ella shook her head. "I have to get ready for work." Ella watched the two for a moment. Dawn seemed perfectly content to play with Jennifer and, she had to admit, Jennifer was wonderful with her daughter.

"How do *you* like being replaced?" Rose whispered as she walked past Ella.

Ella looked at her mother, annoyed, then glanced back at Dawn. As Jennifer went to get the Legos, Dawn held up her arms to Ella, asking to be picked up.

Ella held her for a moment. "Are you having fun?"

Dawn nodded, then held out her arms to Jennifer as she returned.

Jennifer took her from Ella. "I'll take good care of her. Don't worry about a thing. Have a great day at work."

Normally, Ella hated perky people, and she *really* hated perky people in the morning. "Thanks," Ella muttered.

When Ella strode into the kitchen, her mother was stirring the oatmeal.

"Take enough time to eat. It's very, very cold outside right now and you'll need something warm inside you."

Ella glanced at the clock. "I'll just have a little bowl," she said, taking some from the pan, then adding milk and sugar to it. "So what are your plans for today, Mom?"

"I'll leave for the hospital around nine, and I'll be back by the end of the weekend—sooner, if I can talk them into it."

"Mom, don't give them a hard time," she said, eating her breakfast standing up.

Rose shrugged. "They said they want to be extra careful because of my age. But I'm having your brother do a Sing for me, so I'm covered."

"Even so," Ella said.

Ella heard Dawn laughing in the other room, and for one brief moment wished she could have been a full-time Mom. The quality time she could spend with Dawn was always at a premium.

Ella shook free of the thought, knowing it would lead nowhere. She had other duties, and it was time for her to get to work. After washing out her bowl, she said good-bye to Rose, then stopped to give Dawn one last long hug before leaving. Unlike most children, Dawn never made a fuss when she was left. Even at this early age she was independent. Then again, having Rose with her at home had always helped, too. Dawn had never had to feel that she was all alone in the company of strangers.

Ella watched Dawn for a moment longer, then putting on her jacket and bullet-resistant vest, hurried out to her unit. It was in the single digits this morning and she shivered while scraping the frost off her windows.

At least when she got inside the Jeep, the heater was blowing warm air instead of cold. Ella had just turned onto the highway when she saw a large, four-wheel-drive pickup truck coming up from behind her, flashing its lights. Ella didn't recognize the vehicle, but she slowed down and pulled to one side of the road.

Unsnapping the strap of her holster, she glanced in the rearview mirror, trying to see who the driver was. The man pulled in behind her and, as he got out, she saw it was Harry.

"Sorry to come unannounced," he told her, slipping inside the passenger's seat of her unit. "I had to rent a bigger truck so I could get in and out of certain areas of the Rez."

Ella smiled. "Motor pool sedans and two-wheel-drive units aren't much good out here off road, are they?"

He laughed. "That's putting it diplomatically."

"What's up?"

"I've been trying to get a handle on Manyfarms, following up on every lead, but he's managed to drop out of sight. I was wondering if you'd heard anything."

"All I know right now is that it's possible Manyfarms has associated himself with a progambling faction that's been playing hardball and leaning on the Tribal Council," Ella confided.

"I've been thinking a lot about the sniper incident, and something occurred to me. Have you checked out George Branch, that local talk radio guy? He has an extensive gun collection, if memory serves me right."

"I know, but he lives outside my jurisdiction. I considered stopping by and talking to him the other day, but I changed my mind at the last minute." She remembered losing Coyote and the men he was with near Branch's home. "Branch needs careful handling. The last thing I need is for him to launch another the-cops-are-corrupt campaign on his radio talk show."

"Ella—" Harry started to add something, then changed his mind.

"What? You don't have to hold back with me," Ella said. "If you have something on your mind, just say it."

"Just watch your back. Something feels wrong about this case. Call it cop instinct."

"I know what you mean," Ella said slowly. "Watch your own back as well. I received a tip that something big is about to go down, possibly an act of sabotage."

"I overhear a lot of conversations here and there on the Rez," Harry said. "If I get anything you can use, I'll pass it along."

"I've got to tell you, Harry, I sure wouldn't like your job very much," she said. "You should be working with a partner on a case this dangerous."

"I usually do, but on the Rez anyone but an Indian would stick out too much. That's why I insisted on having a certain amount of time to work the case on my own."

"That was probably not such a terrific idea."

Harry shrugged. "I have another two weeks to show concrete results. After that, more deputies will come."

"More feds here?" Ella suppressed a groan. "Things are very tense of the Rez right now, Harry. Make sure they understand that."

"I'll try, but although they'll hear the words, the message won't carry that much impact. Outsiders seldom understand the subtleties of dealing with the People."

As Harry returned to his pickup, Ella's cell phone rang. It was Kevin.

"I need to talk to you. Can you meet me someplace for coffee?" Kevin asked. Ella waved as Harry drove off ahead of her.

"Sure, I think I can swing that. How about the Totah Café?"

"Good enough."

Ella arrived first, and sat at her favorite table in the corner. To her left were the mountains in the distance, fully bathed in sunlight. They were like old friends now, steady and sure.

Kevin approached and joined her a short time later.

"Coffee," he said, signaling the waitress.

"So what did you need to see me about?"

"I heard about the interview your mother gave the news station, and somebody sent me a tape of the network version. It was more than sound bites, which was what I'd expected, but she's really going out on a limb."

Ella looked directly at him. "My mom does and says what she pleases, Kevin. You should know that by now."

"You know what's really strange? I think she and I are going to find ourselves on the same side." He paused, then with a grin added, "She'll think the world has ended for sure."

"So you *have* decided," Ella said, intrigued. "But what about the threats?"

"I'll hire a bodyguard if I have to, but I don't think it'll come to that. I've come up with a compromise that should appease both sides."

"Be careful, Kevin. Sometimes compromises only double the number of enemies a politician has."

"The need for money and jobs is at an all-time high, Ella, and this requires some big decisions and action from the tribal leaders. I've tried several times to get a majority of the council to agree on a referendum, but I realize now that I'm not going to get the votes I need. What I intend to do instead is try passing a limited proposal approving gambling, but only at a test casino in To'hajiilee. That's close to Albuquerque and a large metropolitan area, so a casino there has a greater chance of succeeding. And, more importantly, many of the people living in To'hajiilee are really pushing for a casino.

"I'll also argue in favor of setting up slot machines at shops across the Rez," he continued. "Then we can give the entire program a trial period—say, three years. At the end of that time, we'll review where things stand, then either renew the bill or let it die."

Ella nodded slowly. "That's not bad. I particularly like the fact that it's all on a trial basis."

"We'd also work to keep the overhead down so we can maximize profits. The casino we set up in To'hajiilee can be a remodeled building rather than a brand-new facility, too. I've already looked at a possible site. We'll fancy up the place, of course, but we'll have job openings right away, both in construction and in casino operations. Getting a bank to fund us initially shouldn't be a problem either because of the success the pueblos have had. Hopefully, we can pay down the loan within the first two years, then start pocketing the profits after that."

"It'll be quite an undertaking."

"I know—both getting the proposal past the council and keeping an eye on everything so the tribe doesn't get cheated." He sat back. "Once things get rolling, I'm not going to have any time off. That's why I'd like to go away this weekend. And that brings me to the reason I wanted to see you."

Kevin paused for a moment. "I've been thinking about what you said—that, basically, I need time to spend with my own kid. I really do want to get to know her, Ella. She's my daughter, too. The thing is I can't do that with you or your mother hovering over us."

"We don't hover over you," Ella snapped. "You've been free to take her to your home for visits whenever you've wanted. You're the one who's had problems finding the time."

"I know," he admitted. "And I've come up with a way to remedy that. I've rented a cabin near a ski lodge in southern Colorado, and I'd like to take Dawn with me."

"Skiing? Have you lost your mind? She's barely mastered walking."

"I don't ski either, Ella. I just like the place, and I thought it would be a great chance for her and me to be together."

Ella wanted to say no to the trip, but the fact was that Rose would be in the hospital this weekend, and she'd be working long hours. The decision she needed to make was whether to leave Dawn in Jennifer's care, or with her father.

"Kevin, are you *very* sure you're up to this? You'll have to contend with her potty training, feed her, bathe her, play with her, and never let her out of your sight. It's not easy, trust me."

"I know. That's why I want to take Jennifer with me to help out. It'll work, Ella."

Ella once again struggled with the impulse to say no and simply be done with it, but she also wanted to be fair to both Dawn and Kevin. Her little girl adored her father, and it was undeniably true that they got to spend very little time together. With Kevin's involvement in the gaming issue, his time during the next few months would be at a premium. To deny them the opportunity now seemed wrong somehow.

"All right," she said slowly. "But I'm only doing this for Dawn. She's crazy about you. Personally, I'm not that thrilled with the idea of having Dawn so far away from me for so long."

"I realize that you'll miss her terribly but, if you want, you could come with us. We'd leave Jennifer here, then, and make it a special outing for the three of us."

Ella shook her head. "You know I can't, not now. There's too much going on."

"I understand," he said, disappointment evident in his voice. "So shall I pick Dawn up tonight after dinner?"

"I'll have to talk to Jennifer first. I don't know how she'll feel about going up with you and Dawn to Colorado for the entire weekend."

Kevin gave her a sheepish smile. "I do. I spoke to her—and her mother—about the idea two days ago."

Ella's eyes darkened. "Without telling me?"

"I was still in the planning stage. I wasn't sure I could swing it. At that point all I was trying to do was anticipate your objections and see if the trip was even feasible."

"I'll miss my little girl," Ella said honestly, because she wanted him to know just how difficult this was for her. "A weekend can be a very long time."

"She'll be safe with me. You know that, don't you?"

"If I wasn't positive of that, I wouldn't have even considered the idea. But that still won't keep me from worrying or from missing her."

"I know. But Dawn and I really need some time to share."

She nodded slowly. "All right. But let me break the news to Mom," Ella said. "She's going to the hospital today for minor surgery, and if she finds out that I let you take Dawn without even telling her, there'll be hell to pay."

Kevin gave her a quick half smile. "Oh, yeah."

As Ella's cell phone rang, Kevin stood up and placed a few dollars on the table. Giving her a wave, he left just as she answered the call.

"It's me," Justine said. "I've now gone to four different judges, including my grandfather. No one will give us a warrant to test that fifty-caliber rifle you saw at Arthur Benjamin's place, not on what we have right now. If you're serious about having a ballistics test done on it so we can have something on file, you're going to have to find a way to get him to voluntarily loan us the weapon."

"Okay, but ask Blalock to give you the names of the other shooters in the gun club in Farmington who own fifty-caliber weapons, and ask if they'll voluntarily surrender their weapons for a ballistics test, too, just to reduce our suspect list and clear themselves. There's only a handful of them."

"That group will probably say no—not without a warrant," Justine warned.

"Ask anyway, but make sure they understand it's on a voluntary basis. If I'm going to tip my hand, I might as well cover my back while I'm at it. If we're asking the same thing of everyone who owns a fifty-caliber weapon, Benjamin won't be able to squawk discrimination or harassment. We're just soliciting some cooperation in solving a crime."

"All right. I'll pass your request to Blalock."

"There's also the possibility George Branch has a weapon of that caliber. The man has quite an armory, as I recall. We'll have to check into that. In the meantime, I'll go pay the Benjamins another visit. I can be charming, when required." But it made her stomach queasy to think of making nice to a rattler.

TWENTY
— ✖ ✖ ✖ —

Ella drove to Arthur Benjamin's house and knocked on the door.

Arthur, who'd apparently heard her drive up, answered the door immediately, and beamed Ella a cheerful smile. "Ah, the daughter of our national celebrity activist," he said jovially.

Ella swallowed her irritation. "I'd like a chance to talk to you, Mr. Benjamin, if you have a moment."

"I'm always glad to help the police," he said, and stepped back into the hall, waving for her to come inside. He led the way from the tastefully simple foyer into the distastefully decorated den. The turquoise-and-silver-painted steer skulls that stared back at her through hollow eyes gave her the creeps all over again.

He didn't offer her a chair, but she didn't want to sit down anyway, not here. "Several days ago there was an incident where someone took a shot at me. I assume you read that in the paper?"

"The article didn't say which officer was the target, if I recall." Arthur tried unsuccessfully to look concerned. "But what does that have to do with me?"

"The weapon used was a fifty-caliber rifle. They're relatively rare, but you have one here," she said.

"That explains your interest in the weapon the other day. Do you think *I* took a shot at you? Or perhaps my nephew? It's really his rifle, you know."

"I'm not accusing anyone. It's possible that perhaps someone removed the weapon from this house and used it in a crime."

"Again, what is it you want from me?"

"I'd like you and your nephew to voluntarily allow me to take the weapon in for a ballistics comparison and rule out that possibility. Or take it in yourself, whichever you prefer. We recovered a bullet after the sniper incident, so a comparison is possible." Ella didn't need to tell him that the slug had been in very poor shape, and it was possible no link could ever be made except for caliber.

"No. Definitely not, not without a warrant."

"You said earlier you were always glad to help the police. Doing this voluntarily would make you look good to the public, assuming of course that the weapon is not the one we're looking for—"

"Don't give me that crap. Your boss and I are old rivals. Right now there's probably nothing he'd like to do more than bury my reputation in innuendoes or false charges—anything to get me off his back."

"This has nothing to do with Police Chief Atcitty," Ella said. "But it has everything to do with an ongoing investigation into the attempted murder of a police officer. Now, it's my understanding that you would like to have the job of top cop around here. It seems to me that you wouldn't want it to become known that you refused to do your part to help track down the person responsible for attempting to murder a police officer."

"I could still lose if I say yes."

"Only if the gun checks out as the weapon used. And, even then, it doesn't prove conclusively that you or your nephew committed the crime. We'd have to prove motive and opportunity, and then build a case around it." She paused deliberately, then continued. "Just be aware that if others bring in their weapons to be checked, and you and your nephew don't . . ."

Arthur smiled mirthlessly. "Let me guess—you'd make sure word got out."

"It would, believe me, with or without my help. I'm not the only one who knows that the weapon is here. There are other members of your nephew's gun club that have already been interviewed by the FBI. They're also going to be asked to cooperate and volunteer to bring in their weapons to be test fired."

"All right. I'll consent to have you take my nephew's weapon in—if he agrees as well—but if, as I suspect, a bullet fired from that rifle is not a match to what you have in ballistics, I'm going to make a public stink. I'll say that this is what the PD does to cover their incompetence—going on a fishing expedition hoping the shooter is even more stupid than they are. I will use this incident to make your chief look as bad as possible."

"Asking you and your nephew to voluntarily allow the weapon to be tested wasn't the chief's decision. It's mine. I'm the investigating officer on this case."

"Don't feel left out. I'll claim you've been harassing me." Arthur held her gaze. "I'll be happy to cooperate with the police—but only under these conditions. It's more equitable if we all have something on the line," he added smoothly, then went to the door of the adjoining room and opened it. His nephew was inside, standing by the pool table with a cue in his hand.

Although Ella suspected that Robert Benjamin had heard their conversation, Arthur told him what Ella was asking for and asked if he was willing to go along with the test.

The younger man shot her a glacial look, then unlocked the gun cabinet and placed the weapon down on the pool table.

"This hasn't been fired outside competition and practice sessions," Robert said, opening the bolt action. "If it had been, I would have known. I want you to look it over again, write down the serial number, and take whatever notes you want, but I am definitely *not* going to let you take it in for testing, not without a warrant. I have a lot more to lose if the lab screws up or fakes the results. Anyone who volunteers for the testing is an idiot as far as I'm concerned."

Ella looked at Arthur's expression. He was smiling as

if he and his nephew were sharing a private joke.

Ella handled the heavy weapon very carefully, examining the action and bore, then she pulled out her small notebook and added the serial number of the weapon.

"It was always your decision whether to help us or not, Robert. If the others volunteer, and the ballistics tests on their weapons come back negative, maybe I'll be back to see you again. Let's see if your uncle can put some kind of spin on this that makes you both look good, at least for now. But I wouldn't count on it." She smiled, heading to the door.

Five minutes later, Ella was on her way back to Shiprock when her radio call sign came over the air. She answered it and heard Justine's voice.

"Andrew Talk is dead. Apparently he was either hit by a car or beaten to death. He was found beside the main highway in plain view. Some of the Navajos who drove by are quite upset," she said, then gave Ella directions to the crime scene, a few miles north of Shiprock on the Cortez highway.

"I doubt it was an accident. He was probably killed somewhere else, then dumped there to make sure word got around."

"You mean as a warning?"

"Yeah. As soon as you get there contain the scene. Then look for skid marks or vehicle tracks to rule out the hit-and-run possibility. I'll be there shortly."

Ella switched off the mike. After everything that had already happened, she was convinced that Talk hadn't died by accident. This had the feel of a gangland-style hit—payback for not doing what you're told. She thought of Kevin and threats he'd received. Immediately she picked up the cell phone and called him.

"I wanted you to hear the news from me, Kevin. Andrew Talk is dead, and my guess is that it's a homicide," she said.

There was a lengthy silence on the other end. "Is it

connected to the ones who've been leaning on the Tribal Council and threatening me?"

"I'm not sure yet, but it seems likely. Have you received any more threats?"

"No, in fact I haven't heard from them at all. I was hoping they'd given up trying to force me to dance to their tune."

"Don't count on that. You still planning on leaving the Rez tonight?"

"Yeah. And before you ask, nobody but you will know where I'm going. Well, Jennifer's mother knows, but I trust her to be quiet about it."

"Good. Don't let anybody else know at all, not even your staff."

"We'll be safe, Ella. First, they'd have to find us to do anything and, secondly, I'm still useful to them. Remember I've always been more progaming than against it."

Her cell phone started giving a tone that she recognized as a low-battery warning. She'd forgotten to replace the battery this morning.

"My signal is about to go, Kevin, so I've got to disconnect now. Just be very careful." She placed the phone down on the seat beside her as a reminder to pick up a fresh battery in her office.

Ella arrived at the crime scene ten minutes later. Justine, Tache, and Neskahi were already there. Neskahi was cordoning off the area with yellow tape. Orange cones beside the highway warned oncoming traffic of their presence near the road. Ella parked a hundred feet away from the scene, got out of her vehicle, and slipped a pair of vinyl gloves on just as Carolyn arrived in her van.

With a wave, Ella walked over to meet the ME, slipping on a second pair of gloves on the way. "You know, ever since you got married I never get to see you except when we're both on the job."

Carolyn laughed. "Oh, please. Like we got together

that often before? We were always working."

"Yeah, but we managed some time to talk occasionally, even if it was at the hospital."

"You're right. Lately it seems I'm either rushing around at work, or rushing to get home."

"I guess the other Dr. Lavery gives you enough reasons not to work late."

"Every day is a surprise," Carolyn said with a tiny smile.

As they reached the yellow tape line, Carolyn stopped suddenly and stared at Neskahi. "Please make an opening for me to walk through. I have no intention of doing the limbo underneath this with my medical bag."

Ella looked at Neskahi and shook her head, signaling him to continue working. "When are you going to forgive him?" Ella asked softly as she lifted up the crime scene tape so Carolyn could pass underneath easily.

"Just so you know, he also referred to me as Dr. Chunk to Officer Tache. I don't take that kindly. He'll pay until the day he retires, or I do."

Ella cringed. No one, but *no one*, made a crack like that about Carolyn's weight—not if you planned on continuing to live life as you knew it. Neskahi liked to joke around, and he'd undoubtedly meant no harm, but this was really going to cost him.

"I'll talk to the sergeant. You can count on that."

"No need. And today I intend to once again have him help me load the body into the bag. As far as I'm concerned that will be his job at every crime scene from this day until eternity. Don't you dare interfere with that."

"You're the ME. I wouldn't dream of it," Ella said sincerely.

Ella followed Carolyn to where the body lay. Although she was a seasoned cop, she had to swallow to keep down the contents of her stomach. The left side of Andrew Talk's head had been caved in as if he'd been struck repeatedly by a baseball bat, or worse. Part of his bloody shirt had been imbedded between his ribs, and one of the bones in his right arm protruded from his skin where it had been smashed with a heavy object. Several of his fingers on both hands were split open and askew, probably defensive wounds as he tried to block the blows from whatever blunt objects were used to pummel his body. He was barefoot, and his feet were swollen and battered, as if his killers had begun there, and worked up his body, taking it slow. Small pieces of gravel from the side of the road were also visible atop the body.

Ella took a deep breath, then moved away. Bile burned the back of her throat, but she managed to avoid throwing up. Many of the murders of Navajos that she had investigated over the years had been the result of beatings, and she never could get used to the brutality.

Justine had been hardened even less, apparently. As Ella looked around, she saw her partner coming back toward the yellow tape from a spot farther off the highway. Her face was pale, and she was wiping her mouth with a handkerchief.

While Ella began searching the area for evidence in an expanding spiral from the body, Tache concentrated on photographing the area around the body where several vague footprints remained. There was no splattered or pooled blood anywhere and that told her that Talk had been dead already when he'd been dropped here. From the wounds themselves, it was obvious this was no hit-and-run accident.

Ella went to where Carolyn was working. "See if you can find any evidence that'll tell us where he was killed. From what I can see, he was dumped here after the fact."

"I'll do what I can," Carolyn said, reaching for the tape recorders in her bag. "One interesting thing. The smell of alcohol is still all over him. The beating may have been part of a particularly nasty drunken attack. I'll check his blood alcohol later and let you know more."

"This man was involved in some shady business that

would suggest this is premeditated murder, not manslaughter. If you find evidence that that's *not* the case, then let me know as soon as possible."

"Understood."

Searching for vehicle tracks, Ella found impressions in the hard shoulder that showed where Talk's killers had stopped to dump the body. The fine gravel made it impossible to discern any tread pattern, however, and she found no footprints. Whoever it was had moved fast to avoid being seen, and scattered gravel and rubber marks on the edge of the asphalt indicated they had pulled away in a hurry. It also explained why gravel had been scattered over the body.

As Tache photographed the evidence, Ella joined her partner. "Justine, I want you to interview all eighty-eight, now eighty-seven members of the Tribal Council—not just the leaders of the gaming issue. I want the names of everyone who has received threats of any kind—even if you get them through hearsay. You might also talk to Jefferson Blueeyes. I have a feeling that man knows far more than he has ever let on. And check with those two Anglos we nailed on the vandalism to see if they've ever met Blueeyes. We never did learn how they were selected, and Blueeyes worked in Farmington at one time. You'll need help to do all this, so recruit whoever you think might be interested in working with our unit short-term. But be careful and pick officers you're certain we can trust."

"Consider it done."

"One more thing. The Benjamins refused to volunteer the rifle for ballistics testing. I can't say it was a big surprise, actually. But if any of the others bring their weapons in, test them very thoroughly. At least we might be able to cross a few names off our list."

"Okay. Anything else?"

"That's it for now. Since we're not far away from the hospital, I'm going to stop by and make sure Mom's settled in. On the way, I'll get in touch with Jimmy

Frank and see if he's got anything on Blueeyes. If he does, I'll be in touch."

After Justine went back to the job at hand, Ella got under way. In a few minutes, just north of Shiprock, she picked up her cell phone to call Jimmy, then remembered the battery was dead. Worried about any conversations on the police frequencies being monitored, she stopped at a pay phone beside a convenience store and dialed his cell number.

"I was just going to call you," he answered immediately. "I've been monitoring a meeting between George Branch, Blueeyes, and two other Indian men I've never met—not Navajos. I borrowed one of Tache's cameras when I started working for you, and I took some photos with his telephoto lens. But I'm no photographer, so I can't be sure of the quality."

"Go back to the station and get the film developed. I'll see you there in about forty minutes. And good job."

Ella's spirits were noticeably higher by the time she arrived at the hospital. A photo of any outsiders dealing with Blueeyes and Branch would probably lead to some answers. It was about time they'd had a break.

Ella stopped by the main desk, got her mother's room number, then hurried upstairs. Having her mother consent to surgery only proved how badly Rose wanted things at home to return to normal. To Rose, her home was her domain, and she'd never liked strangers there for any length of time.

As Ella entered the room she noticed that her mother was talking to several nurses and an orderly. For a moment she wasn't sure what to make of it, but as she heard their conversation, she realized that Rose was taking the opportunity to work against gaming, even here.

"Mom," Ella said, greeting her.

The nurses smiled as Rose introduced Ella as her daughter, then they left to continue their duties.

Ella sat down on one of the two chairs and wondered how to begin. She had to tell her mother about Kevin and Dawn, but she just wasn't sure how to bring it up.

"What's on your mind, daughter? I can see you're concerned about something."

Afraid she'd lose her courage, Ella blurted out the entire story quickly, then waited. Although she could face an armed opponent with a steady hand, her mother could sometimes rattle her to the core. Rose was not an easy woman.

It seemed like an eternity before Rose spoke. "I don't like it, but my granddaughter adores him. You're right about that. More importantly, I won't be home, and you'll be working long hours this weekend. With all the unrest around the reservation, maybe having her go with him on this little trip will be a good thing. I don't like my granddaughter's father, that's no secret, but I trust my friend's granddaughter to take care of everything."

"Then it's settled," Ella said, glad to have that issue out of the way. "Have you heard any new rumors about what's happening on the Rez?"

"Only that those who favor gaming are getting impatient. They're calling for a vote. They want the Tribal Council to make up their minds."

"Are they planning to do something to speed things up?"

"I don't know," Rose said, then in a thoughtful voice added, "The reservation has become a dangerous place right now, particularly for our family."

"The department will have things under control again soon, Mom. Try not to worry." Ella stood. "I've got to get back to work, but I'll do my best to stop by tonight. If it's late before I can get away, I'll come by in the morning and we can talk then. When will you have surgery?"

"They've moved it up to four this afternoon."

"I'll try to come back before they take you to the operating room. And, Mom, take it easy, okay? You're here for surgery, not to conduct an antigambling campaign."

"I can do both," Rose said firmly. "At my age, you learn not to take time for granted. There's more life behind me than there is ahead of me, but our tribe still needs me. When my time finally comes I want the People to remember that I was here once, and that I lived a life that made a difference."

"Mom, you've got many, many years ahead of you and you've already done plenty for the tribe. The Plant Watchers keep the old ways alive." It bothered Ella to hear her mother speak this way.

"You'll understand how I feel someday, daughter. But, until then, I'll do what I have to, and you'll have to learn to live with it."

With a sigh, Ella kissed her mother good-bye. As she stepped out into the hall, she saw Herman Cloud coming out of the elevator with a dozen red roses in his hand.

Ella caught Herman's eye just as he spotted her. Surprisingly, it was Herman who blushed, though Ella had expected she'd have been the one to feel awkward.

"How is your mother?" Herman managed, smiling awkwardly, holding the roses down by his side, as if in doing so they became less conspicuous somehow.

"She can use some cheering up. And I think you and those beautiful flowers will help." Ella smiled back, grateful that she wasn't the only one having to cope with the changes taking place in Rose's life.

Outside, sitting behind the wheel of her unit, Ella relaxed, knowing Herman's visit *would* probably improve her mother's spirits. Cheering people up had never been Ella's strong suit anyway. At least she understood the world of a cop.

Ella drove to the station and, as she walked down the hall, she heard Blalock's voice. He and Payestewa were coming out of the squad room.

"About time you got back," Blalock said sourly, following her to her office. "I didn't want to use the radio and your cell phone is out."

"I know. The battery is dead, so I shut it off. What's up?"

"I had a tip from the U.S. Marshal's Service. Manyfarms has been seen in the vicinity of the power plant. Harry Ute couldn't get you on the cell either, so he asked me to get a message to you ASAP, but to stay off the police frequencies. Something's going down over there. Two other non-Navajo but definitely Indian men were meeting with Manyfarms less than a mile north of the plant. Before Harry could move in, the men spotted him."

"Is he all right?"

"Yeah, but he's mad as hell. He lost Manyfarms again. The two others pinned Harry down with handgun fire while he escaped. The last he saw of the armed pair, they were still heading in the direction of the power plant, so he called plant security. But he figures you should warn Big Ed and get your team down there to check things out."

"No need to warn me," Big Ed said, stepping into Ella's office. "It's already too late. Apparently there's a group calling themselves *Hasih*, which means 'there is hope.' They've taken over a smaller structure south of the main plant where the coal cars from the mine dump their loads. Some of the heavy-equipment operators are now hostages. Apparently they're threatening to set fire to all that coal unless the Tribal Council proves to them that steps are being taken to ratify gaming and ease the financial crisis on the reservation."

"Setting fire to that coal would create an enormous, polluting fire."

"It'll also take away electrical power for a million people or more," Big Ed added, "and be hell to put out."

"Are these people crazy? Who do they think they're helping?" Ella asked.

"My guess is that the possibility they might fail to get results from the council never occurred to them," Big Ed said.

"Or they're willing to consider the coal an acceptable loss," Ella said.

"Get over there, Shorty. Assess the situation and report directly to me. I have better communications here at the moment, so I'm staying put, but I'll probably end up moving to a command post near the scene if this drags on." He looked at Blalock, who nodded.

"Are there any negotiators en route?" Ella asked.

Big Ed shrugged. "There's an exec from the power plant trying to talk to them now. Apparently, he received hostage-negotiation training when he worked for a company in Latin America."

"He's not dealing with Latin Americans," Ella said.

"I've got some hostage training," Payestewa said. "Let me take that on when we get there. I can try to keep things from escalating. Is the power plant still operating?"

Big Ed nodded. "Security at the plant has already moved in to protect the main facility. But they only have coal in their silos for a few days before they'll have to start shutting down their generators for lack of fuel. The situation has to be stopped. The *Hasih* can't be allowed to control something that's so critical to the tribe."

"Understood," Ella said.

Ella led the way to the supply room to gather the equipment they needed for the hostage situation, including weapons, vests, and extra communications gear. Ella's SI team joined them, and everyone was soon en route to the power plant, which was southeast of Shiprock.

They arrived in the area from the northeast, coming down the main access road on the east side of the lake that provided the cooling water for the plant. The enormous power plant lay at the southwest end of the lake, and the mines, essentially a seam of coal running in a northeast–southwest direction, were now in operation several miles away, apparently untouched by the *Hasih*. An electric train system brought coal to the power plant from the mines, but it had been shut down for the moment.

Parking on the service road just to the east of the coal storage piles, the group of officers climbed out of their vehicles and joined two police cars and three power plant security vehicles already at the scene. Several hundred yards in front of them, across a large cooling pond, stood a fifty-foot-high ridge of coal extending for a quarter mile or more. Ella could see heavy bulldozers, idle now, clustered around a large hole in the ground beside the mountain of coal. Conveyer belts supported by a towerlike structure extended from below ground level to tall metal storage bins across a tall fence at the south end of the power plant.

Taking out her binoculars, Ella could see people wearing hoods reminiscent of those worn by the Fierce Ones moving along the base of the black mountain in pairs. Assault rifles were visible as well as large athletic bags in the hands of one of the pair in each group.

Ella spotted a tall Anglo in a plant jacket with a cell phone, figured he was the negotiator, and headed toward him. Seeing her, the man closed up the unit and looked at her expectantly. "Thank God you're here. I'm Ron Cleary. I'm the plant manager. Besides all those people with rifles out there beside the coal, there are more in and around the conveyer tower."

He pointed to a low metal building surrounded by a high fence at the southwest end of the plant and crisscrossed by steep conveyer belts, the same structures she'd noticed coming in. "They've taken some of our people hostage and control the conveyer belts that deliver the coal from the grizzly—that big hole the coal is fed into—to the storage bins, what we call silos. This prevents us from keeping the silos full. Once they run out, we'll have to shut down the boilers, turbines, and generators. That'll put us out of the electricity business. I've tried to get them to compromise and give us back the fuel supply. But they're not willing to negotiate until the Tribal Council takes action on the gaming issue. The thing is, I'm not even sure which members of the council I should call."

Ella gestured toward Payestewa, who had followed her. Blalock was with him. "They'll do the negotiating from now on. But, before you fill them in, I need some more information from you. Exactly what happened here, how many are inside, and what kind of threats can they carry out?"

"I noticed something was up about an hour ago. I'd seen several vans crossing over the causeway between the cooling ponds, heading for the coal piles and grizzly area, so I called security and went to check it out myself. By the time I got there, two of the vans were parked outside the conveyor tower. I heard shouting, and when I went inside, I found myself face-to-face with five armed men and one woman, judging from her voice. I can't tell you who they were because they were wearing cloth hoods over their faces. They kicked most of us out, but they kept three members of our office staff, one of the heavy-equipment operators, and two of the crew who operate our conveyor system that delivers coal from the grizzly to the silos."

"Are you sure about the number of armed people?"

"I just saw those in the building. There were more outside, at least three or four, I think. Each person had at least a pistol and a rifle, with several clips stuck in their belts or pockets. The rifles are all assault weapons, like M-16s, and the pistols are semiautos, every one of them. It looked like they'd been supplied by the same manufacturer."

Ella nodded, having noted already that those out by the coal piles had seemed to be armed with the same type of rifle. This hadn't been instigated by Navajos. Since most of the *Dineh* wouldn't have had the money these days for that kind of weaponry, which weren't hunting weapons, she felt sure this hadn't been funded by one of their own. The *Hasih* were being used and manipulated by someone else, maybe the Indian syndicate. But to what end? Was it to create trouble for the police, or were officers being drawn here as a diversion so something else could go down? An uneasy feeling began to creep up her spine, and she felt the badger fetish around her neck growing warm against her skin.

Ella got out her handheld radio and gave instructions to the others to set up a secure perimeter and make sure the power plant and coal silos remained safe. Company guards were already at the mines.

Blalock came up just then and said something about a command post. As she turned around to ask him to repeat himself, the radio in her hand seemed to explode, spraying her with pieces of plastic and metal.

Ella began to drop to the ground at the same time that the explosive crack of a fifty-caliber rifle shattered through the air, reverberating across the lake behind her. It was the sound of death, and it told her that the sniper was back.

TWENTY-ONE
✖ ✖ ✖

Looking around from her prone position, Ella rubbed at the side of her face, brushing away small pieces of shredded radio. There were tiny cuts on her cheeks that stung, but nothing had struck her eyes.

"You okay, Ella?" Blalock asked from somewhere behind her.

"Just a few cuts from pieces of the radio, I think."

Guessing from the sound of the shot that the bullet had come from behind her, Ella jumped up and ran around the Jeep, putting the vehicle between her and the lake. Unfortunately, by doing that, she knew she was also exposing her back to all the *Hasih*'s gunmen.

"Anybody know for sure where the shot came from?" she yelled.

No one answered and the silence stretched out. Then Ella heard someone running toward her vehicle.

"I saw dust kick up from where he fired." Harry Ute came up over from where he'd been crouched behind the SI van a few seconds ago, grabbed her hand, and pointed toward a curve in the causeway that arced around the opposite end of the power plant. A pickup was just pulling away from the spot. A wide canal paralleled the south side of the causeway, and on the north side was the lake.

"Come with me, Ella. If we can get over there right away, we might be able to catch up to him."

Ella glanced at Blalock who gave her a thumbs-up. "I'll get our people in position here."

Jumping into the passenger's side of Harry's truck,

she fastened her seat belt as Harry slid in behind the wheel. Within seconds, he whipped the truck around, tires spitting gravel, and drove toward the causeway skirting the south end of the lake.

"I saw you talking to that tall Anglo when I came in just a few minutes ago. I came across this causeway from the west side of the lake in hopes of getting a lead to where Manyfarms had gone. But I had the strange feeling I was being followed. When I stopped beside the police units, I got out my binoculars and looked back down the road. That's when I saw the pickup parked on the causeway on the inside of the curve. Then, a few feet from there, I saw a man, prone, with this big rifle on a bipod pointing in our direction. Before I could yell a warning, he fired."

The pickup she'd been watching race away had already passed out of sight around the north end of the massive facility, but Ella remembered just how good Harry was trailing a suspect. There was a tenacity about him that kept him focused on his goal until he achieved whatever he set out to do.

"I wish I had a better handle on what's happening," Ella said. "I hate being taken by surprise."

"I've been all over the Rez, Ella, listening to people talk about the trouble that's been going on. The one word I keep hearing is 'éyóní. That's the key."

"Outsiders, foreigners," Ella said, remembering the Navajo term.

As they reached the spot on the rock-and-earthen causeway where it curved at nearly a ninety-degree angle, Harry stopped the truck and they both jumped out. "He's long gone now, but I think this was where he took the shot."

Ella walked over to the edge of the embankment to her left and saw the marks on the ground, including the impressions left by the supporting legs of the bipod that held the rifle steady. There were also boot prints. "I can't remember Manyfarms's shoe size. Do you?"

"Eight, and that print is either an exact eight or darned close."

Ella saw something big and brassy about ten feet away, halfway down the small slope that led to the canal connecting the lake with the cooling ponds. As she inched down the slope, she saw it was a shell casing for a fifty-caliber round. Putting on her leather gloves, she picked up the casing and slipped it into an evidence bag she'd taken from her jacket pocket.

"This should at least tell us something about the bolt mechanism," she said, climbing back up to the road. "And if the bullet didn't go into the cooling pond, Tache will eventually find it, I'm sure. He may not be able to search for a while, though, with those armed thugs around the coal piles."

"Meanwhile, Manyfarms is still playing with us," he said, crouching down to study the vehicle tracks. "He can't be more than a mile or two away from here now, but there are a lot of places to hide, and he may be heading to a friend's home in Shiprock, Waterflow, or one of the other communities. I didn't get a make on the truck he was driving, but the tires are narrow, so it's not a full-sized model. I'm going to stay on his tail."

Harry looked back at Ella. "And you've got to keep your guard up while he's at large. He got too close today, Ella. When I thought you might have been hit—" His voice wavered and he stopped speaking for a moment, looking away. "But you're okay, and that's what matters." He brushed her cheek with his palm, then pulled his hand away. "I've got to get going. I'm going to continue on the route he had to take, and see where it leads, or where he turned off. I wish I could help you with what's going on back there, but I have to stay on Manyfarms's tail and catch him before he gets a third shot."

"I know." Ella wanted to say more, but there was no time. Her cell phone, now with a fresh battery, began ringing.

"I'll take you back to the action, then get going," Harry said as they climbed into the truck.

Ella exchanged a few quick words on the phone, then held up her hand and opened the door to get back out. "Tache is coming up. I'll get a ride with him. Go."

She watched Harry leave, wishing that someday they could actually get together at a time when the entire world wasn't self-destructing around them.

Tache arrived a few minutes later, and she showed him the cartridge she'd found, pointing to the location where the shooter had been. "I need a ride back, but after you've dropped me off, come back up here and record whatever you can find, including those impressions and boot prints."

Tache nodded. "You've got it."

They pulled up next to Ella's vehicle a short time later and she jumped out. Most of the officers were already moving to positions that would allow them to keep the activists under surveillance from a safe distance and prevent them from escaping or gaining reinforcements or supplies. Another group of officers had driven around to a spot near the coal silos where they could watch the conveyor system. Learning that was where Justine and the FBI agents had moved to, Ella drove over to join them.

Standing behind his unit in front of the padlocked fence that separated the conveyor tower and coal piles from the rest of the power plant, Payestewa was busy on the cell phone. Justine had one of the department's sniper rifles, watching the windows of the building with the scope.

"Anyone down here figure out where the bullet went that nearly took my head off?" Ella asked, absently running her fingers through her hair and finding another piece of plastic from the radio.

"Yeah, somebody saw a splash in the water before the sonic boom from the rifle arrived," Justine said. "It was right against the far bank of the cooling pond. I left a marker by the road across from it."

Ella nodded. "That's good news. As soon as we can get our people over there, we can search for it. We might need a diver on a tether, so we'll have to call the state police and ask them to send one of their people over. But until things here are secure, we can't make a move, even though we have crucial evidence there. The perps around those mountains of coal might think they're under attack and start shooting."

Justine glanced over at Payestewa. "Paycheck's doing a great job. I heard him accuse the hostage takers of trying to whack a police officer. They denied it, but now he's busy explaining the penalties of such an action. He's been telling them that whatever they were trying to do has been eclipsed by that one event. With that, he's already taken away some of their control."

Blalock came up then. "We've just been warned by the *Hasih* that those athletic bags they were carrying contain explosive charges. They claim to have enough high explosives to start the coal burning in half a dozen places."

"Will that really start a fire? I thought they used explosives to help mine coal," Ella asked.

"The experts say the mines use low explosives, which are less dangerous. If these people have high explosives, the risk of fire is a lot worse, especially around the conveyer belts, where there is a lot of coal dust. That can also cause secondary explosions," Blalock answered.

"Has someone called Sam Pete?" Justine wondered out loud.

Blalock smiled. "Your one-man bomb squad?" He nodded, then added, "But I've also got some ATF guys coming in with dogs. We don't know how sophisticated the explosives are they have inside and too much is at stake. The ATF guys will have more experience."

"Fine, but don't leave Sam out of the operation," Ella said firmly. "He's a fine officer, and this is his turf."

"All right."

"Has the Tribal Council heard what's going on?" Ella asked.

"The tribal president is having them contacted now. Early word is that they want to keep politics out of this," Blalock answered. "The president has given Payestewa some leeway in making whatever agreements are necessary to resolve the situation peacefully. He'll pretty much go along with whatever we decide here if it'll save lives and protect the plant operations. But they won't give an inch on one thing—he warned us that neither he nor the council will grant them safe passage out of here. He said they're no better than terrorists and, when all's said and done, he wants these people brought up on charges. The extent of those charges, of course, will depend on what they do from this point on."

A moment later, Paycheck hurried over. "I need to find a council member who'll be willing to talk to the *Hasih*. The tribal president can't make it here on time, and so far hasn't been able to find anyone else who's close by. If the *Hasih* don't get a call within the hour, they'll set off a charge just to make a point."

"Any idea how big each charge is?" Ella asked quickly, "or what they're made of?"

Paycheck shook his head. "We've had a few spotting scopes set up, but, according to what they've told me, they're keeping the explosives inside those athletic bags they brought with them. They won't divulge any more details."

"Are *all* the charges placed around the piles of coal?" Ella asked.

"I'm not sure about that either," Payestewa answered. "They won't give me a straight answer. I think some of the bags have been placed underneath the conveyer belt supporting structures. The plant manager, Cleary, said the hostage takers had several athletic bags with them too, and were talking about putting a few in the machines that feed coal into the grizzly, and around the conveyer tower. Some of the other hostages who were released confirmed that."

"Wait—you mean that you think these guys are willing to put the entire power plant out of operation just to make their point?" Ella asked.

"They said that they're willing to pay whatever price is necessary, if it comes to that," Payestewa said. "But there's a chance that it's all just talk to up the stakes and regain some control."

"Someone needs to get in there and check things out."

"Easier said than done," Blalock said. "They've got sentries watching all sides of the conveyer tower and the maintenance building beside it."

"But there's got to be a blind side or an area that's not easily monitored. That building has got several big machines around it as well as the tower. Someone should be able to get in close," Ella argued.

"You're jumping the gun, Ella," Payestewa said. "I think I'll be able to talk them out of there. It's really just a matter of waiting them out and staying in control."

Ella knew that Paycheck and Blalock weren't taking into consideration something that was very important. Navajos knew about biding their time, and they know how to endure. "We may have a very long wait and, before long, the power plant is going to have to start shutting down their generators. Then people all over the West will be cold and in the dark. One of the transmission lines went down last March for several hours after a grass fire, and people in three states lost power and heat."

"I remember that. But the plant here can start trucking in some coal from other facilities, and use cranes to transfer that to the silos. That will stave off shutting down the generators for a while," Payestewa said. "Give me a chance to work. I'm on top of it. But I really need you to find a council member who'll be willing to talk to the activists inside. We're running out of time on that, because whoever we end up with will have to be brought here so I can stay by him, coaching him, and make sure he doesn't make things worse if they throw him a curveball."

"All right. I'll see what I can do." Ella jogged back to her unit, then drove north away from the power plant complex to the main highway. She'd speak to Kevin first. He was seen as progaming, generally, and had a plan for making it happen that the perps might accept.

Ella went inside the Shiprock tribal building twenty minutes later at a hurried pace and walked straight to Kevin's office.

His secretary looked up and, recognizing Ella, smiled. "He decided to leave early for the weekend, but he said for me to give you this if you came by." She handed Ella a sealed envelope.

Ella opened the envelope and found a note from Kevin. He'd taken off while Blueeyes was out of the office, but wanted her to know how to reach him. He'd included the name of the lodge and the phone number of the rental office. The cabins didn't have telephones.

The note continued, "I've arranged to pick up Dawn from Jennifer. She wants to go by her home to check on her mother, who's not feeling well today. She'll meet me at the Farmington airport in time to catch the flight. I would have gone with her, but I didn't want to just hang around Shiprock with Dawn where someone else might see us."

Ella looked at the words again. She hated the fact that Jennifer had released Dawn to Kevin without talking to her first. As soon as possible, she'd have to have a long talk with her.

But now she needed to track down another Tribal Council member who was willing to talk to the *Hasih* before they started blowing up things or setting fires beside the power plant.

Ella stuffed the letter in her pocket and got the secretary's attention again. The very businesslike woman in her early fifties was busy on some reports, but immediately stopped her keyboard entry work. "What can I help you with, Investigator Clah?"

"I need to know if any Tribal Council members are here or in the area. I need their help with a police matter that just came up," Ella said without divulging any details.

"I just got a call from the tribal president. Does this have to do with the situation over by the power plant?" Jefferson Blueeyes asked as he emerged from Kevin's office.

The slender, well-dressed man seemed eager, stepping forward immediately to shake Ella's reluctant hand. "Good to see you again, Investigator Clah—Ella. The president alluded to what was taking place now, and he's been contacting all the council members, as you probably already know."

"What's going on at the plant? Was there an accident?" the secretary asked, looking at Blueeyes, then Ella. "My son works on the graveyard shift. Will he be called in early?"

"The problem is mostly at the coal storage facility, not the power plant itself," Ella explained before Blueeyes could speak again. "But I can't say anything more about it at the moment."

"I can help you track down a Tribal Council member, Ella," Blueeyes motioned her toward Kevin's office. She followed him inside and noticed that Jefferson sat down in a chair beside Kevin's desk rather than in Kevin's seat.

Ella closed the door before speaking. "So the president gave you some indication of the trouble we're having?"

Blueeyes nodded. "He said that Navajo activists calling themselves *Hasih* apparently took over part of the coal storage area beside the power plant. They were going to start setting fires or blowing up crucial machinery unless the council moved quickly on the gaming issue."

"That's it, in a nutshell. I'm now trying to find a

Tribal Council member who'll talk to them. Unless they hear from someone soon, they intend on setting off a bomb to demonstrate their sincerity. That's why I was looking for Kevin."

"He left word with Mrs. Johnson outside that he was going to be away for the weekend. That was a surprise to me because we still had a lot of work to do on his gaming position. Did he leave a phone number with you where I can reach him?" Blueeyes asked.

" 'fraid not," Ella said, keeping the truth to herself for now. She didn't want anyone else to know the details of Kevin's weekend with Dawn, especially Blueeyes, whom she really didn't trust.

Ella looked at her watch. "We have to hurry."

Using the two phone lines they had available in Kevin's office, Jefferson and Ella went down the list Kevin had, but were unable to find anyone who could get to Shiprock in time.

In desperation, Ella tried to reach Kevin on his cell phone, but it was out of service. She'd figured as much, with cell phones being restricted on the small aircraft he and Dawn were traveling in.

As it became apparent that their attempts to find an available council member in time would fail, Ella quickly came up with an alternate plan.

Moments later, she raced to the mine with Blueeyes riding beside her. When they arrived, Ella half dragged Jefferson to where Payestewa was and filled them both in. "Jefferson can say he's Kevin. Their voices are very similar, and they both know the agenda before the council. We can pull it off."

"I don't know about this," Blueeyes said quickly.

Ella looked at Payestewa. "We're down to five minutes. This is our only option. You can brief Jefferson and monitor everything he says. If he gets into trouble, we'll cut off the call."

"All right," Payestewa agreed. "If the *Hasih* get what

they asked for, sort of, hopefully they won't feel the need to take any drastic action."

Three minutes before the phone call was due, Jefferson sat in the crime-scene van, which served as their temporary command post and communications center. Blalock had reluctantly approved their emergency plan, but Blueeyes looked like a trapped man.

Payestewa handed Blueeyes some notes and he began to study them. "What if it goes sour?"

"It won't. You know Kevin's political positions better than the rest of us," Ella said.

"It's time," Payestewa said a moment later, and Ella nodded to Blueeyes.

The call was made, and the phone inside the maintenance building was answered after the first ring.

"You're cutting it close." The voice came over the speaker, turned on so those in the van could hear both sides of the conversation. "Who is this?"

"Councilman Tolino, from Shiprock," Blueeyes answered in a steady voice, then looked down at his notes. "I'm willing to listen to what you have to say, so don't do anything that will harm the *Dineh* or yourselves. We all want this to end peacefully."

Ella watched Blueeyes closely, but now that it was show time, he was coming through like a pro.

"You already know what we want, Councilman Tolino. It's time to get the rest of the council together and do whatever's necessary to bring the People out of this hole you and the other so-called leaders have dug for the tribe."

"I hear you, and now I want you to listen to me and understand what *I* have to say." Blueeyes looked briefly at the notes, then continued. "No vote will be taken while you hold hostages or occupy any portion of the plant. We've gone as far as we can. Threats will not get you what you want. The next move is yours."

Payestewa made a cutting motion across his throat, and Blueeyes hung up the phone.

Ella and Blalock climbed out of the van, looking anxiously toward the coal storage area. Someone wearing a hood came out of the maintenance building and waved his arm from side to side at waist level. Then two disguised individuals crouched beside an athletic bag in the road stood, and walked over to talk to him.

"It must have worked, Ella." Blalock smiled grimly.

"I'm just glad whoever it was didn't know Kevin. I was afraid they'd ask him something Blueeyes couldn't answer," Ella said softly. "We got lucky."

Ella heard footsteps, and half turned. Jimmy Frank was coming up, having arrived along with twenty or more country deputies and law enforcement officers enlisted to help maintain the perimeter. "Excuse me, Dwayne. I need a few moments with Officer Frank."

Jimmy waited until Blalock had walked away, then spoke in a soft voice. "My cousin works at the tribal center, and told me what's going on. She heard that you left with Blueeyes and was afraid you'd end up trusting him too much, so she called to warn me. She's been helping me keep close tabs on Blueeyes at work—who comes to see him, and so on. I was planning to make out a full report that included information I got from her but there hasn't been time. When I heard you were here, I figured I'd better come over and talk to you personally."

"What have you got?" She turned to look at the command post van. Jefferson was outside now, walking with one of the plant managers to a white pickup.

"For starters, Blueeyes has been connected to some borderline shady business ventures these past few years since he moved back from California. First he tried to set up a security alarm business in Farmington, but it failed miserably and he barely avoided an investigation for fraud. After that, he got into real estate, but the land he'd tried to sell proved to have a problem with water rights and access roads. Eventually, he shut down that company, too, filing for bankruptcy and avoiding creditors. That was almost a year ago, and I'm not sure how he made his money until he resurfaced as Tolino's aide. What I do know is that he paid cash for that fancy car of his and the big trailer he lives in."

"I wish we'd have known about this sooner," Ella said, then, with a quick thanks, left to look for Paycheck.

Ella found him by the crime-scene van, and learned that Blueeyes had managed to find a ride back into Shiprock. Jefferson had volunteered to continue calling Tribal Council members in hopes of getting one to come to the site.

Glad that he was no longer around where he could observe their strategy, Ella filled in the young Hopi agent quickly on what she'd learned about Kevin's aide.

"That explains something that was bothering me about the phone call. I couldn't figure out why the man Blueeyes spoke to was so passive. I was expecting a protest from the moment Jefferson started laying down the rules, and when it didn't come, it threw me a bit. Now I figure he must have recognized Jefferson's voice, and couldn't let on without putting him on the spot."

"I wish we knew what was really going on inside there," Ella said, indicating the maintenance building.

"We've been listening in as best we can with a parabolic microphone, and it sounds like there's some dissension, at least between the ones who are outside the building. I don't like this, Ella, because it makes them— and the situation—even more unpredictable."

"I think we need to infiltrate the area they're controlling. We know that there's at least one woman among the *Hasih*, so all I'd have to do is study how they're dressed and get a good look at their hoods. Then I could disguise myself and move in after dark. Their sentries can't be everywhere at once, so with the right timing, I see no reason why I can't slip inside."

Before Payestewa could answer, Blalock approached. "I heard what you just said, and I've got photos that'll help you. I've been taking shots with a telephoto lens, trying to verify how many are inside. I can now tell you that there are more than five armed people in there, but probably less than ten. I think the actual number is more like eight, and at least two appear to be women."

"From what I saw earlier through the spotting scopes it looks like their hoods are all made the same way," Ella said. "I'll get all the details I can from your photos, then ask my brother how the Fierce Ones recognize each other when they're masked. I have a feeling that some of the ones inside belong to the Fierce Ones and are using the same strategy."

"I still think the idea of going in is risky," Blalock argued. "We want them to call it off and walk away, not give them another hostage, especially a high-profile one like you."

Ella looked at Payestewa. "You're the one who's been in closest contact with them. Do you think we can count on them surrendering before they do something stupid?"

"The fact that there's dissension going on makes the situation volatile. I can't be sure of anything except that I have a strong feeling I haven't been talking with the real leader. So far whenever I've asked the guy I'm in communication with to agree to something, he puts me off, then calls me back a short time later with an answer. Twice now, I've had him about to listen to reason, but then he cuts off our conversation. By the time I get him on the line again, we're back to square one. My gut tells me that the person I've been speaking to wants to end this now that they've made their point, but he can't convince whoever's really calling the shots in there."

"Maybe they're just playing for time. Do you think it's possible that this is nothing more than a diversion?"

"What makes you think that?" Payestewa asked.

"Look at the facts," Ella said. "They must know that interfering with the flow of electricity all across the Southwest isn't going to make them any friends. Even those with gas furnaces need the electricity to run the blowers. And any pollution or long-term disruption in power will hurt everyone on the Rez. If nothing else, they'll be breathing polluted air like the rest of us. So what they're doing just doesn't quite mesh. We don't even know for sure that they *can* set fire to the coal or blow up the conveyer belt system."

"The biggest problem we're facing is that we just don't have enough information to go on. We've got to tread carefully," Payestewa said.

"That's why one of us has go in and see what we're really up against," Ella said flatly. "Since I'm Navajo, I think it should be me. Hopefully, if I get caught, they'll be less likely to shoot one of their own."

"It's still a bad idea," Blalock said, "but I haven't got a better one, except to wait them out and negotiate."

"All right, then. I'll make my move after two in the morning, when they're all going to be half-asleep and freezing from the cold. But we've got to keep this from the rest of the officers and the security staff around here too. For all we know one of these people could be working with them, reporting our every move."

"Agreed," Blalock said. "Just remember that you'll probably have to neutralize one of the female members of the group so you'll be safe if anyone takes a head count."

"I'll handle it," Ella answered, plans already forming in her mind. "Get me photos of those hoods, and a shot of whichever woman is closest to my size and shape. Then I'll drive over to my brother's place and make a quick stop at the station. After that, I'm going home to try and get some sleep. I'll be back at one-thirty A.M. or sooner."

"I'll E-mail your home computer color close-ups of their hoods and some photos of the women involved," Blalock said. "The photos won't take long to develop and upload. But, for the record, I still think you're taking one helluva chance."

"We need to know what we're up against. What we

don't know, in this case, might end up hurting a lot of people," Ella said. Although she didn't like the odds against her any more than he did, she knew what had to be done.

TWENTY-TWO
✕ ✕ ✕

Because of the time of year, it was already dark outside when Ella arrived at Clifford's home. Despite the low temperature she found him standing outside watching the stars.

Ella left the unit and went to join him. "Hey, big brother, isn't it a little cold tonight for Navajo astronomy?"

"It helps me think," Clifford said, giving her a smile. Gazing up at the sky, he added, "When I stand out here, the stars always remind me that everything has a purpose. Some of the stars form patterns and that's the work of the Holy People. Others are in a state of disorder, which is the work of Coyote, the trickster. Yet they all provide light when the moon is waning or not out at all, guidance for the hunters, and are seasonal markers as well."

Ella looked back at the house and saw there were no lights on. He was apparently alone again tonight. "Is everything okay?"

Clifford nodded. "My wife and son are still visiting my mother-in-law," he said sadly. "When they're gone, the house seems too big and empty, particularly at night."

She nodded slowly, aware that it would be the same for her when she went home tonight. Neither her mother nor her daughter would be there to greet her.

Clifford turned around and regarded her face thoughtfully in the illumination of thousands of stars. "I heard people talking when I went to the trading post earlier for supplies. I gather that there's trouble at the power plant."

She told him quickly what had happened, then asked for his advice about infiltrating the *Hasih* group. "I need to pass as one of them without arousing any suspicion, so I was hoping you could give me some information. For starters, how did the Fierce Ones recognize each other when they were wearing their hoods to conceal their identities?"

"I'm glad you came to me about this," Clifford said. "Your instincts served you well." He took a deep breath, then let it out slowly. "The *Hasih* members are caught between wanting to keep the Rez separate from the Anglo world, and thinking that it could be a slow death for their families and the tribe unless gaming is brought in. They're trying to do what's right, but they feel trapped."

"We need a way to bring this situation to a conclusion peacefully, if possible, but the longer it draws out, the more unstable it becomes," Ella explained.

"Is it true they plan to set fire to the coal reserves?"

Ella nodded. "We'll do whatever is necessary to prevent that from happening."

"For the first time in my life I'm glad my son and wife are with my mother-in-law."

Ella smiled. "Yeah. My daughter is with her father, away for the weekend. I'm glad she's not at home. A big coal fire will pollute the air with the worst kind of contaminants."

Clifford took her into the medicine hogan where he had a small piñon wood fire burning. He reached into a pine trunk and pulled out a cloth hood. "This is the one I used last year. There are certain things that we incorporated into it, like the shape of the eyeholes, that were meant to help us identify any infiltrators. I have a friend who knows the *Hasih* and how they think. He'll tell me what I need to know. I'd like an hour or two. Can you give me that long, or will you need the information sooner?"

"I plan to make my move at two in the morning."

"Then be here by ten. I'll help you get prepared for what you have to do."

"Thanks, brother. I appreciate this."

"Take your *jish*, your medicine pouch, tonight too." He paused, then added, "How long has it been since you've worn it?"

Ella understood his question well. The medicine bag was seen as a repository of power. But belief said that the *jish* had to be kept fresh and vital through use. To lock it up in a drawer would weaken it. "The truth is I'm not even sure where it is. I'll have to search."

"I'll make one up for you," he said. "At least you have your badger fetish—correct?"

"I wear it all the time."

As Ella drove away, she thought of how different she and her brother were. She placed her faith in her police skills and in the system that balanced crime with law. He believed in the gods and powers that brought order in the midst of chaos. Yet, in the final analysis, they both sought harmony and *hózhq*, a state of blessedness that became a tangible reality when the heart was receptive to the beautiful and the good.

Ella arrived at the police station a half hour later. It occurred to her that the rifle used to shoot at her again, at the mine, could be the same one that the Benjamins had refused to bring in for ballistics testing. Were the Benjamins playing her in some way she hadn't determined yet, or were they just hoping to make her squirm? Either way, until a bullet was recovered that could serve as a basis for comparison, and she had more on the Benjamins than just a lack of trust, there weren't any more reasons to confront them.

Ella stopped by her office to type a quick report for Big Ed, then returned to her vehicle. As she switched on the engine, her cell phone rang. Ella recognized Blalock's voice immediately.

"We have a problem with Branch, the radio talk show moron," he said. "He got wind of what's happening at the mine, and he just made things worse on his program, adding wild speculation to the few facts he had."

"Just what we needed," Ella answered.

"We're thinking of going to the station owners, asking that they have him exercise some discretion until the crisis has ended."

"What exactly did he say?"

"He listed ways those occupying the coal piles and preparation area could wreak havoc with even a small amount of the right explosives. He even read a paragraph from the *Anarchist's Cookbook* on how to place the charges. From the information he gave we figure they could cripple the facility for weeks, maybe months. Hopefully nobody holding those hostages was listening."

Ella knew that Blalock was no more a fan of Branch's than she was. The man was an extreme right-wing ratings-hungry jerk who took every opportunity to undermine the tribal government and local law enforcement. "So now what?" she asked.

"Meet me at his home. He's off the air now and I was told by his producer that he'd talk to me. If he refuses to listen to reason and cooperate, we can lean on his bosses."

"I'm on my way. And, while we're there, will you ask if he has a fifty-caliber weapon in his gun collection? If he does, ask him if he'll volunteer to bring it in for a ballistics test."

"I'll give it a try," Blalock said. "Do you think the sniper weapon could be his?"

"Who knows? All I remember is that he has an extensive gun collection. Unfortunately for us, he could lie about it and we would never know unless we stumbled across the person who sold it to him."

"*I'll* do the asking. Remember that we have to go by the book with this creep, and it's my jurisdiction. Branch is slimy and he keeps score."

As she drove east across the Rez, Ella got an update on the negotiations. For the moment, things were quiet.

Ella checked her watch. Blalock would arrive at Branch's home first, but that was a good thing. Had it been the other way around she would have been tempted to press Branch for answers, and that could have just created more trouble.

Blalock was waiting with George Branch on his farmhouse porch by the time she pulled up beside Branch's monstrous SUV.

"I see you're finally learning to play by the rules, Special Investigator Clah." Branch used his radio voice when stating her job title, emphasizing each syllable. "Jurisdiction is something the courts take very seriously."

She would have given anything to bury her fist into his ever-growing gut but, instead, she simply nodded.

"I understand that you have a question about my gun collection?" Branch asked her as they stepped inside to his living room. He sat down immediately, but Ella and the FBI agent remained standing.

Ella shook her head. "You can address your concerns to Agent Blalock. As you said, it's his jurisdiction."

Blalock's expression was one of pure relief. "We need to know if you own a fifty-caliber rifle, sir, and if you do, may we examine it?"

Branch hesitated. "I did own one, but it was stolen."

"Did you report the crime?" Blalock asked.

"It was over a year ago, and, yes, I did. The county sheriff should have a record of that report. And my insurance company probably has a copy on record as well."

"If you don't mind my asking, I seem to remember that you have an elaborate antitheft system. What happened?" Ella asked.

"There was an accident about a mile from here involving a gasoline truck, and apparently the electricity was down for several hours. I wasn't home at the time. Unfortunately, by the time I got back, my house had been broken into and several of my weapons were gone."

"Did any of them ever turn up?" Blalock asked.

"None. I lost the fifty-caliber, two long-barreled goose guns, and three nine-millimeter pistols. They took several boxes of shells, as well."

"Any idea who might have taken them?"

"No. The sheriff's deputies asked me the same questions, but a lot of people know about my gun collection. When the power went out, someone must have seen it as their golden opportunity." He looked at Ella and then at Blalock. "Why all this interest now?"

"A fifty-caliber rifle was used in a crime recently and, as you can imagine, there aren't that many of them in these parts."

"A weapon that big used in a crime? Hell, it almost takes two people to carry one. It's expensive, too," Branch conceded. "Okay, now that I've cooperated with you, will you give me a statement about what's going on over at the power plant?"

"I'll have to refer you to the news reports. There's nothing more being released to the press or public for the time being," Blalock answered. "And we'd appreciate it if you didn't give the *Hasih* any extra intelligence information about the facility. A little discretion could be a community service right now."

"Hey, they're *in* there now, aren't they? It's not like I'm telling them something they don't know already."

"They may not be as well-informed as you regarding the use of explosives," Blalock said.

"I'll keep that in mind," Branch said. "How come the police don't just raid the place and take their buildings and coal supply back?"

Blalock shrugged. "We always prefer to handle hostage situations without bloodshed, if possible."

Branch's eyes narrowed. "But you've got a plan to take the place back forcibly."

Ella decided to focus Branch's thoughts on the stolen

weapon instead of continuing to play mind games with him. "Crimes like residential thefts are sometimes traced to someone who's already visited the home. Can you associate anyone who's been here to the stolen weapons?"

"All kinds of people come to my home. It's the nature of the business I'm in. I can't vouch for everyone I've met, and I'm sure you can't either. Besides, how am I supposed to remember a year later who might have been in my house? Do you remember all your house guests from a year ago, Investigator Clah?"

Ella hadn't expected an answer anyway, but this was the closest to an honest response she could hope for from the man. At least he had a point.

She continued. "We've had some outsiders on the Rez recently causing trouble. Have *you* had any problems with vandalism lately?"

"I live off the Rez, Clah. What do you mean, 'an outsider'? Navajos are the outsiders in the county."

Branch was too quick and glib with his answers. That was a trait she'd found most often in people who made a habit of telling lies and half-truths.

Blalock looked at Branch, thanked him, then walked outside with Ella. As soon as they were away from the house, Blalock spoke. "I don't think he's lying about the gun being stolen. That's too easy to check up on."

"But it's also possible that the rifle and the other weapons were never stolen, that he gave or sold them to someone and he knows exactly what's going on."

"But we can't prove any of that," Blalock said, then checked his watch. "You better get some rest before you make your move."

"Yeah, you're right."

Ella said good-bye to Blalock, then drove straight home. She was almost dreading the empty house. The thought of not finding Rose or Dawn waiting depressed her.

When she unlocked the door a short time later, Two

came running up to her. She felt sorry for him, and bent down to pet the old but hardy mutt.

"You don't like being home alone either, do you, pal?" Ella scratched him behind the ears.

Two followed her into the kitchen and Ella fed him, then heated herself a can of soup. She wasn't hungry, but she needed to eat. Carrying the bowl into the living room, she turned on the television set. The dog relaxed at the sound of voices and Ella made a mental note to leave the TV on for him until someone came back home.

After finishing her supper, Ella downloaded the photos Blalock had sent her. She had an inexpensive ink-jet printer that provided color capability, so she set the software on high quality and printed the best of the photos.

Returning to the living room, Ella set the photos down on the coffee table, and studied each. From what she could see, getting the hood just right was paramount.

She sat back, mulling things over in her mind. As she did, her gaze drifted over Dawn's scattered toys. Unable to resist the impulse, she reached for the phone and started to dial Kevin's cell phone number, needing the reassurance that Dawn was okay. Then she realized what time it was, and hung up.

There was no sense in waking Dawn up too. Kevin would find out that their daughter lived up to her name quite naturally. She chuckled softly, thinking that Kevin was in for a surprise when Dawn woke with Sun. If he'd had plans to sleep late this weekend their daughter would change that in a hurry.

Realizing that she'd have to get some sleep soon, she took a last look at the photos, then went to her room. She'd just stripped off her clothes and crawled into bed when Two jumped up, settling beside her.

Ella glared at him for a moment but, seeing the hopeful look he gave her, she caved in. "Okay, Two, but just for this weekend."

After setting the alarm on the bedstand to go off in exactly three hours, she turned off the lamp.

When the alarm went off it felt as if she'd only been asleep a few minutes. Ella groaned, then opened her eyes, trying to get her bearings in the dark. As her thoughts became focused she switched on the lamp and got out of bed. Two looked at her, but made no move to get off the covers.

"All right, furball. You get it all to yourself now."

Ella considered a shower, then realized the people holding the hostages wouldn't have bathed for many hours. She dressed quickly, using the photos of one of the members of *Hasih* as a guide, trying to match the person's appearance.

Turning on the TV for Two, Ella stepped outside into the bitter cold wearing her vest over the coat. She'd wear it as long as she could.

As she switched on the ignition, her thoughts shifted to the task ahead. Clifford would be waiting, and it was time to go to work.

TWENTY-THREE
—— ✖ ✖ ✖ ——

Driving to her brother's house, Ella thought about Clifford. She doubted he ever got much sleep when his family was away, and, for the first time, she truly empathized with that.

A short time later, she pulled up near the medicine hogan and Clifford came out and waved at her, inviting her to come inside. The weather was beyond cold as she left the tribal unit and walked across the frozen earth. The gusts sweeping from the mountains to the west chilled her to the bone.

"This has got to be one of the worst winters we've had in a decade or more," Ella said, teeth chattering. The fire in the hogan was low, but it felt wonderful after being outside.

"I think it is." Clifford opened the trunk she'd seen before and pulled out a newer-looking burlap hood. "This is a duplicate of the ones the *Hasih* use. My patient's nephew is involved in the group and this was the hood he wore until it got torn up in the back. I've repaired it for you."

"Who's your patient?" Ella asked, pulling out the color print of the photo Blalock had sent her, and comparing the hood Clifford had with the one in the photo.

"*Hastiin Sání*."

The nickname simply meant "mister old man" but she knew who he meant. It was Pablo Tso, and his nephew, Clyde, had been in school with her. Pablo was over one hundred years old if he was a day.

"Are you telling me that his nephew, my old schoolmate, is one of the men inside the mine's operation building?"

"Yes, and in exchange for the information, I've promised Hastiin Sání that you'll do your best to protect his nephew. But be careful. I'm pretty sure he'll recognize your voice if he hears it."

Ella thought about the boy she'd known. "I can't believe he's involved in this. He was the most nonaggressive person I've ever met. I remember he got called out a few times but he refused to fight until the other guy threw the first punch."

"Yeah, but once he was forced to fight, he always kicked their butts. This type of action isn't really out of character for him if you think about it. The situation the tribe is facing is making many of our people feel cornered."

"Yeah, but if he's anything like the kid we both knew, I can't see him destroying that coal or blowing up the power plant."

"The boy we knew and the man he is could be two very different people," Clifford warned, reaching for a bracelet made of colored strands of leather. "This is one of their trademarks. Wear it on your left wrist. It'll barely show, but they'll see enough of it to know you're one of them."

"Anything else?"

"Be wary of their leader. My patient assured me that he's a dangerous man. I tried to get him to tell me more, but he refused."

"What's the person's name?"

"I don't know. What worries me is that I've never known my patient to be afraid of anything or anyone before."

"Do you think someone has threatened him?"

"Not him, but maybe his wife," Clifford answered. "I did notice that when his wife went outside the hogan to get some firewood, he went to the doorway carrying his thirty-thirty Winchester and kept an eye on her until she got back."

"I'd give anything to know if the leader is Navajo or a member of one of the other tribes in the area."

"You'll know once you hear him talking. When the *Dineh* speak English, they have characteristic pauses that all of us recognize easily." Clifford handed her a *jish*, a medicine bundle in a leather pouch sealed with a drawstring. "This will protect you tonight."

"Do they wear these?"

"Some do, I'm sure. They're traditionalists."

Ella fastened it to her belt, then looked up and held her brother's gaze. "I'm going to be careful, but if anything happens to me . . ."

"You know that Mom and I will look after your daughter," Clifford answered.

"These days I'm never as afraid for myself as I am for her," Ella admitted slowly. "My daughter's father would want to take custody of her, but the way his family feels about ours makes that a bad idea. I also don't think he's prepared to deal with her on a daily basis."

"That's not something that should ever worry you. You'll be fine tonight. Your training and instincts won't let you down."

Ella said good-bye to her brother, then drove through Shiprock to the mine, which lay several miles farther east on the edge of the Rez.

After passing through checkpoints and a roadblock, she pulled up and parked by the line of police units on the east side of the facility. The power plant itself was lit up like a carnival, but the facilities at the south end were in the dark.

Blalock came up to meet her as she walked toward the fence line separating the coal piles and conveyer system from the rest of the plant. "It's been quiet so far. We've cut off the power leading to the conveyer tower and maintenance building, so by now it's probably pretty cold in there. We have a few night-vision scopes and, from what we've seen, the *Hasih* sentries guarding the coal piles and storage bins are taking one-hour shifts so they won't freeze standing outside. We're doing the same with our officers. At least the ones guarding the coal have enough sense not to try and build any fires. Coal dust is supposed to be highly explosive."

"Let's hope they stay smart."

"Payestewa offered to turn some of the power back on if they'll release all the hostages, but they're not ready to do that yet. Their answer was that if we don't mind the hostages being cold too, it's fine with them."

"Have there been any reports of trouble anywhere else on the Rez?"

"You're still thinking that this might be a diversion?"

"Yeah. It's just a nagging feeling I have," Ella answered, reaching for the cloth hood on the passenger's seat.

"We have a plan we think will allow you to get in," Blalock continued. "Payestewa will get them on the phone and again offer a hostages-for-heat swap. At the same time, we'll have two cops scuffle with a TV cameraman who's gotten too close. The cameraman, of course, will be one of ours. While the *Hasih*'s attention is focused on the scuffle and the phone call, you'll have the chance to slide beneath the fence and get under the conveyor belt platform—that tower. The maintenance building has a door on that side."

"Let's hope they haven't booby-trapped that door," Ella said.

"We've watched with the night scopes. They've used the door a few times, but they keep it locked. We got you a key," Blalock said. "One last thing. I'd like you to be wired when you go in. That way if you're in trouble, we'll know right away and can try to protect you."

"With all the heavy winter clothing I'm wearing, hiding the wire won't be a problem, but transmission might be."

"The Bureau has some new equipment that'll do the

job. We'll hear you. If you need us to move in but can't say it clearly, tap your chest twice. The mike will transmit that sound."

"Got it."

"We've been listening with our parabolic mikes, and they haven't been talking very much to each other except a few Navajo words. According to Neskahi, who's been doing the listening, they haven't used any names either. It's either that traditionalist taboo against names, or they're afraid we're listening."

"Thanks. I don't plan to do much talking inside anyway."

Staying out of sight inside a van, Justine helped Ella put on the wire and then adjust it.

"I wish you weren't doing this," Justine said. "The information we have about what's really going on inside the building is too sketchy. There's just no telling what you'll be facing in there. I'll be watching you through a night-vision scope on a rifle when you're in the open, but if you're in the building or out of sight, we can't give you any covering fire."

"I wish there was another way, but we just can't take the chance that they'll decide to set fire to the coal piles and blow up the conveyor belts just for the hell of it. With luck, I'll be able to get close enough to check out the explosives and see how they've been wired to detonate. If they have a remote and we can't neutralize it, we're going to be screwed if we have to assault the place."

"All ready here?" Blalock asked, knocking on the rear van doors. As Ella stepped outside, he handed her the key to the side door.

Ella slipped it inside her jacket pocket as Justine moved into position, rifle in hand. "Let's get this show on the road," Ella said, and slipped the hood on. "Just make sure our own guys don't shoot me."

"Our snipers will be watching for you and they'll keep you covered as much as possible," Blalock said. "But they're the only ones who know you'll be in there."

"Okay, we're all set. I'll see you in a little while."

Ella slipped into the dark shadows cast by the huge power plant, several stories high and fifty yards away, north of the fence. At the moment, the building and its immediate surroundings were lit up like a Christmas tree. There were over a dozen armed security guards and officers making sure it remained out of the hands of the *Hasih*.

She crept closer to the chain-link fence until she spotted the gap at the bottom that Blalock had told her about earlier. Justine was somewhere behind her in the bed of a pickup using the night scope, watching Ella's green image against the hazy background. She knew that the lack of heat from the metal buildings ahead would make it easier to track her.

Hearing the shouting officers and assured that the diversion was under way, she ran to the fence and scrambled underneath, crawling on her stomach to make sure she didn't get hung up.

Ella rolled into the shadows and adjusted her hood again. It had twisted and she needed to position the eyeholes so she could see. Reaching for the key in her pocket, she made a dash to the side door.

The first thing she'd have to do was neutralize and conceal one member of the group that had taken over the power plant. If their numbers were few it would be too easy to spot an extra person. Yet, despite Blalock's warning, she wasn't overly concerned about making sure that the one she put out of commission turned out to be a woman. Wearing the hood and a bulky jacket in the dark, no one would be able to tell which sex she was anyway.

Ella slipped inside and closed the door behind her, leaving it unlocked. There was a faint glow from a battery-powered emergency light, obviously triggered by the loss of electricity. Time and the effect of the cold on its batteries had dimmed its power, fortunately. Two people with assault rifles were huddled against a door on an adjacent wall labeled Storage. A big piece of wood had been wedged against the bottom of the door, and she deduced that was where at least some of the hostages were being held.

Behaving as if she had come inside to get warm, she glanced around casually. Nobody seemed much interested in her arrival.

The two hostage guards weren't wearing hoods, so she slipped hers off, making sure to keep her distance. It was still so dark that facial features couldn't be distinguished except up close.

A tall, broad-shouldered man stood next to the window facing east, speaking on the phone. His hood was on, and he had two pistols jammed into his belt and an assault rifle with a sling over his shoulder.

"We're not going to shoot anyone unless that cameraman moves in closer." The man paused, then holding the receiver close to his chest, repeated what he'd heard from Paycheck to another guy who stood in the shadows beneath the dim emergency lamp. Ella hadn't even seen him until now.

Ella recognized the face the moment he stepped out into the zone where the emergency lamp was directed. It was one of the men she'd seen with Coyote, the man with the pockmarked face and probably the "Indian" who'd hired the low-IQ Anglos to vandalize tribal property. Now there was no doubt in her mind that she was dealing with the Indian syndicate.

He made a slashing motion across his throat, signaling his spokesman to cut off communications.

The one with the phone quickly hung up.

"Let them worry for a while," Coyote's companion snarled.

"I don't know, Gary. This doesn't seem right. We're getting further away from our objectives all the time. We just wanted to get the public's attention about the problems facing the tribe, not turn this into a war."

"Whenever you're forced to take a stand you have to be willing to risk everything," Gary answered flatly. "Stop questioning my decisions. I know what I'm doing. And don't use my name. We know they're using microphones to listen in."

The two men walked away from the phone, which rested on a large metal desk. The maintenance building was essentially one big room containing much of the machinery needed to operate and maintain the conveyer belts. A small office cubicle was at one end. As Ella tried to plan out her next move, she saw one of the sentries come in from outside and walk toward the ladies' rest room, her assault rifle over her shoulder.

Ella moved casually in the same direction, grabbing a roll of duct tape she saw on a workbench, then followed the woman inside.

In less than a minute, the woman was unconscious, and in another two, handcuffed to the pipes in the stall, which Ella had locked from the inside. Her mouth was taped shut so when she regained consciousness, she'd be able to breathe through her nose, but wouldn't be able to yell. Ella had used the rest of the roll of tape to secure her legs to the toilet so she couldn't kick the walls to make noise.

So far, luck was with her. Now wearing the woman's jacket after transferring her own ammunition to it, Ella stepped back out into the main room. Carrying the assault rifle in one hand, she moved toward the small office area. More men had come inside while she was taking out the woman, and were standing around the office door. Ella moved up behind the newcomers, but was careful to stay back far enough so that no one would be able to see her face clearly.

"The Tribal Council still hasn't agreed to meet and vote on the gaming issue, and the police are stalling. It's time to demonstrate our sincerity. Are all the explosives in position?" Gary asked, looking from person to person. He glanced at her only briefly, but knowing that Blalock was probably hearing every word gave her a small measure of confidence. Even if she was discovered, at least the *Hasih* wouldn't be able to achieve complete surprise.

"Yeah," another voice replied. "I made sure on my last patrol."

"All right. Then it's time for our volunteer to go out and attach the detonators. Once he's finished, I'm going to take one charge out into the middle of the road and set it off as a demonstration of our sincerity. Everyone except for the hostage guards needs to be outside in case one of the cops does something stupid, like trying to move inside the fence line. If that happens, the ones guarding the charges will light the fuses and run like hell south or west." Gary looked around the group. "Understood?"

"I better get started on the detonators, then," someone answered.

She recognized her friend Clyde Tso's nasal, high-pitched voice. Even through the hood he now wore, it was impossible to mistake it.

"The line has been drawn in the sand," Gary continued, "and we've stepped over and taken control again. Set the charges, brother, then report back to me when you're done. The rest of you keep watch. When you see me walking away from the bomb, count thirty seconds for the blast and look away so the flash won't ruin your night vision. And remember—shoot anyone who tries to rush the fence, and if anyone gets through, blow this place to hell. Are you ready and with me?"

A murmur of assent went around the room.

"Then put on your hoods, check your weapons, and get outside into position," the leader said.

Ella went outside with the others, staying right behind Clyde. Now that Blalock had hopefully overhead what was about to happen, the risk of law enforcement over-reaction around the perimeter was diminished. But she had to do whatever she could to protect the coal and its delivery system, the conveyor belts.

While the others took sentry positions Ella stuck with Clyde. This wasn't the man she'd known, taking the role of a terrorist bomber. He moved toward the first athletic bag, which was positioned beside one of the massive electric motors that powered the largest conveyor belt.

As he crouched down with a small penlight she stepped closer, silently watching, trying to decide when to make her move. To her surprise, Clyde took a pocketknife and cut the safety fuse away from the detonator assembly instead of inserting it into one of the explosive sticks. But he must have heard her breathing, because he suddenly spun around and slammed her against the wall, his arm pressed to her neck.

"Ease up, Clyde. It's me, Ella. If I'd have known you were going to remove the fuses from the detonators instead of placing them in the explosives, I wouldn't have come up so close behind you," she said, then quickly added, "Blalock, tell Justine not to shoot him, it's okay."

It took Clyde a few seconds to get up to speed, but finally he released her.

"Ella, what the hell are you doing here, and how did you get in? And who are you talking to? You wearing a microphone?"

"There's no time for explanations now. Let me help you finish what you've started now that I know what you really stand for." She looked around, worried someone had seen what had just happened. "Give me the detonators, but be careful. We don't want anyone else to know what we're doing."

"Okay, let's work fast," he said, handing her the small cigarette-sized blasting caps that had safety fuses attached at one end. "But I'll have to connect the one in the road so Gary can carry out his little demonstration. If it doesn't go off, he'll know something is wrong and order the others to start shooting."

"Do you think it's likely he'll get someone else to

come out and attach new detonators and fuses, if necessary?"

"No. We don't have any extra. We had to leave half of our explosives behind because of that."

Moving from athletic bag to athletic bag positioned on coal piles or under pieces of machinery, they pretended to connect the detonators while Ella secretly pocketed the devices instead. As she studied the duct-taped bundles of high explosives, she noted that they appeared to be the same brand and batch that she'd run into before.

The one in the road was the last. Clyde had to use some force to insert the detonator into the normally soft explosives because the cold had hardened the mix, and Ella cringed, realizing that if it went off by accident, she'd end up all over the facility.

"Okay, Ella. Now what? I've got to go tell Gary I'm done. Then he's going to set this one off himself."

"I'll go back inside with you, and stay near the door as if I've been watching your back. Once you tell Gary you've finished, let him know how cold you are and tell him you're going to relieve those two guarding the hostages. I'll join you there once Gary and the others are all outside. We can use the diversion of the explosion in the road to take the hostages out the side door underneath the conveyer tower. There's a place I found where we can get them under the fence and to safety."

"All right," Clyde said with a nod. "But you'd better go with them, Ella. If Gary or some of the other die-hard troublemakers catch you, they'll have all the detonators back. I've cut the fuses off, but they can be reinserted."

"I plan to make my own escape as soon as the hostages are clear, but you can't stay either. If any of them check and notice the detonators and fuses are gone they'll turn on you and have another hostage, or worse."

Clyde nodded. "One thing at a time. I've got to go check with Gary before he starts to worry."

Ella followed silently, carrying the rifle she'd liberated as if she were providing security for Clyde. Gary grunted when Clyde told him everything was set and handed him the penlight, then nodded when Clyde asked for a few minutes inside to warm up.

Ella followed Clyde, watching Gary out of the corner of her eye as he walked outside. The leader stopped, looked back at Ella for a moment, then gave her the thumbs-up and laughed. She returned the gesture, but remained silent, fearing that at the last minute he'd recognize something about her that didn't fit.

Five minutes later Ella was keeping watch while Clyde crawled under the fence, handing his rifle to Blalock while another officer led the freed hostages toward a van. The blast in the road had made her jump although she'd known it was coming, but thanks to the warning Blalock and the others had received, nobody overreacted. Payestewa, she hoped, was on the phone now acting concerned and indignant about the blast, and relating his fears about the safety of the hostages. The rest of the *Hasih* were still shouting and whooping like Hollywood Indians, believing they still held a winning hand.

Ella hadn't told Clyde, but she hadn't wanted to send the detonators with him or the hostages just in case one of them was a decoy working with Gary or his Indian mafia group. Now that everyone was through, Ella made a split-second decision, gesturing to Blalock.

"Here are the detonators and fuse cords." She took off her outer jacket, the zippered pockets full of the devices.

"Hurry," Blalock said, his voice hushed. "Someone's coming out that side door now."

Ella studied the hooded figure who emerged. "From his size and shape, I'm guessing that's Gary." She paused, then quickly added, "I'm going back. If I can get the drop on him and take him out, the others may not continue the standoff once they've lost their leader.

Payestewa might be able to make a deal and get them to lay down their weapons without a problem then."

"Be careful, Ella," Blalock whispered.

She slipped away and ran toward the conveyor belt tower, staying in the deepest shadows. Then, moving quickly and silently, Ella ducked behind a big metal box that said Fire Emergency on the outside and watched Gary pass by.

Ella followed him around the back of the building, noting that he wasn't carrying his assault rifle. Seeing a *Hasih* sentry twenty feet away standing beside a white pickup, she stopped at the corner and watched, reluctant to move any farther out into the open.

"Watch where this guy goes, Justine," she whispered, hoping that Blalock could relay her words in time.

Ella wanted to narrow the gap between them, but before she could find another hiding place, the man walked over to the fence and took off his hood, placing it inside his jacket. Although she was twenty yards away, Ella could see the outline of a Navajo police officer just on the other side of the fence, dimly illuminated by the power plant lights, yet the *Hasih* man seemed completely unconcerned.

Then he signaled the officer by holding his right fist over his heart. The officer responded to the signal by imitating the gesture, but with his left fist, then came over and lifted up a section of the fence, allowing the man to slip beneath.

"We have a bad cop working with the *Hasih*," Ella whispered. "I need someone to keep an eye on the *Hasih* member who just came out of the fenced area on the north side. I'm pretty certain it's Gary—and we need to find out which one of our cops let him through."

Ella went back to the conveyor tower and waited until she was sure no sentry was watching her area. "I'm coming out. Someone meet me over there."

As she reached the exit point, Blalock came out of the shadows. Grabbing her hand, he helped her crawl out. "We've identified the bad cop," he whispered.

"Who is it?" Ella moved behind the cover of a police van.

"Lieutenant Manuelito," Blalock mumbled.

TWENTY-FOUR
✖ ✖ ✖

Justine had identified Manuelito using the night-vision scope on her rifle, and had informed Blalock immediately. But locating the man who'd sneaked past the law enforcement perimeter with Manuelito's help proved tougher.

Ella recognized one of the uniformed cops just coming out of the command center van and took him aside. She'd known Philip Cloud, one of Herman's nephews, since high school, and she trusted him.

"Keep an eye on Manuelito. Don't turn your back on him or let him out of your sight," she said, and told him about the lieutenant's actions. "We need to see who he links up with."

"You've got it. I never liked the SOB much anyway," Philip said, and left for the perimeter just as Justine saw Ella and jogged over to join her.

"Have you heard if we've caught the *Hasih* member who left?" Ella asked immediately.

"No, he managed to leave the facility using a phony power plant ID to drive out past the checkpoints before his description got to those officers," Justine said. "But the officer manning the roadblock does remember what the driver looked like, and his description matches that of the man we saw at the coffee shop."

"That's the one the *Hasih* called Gary, and he was calling the shots inside," Ella said.

"There's our link to the syndicate, then," Justine answered.

"Make sure the officers we trust keep a lookout for

him. Maybe one of our patrols still out on the highway can pull him over," Ella said.

Heading to the command post, Ella and Justine joined Payestewa, who was now on the phone with one of the *Hasih* leaders. It was the man Payestewa had first spoken to. Ella, listening in, verified that it wasn't Gary.

The *Hasih* spokesperson had a different tone now that they'd discovered one of their own bound and gagged in the ladies' room and all their hostages missing. He was offering to have his men put down their weapons and leave the grounds peacefully if the Tribal Council was willing to publicly set the date for a final vote on the gaming issue.

Payestewa agreed to contact the tribal president immediately, then hung up.

"That's a long ways from their earlier demands, Ella. My guess is that they also discovered their explosives are pretty much useless. I'd shake your hand on a job well done, if you Navajos shook hands," Payestewa joked. "Did Blalock tell you what the tribal president did while you were over there wandering around in the dark?"

Ella looked at Blalock, who shrugged. "The tribal president called a special session of the Tribal Council for Monday on the gaming issue. Apparently, the so-called legitimate supporters of gambling used this take-over to force him to act. Payestewa will let the *Hasih* know about this development as soon as our reinforcements arrive. We have another fifty deputies en route just to show the *Hasih* that a shootout would be a mistake. But, since it now appears that they're going to be getting what they asked for, I don't expect we'll have much of a problem," Blalock said.

"With no way to set off their explosives and no hostages, the only leverage they'll have are their weapons, and they have only ten or so people left in there now. We currently have sixty men and women on the perimeter and will have a lot more shortly," Payestewa explained.

"The next few hours should be quiet ones," Big Ed Atcitty said, coming into the command post. He looked cold, but in a good mood. "I've got Manuelito being watched by a couple of officers. No wonder that weasel wasn't having a crime problem in his district—he's been working with the crooks."

"We've got to keep him away from any *Hasih* members we end up arresting here. I don't want him passing them any more information," Ella said.

"With luck he'll lead us to the others," Big Ed suggested. "I need someone to go in person to warn the skeleton crew at the station about Manuelito. Obviously we can't use the radio because he'll hear us. I've already spoken in person to a few key county people, including Sheriff Taylor. But I need to make sure Manuelito doesn't issue any orders and create more problems for us than he already has."

Ella looked at Big Ed. "How about if I go back to Shiprock and have the watch commander send word via land line to the other stations, especially Window Rock? We should also have Dispatch monitor all his calls. Then, even if someone tries to tip him off letting him know we're onto him, Dispatch can alert us."

"That should cover it," Justine said.

"Not quite. We'll also have to disable his cell phone," Ella said.

"Not a problem. I'll get it done," Blalock nodded.

"Okay, then I'm off to the station. I'll be back within the hour," Ella said.

Ella walked back to her unit, put on her bulletproof vest again, pocketed her cell phone, which she'd left in the Jeep, then drove past the checkpoints to the highway. It didn't feel right to leave again before the operation was finished, but Manuelito could cause a lot of harm unless other officers out in the community were warned about his treachery.

By the time she pulled into the nearly deserted police station parking lot, tension was making her entire body ache. As she stepped out of her unit, she heard another vehicle approaching. A beige sedan screeched around the corner, one of its front tires hopping the curb as the driver hurtled into the station parking lot, heading straight toward her.

Ella yelled, and, overcompensating, the driver swerved and slammed on the brakes. The car skidded and struck the concrete barrier at the front of a parking space, hopped it with a crunch, and came to rest straddling the concrete rail.

Ella ran to the car and found the driver slumped over the steering wheel. As she threw the door open, and the dome light came on, she could see that the upholstery was soaked with blood. The seats began steaming slightly as the cold outside air hit the warm, wet fabric.

Ella pushed the driver back gently, trying to figure out who he was, but his features were covered in blood, swollen and badly distorted from the results of a beating. There were slashes on his arms, some caked with blood, others still bleeding onto the car seat and onto his clothes. She couldn't remember the last time she'd seen this much blood coming from someone still alive.

"Ella," he whispered.

Her heart froze. The voice . . . she knew it. Seeing the watch commander coming toward her from the entrance, she yelled for him to call an ambulance and the EMTs. With a quick nod, he turned and ran back inside.

"I had a little trouble getting away," the man whispered, then coughed, and more blood came spilling out of his mouth. "I blew my own cover."

"Henry?" Her heart was beating overtime. She wasn't sure how someone with all the apparent knife wounds he'd suffered could still be alive. Had he been shot as well? "Don't talk," she said. "Help's on the way."

"Listen. Not much time. Tried to warn you. Cop on the take caught me trying . . . to get message to you.

Found out about him too late. He killed the councilman's girlfriend, then the councilman. He told others to use your daughter to ensure Tolino's vote."

Hearing her child mentioned, Ella's blood turned to ice. She swallowed, forcing herself to concentrate. "Have they taken her?"

"Don't know."

"*Who's* going after my daughter? Tell me." Ella pressed. If it was Manuelito, she'd kill him herself.

Henry's eyes closed, and his body went limp, slumping sideways onto the seat. Fear clutched at her stomach and she reached for him, praying he wasn't dead, but before she could check, someone pulled her back.

Instinctively, she started to resist, but then saw it was the watch commander with a blanket and emergency stretcher. "Paramedics are on the way. Help me get him onto the ground. We need to stop that bleeding."

Ella helped lift Henry Estrada out of the car and onto the stretcher. Covering him as much as possible with the blanket, Ella and the watch commander applied pressure to the worst of his wounds with compresses from a first-aid kit. Every instinct she possessed screamed at her to run inside and call Kevin to warn him, but to leave, for even a second, might take away Estrada's chance at life. Torn, she told the watch commander about Manuelito, warning him not to use the police radio to pass the warning to other Navajo officers.

As Ella applied pressure to the brachial artery in his upper arm, stemming the flow of blood to a long cut in Henry's forearm, she listened anxiously for the paramedics and an ambulance. Then one of the secretaries came outside with another blanket. Ella shifted her attention for a second. "Reach into my jacket, get my notebook, then go inside and call Kevin Tolino. His number is on the back inside cover. Warn him that our daughter's a target. If you can't get him, call the Colorado State PD and send them to find him at the Pine Bluff Lodge."

"We all have first-aid training. Let me handle this while you make the calls." Shifting positions, she took over for Ella.

Ella stepped away and flipped open her cell phone, punching out the numbers as she hurried back to her unit. Kevin's number rang and rang, but no one answered. Fear clutched at her heart. Were they just asleep and couldn't hear the phone, or had Dawn already been kidnapped? Next, she tried the lodge office, but all she got was an answering machine at this hour.

Ella started to shake, and knew it wasn't from the cold. Her child was in danger. The knowledge tore at her, undermining her even as she tried to stay focused.

After learning via her cell phone that the scheduled flight had taken off on time with all but one of the listed passengers—they wouldn't confirm Kevin and Dawn's presence unless she came to the counter and identified herself as a police officer—Ella knew she'd have to go to the airport, at least.

Ella climbed into her unit and switched on the ignition. She'd drive to Farmington to confirm that Dawn and Kevin were on the flight. If so, and she was still unable to get Kevin on the phone, she'd take the next airplane that could get her close to the Colorado ski resort. The Pine Bluff Lodge was only a few miles from there. While en route to Farmington she'd notify Big Ed and alert the Colorado cops.

She was just pulling out of the parking lot when her cell phone rang. She opened it with one trembling hand, but it wasn't Kevin, it was Big Ed.

"Have you sent out the warning?"

"The watch commander knows, but I . . . Something's come up," she said, filling him in, her voice shaky. "Don't let Manuelito out of your sight," she almost begged. "If they've gotten to her and Kevin, that man may be the only one who can tell us where my daughter is."

"I'm placing him under arrest right now, as soon as we hang up."

"Fine with me." Her voice was still weak and strained.

"But there's something I need to tell you. Dispatch called. They know we're handling a crisis situation, so they didn't call you directly, worried about your cell phone ringing at a bad time. Jennifer Clani tried to reach you earlier."

"Did she leave a number?" Ella asked quickly, remembering she'd hadn't taken her cell phone with her when infiltrating those holding the power plant's coal facility.

"She's at home," Big Ed answered, then gave her the number.

The news stunned her. Not even taking time to say good-bye, Ella disconnected the call, then dialed Jennifer's home.

"I've been trying to contact you," Jennifer sobbed. "I missed the flight with Dawn and Mr. Tolino because I found two flat tires on my car. I couldn't get there in time. I called Mr. Tolino's cell phone number as soon as I could get to a phone, but I got a message that said it was out of service. I tried again later, but all it does is ring. No one answers."

"I'll keep trying, Jennifer. If you hear anything about where Kevin and Dawn might be, let me know immediately but don't tell anyone else." She gave Jennifer her cell number, then hung up and redialed Big Ed.

He was at the command post, but sounded out of breath when he answered the call. "Chief, I need you to call the local sheriff and state police and see if they can go to the lodge now and check things out for me."

"I've already done that," Big Ed said. "Miss Clani gave me the number earlier. And I've got some news you need to hear, Ella. First, I want you to know the hoodlums calling themselves *Hasih* have struck a deal with Payestewa. They'll be setting down their weapons and coming out as soon as the tribal president arrives and they can see the document calling for the council vote on Monday. They want the press here too to hear the announcement so that the tribal government will be under public pressure to keep their side of the bargain."

"I'm glad that's being settled," she said, her thoughts miles away.

"But there's more, Ella. With the extra deputies arriving and relieving some of the cops who'd been on duty since the start of this, there was some confusion for a while. Taking advantage of the activity, Manuelito apparently slipped away on foot. His vehicle is still here."

"If that man gets anywhere near my kid—"

"I don't think you'll have to worry about Dawn or Kevin. There are forty council members who have expressed their intention to vote for gaming, and about that same number are expected to vote against. The rest are undecided. Both sides will need forty-five out of the eighty-eight for a majority, or maybe that will be forty-four out of eighty-seven now. Either way, they need Kevin to vote progaming, and they can't afford to harm either of them if that's going to happen. My feeling is that they'll keep Dawn as leverage and release Kevin."

"That should invalidate the entire voting process on this," Ella argued.

"Not unless solid, incontrovertible proof that our Tribal Council members have been coerced comes to the surface. As things stand now, the majority of the *Dineh* are demanding that the Tribal Council act. This is bigger than just pressure from the *Hasih*."

"Nobody takes my daughter away from her family, and she's not going to become anybody's political pawn. I'm going to find an airplane to take me to the Pine Bluff Lodge," Ella said coldly. "I'm getting my daughter back."

"That's what I'm counting on. I'll make sure Colorado officers are there to meet you when you arrive and back you up all the way."

Ella reached the Farmington airport on the west end

of the city ten minutes later. After briefly alarming airport security when they saw Henry's blood on her hands and clothes, she confirmed that Kevin and Dawn had departed as scheduled for Colorado. The same carrier offered a charter service that could take her to the airfield closest to the lodge on a smaller aircraft. It would be a bumpy, uncomfortable ride, but she'd be there less than forty minutes after departure.

Black despair churned inside her, but she tried to focus on the task she had to perform rather than on her emotions. She had to stay in control of herself now. Nothing she'd ever done, nothing she'd ever do, would matter if when Dawn needed her most she wasn't there for her. It seemed a bitter irony that after all her concern and care, it was Kevin and his job, not hers, that was the reason for their daughter being in danger.

Forced to wait until the aircraft was ready, impatient for news, and unable to get a connection with her cell phone to Colorado, Ella used a pay telephone at the Farmington terminal to call the sheriff's office in the Colorado county where the Pine Bluff Lodge was located. She had to wait less than thirty seconds before a detective named Mike Brown was on the phone.

"I have some news on an incident that has a connection to Mr. Tolino, Investigator Clah," he said, alert and all business despite the very early morning hour.

Detective Brown hadn't said "bad" news, so she continued breathing.

"We did some cross-checking on a call we received late last night. Our dispatcher received a report of shots fired and this led officers to the Pine Bluff cabin Mr. Tolino had rented. Unfortunately, the place was deserted by the time the deputies arrived. There's evidence that a short but intense firefight took place, and two vehicles left in a hurry after that. Windows had been shot out and some of the furniture looked as if it had been used to block doors or to provide cover from gunfire."

"What else?" she asked, her voice unsteady.

"No blood, first of all. But we noticed what look like nine-millimeter rounds lodged in the solid door-frame. I think they may have come from Tolino's gun. Your chief did some quick checking for us and we learned that Tolino owns a nine-millimeter Beretta and has a permit to carry that weapon. We found more nine-millimeter brass inside the cabin—a total of six cases, I think."

The prickly sensation all over her body and the knot of ice in her stomach were all signs that she was close to losing control. Her mouth was completely dry and her tongue felt glued to the roof of her mouth. She wanted to say something, but she wasn't sure her vocal cords would work right.

"You okay, Investigator Clah?"

"Yes," she managed. "Has a crime-scene unit been to the cabin already?" she asked, hating the way her voice had broken on the last syllable.

"They're on the way. We've had some break-ins in the area recently, so they were out on another call. I just came from the cabin after a cursory look around and a few quick interviews with local citizens. I'll be joining the team shortly. I was just on my way there again when your call came through."

"Did anyone in the area hear anything?"

Detective Brown paused a moment, then continued. "A guest at the nearest cabin, the same individual who reported the disturbance, heard eight or nine gunshots in a short period of time, maybe two minutes, then right after that, the sound of two vehicles racing down the road, one after the other. The cabin guest called the station from his cell phone. The cabins themselves apparently don't have telephone service."

"I need that cabin and the surrounding scene gone over with a fine-tooth comb. We need to know exactly what happened and where they might have gone if we're going to find my daughter," Ella asked.

"You can count on our crime-scene team. They're experienced professionals and won't let up until the work is done. Knowing that a fellow officer's child is involved will make us work just that much harder. Mr. Tolino and your daughter will be found, Investigator Clah, if they're anywhere in the state of Colorado. You can take my word for it."

"Thanks, Detective Brown. Please contact me immediately if you get any kind of lead. I'll join you as soon as I can." Ella hung up, her voice shaking again.

She focused on the rage that darkened her mind, allowing it to flow through her, giving her strength. Someone had come after her daughter, endangering and terrorizing her. Ella nurtured her anger, knowing that, unlike fear, it didn't stop her from thinking—it just added to her determination.

TWENTY-FIVE
✖ ✖ ✖

Ella was walking toward the small airplane parked on the concrete pad when her cell phone rang. It was Big Ed again.

"Don't make that flight, Ella. I have some new information for you, and it's good this time. I just got a call from Kevin Tolino. He has Dawn with him, and is taking a roundabout route to a hiding place where he'll be safe. He said he can't trust the police, so he's not saying where he's going. Tolino heard his attackers mention Manuelito and feared that there might be other bad cops in the department. The lawyer's keeping a cool head, but he's scared. At least he thinks he's lost them—for now," Big Ed added. "And the last thing he said was to make sure you knew that Dawn is tired but unhurt."

Ella couldn't speak for a moment, her heart was beating so fast. "That's a relief. Did he say why he didn't call me directly?"

"He said he tried, but couldn't get a connection. It may have something to do with your location compared to mine. Either way, you can skip that trip to Colorado," Big Ed replied. "I'll call the sheriff's office up near Pine Bluff and fill them in on Kevin and Dawn."

"Thanks. Talk to Detective Brown, if you can. I have a feeling he knows what he's doing. Did Kevin say anything else, like what happened?"

"Before the cell phone he was using lost battery power, he was able to tell me a few details. Men had come up and tried to break into the cabin, calling by name for him to surrender. He had fired shots to pin them down long enough to drive away with Dawn. He'd been forced to leave his cell phone behind and he couldn't stop long enough to use a pay phone because of the close pursuit. Later he'd eluded the men long enough to stop at a gas station, where he found another vehicle with the keys in the ignition, and changed transportation. After a while he discovered there was a cell phone in the console of the car he'd just stolen. That explains why there was a delay in getting word to us," Big Ed said.

"If he's in trouble and looking for a place to hide, he'll head for the Rez. It's time for me to get back home. I'm going to see if I can track him down."

While driving back to the Rez from Farmington, with the sun just coming up in the east behind her, Ella checked the local radio stations for news on the power plant disturbance. The crisis at the power plant was apparently ending, and those involved had begun to surrender to an estimated two hundred armed law enforcement personnel. The tribal president had publicly announced that the Tribal Council would decide the gaming issue no later than Monday.

Despite the good news coming in, every nerve in her body was screaming with tension. Ella leaned back into the seat cushion of her vehicle, reduced the speed she was traveling to the official limit, and tried to clear her thoughts. She needed to calm her fears and focus on one thing alone—finding her daughter.

Pulling herself together, she thought of at least one person who might be able to help her find Kevin. This woman, more than most, had connections when it came to tribal politicians.

Ella drove directly to Abigail Yellowhair's home, which was west of Shiprock and about forty minutes from Farmington. When she arrived, Abigail herself, fully dressed already, answered the door of the luxurious clay-tile-roofed home, then stared at her with concern.

"You look positively exhausted. What's wrong?" she asked, ushering Ella inside quickly out of the frigid winter air and bringing her a warm mug of coffee.

As Ella stared at the cozy room, so warm and hospitable with a piñon fire going in the massive corner fireplace, she wondered if Dawn was inside a building and comfortable, or still sitting on a car seat on some back road, shivering from the cold? Had Kevin made sure she'd eaten? She had so many questions and so few answers. Swallowing hard, Ella brushed a strand of hair away from her weary face and forced herself to look directly at Abigail Yellowhair.

"I have a problem." Ella told her quickly about the attack on Kevin, and then how he'd fled with their daughter, searching for refuge. "You know Kevin's current circle of political and business friends better than I do. I was hoping you could help me track him down."

"Give me time to make some calls. I'll find out everything I can for you. This attack on another one of our council members worries me very much. I've heard rumors of an Indian group trying to force the passage of gaming on the Rez."

"Do you know anything about them that I could use?"

"No, that's all I know."

"More importantly right now, will you help me find my daughter and her father?"

"I'll need an hour or so to track down some contacts. Would you like something to eat, or maybe just rest for a while?"

"Thank you, but I need to be out looking, even if it's just driving around. I'll have my phone with me."

"I understand what you're going through, worrying about a child." Abigail Yellowhair had lost her own daughter just a few years ago, and her face turned dark at the memory. "I'll get back to you as soon as I can."

Ella left Abigail her cell phone number on a business card and walked back to her unit, realizing that there was nothing more she could do until she got more information except drive around and hope for a lucky break. But one responsibility remained. She had to tell Rose about Dawn. If she held back now and Rose managed to learn what had happened from anyone else, like Jennifer or the Colorado officers, she'd never trust her again.

Resigning herself to the task, Ella took the ten-minute drive back to the hospital in Shiprock where Rose was a patient. She would have given anything to avoid delivering this news to her mother, but there was no way around it.

Ella entered the hospital through the main entrance, then went upstairs to her mother's room.

Rose's expression brightened the moment Ella walked in. "Good news, daughter. The surgery went so well, I may be allowed to go home this afternoon! I think it's because your brother did a chant for me," Rose said, then stopped as she regarded her daughter thoughtfully. "I'd heard that the trouble at the mine had ended peacefully. Is something else wrong?" she asked, the heightened perceptivity mothers possessed out in full force.

Through sheer willpower Ella held herself together, forcing her voice not to crack as she told her mother everything she knew. After she finished, Ella swallowed back the bitter taste of fear that lingered in her mouth. "I swear I'll find her, Mom."

By then Rose was shaking. "Why didn't you call me? How long have you known about this?"

"An hour or two, not much more. I've been running around trying to get a lead since I heard, and the officers in Colorado are checking for any leads on their side of the state line. Now I have to wait for news or hope I can uncover a clue on my own."

"Use your instincts," Rose said firmly, sitting up in bed. "Your intuition is your gift—one you know how to draw upon."

"Mom, I'm using everything I have as a cop and as a mother, but I don't have any idea where to look next!"

Ella felt tears spilling down her cheeks. Impatiently, she wiped them away. If she let herself fall apart now she'd lose the focus she needed to help Dawn.

"Listen to me, daughter," Rose said sternly. "You can't use your instincts properly until you cast your fear aside."

"When I think of what may have already happened . . ." Her voice broke and she swallowed.

"Stop it," Rose said flatly. "You're a police officer. That's the side of you that has to come through and take over now. Go and do whatever it takes to find her and bring her back."

Rose gestured to the badger fetish Ella wore around her neck. "Use the animal medicine you were given when you accepted that gift. Badger medicine teaches you to defend what's yours and keep your eyes on the goal. Most important of all, it teaches you to *persist*. Call upon that medicine now, daughter. It'll work for you and against your enemies."

Ella nodded, then leaned down and kissed her mother good-bye. "I'll be back as soon as I can."

Ella wrapped her hand around the badger fetish. It felt warm, and for a moment she could feel the sheer power of beliefs that Navajos had cherished for generations coming to her aid.

Leaving the hospital with fresh energy in her stride, she hurried to her unit. She was just unlocking the door when her cell phone rang.

"It's Abigail," the voice on the other end said.

Ella's pulse began to race. "Do you have something for me?"

"It's a lead—nothing more. I spoke to a friend of mine, and while we were talking I remembered something you may find helpful. There's a cabin on the western, upper slopes of the Chuska Mountains east of Round Rock and on the Arizona side. Our council sometimes uses it as a retreat during the summer. Right now it's probably empty, but Councilman Tolino knows about it, and he could have reached the cabin in a four-wheel-drive vehicle."

"If he didn't take a direct route, he probably went southwest from Colorado to Mexican Water and down to Rock Point. I'll need directions from Round Rock to the cabin." Ella knew this was a real possibility. She wrote the directions down, then contacted Big Ed to ask for backup.

Ella filled him in on her conversation with Abigail, then told him where the cabin was located. Instead of replying, there was a sudden silence at the other end of the line. "Chief?"

"If that's where Tolino took your daughter, we may have a problem," he said slowly. "We got a report from an officer just coming on duty at Window Rock. He saw Manuelito in the Lukachukai area an hour ago before he knew his lieutenant was on the wrong side. Lukachukai isn't very far south of the cabin site. It's possible Manuelito has also guessed where Kevin might have gone and the syndicate sent him over there to check it out."

"At least Kevin already knows that he can't trust Manuelito," Ella said, then paused, gathering her thoughts. "But Kevin and my daughter are still in trouble. I have to get over there as soon as I can. I'm going to need a helicopter, Chief, and I want their pilot briefed that we may be flying right into the middle of an armed situation."

"It would take an extra half hour for the county to get a helicopter here, and the state police or military jobs are even farther away. You want to use *Angel Hawk*? The hospital has worked with us twice before in an emergency."

"Yes, especially if Jeremiah Crow is the pilot. He's ex-military and cool in a crisis."

"I'll see to it that it happens. I'll have things set up for you by the time you get to the hospital."

"I'm in their visitor parking lot now, Big Ed."

"Good. Just get whatever gear you have on hand, especially your vest, and go up to the chopper pad. Backup will be dispatched to the cabin, but keep in mind that their ETA will be longer than yours because they're on the ground, and the roads are going to be bad this time of year up in the mountains. I'll try to get some personnel there via county chopper, but don't count on it."

"Ten-four."

Ella drove around to the rear parking lot and climbed out of her Jeep. She grabbed her flashlight, extra pistol clips, then retrieved her rifle and a bandoleer of ammunition. Remembering the binoculars she'd kept in a box on the floor, she added them to her gear. Fully equipped, including her FBI loaner vest, she ran up the outside staircase to the roof of the building where the helicopter was stationed.

Jeremiah Crow was already in the chopper, the engine starting up, as she came into view.

Ella climbed up into the helicopter, then fastened her seat belt. The Navajo EMT, Glen McDonald, was in the copilot's seat studying the chart in his hands, and never looked up.

"Have you been given directions?" she yelled to Jeremiah, a hardy-looking Navajo man in a leather jacket and baseball cap.

He turned and gave her a half smile. "Roger that, Investigator Clah. Flight plan's already been logged, too. The trip will take thirty-five minutes, give or take, depending on wind conditions over the ridges."

"Remember, I don't want *Angel Hawk* to draw fire in case shooting starts. You're my kid's ticket out. Just get me down close to that cabin."

The trip seemed to take an eternity. Yet the noisy, stomach-churning roller-coaster ride merited nothing more than a passing thought to Ella. The need for action was drumming through her, and underneath that was an almost overpowering fear her rescue attempt would come too late.

The EMT offered her a chocolate bar, and she accepted it gratefully. Up in the mountains she'd need some energy reserves to support her once the adrenaline rush gave out.

As they approached their destination, having circled in from the north past Beautiful Mountain, Jeremiah pointed to a snow-covered clearing below, east and up-slope of the cabin, which was barely visible. It seemed odd seeing moisture in any form on the Rez these days, but at the moment, it was just another problem she'd have to deal with.

"There's no place to set down any closer," Jeremiah said. "There are too many trees and ravines, and the parking area in front of the cabin is just too small. We can use the clearing, or go down the mountain until we find a wide spot in the road. It's up to you."

"The clearing," Ella answered. "Then stay with the chopper. I'll take care of the rest." She pointed to her handheld radio, and he nodded, acknowledging how they would communicate.

Jeremiah dropped the helicopter down quickly, and Ella felt a sinking feeling at the pit of her stomach, much like the sensation she always got in elevators right before they came to a stop.

The moment they touched down, she jumped out into six-inch-deep snow, still a bit dizzy from the landing, then jogged away from the chopper. As she headed to the cabin, the pilot cut the engine and the noise level dropped off quickly in the sound-absorbing forest.

She was about two hundred yards away from the cabin when the sound of gunfire erupted from below. Adrenaline shot through her, and she increased her pace, running high-stepped across the crusty surface.

Ella hurried downhill in a diagonal direction, making sure she remained among the long-needled ponderosa pines for cover, and advanced to a point where she could see the cabin clearly. The SUV Kevin had stolen was in the road, blocking two other vehicles where the forest path was at its narrowest point, downhill to the west.

Two or three men were behind the SUV Kevin had stolen, close to the southwestern corner of the cabin.

Using her binoculars, Ella gave the front, back, and closest or eastern end of the rectangular log structure a quick once-over. That's when she discovered the tip of a rifle barrel poking out from inside the front cabin window closest to her, at the southeastern quadrant of the cabin. From what she could see Kevin was managing to keep them at bay. With no back door or windows on the north side, they'd been unable to get around behind him, and the side window she could see was heavily shuttered. If the west end was the same, their only access was from the front.

She moved ten feet to her left to get a better angle on the front of the building, which faced south. There were two front windows, one on each side of the door. A man was lying beside the front window farthest from her and closest to the vehicles, squirming around with his arms, trying to remove something from his leg. A closer look with her binoculars revealed he'd been caught in a coyote trap. The snow around his leg was stained crimson. At least two more men were in the trees on the south side directly across from the cabin, firing what sounded like pistols at the window where Kevin was positioned.

As she evaluated the situation, a fourth man with a shotgun emerged from around the far end of the house and rushed the door, dodging past the man in the trap. Fifteen feet from the door the man tripped, caught in an outstretched rope buried a few inches beneath the snow.

His shotgun flew out and struck the ground ahead of him, discharging into the air. It came to rest beside the small porch. When the man tried to crawl forward to grab it, Kevin fired a shot with his pistol this time, and the bullet ricocheted off the stone porch. The man yelled, and grabbed his face, apparently struck by fragments of stone. Moving quickly, he rolled up against the south wall, out of Kevin's view. Blood still streaming down his face, he pulled out a handgun and reached up for the windowsill above his head.

Letting the binoculars dangle from the strap around her neck, Ella flipped her rifle off safe and found the man in her telescopic sights. She aimed low to avoid any portion of her bullet entering the cabin, and squeezed the trigger gently, catching the man in the side just above his belt. He sagged to the ground, dropping his pistol.

The shot announced her presence, and created a flurry of confusion below. The men in the trees across the clearing from the cabin began firing blindly up the hill while scrambling for better cover toward the west end. Ella used the opportunity to change her own position, moving farther downhill and more to her left to outflank them and maintain cover for herself.

The pair that had fled from the trees made it downhill to their blocked vehicles, putting Kevin's SUV between them and her. Through the rifle scope Ella caught glimpses of Jefferson Blueeyes. She didn't recognize the Indian beside him, but she got the impression he wasn't Navajo. If she'd had to take a guess, she would have said that it was one of the two who'd been with Henry Estrada that day at the coffee shop.

She suddenly saw two more men to her right and below her, moving through the forest behind the cabin, bringing the number to at least four still actively involved. Both stopped behind rock outcroppings and started firing in her general direction with handguns. Obviously they still couldn't see her among the shadows, but hoped to pin her down and throw off her aim. To her, that clearly meant the attackers were about to make a move somewhere else.

The man with Blueeyes suddenly broke out from behind the cover of the closest vehicle and made a dash for the window at the southwest corner, the one where two of their comrades had fallen already.

Ella raised her weapon but, before she could shoot,

Kevin fired. The running man grabbed his thigh, fell to the ground, and crawled back around the west end, out of sight.

"Way to go, Kevin," she whispered. He was obviously running from window to window, trying to keep an eye on three directions and, so far, had done very well for himself. Now, with her there, he'd only have to guard one position.

Ella moved a little more to the south and downhill, trying to find a clear line of fire so she could take out Blueeyes, who was still behind the vehicles. But, almost as if sensing the danger he moved around so that he had cover on three sides.

Ella knew time was running out. She had to take out two or more of the gunmen before Kevin ran out of ammunition for his rifle and pistol or was struck by a lucky shot. Hopefully he'd placed Dawn in the tub in the bathroom where she'd be safest.

Suddenly she heard the sound of roaring vehicle engines from somewhere west, down the mountain. Relief flooded through her. Reinforcements. They weren't going to be alone anymore. The odds had now shifted in their favor, and the ones trying to take Dawn would have to fight it out, surrender, or take to the woods on foot.

Her cell phone rang. "Ella, this is Blalock with the cavalry. We're staying off the radio just in case, but I've got walkie-talkies for the others that they'll have a hell of a time monitoring. I'm about an eighth of a mile below and west of the cabin, coming up the road. What's your situation?"

Ella directed Blalock and the team toward the cabin, moving in from her left, right, and up the road, forcing the attackers into the center, where they'd eventually be caught by gunfire coming from all four directions. Five minutes later, Ella saw Blalock beyond the vehicles, moving east up the road but staying within the tree line.

"I'm directly opposite you right now, in the trees above the clearing. They still can't see me here in the shade against the bright sky," Ella whispered into her cell phone. She hadn't seen any of the gunmen below move in the last five minutes, but she broadcast their approximate location. "I'll keep the phone open and in my jacket. If you say something, I'll hear you."

"Good enough."

"How much help did you bring?" Ella asked.

"We didn't have regular manpower to draw from," Blalock replied. "Most of the officers and Big Ed had to run to check all the bridges between Shiprock and Farmington. One of the *Hasih* in custody decided to announce that explosives had been planted on three area bridges, and that those had remote timers. Payestewa and every other cop available is on that assignment now, as well as the ATF. With so many local officers just coming off that long standoff at the mine, and all our extra help headed back across the state, we've almost out of manpower."

Ella listened, but her mind was only on the events unfolding before her now. "So who came with you?"

"Officer Goodluck, and two deputized volunteers we've worked with before, your brother, Clifford, and Wilson Joe." Blalock responded.

"I believe there are three able-bodied men left down there. The other three are wounded or dead."

"Only three? Are you sure of that?"

"No, I still have a blind spot, the west end of the cabin. I just shoot at anyone I see that isn't Kevin. I figured we'd take them out one by one until no one but us good guys were left standing."

"Henry was right about you being part pitbull. Nothing ever makes you back off."

"You've spoken with him?"

"Briefly. He's really messed up, but the doctors say he's going to make it."

"That's a relief." Ella, who hadn't taken her eyes off the perps below, spoke quickly, bringing their focus back to the present. "We've got trouble," she said.

"Somebody managed to start the stolen SUV. The tires are spinning right now, and he's not making much headway, but it looks like he's planning to ram the front of the cabin. He's got one of the others with him."

"Everyone with a sight line try to take out the engine or driver," Blalock announced, obviously using his radio and the cell phone at the same time. "Don't hit a tire, that'll just give him more traction."

Ella quickly sighted in on the engine and fired, scoring a direct hit right above the radiator. Almost simultaneously, two other shots rang out. The windows of the SUV shattered, and the engine whined, and started smoking. The vehicle, spinning badly already, slid around nearly ninety degrees, striking the porch with its right rear tire.

Black smoke, then orange flames, began shooting from around the engine compartment, then the hood blew open with a fiery roar. The men jumped out in a panic and slipped and stumbled back to the other vehicles, diving underneath them for cover.

"Ella, your brother says that he's south, in the trees across from the front of the cabin. He'll keep them pinned underneath the cars," Blalock said through the open line of the cell phone.

"Good deal!" Ella said, moving straight down the hill toward the cabin, being careful not to trip on a fallen branch or tree stump.

"Wilson's close enough to see two men crouched down low at the northwest end of the cabin, toward the back," Blalock said. "They don't know which way to run, and can't move toward the vehicles without coming into my field of fire."

Ella continued downhill. Nothing was going to stop her from getting to her daughter now. Hearing someone to her right and above her, she dove behind cover, wheeling around with rifle up.

"It's me," Justine whispered, then stepped out from behind a tree, and, at a low crouch, ran over beside her.

"I came to give you this." She handed Ella one of the two walkie-talkies she had clipped to her belt. "I was with Wilson, but ran ahead and came around on the uphill side. I'll cover you. Don't worry," she added grimly. "I finally got my score back up at the police range."

Ella raced down the slope and quickly reached the shuttered window at the east end of the cabin. She stood to the side, and directed her voice toward the window. "Kevin, it's me, Ella. Open the window."

To her left, behind the cabin, was Wilson somewhere in the brush. Her back to the wall, she saw Justine nod from farther up the hill.

She heard the window being opened, then the shutters were unbolted and swung open with a creak. "Okay. Climb on in," Kevin mumbled, his voice weak and weary.

Ella put her rifle on safe and placed it inside, standing in the corner of the window, muzzle up and away from her. Then she pulled herself up and over, landing on the wooden plank floor in a crouch. Looking around as she grabbed her rifle, she saw that Kevin had moved down to the far window, looking back and forth between the outside and an opened half door in the floor that apparently led down to a cellar. Fumes from the burning vehicle had drifted in through the broken windows, but the circulation caused by the air from the additional window she'd just entered through was helping disperse the smoke.

"Where's—"

"Down in the cellar, covered by a dozen or more blankets. She's got a flashlight 'cause she hates the dark, but she's okay," Kevin said.

Ella set down her rifle and hurried across the room. She quickly climbed down the crude wooden steps into the cool darkness. The place smelled earthy, as with all old cellars. A flashlight beam shined in her eyes.

"*Shimá!*" Dawn dropped the flashlight and scrambled

out of the covers of an old bed just as Ella reached her, jumping into her mother's arms.

Ella held her close, comforting Dawn even as it comforted her to hold her daughter. But there was no time for more than that now. "Stay here, under the covers, just a few more moments, pumpkin." Ella set her back down on the bed, covered her with blankets, then handed Dawn the flashlight. Quickly she ran back up the stairs.

"It's me, I'm coming in!" Justine yelled, then opened the front door. The lock had been shot away already. "We have all but one of them in custody now. Whoever it was slipped past Wilson and Blalock somehow. Wilson caught a glimpse of him as he ran into the woods, and thinks it's Blueeyes. He's headed down the road toward our vehicles. Blalock's following him."

"Guard my kid, Justine. I'll be back," Ella said, anger in her voice as she checked her pistol.

"You going to join Blalock?"

"You bet. Jefferson Blueeyes made my life and my daughter's a living hell. He's not getting away, and freezing up on this mountain would be too good for him."

"Better let FB-Eyes know you're coming," Justine yelled out as Ella headed out the door.

Ella nodded to Clifford and Wilson, who had the prisoners sitting on the ground with their backs to the wall, but continued past the vehicles and downhill.

She contacted Blalock on the handheld as she hurried along the trees at the left side of the road, following the tracks in the road itself but staying out of sight from anyone covering the open area.

"I'm ahead of you, on the right side," Blalock whispered, "but I'm going to try to intersect the road just past where we parked, and cut him off from below. With luck, we'll trap him between us."

"I don't want this sleazeball to get away. Good hunting."

Ella pushed forward for a hundred yards, and spotting

something in the road, stepped out briefly from behind a tree to take a closer look.

"Ella, get back!" Blalock yelled over the radio.

She heard the gunshot almost at the same time she felt the bullet strike her chest. The force knocked her back into the snow-covered brush alongside the road. Pain made it impossible for her to take a breath, and her eyes teared as she tried. Afraid that she might lose consciousness any second, Ella tried to raise her weapon to defend herself. But her hand was empty. The pistol was somewhere in the snow.

TWENTY-SIX

✖ ✖ ✖

Blalock came up to the road on the other side, then sprinted and slid across the narrow lane, firing toward the tree line where the shooter had taken cover. Grabbing Ella by the collar, he dragged her farther back among the trees, where he sat her up.

"I feel as if I've been kicked by a bionic mule," Ella gasped, looking down at her jacket to take a look. Although the round hadn't penetrated the special vest, she'd been struck right above the breastbone and her entire chest ached. "I'm going to have trouble moving for a month."

"You're alive and you haven't sprung a leak. Take it as a win," Blalock said, his eyes now glued on the trees again. Spotting something in the snow in a footprint he'd left, FB-Eyes crawled over and retrieved her handgun. "You might need this, Clah."

She nodded, checking the weapon for any blockage of the barrel or action automatically. "Blueeyes was in the road. The round couldn't have come from him. It was someone on the other side."

"It was Manuelito. I saw the SOB. He was using Blueeyes as bait to lure us out into the open. I was trying to get a clear line of fire so I could take him out, but I lost him for a second, and that's when he fired."

Ella struggled to her knees with a groan. "We have to split up. Go after Blueeyes. As much as I want that weasel, I should take Manuelito instead. He's a Navajo cop and deserves to be taken down by one of his own."

"Before you go, Ella, keep in mind that Manuelito was probably the one who fingered Kevin and your daughter.

After he was spotted near Lukachukai, Big Ed found out Manuelito had provided security a few times for tribal meetings up here. He knew Kevin had been to the cabin, and must have guessed he would head here."

Cold anger strengthened Ella's resolve. "Let's go."

They took positions on both sides of the road, and advanced downhill, covering each other as they moved from tree to tree.

When they reached a switchback in the road, Ella spotted someone trying to start one of the vehicles that had brought her reinforcements. She moved forward, but the man saw her, jumped out of the SUV firing, and ran behind cover, ducking behind a large rock. Catching a glimpse of his face, Ella saw that it was Blueeyes, but someone else was across the road dead ahead, hiding in the brush. She could see the shoulder of his jacket from where she was crouched. That had to be Manuelito.

Ella came up with a plan and called Blalock. "I'm going to sprint across the road," she whispered into the radio. "That should draw fire from Blueeyes. When he peeks out, nail him. I'll keep on moving to your right and come out behind Manuelito. Right now he's across the road from Blueeyes, but around the bend in the road so you can't see him from your position. As soon as you neutralize Blueeyes, move up so you can keep watch over the vehicles. Manuelito will have no place to go without breaking cover."

"Okay, anytime you're ready," Blalock snapped.

Ella took a deep breath, then sprinted across the road, hoping she wouldn't slip or trip over a rock. Just as she reached the trees, she heard three quick shots, one of them going wild somewhere over her head.

Ella, glad she'd left her rifle behind so she could maneuver easier, kept her eyes on the tree line ahead, watching for Manuelito. As she'd expected, Manuelito was on the move again too, but he could only go downhill without coming into Blalock's line of fire, or into the forest directly in her path.

Anticipating his attempt to flank Blalock, Ella moved into position where she could cover the FBI agent's back, and waited. Less than two minutes later, Manuelito appeared in shadows, crouched low and searching the trees ahead of him. Three steps later, she had the rogue cop in her sights.

"Drop your weapon or die."

Manuelito froze in his tracks, looking around anxiously until he saw where she was crouched behind a fallen tree.

"Clah, have you flipped? I'm here to help you." Slowly he moved his gun hand in her direction.

"Set your weapon down," Ella repeated very clearly. "And don't move your hand another inch. You probably have a vest, but I'm close enough to double tap you in the head, and I've already taken up the slack on the trigger."

Manuelito very slowly placed his weapon on the snow, then, following her orders, turned away from the pistol and went down on his knees, hands locked behind his head.

"You've got nothing on me," he spat out.

"I think you'll be surprised just how much we do have. More than enough to put you behind bars for twenty years or more. You're going to be an old man before you get out again." As Ella handcuffed him, Blalock came up with a grim look on his face.

"Blueeyes?" she asked.

"Dead."

She nodded once. "Help me pat down this lowlife for a backup weapon or two, then he's all yours. I want to get back to my daughter."

By the time Ella and Blalock returned with their prisoner, the county's police helicopter had arrived on the scene, bringing Sheriff Taylor and three tired but heavily armed Navajo cops, including Philip Cloud.

The wounded prisoners were given medical care, then left for the hospital in *Angel Hawk* with Officer Cloud guarding them.

While Blalock and one of the tribal officers drove back with Manuelito in custody, Ella, Dawn, and Kevin caught a ride in the county chopper with Sheriff Taylor.

Ella, content to have her daughter safe, held her tightly, and it wasn't long before Dawn went to sleep, bundled up in a blanket. Ella glanced over at Kevin, who was sitting beside Sheriff Taylor.

Her daughter's father had shown bravery and ingenuity and had kept their daughter safe. She'd always be grateful to him for what he'd done. "My mother's in the hospital," Ella said. "I'd like you and Dawn to pay her a visit as soon as we land."

Kevin shook his head. "I'm the last human being she wants to see right now, especially after what's happened."

"Not after I tell her what you did for her granddaughter. She's safe because of you, and I have a feeling that's going to cut you an enormous amount of slack for a while."

He smiled wearily. "I'll believe it when I see it, but I'm willing to give it a go."

"It's time, for Dawn's sake, that there was peace between you and my mother."

After they landed, Ella carried Dawn and together with Kevin went to Rose's hospital room. The moment she saw Dawn, Rose's entire face lit up.

"Come here, little one!" Rose held out arms, oblivious to her bandaged hand.

"I wasn't scared, *Shimasání*," she said. "You said I should never be scared."

Rose hugged her. "That's right."

Ella told Rose about Kevin's efforts briefly, couching the details because her daughter was present, but Rose was adept at reading between the lines.

Rose looked at Kevin and nodded once. "For what

you did, you have my respect and my thanks."

"She's my daughter," Kevin replied quietly. "I would never let anyone harm her."

Rose met his gaze and in the look that passed between them Ella saw a new understanding. They would never be friends, but there would no longer be open warfare between them.

As Dawn began playing with the vase of flowers by Rose's bedside, Jennifer Clani came into the room carrying a big potted plant. The minute Dawn saw her, she hurried over, holding out her arms, asking to be picked up.

Rose and Ella exchanged glances. There was nothing they could do about this now. As far as Dawn was concerned, Jennifer was family, too. And, in the long run, maybe that wouldn't be so bad after all.

"Would you like me to take her home? I can give her a bath and something to eat." Jennifer asked Ella.

Ella nodded. "I need to go to the station for a bit, and Kevin will have to come with me to fill in some missing information and speak to the Colorado authorities about what happened up there. If you could look after her until I can get home, I'd appreciate it."

As Jennifer carried Dawn out, Rose gave Ella a warm smile and took her hand, squeezing it gently. "I'll be home later this afternoon."

"You're being released?" Ella asked, relieved to hear it.

"Yes. I've already arranged for a ride."

Ella nodded. She didn't need to ask who was providing Rose with transportation. "I'm glad to know you're going home, Mom."

"Maybe we can give my granddaughter a little party tomorrow—a homecoming. It'll be good for her. My granddaughter is growing up and needs to be around other children."

Ella nodded. "I've been thinking of sending her to day school for a few hours each morning. But I'd want our home helper to go with her. I don't want my daughter anywhere alone—at least not for some time."

"This was frightening for all of us," Kevin said. "But don't start smothering her."

"I wonder if I should take her to a doctor," Ella mused, glancing at Kevin, then at Rose. "I don't want what she went through these last two days to haunt her for the rest of her life."

"I don't think you'll have to worry about that," Kevin said. "Even at the height of the chaos back in the cabin, the only thing that bothered her was the noise. I was worried as hell, but she took things calmly, as if it was just some big TV show. She said you'd come for us," he told Ella, "and that you'd bring her uncle too. She was absolutely certain we'd be fine."

"She's far from ordinary, isn't she?" Ella said rhetorically, pride in her voice.

"Spoken like a proud mom," Kevin said, and laughed.

Ella looked at Rose and knew that to her mother that statement had been more than a casual remark.

After saying good-bye to Rose, Ella and Kevin went to the elevator.

"Let me meet you at the station later. I'd like to talk to some other councilmen and apprise them of everything that happened."

"All right. I'll see you then."

Ella headed to the station feeling more at peace than she had in a long time. Manuelito was no longer a threat and her testimony along with that of Payestewa and the other officers would ensure that the former cop would be in prison for a very long time.

On the way, Ella got a call from Dispatch. Justine had radioed from the cabin, where she'd remained to process the scene, and reported that a monitor to a listening device had been found on Blueeyes's body. This suggested that a bug had been placed in Kevin's office somewhere, and explained how the syndicate had initially known where Kevin had gone with Dawn for the weekend.

As Ella finally pulled into the station's parking lot, she saw that it was nearly empty. She'd have to check the status of the PD's situation with the bridges and the threat of explosives, then go wherever she was needed. On her way inside, she met up with Sergeant Joseph Neskahi, who was just coming out the door. His arm was in a sling.

"What happened to you?" Ella asked.

"I was helping search the old Shiprock bridge when I slipped on a pipe and nearly fell into the river. I'm okay, but I'll have a broken wing for a while."

"So what happened with the explosives?"

"There were a few sticks on each of the bridges, way out in the middle and underneath at key structures. But it turns out they didn't have any detonators. It was just another diversion to wear us down and keep us occupied while they made their move on Councilman Tolino. Some of the officers have now finally been sent home to get a little rest, but I was on my way to find you. I've got a message for you from Big Ed. Harry Ute called him and said that he's got some volunteers as backup and he's closing in on Manyfarms."

"Who's backing him up?"

Before he could answer, a rifle went off somewhere close by, and a cinder block in the station wall a few feet above them literally exploded, showering them with chunks of debris. Ella grabbed Neskahi roughly and pulled him down to the pavement behind her Jeep.

Neskahi groaned. "Damn, that hurt," he said, rubbing his shoulder. "What was that? It blew a hole clear through the wall."

Ella had her pistol in one hand, her radio in the other. "We're taking fire from a fifty-caliber rifle out here," she yelled to Dispatch inside the station. "Keep everyone away from the west side of the building." Ella looked around, trying to see where the sniper was without becoming a target again.

"Where the hell is he?" Neskahi looked around the

front tire, keeping below the silhouette of the vehicle.

"Across the road, and high enough to see us over the Jeep. Stay down," Ella answered. It was suddenly very quiet, and she could hear the engine of the Jeep ticking as it cooled.

Neskahi looked at where the round had struck. "I can see a light fixture on the ceiling inside the station. That bullet must have gone halfway through the building. Hope nobody was in the wrong place at the wrong time."

Ella's handheld suddenly squawked with static. "I've got Manyfarms." She recognized Harry Ute's voice. "You can relax now. I'll be the station with the prisoner in a few minutes."

"Where was he?" Ella stood and looked at the houses across the street.

"On the roof of the green garage," Harry replied. "The second house down the side street."

Ella saw someone waving at her from the roof, which was about two hundred yards away, then the person disappeared down the other side.

She waited in the parking lot along with the watch commander and Sergeant Neskahi. At least nobody had been hit in the station. Five minutes later two vehicles came up the street and pulled into the parking lot. Herman Cloud was driving the sedan. Harry Ute sat in the back with his prisoner, the tall, slender, Artie Manyfarms, who was lying against the car door, dazed, with his hands cuffed together behind his back. A trickle of blood ran down the side of his face.

Herman's faded green souped-up pickup pulled up next and Ella recognized two older men in the truck. They were contemporaries of Herman Cloud and old-guard traditionalists, and like Herman, were dressed in flannel shirts, bulky Levi's jackets, and wearing worn felt cowboy hats.

"Thanks for helping us when we needed you," Ella said to Herman, then waved and smiled to the men in the pickup.

"The marshal did all the hard work," Herman said, climbing slowly out of the car. "He crept up behind Skinny Legs there," he added, gesturing to Manyfarms, "and stepped on his buffalo gun. The bullet went wild and the marshal was all over him after that. He grabbed the rifle and whacked the damned idiot on the side of the head real good."

As Herman opened the door, Harry half dragged Manyfarms, who was just starting to get back enough energy to resist. "I'm sorry that the gun went off before I could get to him. Was anyone hurt?"

"We're fine," Ella said. "How did you catch up to him?"

"I've been one step behind him, checking out every report of stolen vehicles since he fled from the power plant the other day. When an officer in town spotted one of those vehicles, I was notified. Unfortunately, the officer lost sight of the stolen truck, but the last reported location was in the area around the station, and that sent off warning signals to me. I decided to hedge my bets, round up some volunteers to watch my back, and check out the neighborhood.

"After driving up and down each street, we finally located the truck, which was on the hot sheet, all right. One of the guys decided to climb up a tree so he could see into the backyards without going door to door, and he spotted someone sitting on the garage roof right across from the station. We got close to the house, and I went up the ladder, not knowing if it was just somebody working on his TV antenna or snaking out a clogged drain.

"When I saw that it was Manyfarms lining up on the station with that big rifle of his, I knew I had to act fast to neutralize him."

"I'm glad you succeeded," Ella said with a shaky smile.

"Yeah, thanks to us," one of the old men who'd ridden

in the pickup said, laughing and making a muscle with his skinny arm.

Manyfarms eyes were now lit up with anger, but he still hadn't said anything.

"I better take him inside," Harry said, cocking his head toward his prisoner. "He's going to have a lot of years added to his prison time now, Ella. Count on it."

Hours later, the station was almost back to normal manpower levels. The FBI agents, Ella, and Justine met in the chief's office. "I managed to get a match on traces of blood I found on Manuelito's night stick," Justine said. "They belong to the murdered councilman, and a security camera from a bar's parking lot shows Manuelito's vehicle was there briefly just before the councilman was beaten to death."

"We'll offer Manuelito a deal, and see if he'll testify against the others," Big Ed said. "Who knows, maybe we can get him a private cell. Cops don't do well in prison."

"I also got a clue concerning the selection of those particular Anglos hired to do the vandalism," Big Ed added. "The one named James Little had his lawyer give me a list of the 'Indians' he and Smith did legitimate carpentry work for during the past few months. It turns out they built a porch for Jefferson Blueeyes."

"And now that Officer Tache has found the bug in Kevin Tolino's office phone, another answer is confirmed." Ella smiled grimly.

"We'll have a tech from the Albuquerque Bureau sweep all the tribal offices for bugs. But right now, Payestewa and I have to get back to my office," Blalock said. "Unfortunately, our job's far from finished. Now that we have several of the syndicate players under arrest, we need to check out known associates and deepen the investigation on a federal and state level until we locate all the others linked to the conspiracy. Henry Estrada is out of danger now, and is going to be a key witness. He knows how the syndicate operates all across the West, and can identify a lot of the players by photographs though they never used their real names. Apparently, he's even served as a personal bodyguard to several of the men who've been controlling some of the pueblo casinos from behind the scene."

"Henry is a tough man. I'm going to pay him a visit as soon as I can. But what about George Branch?" Ella asked hopefully. "Has anyone linked him to the conspiracy yet?"

Blalock smiled. "We'll never get that lucky. The serial numbers on that fifty-caliber rifle have been filed away. They can probably be restored in the laboratory, but even if the weapon turns out to be the one 'stolen' from Branch, he's already covered his tracks. That slippery worm oozes away every time."

"Unless someone needs the paperwork right away, I'm going to head home," Ella said, standing up. "I'd like to be with my family right now. I can come back first thing tomorrow and work on the necessary reports." Ella looked at Big Ed, knowing it was up to him. "Is that all right with you?"

"Sure. In fact take a few days off, Ella—*after* you fill out the reports tomorrow," Big Ed said. "You've earned it."

After washing away most of the blood, dirt, and grime of the last two days in the women's rest room, Ella drove back home, still riding the adrenaline high that came from the events of the past several hours. Experience told her that she'd have to find a way to work off some steam before she went to bed or she'd lie awake for hours.

As she parked in the driveway by her mother's pickup, she saw headlights in her rearview mirror. A moment later, Harry pulled up and came out to meet her.

"I know it's late and you've had a long day, but can you give me a few minutes?"

"Sure. In fact, I'm still way too jazzed to take it easy. Can you stay a bit?"

Harry nodded, then smiled. "Maybe even longer than you want. I just got word and I'm accepting a post out here. I won't be around the corner, not exactly, but Albuquerque is only three or four hours away."

"I've always liked car drives," she answered with a happy smile.

She'd been wanting some time alone with Harry, and knowing Dawn would be asleep already she asked him inside and into the den, where a warm fire was going in the woodstove. Rose was probably tired and would leave them alone. She was certain of that.

Harry sat beside her on the couch and, as he draped his arm around her and pulled her closer, someone knocked at the door.

Ella suppressed a groan. "Don't go anywhere. I've got to answer that before they wake Dawn up."

As she opened the door, she saw Herman Cloud on the porch, a large paper bag in his arms.

"Your mother said for me to just come in, but I saw the marshal's truck and thought I'd better knock. I didn't want to surprise you." He was holding a bucket of chicken from Shiprock's busiest fast-food place. "Here, you can take this. I've got a lot more in the car."

Ella looked at the size of the bucket, then back at Herman. Her mother couldn't eat this much chicken in a month. "Which army are you planning to feed?" Then she saw another set of headlights in the driveway, and more coming up the road.

"We'll need it all, daughter. I've invited some friends to the house," Rose said, coming from down the hall. She was dressed in a long blue velvet skirt, and her salt-and-pepper hair was fastened back and then twisted in a bun. She had her best burgundy velvet blouse on, and a silver-and-turquoise squash blossom Ella hadn't seen her wear in years.

"Am I the only one who didn't know we were having

a party?" Ella asked, bewildered, as the same men who'd helped Herman and Harry capture Manyfarms came in with a cooler full of soda pop and ice.

"Our friends are always welcome," Rose said, giving Ella a stern look. "But don't worry. We'll all keep our voices down so we don't wake my granddaughter."

Everyone complied instantly, dropping their voices to barely more than a whisper as they walked into the kitchen.

Ella closed the front door then, looking back toward the den, saw Harry coming out to join her in the living room.

Maybe they could sneak out the front door. Ella was about to suggest it to Harry when another knock sounded at the door. Harry smiled, and shrugged. Ella sighed and went to answer it. It was Kevin, cleaned up and wearing a warm-looking sweater and gray slacks.

"What on earth are you doing here? I expected you'd go straight home and crash early tonight."

"I came to bring you some news," he answered, stepping into the living room and nodding to Harry, who nodded back.

Hearing his voice, Rose came in from the kitchen.

Seeing her, Kevin cleared his throat. "When the tribal president learned that I'd returned, he called for an emergency council meeting this afternoon instead of waiting until Monday. We met in Window Rock about two hours ago, and finally took a vote on tribal gaming. A proposal for casino and video gaming came out a tie, forty-four to forty-four, including the vote of the new appointee. The tribal president abstained, so the proposal failed. Then the president called for a gaming referendum to take place in June, assuming funds can be scraped up. If a majority of the People choose gaming, the council will reconsider the issue in July."

Rose smiled widely, then quickly went into the kitchen to tell the others.

Ella chuckled. "You've just made her day."

"There's more," he said, lowering his voice to a whisper. "Everything that's happened—how they bugged my office, tried to coerce my vote, and how I came under attack during a time when I had my child with me—will come to light soon. I expect the news will help my career and that's a plus, but there's a downside, too." He paused. "I received this note when I went back to my office. I still don't know how they got in because my door was locked."

He handed it to her, and Ella noticed two jagged holes in the paper. "How was it delivered?" she asked warily.

"With their usual flair," he answered. "They used my own letter opener to pin it to the back of my door."

Ella opened the sheet that had been folded in half and read the message.

You won a battle, but not the war. Don't plan to be around next election. You're worth more dead than alive to a lot of people.

"So now there's a price on your head," Ella said softly. That meant that there was probably one on Manuelito's head, too, not that she was sorry about that. "You'll have to hire a bodyguard, Kevin, someone who really knows the ropes."

He nodded. "About Dawn . . ."

Ella paused. It was Kevin's right to see his daughter. He'd certainly earned it. But with a price on his head, new rules would have to be set up. "You can see her anytime, but I don't want you to take her away from here unless I can come with you."

He nodded somberly. "I've been thinking that I should come over and visit both of you more often."

Ella looked at the man who was the father of her child. To say she had no feelings for him would have been to lie to herself. But there was another . . .

At that moment, Harry came up from behind her and placed a hand on her shoulder. "Everything still okay?"

Ella looked back at him and nodded. All she'd wanted was some time alone with Harry. Now, as always, her life was suddenly complicated again.

"Come in, Kevin. Join Harry and me and have something to eat," Ella suggested, conceding that tonight was going to be for the whole family.

As she led both men into the kitchen, she saw her mother standing beside Herman Cloud. Had life always been simpler for Rose? Why was it that Rose never failed to know what was right for her?

Harry took Ella's hand and pulled her back into the living room. "Kevin's your child's father. But that's the past. Don't confuse it with the present. Or the future."

She was still trying to figure out how to answer when he pulled her against him and kissed her tenderly. Then, before she had time to answer, he smiled and walked out of the house.

Ella stared at the door as it closed, then slowly matched Harry's smile.

Rose stood in the doorway watching Ella looking out the window as Harry drove away. New alliances and relationships were becoming a reality now for both of them. To be sure, it was an uncertain time, filled with second thoughts and doubts. But life and change were as one.

Changing Woman, who was at the center of Navajo beliefs, stood for creative feminine power—life restoring itself in an endless array of new cycles. Her daughter would follow her own destiny, as would Dawn, whose life had yet to be defined. As for herself, she'd found that life brought a different kind of peace to those her age—one that would give her the confidence and courage to walk a new life path for herself and for her tribe.

TRACKING BEAR

THE NEW ELLA CLAH NOVEL

❌ ❌ ❌ ❌

Available from Forge Books

April 2003

The college was a modern facility with core classrooms and offices constructed in an architect's interpretation of giant eight sided hogans.

Wilson Joe, a popular, good-looking professor about Ella's height and a year older, sat alone in his office grading papers. Seeing Ella, he beamed a smile. "Hey, stranger. I haven't seen you around much lately."

"Work and family. That's my whole life in a nutshell."

"How's Dawn? I heard that she's going to day school."

Ella smiled. Everyone tended to know everyone else's business in this community. "Yeah, and she loves it. I think it's good for her. She needed to be around kids her own age. She's learning Navajo and English and seems pretty comfortable with both—though I have to admit she makes up her own words with alarming frequency. *Shush* is bear in Navajo, but she calls her teddy bear Shooey." Ella paused. "I sound like one of those mothers who's convinced *everything* her child does is adorable."

"And you're not?" Wilson laughed as he walked over to a small coffee port on the counter, carrying his cup. "You've got your life organized the way you want it," he said, pouring her a cup of coffee without asking, then topping off his own mug. "I envy you that. I wish I could get my life more on track. Justine and I . . . well, we have things to work out." Ella nodded and said nothing. Wilson continued, "But you didn't come to talk about this, Ella. What's up?"

"How well do you know Professor Kee Franklin? I understand that he guest lectures here."

"Dr. Franklin conducts demonstrations and lectures often. He's a very gifted professor, and an inspiration to my students."

"Do you know him on a personal level?"

Wilson shook his head. "We've made small talk and discussed the *Dineh's* relationship to science and technology, but that's about it. Why do you ask? Is he in some kind of trouble?"

"Not the kind you think. Have you heard that a tribal officer was shot and killed?" Seeing him nod, she added, "It was his son."

Wilson took a deep breath. "That's going to devastate Dr. Franklin. His son was the world to him. They hadn't been close while the boy was growing up, but their relationship improved since Kee moved back to this area."

"When I gave him the news he took it really hard," Ella said. Hearing someone approaching, she turned her head and was surprised to see her mother standing there. "Mom! What on earth are you doing here?"

"You're not the only one with business to attend to, daughter," Rose said, taking the chair Wilson offered, then glancing up at him and folding her hands in her lap. "I came to get your opinion on the proposed 'nuclear casino.' You explain things to people every day in words they can understand, I figured you could speak plainly to me about it."

"Would you like some coffee?" Wilson offered, waving toward the pot.

"No thank you," Rose replied, then got right to the point. "What do you think are good reasons for building this nuclear power plant, Professor?"

"You have to hand it to the New Traditionalists," Wilson said. "They've come with something original that could add a whole new dimension to the energy industry in Four Corners. If it passes and a nuclear facility is constructed, the electricity produced could bring our tribe a great deal of revenue. Right now the many outsiders operating the coal-fueled power plants, the mines, and so on, have a lot of control over what happens to our land. But with a nuclear power plant here, owned and operated by the tribe, those days would be over. We'd be calling our own shots at last."

"What I'm most concerned about is the safety issue," Rose said. "It's only clean energy when everything goes as planned. The Holy People warned us that certain rocks should stay in the earth. When the *bilagáanas*, the white people, came to our land during the Cold War and council elders allowed them to take the uranium out, the mining ended up causing disease and misery. We can't afford another mistake like that. Polluting our scarce water supplies is unforgivable."

Wilson spoke. "It should be different now—with scientific knowledge that simply wasn't around before. And the public is a lot better educated. Do you realize that at current prices, we can make an estimated one billion dollars mining our own uranium and running the power plant—that is, if the plant is allowed to operate for twenty-five years."

"Even if we make more money, that still won't guarantee that we'll find harmony and walk in beauty," Rose said. "Even a small mistake could be a disaster."

They talked for a few more minutes, then Rose took her leave. "Thank you for your time and your thoughts, nephew," she said, using the term as a sign of affection, not kinship.

"Mom, wait, and I'll walk back to the parking area with you," Ella said.

As Rose went out to the hall, Ella glanced back at Wilson. "I need a lead that will point me to Officer Franklin's killer. If you hear anything, from your students or elsewhere, give me a call."

"You've got it. I'll start by finding out if the professor's son ever attended classes here."

Ella joined her mother as they walked back to their cars. They were nearing the parking area when a young woman in her early twenties, wearing jeans and a sweatshirt, saw them and came over. Four other young women followed her.

"Aren't you Rose Destea, the traditionalist who is trying to turn everyone against a tribal nuclear power plant? I read what you said in the newspaper."

"You are right about my name. And although the newspaper gave a distorted report of my comments, I do have many serious questions and concerns about the NEED project. But people are free to make up their own minds." Rose spoke calmly.

"My name is Vera Jim." The woman stepped right up to within a foot of Rose, but Rose didn't flinch or give ground. "People like you are the tribe's biggest enemies. You're so used to living in poverty you can't see that the opportunity has finally come for the rest of us to break out of this cycle of misery. New Traditionalists provide leaders who can improve our standard of living, but there is always someone like you to stand in our way."

"I am *not* an enemy of the tribe," Rose said sharply. "The only ones who truly undermine who we are as The People are the ones who show no respect for our ways."

Ella was surprised by how well Rose was handling things, though she could tell her mother was furious with Vera Jim. Vera suddenly pushed Rose hard.

"*Your* ways suck!" Vera snarled.

As Rose staggered back, Ella steadied her mother quickly, then, in an instant stepped up to Vera, pinning her against the trunk of a cottonwood tree so she couldn't move.

"You have assaulted a member of our tribe," Ella said. "I am a witness and a police officer."

"Daughter, let her go," Rose said. "There's enough division among the *Dineh* as it is."

"Mom, you can press charges—"

"No. That's your way, not mine. Common sense and respect for their elders isn't something you can force into a person. If they haven't been raised properly, they have to learn it by themselves."